Fate and Fair Winds

I0674386

Edge of Empire Series

World Turned Upside Down

Dory Codington

Dory's Historicals Press
doryshistoricals.com

ISBN 10: 0-9963226-3-9
       13: 978-0-9963226-3-8

Library of Congress Control Number: 2016912688

Published by DorysHistoricals Press, Newton, MA 02458

DorysHistoricals Press 2016

Second Edition

For Ellen who met Rebecca first, and who helped her come alive.

Tallulah, who knows that dreams make good stories.

And, as always –

To those who won and those who lost the American Revolution.

Preface

September 22, 1776.

Simm watched the hanging with disgust. Why would the young man pretend to be a spy when he had no skills and no natural ability? As far as he could tell there had been no secret inks, no codes, and little effort to hide his actions from strangers. Maybe the world was better off without such fools – fledglings who fall out of the sky, only to die on the ground. By all accounts he'd been a decent young fellow, a schoolteacher whose loyalty exceeded his ability.

Simm turned Artemis north. He needed to change out of the bright red uniform and return, in civilian wear, to his rented rooms at the nearby Dove Tavern as plain John FitzSimmon, neither a Major in His Majesty's Royal Army nor the fifth son of a duke.

He rode along the dirt roads to the north of the town. He supposed Manhattan had good points to it. Mostly wooded, it had clearly grown without a plan, and it bothered Simm's sense of order. It had rows of the most beautiful houses he'd yet seen in the colonies, but its opulence seemed shown-off without any sense of propriety or modesty. New Yorkers, it seemed, would improve their lots without a care to the state of the streets or town planning. Simm had even preferred his year in Boston, with its red brick houses, muddy streets and rebel attitude. At least there, people were indoors on Sunday afternoons, at home with family and friends. These few weeks in New York had almost convinced Simm that tavern living was normal. He would be delighted to move on.

September, even before the hanging, had been especially busy as well. He had been adjunct to the Howes as they and the Adams cousins, John and Samuel, had tried to come to any sort of conciliation with the colonies. The process had been contentious, and neither side was willing to move beyond stated goals, and those were fixed before anyone set foot on Richard Howe's ship.

So much for the alleged unity of Englishmen, for truly no group was ever more English, and yet so bound to remarkably disparate views. The meetings had failed, but there were men there whom he now felt to be brothers, even those Washington had sent as observers. Brothers, yes, but not friends – that was the way of war, and the way of families.

Simm assumed that he had been asked to help the Howes because two of his real brothers sat in Parliament. It was never a bad idea to have political power behind a plan. He was glad that he brought more than family connections to the negotiation team. He was good at seeing, at a glance, where pieces fit together. It had become Simm's work in the army to unravel knots and finish puzzles. More recently, he had been sent to sort out crimes involving the army and the civilian population. This work for the Howe proclamation for peace, as it was to be called, was one more puzzle for him to work on.

He considered these things as he made his way out of the regimental office, without a wig and dressed in a dark blue waistcoat and beige breeches. He threw his dark cloak over his shoulders and mounted. The ride from there to the Dove was not far, but far enough, and in another part of town entirely. It was important that no one at the tavern knew the

Major, and equally important that no one around headquarters knew the civilian John FitzSimmon. Not that Simm was doing anything illegal or treasonous, but it was so much easier to find those who were doing those things if he were barely noticed.

Simm had been involved in war since he'd joined his regiment at eighteen. He had grown to see the planning and negotiations that went on behind the battles as a chess game, with players assigned their parts. This fell apart when criminal activity, espionage and political corruption complicated the process. It became especially complicated when crimes were committed upon the people whose obedience and loyalty was needed for the political process to work.

Spies. His mind shifted back to the young schoolteacher he had met only days before. Nathan was too bold, really, but, all in all, it was sad that the General couldn't just give him a good switching and send him away like the foolish schoolboy he was imitating. Simm didn't like spying, not even that done for the army he supported, and he despised that done for his enemy. But years in the army and at war had taught him to respect those who were good at their craft. Those truly skilled, and working against him, he had not met. Simm suspected that if they were good enough, he and they would never meet. Not meet, that is, until that day when their skills failed, and they weren't as good as he was.

Simm had found these last weeks of military negotiations difficult and distracting. He had jumped back into the work when orders reached him at Trenton on his way north in late August. He had spent the spring and summer meeting people while traveling through the colonies, and it had been one of the best voyages of his life. Not only had he completed a mission to help General Howe understand the American people, if there was a unified people to be understood as such, but he had also seen to family business, speaking to shipping agents in all the port cities on behalf of the family shipping firm. More than that, he had seen his closest brother, in age and temperament, twice during the summer. Fortune and the weather had both been kind, and he had met up with Jason when his ship, the *Good Queen Bess*, was in port at both Charleston and Philadelphia. It was a good and valuable trip, one that could not have been accomplished had he been required to wear his uniform.

After he completed his journey, he headed into the Jerseys and received new orders. Although he had expected to make it back to New York before resuming duties, the realities of war interfered. The region continued to be one of colonies in chaos. There were regular reports of rape and plunder being committed by British soldiers against townsfolk. Many of these people had already sworn loyalty to the King, and the soldiers' conduct was making it more difficult to avoid further warfare. This thuggish behavior had been expected of the Hessians. It certainly was not approved, but for British soldiers under General Howe this was treason, and Simm had been responsible for shooting or hanging men without trial. The purpose of his work was an almost impossible attempt the calm the countryside.

The Americans, at their end, did not make his task easier. Farmers throughout the Jerseys fought from their own fields, put the gun over the hearth, and then went back to work in the barn. Simm did not approve of their behavior any more than he could approve of the mayhem wrought by the two armies sent to subdue the rebellion. During his time in America, stationed with Gage and Howe in Boston and New York, visiting his brother north of Boston, and then on other travels, he had begun to believe that some sort of separation between the colonists and Britain was inevitable. He had never put this theory forth directly to either his American friends, most of whom knew him to be a British soldier, or to his commanding officers.

The clop-clop of Artemis's hooves on the hard-packed road gave him a few minutes to let his mind follow its own route. And, as it always did now, it slipped back to the previous summer in Philadelphia, and a certain American girl searching for her own meaning of the Declaration of Independence.

Simm had met his Columbia on the dock on a Monday morning. Rebecca was sitting with her sketch pad next to the *Good Queen Bess,* working on an amazing lovely quick sketch of the ship. He had offered to buy it from her at a price they had negotiated over lunch. He had taken away from their meetings only that sketch, a small cutting of rosemary tied with a few strands of silky blond hair, and a name, Rebecca, one of the sweetest and most common names in the English world, and one that would be impossible to track – just as his first name, John, the only name Simm had left her with, would be.

Chapter 1

Philadelphia, Pennsylvania: Late July, 1776   The summer heat had not yet reached the city as Rebecca headed toward the river. The bustle of the early morning, of the day just beginning, was so much more pleasant to her than her own chores on the quiet farm, that she snuck away to make this journey as often as she could. Walking the five miles to the piers on the river should have made her tired, but, as usual, the busy seaport had the opposite effect. She breathed deeply of the free wet air as she cleared her father's voice and his angry threats from her head. Today it had taken too long to finish her work and leave the farm, because Jasper Willent had revealed that he'd spent her dowry on land a neighbor offered. This left her with nothing of the money her mother had saved for her. To top off Jasper's theft, he'd had an offer for her hand in marriage without a dowry. He was too happy to tell her about it, even as it made her skin crawl and blood boil just hearing about it.

Herodius Smith, widower and father of a gang of endearing but unruly brats, needed a new wife. He didn't need a wife's dowry to sweeten the marriage, Jasper was delighted to report – Rebecca's youth and beauty would be enough. Mr. Smith would even give Rebecca's father the three-acre parcel at the far end of his land, the piece that connected the original Willent farm with her brother Hackett's pasture, when the marriage took place.

"You are willing to sell me to the old, smelly, bag of rotten bones and teeth for three acres?" Rebecca had screamed at her father that morning as she came in with the eggs she had just gathered.

Jasper Willent shrugged. "Gosh, Becky, don't put it that way. He was a good looking man when he was young. I'm sure you can clean him up a bit after you're married."

"And! What did you do with my dowry?" Rebecca tried not to scream, but it was getting harder, "Mother saved egg money to make sure I had something. I know it's been hard having six children, but there are only two of us girls, nothing to *tax* you!"

"Sorry, Becky, but that dowry went to make sure the land was secure."

"Your land! You mean you spent my money to buy Hackett's field and you intend to use my marriage to that disgusting man to secure the rest. Don't think much of your sixth child, do you, Da?" She tried not to, but failed, spitting out the last.

"Honestly, girl, I hadn't thought much either way till your mother died last year. Now I figure you should be put to some use, since you haven't pulled your own weight around here much."

Rebecca grabbed a bonnet, her bag and a few pennies, and fled the farm. Usually she changed into something appropriate for the busy town, but today she was so angry that she walked from the farm in an old gown used now only for farm or housework. It was a simple cut of pale rose and blue with a matching long jacket. Now it was slightly dusty from a morning of gathering a few eggs and milking the two cows.

The smell of the tidal river and the sight of ships, masts and figureheads, sailors on the ships, and workers on the docks, thrilled her every time she saw them. She found energy in knowing that they caught the wind and went anywhere, everywhere in the world. She found her favorite spot on the pier, out of the way of the hustle and bustle that was the daily work of the place. There she pulled her drawing paper, her penknife and pencils out of her satchel. As she settled into watching, she let pencils in her skilled fingers draw the river and the ships.

Some days she sketched the entire scene, and on others she drew just one ship or even the small boats, tugs, dories and dinghies bobbing beneath the ships. She tried to capture the energy and movement of the busy port, and tried not to think about the war and the danger her brother was in just then in New York. Nat wrote occasionally, mostly to ask her to stay aware of ships and troops moving up and down the river. Nothing like that had happened, so she had continued to sketch what she liked.

Rebecca would have loved to set up an easel and paint the ships, but she didn't have the money for paints, and had never had the chance to develop that skill. She had no doubt that she would be as good with oils as she was with pencils, and often saw her work on canvas even as she was working in charcoal or pencil. But with her father being so stingy as to sell her to an aging farmer, paint, canvas and easels were not for her.

Sitting off to the side of the working men, she spent most mornings outlining the ships or completing a sketch she had started the day before. Once in a while, a captain or ship's owner offered her a shilling or two for the piece, and she was happy to sell. This morning, she had begun a pencil sketch of a ship she had not seen before, the *Good Queen Bess*. She was a beauty. Double-masted, she was painted like a robin in brown and red with blue and white trim. The pretty ship was crowned with a striking figurehead of a redheaded woman.

She did not look like a standard Queen Elizabeth – no, this Bess was smiling and looking with joy out at the world. Rebecca could not help but sketch the ship with great care.

Simm had walked from his rooms to the pier to meet his brother, Jason, captain of the *Bess*. It had been a pleasant breakfast. He didn't see his family often, and Jason was the only family on this side of the Atlantic. But the man was captain, and busy with his ship. So, feeling like his short vacation should not be wasted by watching his brother shuffle papers and yell at the mate, Simm had left to wander the river front.

Rebecca did not notice the well-dressed gentleman looking over her shoulder. Lost in her own world, she was absorbed with ships and bird cries. Just at the moment when a shadow fell across her page, she heard a crisp English voice. "Excuse me, Miss? I'm sorry to interrupt you, but you're penciling my ship. And I was wondering if, when you're done, you'd let me have it for a crown. You haven't any colors, have you?" His voice and accent were truly beautiful, Britishly mellow – no New England whine, no foppish Virginia drawl, no Pennsylvania German lilt, or Quaker "thee" and "thou."

Rebecca was struck by the loveliness of his voice and the generosity of his offer. Speechless, she nodded "yes." A few last strokes on the red-haired beauty that was the figurehead of the *Good Queen Bess,* and she was finished.

"It's done; would you like it now? And no, I don't have colored pencils, sorry." Rebecca rolled the paper and handed it up. She nearly gasped when she turned to see who her benefactor might be, and found herself staring into blazing blue eyes looking down at her. They were dark, almost black, but in the sunny morning, gray flecks brightened them into an icy shimmer. The face and voice belonged to a man who should be wearing a white wig in the latest style, but instead, his dark auburn hair was tied into a perfect queue. He was tall, relaxed in his stance, and slender, made for horses, dancing and charm. Rebecca, who had been raised in a world of farmers and tradesmen, had never been near a highly-skilled gentleman, let alone seen one up close.

To ask even a Pennsylvania farm girl at what he was *skilled* would be to mock her. He had a commanding serenity around him; he stood at ease on the busy dock, as though no movement affected him, as though nothing would move until he was, somehow, consulted.

"Yes, thank you. Let's see what we can do about colors. Where is a shop that would have some?" Simm handed the gold piece to Rebecca as he assessed the artist. She was under twenty, probably eighteen; shiny blond hair; blue-eyed and soft looking. Now he looked more closely, letting his eyes roam over her. This was not merely a run-of-the-mill British American. At first glance, she did seem to be a fairly typical blond, blue-eyed pretty girl. But there was something different about this blonde, something vibrant and unexpected.

He watched at her blond hair playing with the summer breeze coming off the river. Maybe earlier this morning she had brushed and pinned it into order, but now, unruly corn silk blond hair escaped both a white cap and a delightful flat hat with a striped blue ribbon that matched a faded and outdated, but once pretty, gown. And she would never convince him that she lived nearby. Although she didn't have hay in her pockets, she did have pale freckles tickling her nose, attesting to having chased hens through the barnyard, lambs around the pasture, and weeds from the kitchen garden. She wore a neckcloth of the same blue, only a truer color that brought out the pink of her cheeks and the blue of her sea-gray eyes. It was clear that the neckcloth had been demurely tucked into the neckline of her shift, but the wind off the water and her own work with pencil and paper had allowed the pretty cloth to stray, revealing luminous skin and hinting at luscious breasts just hidden.

Simm caught himself staring and wishing that he were a lamb being chased around the pasture. He stopped himself from staring, feeling exposed and rude, but he watched as she packed away her artist's supplies and deposited the crown deep at the bottom in a very unusual leather bag.

"The bag. It's Bill, our prize bull. I should say *was* our prize bull. He was charging and huffing at a thunderstorm instead of going inside the barn or lying down in the rain like a sensible animal, and was hit by lightening. Fool beast." She went on explaining as she packed. "Sunday dinners for weeks, shoes, a saddle, Nat, he's my brother in the army, got the saddle, and I got a misshapen piece of leather, so I had this bag made. Had to pay for it myself, of course, but it's unusual and suits me, and of course it's Bill. I should say it reminds me of Bill."

Rebecca realized that she probably made little sense, and that this god who fell from his heaven would merely assume she was daft, or an idiot, and walk away without another word, so she stopped talking.

Simm was entranced. This blonde pixie was weaving delightful nonsense even as she seemed so sad. This was fun, in a world coming apart; could this summer's day be something simple to cherish? That idea, and its simplicity, almost overwhelmed him. Instead of overanalyzing as he usually did, he jumped into the silliness of the alliterative tongue twister.

"So the bag is Bill the prize Bull caught running, ranting

and raving in the tor-*rential* rain?" He emphasized the second half of the last word.

"Oh." Rebecca hesitated trying to think of another one. "Bill the bull, buffed and blundered until lightning, illuminating the heavenly heights aimed arrows at the arrogant animal." She finished gazing into Simm's laughing eyes, caught up in his pleasure at the simple wordplay. "I can't go on, Sir. I confess to using up all my cleverness for one day."

Simm smiled at Rebecca, his deep eyes shimmering with laughter. When was the last time he had laughed? He hadn't engaged in foolish play for an eternity – what seemed like decades, but probably was just years. Men at campfires and on march joked, usually at someone's expense, often about a woman or two who'd ended up-ended, or a man caught by an irate husband. Not at all like playing with the image of a large bull charging at raindrops with this lovely young American lass.

"Miss, I'm sure you have all sorts of cleverness, probably stored deep in that fine bag. Thank you for that play, I feel like I haven't been silly in a very long time. And thank you for the sketch. I'm John." He put out his ungloved hand.

"I'm Rebecca, and honestly, I'm glad you laughed. I also needed that. By the way, I do try not to go around unescorted, but there is never anyone who wants to come with me." She extended her right hand and shook his, wondering as she did if she should have placed it delicately in his for kissing. "It's nice to meet you, John." Simm shook her hand gently, and then turned it within his own larger, darker hand. Slowly he lifted it and just brushed his lips over the top of her hand, so that the kiss was the merest whisper.

Rebecca tried not to gasp. She tried to behave as though she had her rough, strong hand kissed everyday by handsome strangers. She inhaled sharply trying not to lose the rhythm of her own breathing. She was used to men ignoring women's attempts at egalitarianism. American men did not shake or kiss women's hands; those that tried to, failed. She smiled with a wistful sadness that Simm didn't quite understand. A kiss like that might have to last a lifetime at least, she told herself, as she prepared to walk back home to her farm and her father's anger. A kiss like that was wonderful, but it really wouldn't see her through a lifetime of marriage to Herodius Smith.

Simm interrupted Rebecca's thoughts, "Mistress Rebecca, could I buy you some lunch, or breakfast, or whichever you haven't eaten yet?" Spontaneously, he took her hand and placed it on his free arm. At the same time, he took the heavy leather bag from Rebecca's shoulder and put it over his own. He steered her away from the busy port and onto the main street, crowded with shops and houses that ran parallel to the river.

Rebecca realized, as she let Simm lead her away from the workers on the pier, that she should say no to the offer of lunch. She should not go off with a man, even a known friend, without a chaperone. And this man was certainly not known – in fact, he was absolutely the definition of unknown. And yet the day hinted of new and exciting things, and really, he was a most beautiful man. Her better self reminded her that she should insist that he allow her to go home, give her back her bag, say good-day, and leave quickly without looking back.

But, said the Rebecca who had learned just that morning that being a dutiful, well-behaved daughter led to punishments of its own, there was lots of time to get back before dinner. "I could go home," she considered as they walked, "I could give up this adventure before it really begins, or I could declare my independence just once before I submit to father's tyrannical will."

There was something about this day and this man that spoke of adventure. Maybe it was the slight shift in the wind, maybe it was that ship, the *Good Queen Bess,* and the energy it radiated, or maybe it was the man himself, and his obvious status and power, so unlike the farmers and tradesmen she was used to. Whatever it was, today, Rebecca vowed to herself, was not going to be like every other day in the life of Rebecca Willent.

Rebecca let Simm lead them away from the dock, enjoying the companionable silence. The day was getting warm, one of a series of hot mid-summer days that had the town sweltering. As hot as it was, getting on to noon, Rebecca was sure that the tingling energy generated from her hand laying properly demure on John's fine linen sleeve, had nothing at all to do with the sun.

"Very well, lunch." Rebecca said with conviction and smiled, catching his eyes with hers and holding his gaze for just a moment. In that moment she became convinced that today was indeed going to be the start of an adventure.

John FitzSimmon was a connoisseur of beautiful women. In some circles back home, those rare times when he'd been home, some might have called him a rake. It was a persona he had put away, a skill he had not thought to use in America. Most of the time it was simply inappropriate. The rest of the time, it was felonious, and he was not interested in being court-martialed over a local girl. Rebecca, walking so near his side, her hand on his arm, her footfalls matching his on the cobble street, did not correspond with his previous experiences. Most of the American girls he had met in the towns and on his travels had been too shy or too bold. He supposed it was the distance from major cosmopolitan centers that shaped their personalities. The lack of sophistication in colonial life at the edge of empire, within a generation of life on a dangerous frontier, had created the American need for a toughness of spirit. That formidability had created women Simm neither recognized nor had any interest in pursuing. The girl on his arm felt different to him.

Rebecca was gentle in spirit and sweet enough to be like her more-shy sisters. She was clearly an intelligent and clever girl who knew how to take care of herself, but there she was, alone on the pier, drawing pictures, and doing it very well, too, he thought to add. Maybe it was foolish of her, being at the river by herself on a weekday morning, but it showed an attractive boldness, and anyway, all good artists understand that good light won't wait for a chaperone. To Simm that spoke of a kind of bravery, a willingness to risk something in order to get things right. Her young beauty was intriguing enough, but that simple courage could drive him to do things he had rarely done this side of the Atlantic.

She had fixed her fichu as she had gathered her things, but he had a fine memory and an even better imagination. Those now-hidden breasts, full and heavy, were certainly the work of the gods, and he had an unusually strong urge to see just how quickly they piqued and rose to meet his lips. Her skin was soft enough for touching, and just pink from the sun in the high summer. He suddenly needed to see what sweet color it was where the sun never kissed it.

Thinking it might be wise to slow down his runaway imagination, he looked at her face instead of concentrating on the sway of her hips and the rise of her breasts as they walked. Not quite sure how it happened, Simm realized that he had moved her decorous hand off of his arm and put his own arm around her waist. Now he could feel her move with only a few layers of clothing between them.

He expected her to say something and stop him. Clearly, she was not a wanton hussy at the pier to ply her trade. She was obviously kindly brought up, most likely on a nearby farm. That she did not haul off and hit him as he played with the fabric of her jacket, drawing lazy circles on her back over her shift as they walked, aroused him more than her beauty.

He told himself later that it was a test. He told himself that it must have been Rebecca's fault, but as soon as they rounded onto an empty street off the busy road, Simm pulled Rebecca into his arms and kissed her. He knew he should stop, but he did not want to stop. Instead of pushing her away and apologizing, he pulled her closer. His hands slid under her jacket with only the merest of summer stays and a thin linen shift between them, and he deepened the kiss. Instead of pushing him away and screaming as he knew he deserved, she shocked him by putting her arms around his back, lifting her lips to meet his, and allowing him to deepen the kiss still further.

Rebecca had never been kissed. That was not quite right, but if this was a kiss, the fumbling, insecure meeting of mouths on the way back from market day did not deserve the name "kiss." Now she merely allowed herself to react. She had no previous knowledge to relate this to, no way of knowing what was happening. So she drifted with new sensations she had not known existed. Her heart started to pound. She put her arms around John's tempting chest and into his hair, pushing her breasts hard against him and holding him as close against her as she could. In seconds it ended.

Simm stopped, pulled his hands off her back and pushed

her away.

"Oh my god, Miss Rebecca, I'm sorry. But it really is your fault."

"My fault?" Rebecca felt as if she had fallen from the hayloft onto the barn floor. She wanted to lean into him for support and to ease parts of herself that suddenly felt abandoned. But John was holding her off at arms length away from himself. So she gathered herself together and stood up. That kiss would not be the last. She almost stamped her foot in disappointment. It had held layers of potential. Yes, it was intense and powerful, but it would not be the final word on her adventure. A little shaken, but not deterred, she replied – "My fault, Sir John, why is that?"

"It is your fault for having those rose-colored, kissable lips."

"Oh." Relieved that he was not going to abandon her, she squeaked out a response.

He put a few inches between them and put her hand decorously back on his arm, and they continued toward the center of town. Rebecca expected him to talk of lighthearted things, such as the weather, but Simm surprised her by being honest.

"I'd claim that I was as surprised by that kiss as you were but, truthfully, I have been wanting to do that since I spied you sketching on the pier." From that, he did move on to mundane topics, and Rebecca gave polite responses and contemplated that kiss.

Rebecca had no answer to her question. Nothing in her experience or even upbringing had prepared her for an assault of that sort. She knew she was to scream and try to fight if a stranger attacked. She knew how to kick a man and run for help if she were scared. But no mother ever taught a daughter what to do if she wanted an adventure and felt abnormally safe with the stranger. Were there no rules to follow if she wanted him to do it again?

Rebecca allowed a deeper instinct to take over, one that she did not know she had. He had subtly pushed them apart as they walked. She moved infinitesimally closer. As they walked, she started making the same little circles on Simm's arm that he had drawn on her hip a few minutes before.

Rebecca had never done anything so bold and so sensual to anyone before. She was therefore surprised at her own reaction to touching Simm, even through his clothing. She could hear that his breathing had quickened slightly, and his polite chatter had slowed and then stopped. Maybe he didn't like being annoyed while walking to lunch, and was too polite to make her stop, but she didn't want to stop. As she touched the fine linen of Simm's jacket, her own breathing changed and she almost needed to sit. Instead, she stopped walking and turned to face him. Rebecca carefully took her hand off of Simm's jacket and looked up into his dazzling ice- blue eyes.

Simm was flabbergasted that Rebecca did not haul off and slap him. He should never have allowed her to play with the fabric of his jacket like that. Of course, she was just enjoying the fine weave of the linen. He knew he should not have allowed himself to become so aroused. He was ready to send someone for his horse and take her straight home. As he was about to move away and act like a gentleman, he noticed that Rebecca had come to her own senses and had moved away from him. He looked at her to get his own bearings, but instead of glaring up at him and announcing that she never wanted to see him again, she put her hands on his chest under his jacket. She stepped in closer.

Rebecca put her head against Simm's chest. She moved

her hands from the front to the back of his body and hugged him to her. She felt him harden, and the power that gave her made her smile. She raised her mouth to his and, in a flash, he covered it with his own.

Simm had been indulging in improper thoughts about the pretty American since he'd spotted her on the quay. But to have her looking at him like that, instead of hitting him and running away, was the real shock. He cradled her cheek and lifted her mouth to his. She deepened it by pulling him even closer and entwining his tongue with her own. "Oh, my lady," he thought as he deepened the kiss further, "I know there is a story behind this." And before he completely lost all ability to think, Lord John FitzSimmon, fifth son of the Duke of Chardon, and Major in the 23rd Regiment of Foot of His Majesty's Armed Forces, made a silent vow to this unknown beauty that had most literally fallen into his arms: that before he found her naked in his bed, he would have the whole story and judge whether he was good enough for this American goddess, this Columbia.

Rebecca had found the sensations involved in kissing and now touching John's body through the few layers between them extraordinary, and didn't want to stop. Growing up with four brothers and all their friends, she had been kissed by a boy or two. The encounters had been mildly enjoyable, but had led to nothing of much interest. Jimmy Slokes had gotten her alone in the barn last summer, and she had let him kiss her and take off her bodice, but he was the only one who'd enjoyed it. So, when Jimmy had pushed her down into the straw and then put his hand on her leg, she had pushed him out of the loft. That clumsy pairing bore no relation whatsoever to this. Rebecca felt John deepen the kiss. She opened to him, allowing herself to fall into the sensations that being touched and touching created. She wanted to unbutton his shirt right there in that alley, but stopped herself from going that far. Instead, she slid her hands inside his silk waistcoat to feel the shape of his back through only a shirt of fine linen.

Simm felt himself harden as Rebecca caressed his back. It just would not do to take her on the sidewalk in an alley. They would probably be arrested, and that was no way to remain incognito. He kissed her neck lightly, and moved just an inch away, enough to let the weak breeze find an opening. He left his hand on her back so that he broke the moment without breaking the mood.

"Lunch! I remember I promised you food."

"Oh, I'm sorry, I... I... I...." Rebecca was so flustered that she wanted to cry.

John put his mouth close to Rebecca's ear. He growled in a whisper, "No apologies, Becky... never."

Rebecca was not sure what that meant, but accompanied him down the street, almost stumbling until she got her feet under her again. Simm held open the door to the dining room of a small, beautifully-appointed inn. It was full of people laughing, talking and eating what appeared and smelled to be good food. Rebecca had not noticed being hungry, but she happily let John find a table and order lunch. After she had finished her soup, she looked at the people in the room around her. There was an interesting variety of people here at lunchtime. They were near the port, so there were well-dressed sailors, captains and other officers, the businessmen who handled the shipments. There were women, too, but not many. Most seemed to be wives meeting husbands for lunch. There were other sorts as well, the overdressed ladies who kept men company. Rebecca tried not to stare .

They chatted gently of family, neither of them revealing anything that would identify or embarrass him or herself. Simm was willing to say that he came from English gentry and that he and his brothers owned the *Bess*. The figurehead on the ship was a likeness not of Queen Elizabeth, but of his mother, called Libby, a famously outspoken Elizabeth of this day. The glorious red hair on the carving was another similarity between the Elizabeths. All the first girls in his family tended to ginger, he mentioned with a laugh.

Rebecca was only willing to admit to living on a farm not too far from where they were, that she had many siblings, and that she was the youngest. Her father, she said, did not really care where she spent the day.

They ate the rest of their meals in near silence, each wanting to say more but unable or unwilling to reveal more.

After a small plate of fruit was served and eaten, Simm offered his hand to Rebecca. "Rebecca, I propose that we have coffee and dessert elsewhere, and on the way I would like to buy you those colored pencils you said you don't yet have. So you see, although they are my gift to you, I buy them with only the expectation that you use them for the completion of the art I already purchased from you."

Rebecca rose with him and they made their way to the door before she answered. "Yes, John, I do know a shop near here. It's where I purchase my papers and pencils."

With her hand resting on Simms's arm and her bag again on his shoulder, they walked down brick streets past shops with clean windows and beautiful items in each. Simm had not seen an American town with such an array of goods, although he had assumed that Boston, before the occupation that came after the damned fools dumped the tea in the harbor, and New York, before its fall to General Howe, would have looked like this as well. He got great pleasure from watching and listening to Rebecca enjoy the pretty things in the windows. She knew many of the shops and their goods. Also she could tell quality when she saw it, to a detail that surprised him in the colonial. This Rebecca was proving to be a puzzle that he felt inclined to solve. She was weaving layer after layer of a mystery whose depths he almost desperately wanted to penetrate.

With the largest collection of German kohls the store sold in her possession, they walked back out into the early afternoon heat. Rebecca kissed him gently on the cheek to thank him for the gift, as one would thank a brother or an uncle. He wanted to grab her and kiss her again in response, but instead he picked up her bag again, noting that the new pencils added quite a bit of weight to the bag that was Bill.

A few blocks away, and down seven steps, they entered a dark, cool coffee shop called by an obvious name: *Coffee Joe's*. Joe, the proprietor was an old forty. His hair was a dirty gray, he needed either a beard or a shave, and his voice was scratchy, but his food was good, his ale was dark, and the coffee was hot. He did not serve tea, and said he never would again "since the damn tax."

The large hearth was cold, with only a small stove heating water for the coffee. People were eating lunch, as well as various pies and pastries. "This is nice." Simm whispered into Rebecca's ear as they entered. The tavern was occupied but not crowded. There was little outside light since the room was below ground, but the cool and the dark was a pleasant relief from the bright summer heat. What light there was was supplied by cheap candles in jars and a few oil lanterns. Simm ordered cider and a piece of chocolate pie for them to share, and escorted Rebecca to a clean, bare table, near enough to a window to see the ship of her drawing. He pulled out the scroll and handed her the leather bag with the new pencils.

They drank cold cider while Rebecca worked on the *Good Queen Bess*, adding just enough color to give it dimension without coloring in the entire sketch. When she had finished, she sat back and watched Simm, calmly observing the diners in the room. He had eaten a bite or two of the pie, but was waiting for Rebecca to join him for the rest. He put a piece on a fork and slowly put it in her mouth as she was wrapping the pencils and putting them away. She looked up and into dark eyes, looking at her with such hunger it made her heart pound in response.

They finished the pie, deliberately licking their forks and falling into laughter as they got messier and sillier. When they were done, Rebecca turned to Simm to explain something that had been on her mind since they entered the dark tavern. "John, I hope you don't think I do this sort of thing with men I meet at the pier. I mean, honestly, I don't know what I'm saying, not with men I meet anywhere."

"Mistress Rebecca," Simm had cleaned his hands and face with a napkin and was drinking again from a cold tankard. "Please don't think I would ever think that of you. In fact, I'm very sure you have never shared pie or done anything like this before, and if it helps you, quite honestly, neither have I."

Simm went to the front of the tavern to get more cold cider. He watched Rebecca from the other side of the room. She was repinning her hair, something he had seen her do, even with cap and bonnet in place. Intrigued with how her hair seemed to continuously expel pins, he was determined to ask. He put the two tankards down on the table and sat close to the bench on the side of the table against a cold chimney, casually draping his left hand on the back of the bench. "Rebecca, I can't help but notice that you continually push hair-pins back into your hair. How many are in there?" He put his hand into the back of her hair and started pulling out pins. As he did so, he rubbed her head and undid her plaits beneath the cap. Rebecca attempted to maintain her demeanor while he drove her to distraction by playing with her hair. She chatted with him meaninglessly, and kept a bland and appropriate smile on her face.

Simm wasn't fooled by her falsely-calm demeanor. The color of Rebecca's cheeks was giving away her arousal, and again he had to stop himself from falling on her and taking her on the table. His reaction to her reminded him of Bill the bull, and he'd probably meet the same end, if not from God then from an angry father, brother or jealous boyfriend. These American farm girls were closely watched, and he was increasingly cognizant of why that should be.

"Ten, there are ten pins holding your hair to you head. Now, if you take off your cap, does all the hair fall on the floor?"

Rebecca shook the desire out of her body with a deep breath. "Hair, floor? No just a limp mess that won't behave itself and stay up and out of the way." She giggled as she insulted her hair. Actually, she liked it; it was smooth and soft and misbehaved, just like her.

"John, you should know that I like my hair. I just can't make it fit social expectations without pins, lots of pins. And if we don't find all the pins you've been removing from my hair, I won't have any until this blasted war is over."

"What does the war have to do with hair pins? Are you rebels refusing them, like tea?" Simm tried to make his voice light, but really this conflict over taxes and tea had him weary.

Every British citizen was taxed, not just these Yanks.

"No, not like tea. I don't think they're taxed, at least not yet. They just don't get through the blockades, and we don't make them here. No industry, you know– you keep it all for yourselves, selfish and no pins."

"I had no idea, I don't believe Tom Paine mentions pins in *Common Sense*, or Thomas Jefferson in your 'Declaration of Independence.'"

"Now, you're just being mean."

"I'm sorry, it was just the thought of all this horror coming down to hair pins."

"I think hair pins are really why people are mad – industry really, John." Rebecca continued, looking him over and deciding that something serious needed to be asked. "Are you really a ship owner, or is there more you're not letting on?"

"I really own that ship, or at least I own a portion of a company that owns a number of ships, but I have been in America awhile and I think what is happening is sad. Our countries are more alike than you Americans know, and your battle is one we have fought before and will again. It really is part of an Anglo tradition. What worries me is not that we fight, but that your government wants France to help America against Britain. France won't help America for the good of America. They will help your cause only for the evil they can do to Britain. And I don't think America, as a new nation, will be able to defend itself from France without Britain's help.

"Uff, I'm sorry, I tend to go on about this. My family actually argue for the American rebels. They say the King should leave the colonies alone and let them grow. But meanwhile...." John let his thoughts and his voice trail off.

He began, in an efficient and businesslike way, to gather Rebecca's pins. Then, in silence, as if the orchestra changed from a reel to a minuet, the world slowed and whirled as he slowly put his left hand inside the slit on the right side of her old-fashioned skirt. Purposely just brushing the side of her thigh with his fingertips, he pulled the pocket to the outside of the skirt. He opened it, dropped the pins into the pocket, and pulled the drawstrings closed slowly, holding the thin fabric of the pocket in his left hand he moved his hand into the opening of her skirt, and brought the pocket inside, placing it back onto her right thigh. He let his hand remain still on Rebecca's leg, waiting for her to say something, or move in some way that would indicate that he should leave her alone. Instead, she tilted her head sideways and slowly licked cider from her lips, staring into his eyes with her own wide with wonder and showing no fear at all. She shifted on the bench, not away but toward him, spreading her legs slightly under the table in response to his fingers beginning to knead her leg.

While his left hand was busy tending to Rebecca's thighs, his right hand clutched the tankard drinking and encouraging her to drink as well. If anyone had bothered to look into their secluded corner they would have seen a couple drinking from pewter tankards, and Simm wanted to keep it that way. But he also wanted to enjoy this dark corner and some of the pleasures such a place could bring.

The sun had moved away from their window, putting the little table deeper in shadow as day passed noontime. Rebecca gave a start and moaned softly into her cider, looking up at Simm and hard into those blue eyes, as he moved his hand from the pocket to the soft skin on her inner thigh. He moved slowly, partly to heighten the experience for them both, and also to allow, to give her time, to shift her body away from him, slap him or tell him to stop. She didn't.

"Brave girl," he whispered into her ear, as he continued to

work his hand closer to her inner secrets, all the while drinking cold cider and looking into her hazy blue eyes which had turned dark gray with desire. She opened her legs a bit more, willing him to take her to places she had never been. She put her head on his shoulder as he played with the hair between her legs and mirrored it with that beneath her cap. Rebecca was experiencing tremendous sensations as Simm continued to tease and torture her most secret delicate parts. She turned and bit his shoulder, then looked to see if anyone in the nearly-empty tavern had noticed. They hadn't, but she covered her own mouth and gasped as he pinched her thigh gently.

She moved her right hand into Simm's hair, playing with the soft hair beneath his queue. She wanted to tear apart the neat style and make him wither as he was making her, but she knew that she did not know how – and it wouldn't have been subtle enough for a tavern dining room. She lifted her right leg over his left leg, wishing that the layers of clothing would evaporate like the drops of water from the tankards. Simm wanted to cover her mouth with kisses and cradle her breasts with his hands. He wanted to suck them till she screamed begging for him. He whispered all that and more to her as he caressed and teased. Rebecca looked into John's eyes and saw kindness and raw desire.

There was a small part of her that knew this was wrong, but that part could not tell her why. Her situation was wrong, too. This didn't hurt anyone. This was not a mistake – it was some kind of fantastic dream. She floated lazily in gentle ecstacy, until sensation caught up and ran past her thoughts, pushing all rational thought out of her mind. She drifted, trying to keep her face expressionless as Simm played with the delicate layers of skin between her legs. She felt herself sinking through an endless cloud; her body shuddered with release, and John's two strong arms were around her, holding her, her head buried in his chest, safe, hidden from the world and the rest of the room.

In a few minutes, her breathing returned to normal, and he reluctantly reminded her that they had to get going, and that she had to be home. He helped her fix her skirt, put her bonnet on her cap, and tied it for her. Lastly, he handed her the leather bag, letting his hands linger over her jacket as he put it over her well-formed shoulders. Simm needed those minutes and more to recover his own calm. The softness of her skin, the smell of her desire, her moistness as she had welcomed him, jolted him into something deeply human, needy and elemental.

From the first moment on the pier when they had met there had been no artifice on his part. By necessity, there were half truths. This was, honestly, something he needed time to think over. "It would probably be best," he mused to himself as he adjusted his britches and collected his wits, "if I avoided anything and anyone that will lead me this close to truth-telling." But instead of dismissing her and eliminating his problem before it occurred again, he surprised himself. He spoke softly, not wanting to break this mood they had created in their corner of the coffee shop. "Rebecca, this has been an unexpected meeting. I know you may hate me and never want to see me again. You are probably shocked and horrified by my behavior and forwardness. But please know that I want to see you again. So, I will be here, at this table, every night this week from five thirty till eight o'clock starting tomorrow, Tuesday. If you don't come, I will understand and miss you. If you do, I will be happy. But.... " He stood in front of her to stop her movement toward the door. Speaking very quietly, he continued. "If you come back to me, please come with the truth so that I believe I am not destroying your life by taking you into my arms."

With that, Simm offered his arm for the last time that day and escorted Rebecca up the seven steps and back into the bright sun of the afternoon, leaving Coffee Joe's behind them.

Chapter 2

Rebecca's secret adventure made her deliciously happy all week. She simply couldn't believe that such a wonderful accident had occurred simply because she had been sketching the ships on the pier. It balanced the scales that her father had tipped against her a few days before. Words with her father had run round and round incessantly in her head since the first hints a day before, like stirring a soap pot. With her mother gone, he'd started; knowing that Rebecca had been his wife's last and favorite child, he found he did not have the patience for fathering. Friday afternoon he brought it up again, seemingly searching for Rebecca's acquiescence to his plan.

"Da, you don't have much to do with me and we handle the farm chores well together, don't we? I'm not much bother." Rebecca assumed that this conversation, like so many others, was an attempt to make her do her chores more carefully.

"Becky, that's not what I'm talking about. You'll always have plenty of chores. Life is like that for people like us, but what I am saying is that Hackett will need this house when the next babies come, and he should have it."

"There's room for me. I'll stay in the attic or something. Da, what are you really saying?" Rebecca knew from his stance that this conversation would not be like the others.

"Well, Becky, you know Smith, down the road, has offered me his back pasture for your hand, and that set me to thinking."

Rebecca knew very well who Herodius Smith was. A vile-smelling widower who had seven children and wanted Rebecca to keep his bed warm. He had plenty of land and plenty of help with the children, who were all pretty and fairly well-behaved. Herodius had been pinching and grabbing at Rebecca since she was fourteen, so his interest did not surprise her.

"Thinking what, Da?" She knew now that she had no chance to talk herself out of his arrangement, especially if it meant land for himself and his oldest son.

"Thinking that you'd turned eighteen last spring and were still not hitched. This is a good offer."

"For you, Da, not me."

"Aw Becky, why do you say that? He's a generous man, likes you fine. Those children need a mama, but they're pleasant for a large brood. He'll be good to you, probably have lots more wee ones. You won't lack for anything."

"So, you'll give my share, the share of the land Mother insisted you put aside for me, as well as my dowry which you already explained you used, for Hackett for his growing family, and sell me to the neighbor for more land. And now with Mother dead and Nat gone, Hackett would see the injustice, but he benefits, so there is no one here to object, NO ONE!"

"Becky, it's not as bad as all that."

"Bad or good Da, that's the truth. We had this conversation yesterday and the day before, Da, you are not going to change your mind, and I am not going to be happy about it, no matter how many times you bring it up. But give me another year – nothing will change between now and then."

And she had stormed off to do the milking and collect whatever eggs the layers had scattered around the farmyard.

This time, before she left for town she planned carefully. She put water on the hearth to heat, and grabbed a towel and an old shift for a cold swim in the stream that ran between the woodlot and the pasture. The cold water on the hot day felt wonderful, and she wiped the anger from her muscles as she tread water and rubbed sand into her skin to get the dirt out of her hands and soften her feet. The wash water was warm when she got back, so she filled a large kettle and brought it to her room where she washed carefully, choosing a clean white shift and her nicest summer gown. She tied her own stays as tight as she could get them in the front, and turned the corset around, pulling her breasts up so they would just mound beneath the silk fichu Aunt Amalia had given her the Christmas before. She dressed herself as well as she could, wishing for a sister or friend to help her with laces and strings. She tied her soft leather boots over silk stockings and put her best bonnet on her head, leaving off her mop cap.

She wasn't dressed for walking the miles between the farm and the town, but asking for a ride from her father was out of the question, as was borrowing a horse or hitching one to a wagon, so walking it would be. She tiptoed through the kitchen garden and past the front window where her father sat, reading the newspaper, almost ready to go off to Hackett and Jane's for his dinner. "Let them feed him. He won't eat my cooking unless he has to," she fumed to herself as she set foot on the road, willing her feet on toward her assignation.

"Well, father can sell my virginity to all the neighbors if he wants. I don't have to deliver it, do I? If it is a commodity, like gloves or tea, then like a good merchant I will deliver where I feel is best. " Rebecca focused her wrath into decisive action as she walked toward the Philadelphia River on that hot Friday night. She would not let her father sell anything; she would give it away to an adventure – give it to fate in the person of a man who amazed and excited her. With John, whoever he was, she would create a memory that would belong to her alone. It would be, definitively, her Declaration of Independence. Should those men be allowed to cause all that trouble and leave her the victim of a different tyrant's will? No!

The sun was getting low in the sky behind her as Rebecca walked toward the town. It was uncomfortably warm. She slowed just a bit so she would not arrive dripping and out of breath. Her breathing was labored anyway, as anxious as she was about the meeting. The early August air was damp, with thick, oppressive storm clouds building to the south. There were the beginnings of rumbles as well, moving up the river on whatever air current the clouds could find. Maybe, she thought, there would be a storm strong enough to bring an end to this heat. She walked just a block away from her Aunt Amalia's fine house through the surrounding neighborhoods, hoping none of her neighbors would recognize her. She pulled her bonnet closer around her face, relieved when squares of fine houses gave way to the crowded riverfront area. Rebecca turned south and walked closer to Coffee Joe's shop, determined not to be a coward.

Town and harbor scents mixed with the air of the impending storm. Joe's was only a few blocks more. She was glad she knew the town as well as she did – at least this part of the adventure did not cause fear. Rebecca stopped in front of the coffee shop and asked herself one more time if this was what she wanted to do. She stepped aside as a man in black walked out of the door, brushing by her into the darkness, turning to stare briefly as he walked away. She did not recognize him, and ignored the feeling of evil that crossed over her. Assured that she wanted to enter, she walked down those seven steps and into the dark, smoky tavern.

Rebecca took a minute to adjust to the dim light in the tavern. She found Simm sitting, affecting a bored nonchalance and nursing an ale. His eyes lit when he spotted her. He stood and walked forward, dropping a few notes on the table behind him. He led her out of the coffee house. Once they were away from the side streets and onto a pleasant street of shops and homes he offered a short explanation. "I hope you don't mind; we have to eat somewhere other than Joe's. I've been sitting there all week, and I'm sure he is as sick of me as I am of that dingy place."

He looked over the girl who appeared as much a gift from the gods as a Philadelphia lovely, so pleased that she had undertaken the next step on her adventure. Simm took in her perfect gown, its bright summer colors in nearly the latest Parisian style, and her lovely bonnet. Clearly his farm girl was more than he had at first thought. He raised Rebecca's right hand with his left and brought it to his lips for a kiss. That elegant kiss surprised Rebecca. It did not whisper seduction or nighttime wonders; instead, it politely brushed the top of her fingers and told her how glad he was that she had come.

Simm led Rebecca to a small place below the main dock. She could smell the good food before they reached the door, and knew with the first steps inside that this was an establishment known for its food, not its elegance. They were each served a large bowl of fish chowder with lots of fried bread. The people around them all seemed happy. There were families and couples, visiting and chatting over good food, and there were sailors far from home enjoying a good meal instead of their ships' rations and grog.

Rebecca felt overdressed. She was, after all, in her very

best gown, but John sitting across from her was nearly as finely dressed, and no one was paying any sort of special attention to them. Soon, she adjusted to the good will and good food and settled in to enjoy herself. She ate the delicious food in near silence, not really tongue-tied, but unsure how to initiate conversation with a man who really was still a stranger. She let him do the talking and engage her interest in various things. He asked careful questions, and skillfully steered the conversation onto general topics, away from war and family politics. They took their time over a bottle of good wine Simm had brought from his rooms.

Simm watched Rebecca enjoy the food. He refilled her glass with the wine often enough to loosen her tongue when he felt the time was right. He didn't want her to get very drunk, but he needed the truth before he did something that would have them both hating him. And though he could not say exactly why, the thought of Rebecca leaving with bad memories of this evening had him wanting to crunch glass. They finished eating as night crept over the bright summer day, offering a slight relief from the heat.

When the wine was gone, and the mood of the crowd in the small dining room changed to a more raucous affair, they edged toward the door. They made their way through the incoming revelers and out into the night air. Behind them, they heard someone begin to rail against the British Parliament and the King, but Rebecca was happy to ignore politics for just this once. Simm pushed through, and away from the crowd, before anyone could approach him and ask his opinion. Honestly, he didn't have a ready answer to the question of American independence that would be coherent to anyone, certainly not himself.

Simm was happy to walk with Rebecca beyond the lights

and crowd of the busy pier toward the river. Dark storm clouds moved in, and the air had gotten closer during the short time they were at dinner. The clouds chased the moon now, and it was certain that the storm, when it came, would bring real change from this heat.

Rebecca was surprised at how happy she was to be with John, and how relaxed. It was hard to believe that she had only met him a few days ago. She felt as if she had known him forever. She felt his body next to hers, aware of every inch of him as they moved in tandem down the narrow road. Rebecca wanted nothing so much as to stop and touch him. What an extraordinary feeling, that was. She shuddered in anticipation.

Simm felt Rebecca shudder. His first reaction was that she might be frightened or cold. The night was far too warm for the latter, and he sensed no fear in her bearing. Her step along side his was strong and determined, leaning close to him, and, surprisingly, not trying to run from him.

Off to their left was a sandy marshland used by fishermen to mend nets and store their small boats. The night was not dark, so they walked down toward the water between the upside- down boats, making a path in the sand. Rebecca found a big rock not far from the water's edge and climbed on it to watch the moon and the water. She sat still, facing away from him. She was sure that Simm was watching while she took off her bonnet, and let her hair free in the quickening wind. She carefully unpinned her scarf and jacket, and stored the pins safely in her small reticule. She untied her neck scarf, and let it flutter to the sand. Her unpinned jacket was loose and she took it off, delighted with the feeling of the wind on her skin. Her body burned with feeling him watching her, his blue eyes devouring her. She felt very much like prey. But unlike the mouse, she wanted desperately to be toyed with and consumed by the cat. So she leaned back in the wind, letting her breasts tempt at the edge of her stays, white orbs glowing in the drifting moonlight.

Simm knew Rebecca could probably feel his eyes feasting on her. Even in the low light of a cloud-swept night, he could make out the outline of her body leaning back on that rock, and imagined running his hands over the skin that the wind was kissing first. There was, however, the task he had presented himself of unearthing Rebecca's truth. He needed to hear why she was so willing to engage in unsanctioned, unsanctified sex with a virtual stranger, one who, however handsome and charming – Simm chuckled at his description of himself – was certain to disappear, destined never to return.

Thinking that he would never seeing her again brought an unexpected sadness. Rebecca was just beautiful and interesting enough that he would want to see her again. But for the vagaries of war, the winds of fate and ill weather, and all things that made such relationships impossible, he would wish for something different. But what was it in her life that drove her off the warranted path and willing, even anxious, to accept the ministrations of a stranger?

Simm walked down to Rebecca's rock and stood behind her, running his hand through her hair, fighting with the wind for control of the silky stuff. She spun around and put her arms on his shoulders, pulling him down to her for a kiss the likes of which he did not think he'd ever experienced before. He deepened it; their breaths mingled as one, and Rebecca ran her hands under his waistcoat and over his chest while he kept his own hands still at his side. When at last the rhythm of the kiss demanded that they stop for a minute, Simm pulled away and drew Rebecca onto her feet in the sand.

He picked up her things and stowed them in the large pockets of his jacket. Then he began to walk down the beach. Rebecca ran after him on the rough gravel, trying to catch up. She knew something was holding John back, but she had no idea what it could be. Finally near enough, she walked beside him, matching his steps. She looked at him to try reading his face, but it was too dark to see anything there.

"John, what is wrong? Did I do something wrong, something to make you angry? You can just take me home if you'd rather."

They had stopped by a small hut and some vessels pulled onto the highland. Simm stopped and looked down at Rebecca in the dark night. He groaned at the thought of leaving this unfinished. "No, Rebecca, you've done nothing. I am not angry. But I do need understand why you are willing to be here with a man you don't know, to throw away your innocence so blithely. It's not that I don't want you, but before ... I need to understand you, I need to know that you understand what is happening here."

"Why, what?" Rebecca did not mean to tease, but she was just confused and aroused enough that she really did not understand what he had asked of her.

"I feel you don't want to expose all your secrets. But I must understand why you are running at this choice." John asked gently, "I assume you are a virgin?"

Rebecca nodded yes. "Oh, I see. I don't mean that it is all a terrible secret. You want me to explain why I am on a beach, flirting with a dangerous rake on a dark night? Like the man you are, you are worried that I am throwing my virginity away without love or marriage; without even the promise or prospect of either. And you wouldn't want one of your sisters out here with the likes of you, now would you?" Rebecca spoke quickly, trying not to show the edge of her anger, but failing.

Simm shook his head, chagrined to have rousted her ire, but not sorry, for such often leads to the truth.

"I'll tell you what you asked. I am not sure the explanation will make you comfortable, but I will try. The short answer is that I don't want to give Herodius Smith his money's worth, but I suppose you want the long answer."

Rebecca sat on the damp ground right where she'd been standing. She fixed her skirts around herself, leaned back to watch the clouds move across the sky, and began to speak in earnest. Simm quietly joined her on the ground and listened.

"I am the sixth child, and the second daughter. My father had money for my sister's dowry four years ago. But he hadn't saved enough for me. My mother, who died of an infection last year, made sure that she saved her egg money so that I would have something. My father told me, this past week, that he took that money and spent it on a piece of pasture that connects my father's land with the land my brother Hackett grazes.

"I have four brothers. The oldest, Hackett, lives on an adjacent farm with his wife and two daughters. Two brothers have moved away, one west over the Alleghenies, and one south to the Carolinas or Kentucky. The last brother is a captain with the American army in New Jersey. Father is a Tory. And he suspects that I share Nat's sensibilities. But that is no excuse for what happened." Rebecca sighed and pulled her knees closer to her body, lost now in her tale.

"We have a neighbor, Herodius Smith. He is a widower with seven children under the age of twelve. The children are sweet-tempered most of the time. They have all the women in the neighborhood fussing over the 'poor motherless waifs.'

But Herodius – I think he was a nice man when he was young – is now brusque and a bit mean. He does not bathe or take care of his teeth. He drinks too much, and he had been grabbing at me and pinching more than my cheeks since well before his wife died, when I was fourteen. Sometimes when he sees me, even from across the road, I feel him leering and hear his lewd muttering.

"It turns out that Herodius owns a piece of land that would complete my father's crop and pasture land. So instead of my father trying to protect his daughter and youngest child from the lewd and nasty neighbor, he has found a way out of my dowry trouble, one that would solve his land problems as well.

"Father has decided to sell me to Herodius Smith for the back pasture Herodius does not currently use. It's adjacent to my brother's land. Generously, Father is giving me until my nineteenth birthday to move out of our house so that my brother and his growing family can move in. If I do not, I can marry Smith. Father can't make me of course, but he would offer no safe alternative, if I cannot find a better way.

"John," She turned to him and put a hand on his cheek. "I think you are beautiful, and truthfully I want to touch you in places I barely know exist. But it is more than wanting you. I want something wonderful. I want an adventure. If I must marry Herodius Smith and become the mother of seven at nineteen, I understand that I must grant him the pleasure of mauling me every night, but I will not grant him the pleasure of taking my virginity. It is my very small declaration of independence. I will decide with whom I will lay my first time. And I decided that a beautiful chance-found rake will be perfect." Rebecca was slightly embarrassed by her forthright speech, but felt he deserved to understand that she really expected nothing more of him. She hurried to answer the next, unasked question.

"John, if there were a child between us I would be delighted. And to bring my bastard into that marriage, with all his brats, he'd not likely notice anyway. Herodius Smith may get my body every night from next summer till forever, but he won't get my soul.

Rebecca looked sideways into Simm's ice-shiny eyes. "When I met you on Monday morning, I had just finished being told by my father that I would be marrying Herodius. After that extraordinary lunch, I realized that I would be a fool not to follow where the fates are leading. I would be a fool to walk away from such a gentleman. I am sorry I seem too bold, but that is the whole of it."

Simm imagined that things like this happened often enough to be mundane, but it saddened him. He didn't think Rebecca was bold to try to take some control of her life in a time of building chaos. His instinct was to save her, but that was impossible and impractical. He knew that this war pulled him in one direction as it would push her in the other. Rebecca's choice was a reasonable reaction to an unreasonable transaction. His body reacted swiftly, hardening at discovering himself part of her life. Of course, rationally, Simm felt honored to find that he was the recipient of that decision. Suddenly, reason and rational thought were not playing very loudly in the symphony of his body's reaction to her, her body and her story. He would kill, however, if he found that such a man was raising his child, but that would likely not happen, and surely he would never know.

Simm reached over and put his hand on her back, as much for simple human comfort as to initiate physical contact. He really had no words or wisdom to offer. He understood she was being impetuous, and that her boldness could too easily get her into unknown trouble. But he also recognized that he, unlike many men, would not put her life or dignity in peril. Smiling ruefully, he forced himself to admit that he desperately and selfishly wanted to run his hands and mouth over Rebecca's luscious body, to teach that soaring spirit how to moan, beg and cry in a very earthy way. And he admitted that he had been dreaming of repeating and adding to their first meeting since they had parted outside of the tavern.

He pulled Rebecca off the wet sand and into his lap, running his hands slowly through her hair. He kissed her and blew gently on her bare neck and shoulders. Rebecca turned just enough to face Simm. She let her body melt into his, feeling his hard, beautifully-muscled chest push against her breasts. Rebecca reached for Simm's hair and pulled it out of its queue. She kept her hands in his hair, deeply rubbing his scalp through it and noticing that, as she stroked, his breathing changed and deepened.

Simm reveled in Rebecca's hands running through hair that was usually covered with a stiff, formal wig, and almost drove him past a point of gentlemanly restraint. While opening his mouth to cover hers, he heard her voice tease at his drifting mind: "John, why don't you need pins in all this wonderful hair?" There was no answer, really, because most days he covered his head with a wig cap, where most men shaved theirs. Rebecca's teasing questions were leading to places he could not go, so he ignored her words and let sensation wash over him. She opened her mouth to his, her tongue answering his questing one, as he deepened the kiss and claimed her with only his mouth. Her body ached for him to touch her, to tease her, to pleasure her. She pushed against him, aching mindlessly for what she did not know.

She began to undo the buttons on his waistcoat, putting her hands inside his vest against the lovely soft linen of his shirt. She ran her fingers over his arms and chest, the touch making her dizzy with need. Simm gently pushed her hands off his chest and let her fall away from him till she caught herself, leaning backwards from his lap, her breasts forced upward by the motion, mounded ripe and full over the top of her stays. Rebecca let her body react with wanton pleasure, as he leaned over her exposed neck and chest to rain kisses over her neck and the aching mounds.

A large drop hit the back of Simm's neck as he was ravishing Rebecca's very fascinating neckline, wondering at what point her nipples would simply pop out as she was leaning back. He had just reached the conclusion that he was going to go in after them, and was looking forward to the expedition when the heavens opened with a large thunderclap.

Simm lifted Rebecca to her feet and quickly realized they would stay drier if he carried her. He lifted the still-dazed Rebecca into his arms and headed across the open marsh to a sail-cloth-tent left by some painters on the beach. He ran with Rebecca in his arms along the strand, running as hard as he could. In a moment she shouted over they roar of rain and thunder that he should let her down. Hand-in-hand they ran the last stretch, her skirts dragging in the wet sand, and fancy half-boots slipping over the stones. Simm got to the opening a split second before Rebecca. He held open the flap as they slipped in, laughing hard, just as the downpour worsened.

Lightening lit the interior just enough to reveal a small lantern in a corner. Simm lit it, but kept it well away from the paint and used rags. In the low light, they could see that the makeshift tent covered a dinghy that had been brought in, away from the impending storm. Low and crowded, most of the room inside the tent was taken up by the useful boat, but it was dry. Rebecca was still aroused, but now bleary and confused as well. She did not know what to do next, or whether her plans were ruined. Her desire had not lessened, but the run across the sandy marsh and the cold rain on her head had jolted her back to reason, and now she was not sure what she wanted.

Simm sensed her change in mood. He did not immediately resume his attentions to her lovely body. Instead, he climbed into the boat and offered his hand to help her join him.

"I'm afraid the only way to be at all comfortable in this abode is to get into the boat." Simm was glad the painter had removed any benches or seats that would have bisected the little boat's length. He sat toward one end of the dinghy and motioned for Rebecca to sit near. The boat was so narrow they were forced together in the slightly-wider middle, even as Rebecca sat as far away as possible.

"Rebecca, we could wait out the storm. Then I could accompany you home, wiser perhaps, but not changed." He emphasized the last word, as he reached out the length of his arm and let a finger run through her damp hair, her smell overwhelming him in the small quarters. He hoped she would refuse his gallant offer, but he would not take it off the table. She shifted her body in the boat. Rising slightly to free her skirts that had been tightly trapped under her legs, she turned away as she sat, so that her back leaned against Simm's warm body. He carefully did not touch her with his hands, keeping them stoically at his sides. She sat very close, very still. He could smell the warm, moist sweetness of her hair. He buried his face in her hair, praying that she would agree to stay with him, wanting almost desperately to pull her closer and resume his pleasant torture of her stays and breasts, now that they were once again nearly within reach of his hands.

She appreciated his generous proposal. It was obvious, she noted now that she was again close to his body, that he had not stopped wanting her. She smiled in the dark of the tent. The option to leave or stay was hers. "John," she spoke softly but surely, "you are kind. I can tell that, but I embarked on an adventure and I am determined to follow it to its conclusion. I live on a farm; I know what you want." She reached back and put her arms around his neck, offering herself to him completely.

Simm kissed her neck and moved his hands to let his finger play with her breasts, so delightfully within reach and peaking back at him. "Ahh", he murmured in her ear, "just where we let off." The torrents of rain on the small tent added just enough noise and chaos so that he didn't try to muffle her moans as he lifted her skirts and let his fingers roam over her thighs and buttocks. As her breathing changed and she nearly reached the edge, he lay down in the little boat and pulled her to his side.

Simm understood what Rebecca wanted, but he wanted to give her so much more than the quick roll she had come for. He would make that second offer, but first she must be satisfied that Herodius would not take her maidenhead, that "John the Rake" would play the role she had cast for him. The narrow boat did not allow for the foreplay he would have wished for her, he considered as he ran his fingers through her damp hair and pulled her against him, covering her mouth with his. Rebecca pulled up her wet, sandy skirts, and put her leg over his, straddling his tense body. He let his fingers find the soft folds between her legs; he gently opened them and rubbed, making her moan as he drew little circles around her precious nub. Her hips moved against him and he felt the moistness of her need flooding his fingers.

Simm needed no more stimulation. The entire evening full of kisses and teasing had been enough. He felt he had been ready to take her from the minute she appeared at the coffee shop. Now he would have wished for more light so he could see her face, but he allowed himself to believe she felt the same urgent desire he did. He moved her under him, unbuttoning his britches and letting his shaft spring free as he did.

She hesitated just a second, and then helped him pull her skirts up and out of the way. Simm wished this could be a bit more genteel, but decided that lying in the boat in the rain was actually rather exciting. He spoke softly right into her ear, "Rebecca, imagine we are on the ocean in our little boat, covered by the tarpaulin from the wind and rain, being tossed and turned in the storm. But I want you so badly I won't let a simple thing like a tempest get in the way." He leaned over her and kissed her, absorbing her smell and essence from deep within as he rose above her. He entered her and felt her body's attempt to block the intrusion, and she cried out and bit his shoulder in surprise.

"Don't stop, John, please. I'd rather you hurt me." She emphasized the word "you," and buried her face in his shoulder, trying hard not to cry.

Simm stilled for a moment, then insistently rained little kisses on her face till he drew her mouth back to his. He kissed her deep and hard until she regained her arousal, then he rose high enough not to do the thing halfway, and broke through the membrane. Rebecca gave one more little cry, then put her hands on his face and pulled him back to her to kiss.

She started moving her hips under him, encouraging him and convincing him that she wanted this very much.

Simm was overwhelmed. She was so lovely, so with him in the present, and yet he had hurt her to the point of tears. He stuffed those emotions away and resumed the delightful task of taking this bird on her first flight. There was barely room to move, and Simm felt it was too quick. As he pulled out, he hoped she would not be too sore.

Rebecca felt the pressure of Simm's manhood against the barrier of her maidenhead. The thought of dirty Herodius having the pleasure of taking her innocence horrified her, so she rose and pushed against John, even though she could tell he didn't want to hurt her. Oh, the sensations once he was through, though. She began to feel as if she were moving in that boat on the sea, tossed by the big waves, but the ocean was warm and safe and she crashed down, shivering with overwhelming sensation into John's arms. "John, that was wonderful, thank you so much." Rebecca spoke once she had her thoughts and breathing under control.

"Oh lady, I wish I could see in the dark that you are happy with your short voyage in our little boat." Simm pulled her into his arms, smelling the perfume of her sweet soap and their sex. He wished she were naked laying on silk sheets, reflecting candlelight from her soft pink body, instead of fumbling for skirts and half-unbuttoned britches. He leaned over her and gently kissed her lips, following the line from her lips to her breasts, still covered with corset and shift. "I really must do something about that," he spoke to her chest.

"Rebecca, my dear lady," Simm teased her soft skin with his tongue and lips. "I can't help but feel that your adventure would come to a premature end if we were to part just now. It would have been inappropriate to invite you to my rooms earlier this evening. But now, my lady, you must agree the barriers of propriety have already been breeched, so let the fates have their say and let me show you real pleasure." He held her close. Feeling her heartbeats in his own chest, he whispered softly into her ear. "Becky, I, too, want your adventure to create memories to last a lifetime. Let me do that for you. Come with me." He felt her nod in assent, so he lifted her onto her slightly unsteady feet and they crawled out of the tent into the fresh air. The storm had moved on, leaving cooler dry air and a starry sky. Simm reached back into the tent to cut the flame of the small lantern, and then closed the flap, sure that they had done no damage.

The wind blew from the northwest as Simm and Rebecca walked toward his rooms. They were in a section of town Rebecca knew well, not far from her Aunt Amalia's, but she said nothing. So far, although it had remained unsaid, it had been important not to give last names or anything that would identify each to the other. Certainly, they both understood that the names "John" and "Rebecca" were as common as dirt. Once they parted, they would have no location or identity.

Simm was relieved that Rebecca had agreed to come back to his rooms. Not only was his own desire barely quenched, he had an equal need to pleasure her beyond reason and make an imprint on her that would last her a lifetime of farm chores and Herodius Smiths. There was a bit of the practical he wanted out of the way before they began, so that all cares would be banished, and her mind and body relaxed and ready for the pure sensation and pleasure he had in mind. "Rebecca, by the by, I promise to wake you at sunrise so I can help you get back to wherever you need to be."

Rebecca read the truth in Simm's kind and forceful declaration. Not only would he make sure no one would know that she had been out all night, but she was to have no expectations of him, nor he of her. She understood his meaning; it matched her needs perfectly, but even so, a bit of sadness crept in and teased at the edge of her thoughts. She carefully put it away to deal with after this wonderful night. She murmured agreement, nodding that he should wake her, and she would quietly take her leave, taking nothing but memories and leaving nothing of consequence behind.

They walked the short distance to Simm's rooms in silence. The intimacy of the very recent past was too fresh, and, along with the anticipation of the immediate future, it was all overwhelming enough to quench speech. It was good to be out in the freshening air for a little while. Rebecca enjoyed the people around her walking together and laughing. The brisk and pleasant wind that blew the violent storm away had changed the mood of the town to a more lighthearted one, as Simm led Rebecca back to his rooms.

Simm noticed how quiet Rebecca was and hoped she was not scared. Anticipation was to be expected – he himself was nearly breathless with getting the beautiful, rosy blonde, breathless and needy, on his clean sheets. He stopped at a newly-built brick building, in a row of similar houses on a nicely designed square. He motioned for Rebecca follow him on tip-toe through the gate and around back into the small yard. He unlocked the back door and lifted the latch to let them in.

"My landlady sleeps lightly at the front of the house. Going in the back like this will let her slumber." Simm spoke softly. In the dark of the stairs, he pulled Rebecca hard against him for a kiss, ravaging her mouth and leaving her slightly limp. Quietly, he led her up the narrow staircase to the third floor, the top of the narrow house. There was a puddle of rainwater near the open window. Simm dropped a towel on the water and opened the windows still further. The northwest wind blew into the room, bringing cool air. In a short time, the wind from the open windows had chased the summer heat from the room.

Rebecca sat primly on the edge of the crisply-made bed, her knees together and arms crossed. She was not sure now what was now expected of her, or of what she expected. They had done *it* and that was as far as her imagination roamed. And it was very nice, far nicer than Herodius Smith would ever be, much more pleasant than Herodius would have been. The delightful floating and shattering at Coffee Joe's and in the tent had been wonderful and nameless, so perhaps there was indeed more. She had no idea.

She looked around the room, lit now by a glowing oil lantern. It was a simple room, no doubt rented for convenience rather than beauty. There was a small chest of drawers and a traveling clothes press with a shaving kit on a shelf. She had expected quality, and his things spoke of nothing else. She admitted to a small irritation at not learning anything further about John the rake.

But now he was on the floor at her feet, slowly and carefully removing the shoes and stockings. He shook the sand out into a corner, and returned with a brush for the hem of her gown. He pulled her to standing and continued brushing off the mud and sand with the stiff brush.

"I should apologize for not commenting on your gown earlier. It is lovely, but my error must be excused when all I could see was the wearer." He started now at the waist of the gown, brushing the sand down and off the fabric. He quickly addressed the bodice, making her turn in a dance pirouette to shake off the remainder. "Now that we've made you look respectable for tomorrow, let's get you unrespectable for tonight." He declared the project complete, and let his sentence trail off as he looked at Rebecca, taking in the whole.

He felt a version of the way a child felt at Christmas when discovering a great wrapped box. Simm had noticed right away that Rebecca's looks were beyond "pretty," but it was at the moment he watched her turn, shaking the sand off her gown in the lantern lit room, that he realized she was truly beautiful. He had been taken by her careful study and skilled drawing; by her ready laughter and bright eyes and smile. He certainly felt the pain of her situation at home, and her need to control her future in some small way. Looking at her sitting nervously again, demurely on the edge of his bed in the small attic room, the light making her skin glow and her eyes sparkle with excitement, he thanked the fates that had brought this work of the gods to his bed. He wasn't surprised, after the events of the past week, that she was here, but he was enormously pleased to think that for a short while he would possess such a treasure.

They had been moving in banal conversation, with Simm only commenting on the quality of the brush or the cool air blowing in the room, and Rebecca responding politely, adding nothing. He finished and swept the sand into a neat pile in the corner. She watched him stand up and turn to stare at her. It was a hard stare, but not unkind, and she was not embarrassed by it at all. So she took her time and returned the look. His clothing was not of the finest, nor were they clothes of a laborer. She wasn't sure, but the clothes he had chosen for his morning walk along the pier on Monday morning seemed finer. These clothes seemed more everyday, as though he had chosen not to be seen at all. She was certain it wasn't because of her. Perhaps it was because he was an Englishman in a town with so many Patriots. Whatever the reason, she didn't bother to care. The man in the clothes was noticeable enough.

It had been a strange evening, and Rebecca was almost ready to give up even trying to catch her bearings. She stared for a long moment at his clothes, and then up, deeply, into his bright blue eyes. He returned her gaze. Ensnared, she could not look away. She looked into his eyes, and her senses reeled with memories of tastes and touches she'd known in the dark tent. Those memories were enhanced with what she saw before her. She had run her fingers through that now-unruly hair. She had felt the strength of those arms around her, and run her hands over the muscles of that lovely body. She blushed as she realized that those firm thighs had laid against her own. She licked her lips in anticipation of combining touch with sight.

Simm saw Rebecca lick her lips as she stared at him. He had never considered himself a morsel of delight, but he was glad to have the chance to be one.

"John, I am glad I am here. You do know that?" Rebecca stood from the bed and walked to where he was standing, her arms relaxed, open at her sides.

"I think I do. You did just lick your lips." He pushed her silky hair away from her face, running his hands through the now-familiar strands. "My Lady Rebecca, let me make this night one that will last you forever."

Rebecca shuddered as Simm helped her off with the brocade bodice she had unpinned long before on that windy rock. He carefully lifted her out of her skirt and petticoat. He placed the well-made garments, carefully folded, on a bench along the wall. He turned back to Rebecca, her corset still holding her lovely breasts tight under the soft summer shift.

Simm walked behind her and untied the knot at the back of the corset, pulling strings until it hung loose, liking the disheveled, wanton look that was so different from the girl he had met earlier that evening. He sat in a stuffed armchair and pulled her to him, still on her feet and facing him, standing between his knees.

He murmured something she heard as "finally and yumm," as he lifted one breast over the top of the corset. He held her breast in his hand like a piece of ripe fruit, and licked the nipple, giving little kisses to the pink aureole around it. Then he slowly pulled out her second breast, so that they hung over the top of the undergarment instead of innocently hiding behind it. He lifted one in each hand and took turns, suckling one and then the other. Rebecca, who had never touched her breasts other than to wash, was amazed at the sensations this caused. She swooned and swayed, as she was having trouble staying on her feet. She felt a tightening deep inside and low, as other parts of her body came alive and demanded attention. Finally, she swooned forward into Simm's arms, her knees too weak to hold her up.

Simm did not let up his gentle assault on Rebecca's beautiful body. He lifted her into his arms for a short moment, letting her catch her breath, then he put her back on her feet at the side of the bed and lay her on her back on the soft mattress, her feet still on the floor. Rebecca started to work the strings of her shift, but Simm grabbed her hands to stop her, holding them over her head with one hand while the other continued to circle the erect sentries her nipples had become, saying, " no lady, don't touch," in a quiet, commanding voice that made it clear that she was not to touch her own clothing or body.

Those simple words resonated with her, and she

understood that he would do whatever he felt necessary to pleasure them both, and she should allow him to lead. She had known him less than a week, but she was sure that whatever he wanted to do to her would be wonderful, so she trusted, and kept her hands governed.

Simm continued to concentrate on her breasts. They were perfect, and caused such delightful responses. He had seen a miniature that a woman artist had painted of one breast. If he were to obtain such a piece, no artist's work could rival the soft pink and pale white mounds he was now playfully tormenting. He watched her in the flickering lantern light as she turned soft pink, glowing with arousal as the aureoles reddened and her nipples hardened. He was enjoying her reaction to his touching and deep sucking, but he was lost in his own sensations as well. She was so sensitive to every touch, and so delightfully aroused he did not want to break the spell by slaking his own need. As it was, he was barely aware of his throbbing need, lost as he was in her soft, quickening breaths. He was lost in the wonder of feasting on ambrosia; he did not want that to end.

It was too much for Rebecca. Her hips began to writhe as they searched in vain for some respite. "Oh Lady, calm, I will soothe you soon enough," Simm cooed as he pet her thighs and hips over her shift. Simm took his hands and lips away from her rigid breasts. He stood to the side of the bed and removed his jacket and shirt. His cravat was long gone. He watched Rebecca writhing on the edge of the bed, trying not to touch her needy body; keeping her hands over her head so as not to soothe her own breasts as they pulsed, calling back to him.

Without touching her body any more than he needed to, Simm sat Rebecca forward, unlaced her corset, and pulled it over her head. He loosened the drawstrings of her chemise, letting it hang lower, allowing him full access to her breasts, which could now fall naturally. He leant down to suck on them again before the tension in them eased, and stopped only when he heard her begin to moan and shift her body uneasily again. Rebecca noticed, with a small bit of remaining sanity, that Simm had shaken and neatly put all her clothes neatly aside for the morning, as she fought the need to beg him to finish her, or let her die.

Simm spoke softly into her ear. "Rebecca, enjoy the sensations, the petit mort will come soon enough. I promise."

Now she wore only her thin, nearly-transparent shift, which was untied and formless. Half- naked, her breasts hanging loose, he pulled her up to a sitting position and briefly kissed her. She tried to put her arms around him, to pull him to her, but he moved slightly away again. She opened in that short kiss, wanting his hard body against her soft, needy breasts. Instead, Rebecca felt Simm pull her gently upright so she was standing. He took her in his arms to hold her tightly and kissed her very hard, and again on weak knees, she opened to his kiss.

It was hard to stand, but she was determined to try if that was what he wanted. Her feet barely held her. She felt strange with her breasts free from her linen shift, but the pleasure of being held in his arms was overwhelming, so she remained standing. He held her close in his arms, feeling her need and wanting her desperately for those few moments. Then, in one swift motion, he simply let the shift fall to the floor, leaving her completely naked. Simm inhaled with lust and anticipation. "Oh, my lady you are so wondrous." He gazed full on the girl in the middle of his room. Her beauty was obvious, but her bravery was breathtaking. Most young women would have fled, or at least screamed, but as stunned as she was at finding herself naked in a man's room, she continued to approach her adventure with courage.

Rebecca stood in the middle of the room, shock registering on her face at her nakedness. She was relieved when Simm lowered the light from the lantern and lit two candles on either side of the bed. He sat in the armchair and just looked, reveling in the pure wonder of the beauty of Rebecca. He smiled with joy. He even confessed to himself that he enjoyed her discomfort, especially as she was obediently trying not to cover herself with her hands.

Rebecca gasped. Every nerve ending was either aroused or scared. She did not know what to do next. She wanted to hide, to cover herself somehow, but she had promised not to use her hands on herself. It was not that she feared punishment, but she did not want to disappoint the man who sat staring at her, looking very much like a dog who had been given the soup bone. Parts of her believed that it was all too much. The other parts of her couldn't wait to find out what John, her rake, had planned for her next.

Simm saw the fear flit across Rebecca's face, and her valiant efforts to master it. He might have stopped and simply taken her into his arms and made fabulous love to her, but he needed to make this night different from any other, so that it would be scorched into Rebecca's memory. If he had been a crueler man, in possession of such perfection, he might brand or scar her, leaving his mark on that perfect body. But his only brand was memory, one she could use for a lifetime with Herodius Smith. And so she would never forget the man who had branded those sensations into her memory, he planned to continue her exquisite torment.

He lifted her up, cradling her close for just a moment, and

placed her on the bed, back up, her luscious bottom ripe for touching. He lay next to her and whispered in her ear, "Rebecca, my lady, fear is not always a bad thing; sometimes it saves us from danger; sometimes it sears memories into our minds, making us remember what we might otherwise forget." He rose and left the bed.

Rebecca turned her head toward Simm's footsteps, but she could not see him, nor tell what he was doing. She was aware of anxiety, but being face-down she felt less vulnerable and exposed. She was able to make out sound. She heard a bottle stopper being pulled and smelled a heady perfume of some kind.

Simm sat at her feet. Rebecca started as hot oil dripped on and was rubbed deeply into one foot, and then the other. He massaged each toe separately and then together. Then he worked up each leg, rubbing the heady oil deep into her calves and thighs. He teased just a bit between her legs, slowly working the oil into delicate skin and lingering at her upper thighs a moment. He did not stay to further stimulate her soft, needy lady parts, but moved to her buttocks, which he pushed and grabbed until she started to squirm.

He left her butt and worked the muscles on her back. It was easy to rub and then touch them, and it was less shocking to her, so Simm did not dwell there. Giving a relaxing massage and letting her fall into a stupor would not suit either of their purposes this night.

Being rubbed with the oil was very pleasurable, and Rebecca returned again and again to a relaxed state. She felt John's strong hands pulling at the muscles of her thighs, lulling her into blissful relaxation. She lolled, deep in that state, when she felt his hands move up her legs and move them apart. He worked his oily fingers up and down her inner thighs, teasing at the tender junction between her legs until she woke again and gently began to moan.

As he played with her legs, he occasionally let a finger or two tease further, deep into her sensitive needy body, but only for brief moments, and he offered no relief. He had stepped away, just as she achieved a new height of arousal, to try to calm his own needs. He listened to soft cries that were turning into frantic pleas for release. At this rate, he thought from across the room, I will need to run into a cold lake.

"John, please." It was the first time she had begged, and Simm was moved. He came back to her and gently turned her over, moving into her raised arms as they reached for him. Their mouths met as Rebecca ran her hands over his back, pulling him onto her, her legs wrapped around his back, pulling him onto her as her hands greedily found his hair. He broke the kiss, extracted himself reluctantly, and pulled away. He had shed his waistcoat and shirt. He was still wearing britches as he lay next to Rebecca on the bed.

She calmed herself as he had insisted she do, and turned onto her side to gaze back at him. He was as beautiful as he kept saying she was. His hair was long and loose, a dark brown that showed bits of bright red when the candlelight hit just right. His eyes were a deep clear ice- colored blue that should have been cold, but betrayed the man by radiating heat. His chest was lean, with strong sinewy muscles rippling in intriguing ways, and covered with soft dark hair. She dearly hoped to have a chance to explore his body as he had hers. He still wore britches, but she knew already that his legs were muscled and long. He had an ease of movement she had noted at the dock, but for this night he was hers to touch, to look at boldly, if she wished.

Simm tolerated Rebecca's intense inspection for a few

minutes, but knew he must move on before he reacted and took her into his arms as his restless body demanded. He was tempted beyond words, but he firmly pushed her back down onto her back so she was staring at the shadowed ceiling, and not into his eyes. His voice was warm and teasing when he said to Rebecca, "There will be a time to meet me halfway, my lady, I sincerely hope we get there, but we won't if you don't let me tempt you further." He held the oil to a candle and held the bottle in the flame, turning the rich liquid until it was uniformly warm. He returned to his lady, lying calmly and obediently on her back.

He unstoppered the bottle and let a drop or two fall lazily on each breast. She gulped as the hot oil touched delicate skin, but no real pain ensued, so she calmed. With Rebecca almost in a trance, Simm rubbed the oil into her nipples, using both hands at once. Now, as she became aroused, she was noticeably uncomfortable. He abandoned her breasts and dripped drops of the hot oil between them. Drop by drop he dripped the oil down her body till he let an especially big drip hit her navel. She jumped as he began to massage the oil into her belly, and lower where she had been pleading to be touched.

"My Lady," Simm cooed as he rubbed oil into the hair at the v of her legs, "let me look at you, so alive, so willing. You want the little death, as the French say. I know you do, but it won't be the end." He teased and rubbed as he spoke soothingly into her ear. " Women are really much more elaborate then men are. Men are like the ram – one ewe and we need a while to sleep. But women, if handled just right, don't need the rest. My lady, I am in the mood to keep you going till I am ready to let you rest. I promise, Rebecca, this won't kill you."

He spoke calmly, though his arousal was driving him mad. As he rubbed the tip that would bring her release, his other hand had returned to soothe her belly and breasts. His finger moved slowly up her body to find her pink lips and delectable mouth. He put a finger in her mouth and urged her to suck and please his hand as she was being pleasured.

It was hard for Rebecca to keep her mouth moving on Simm's finger. She moaned and cried for him to finish, but he was enjoying watching her pleasure and anguish as her hips moved and she growled with need. He let her struggle with her desire for a few more minutes until finally, moving his fingers deep into her, he rubbed her own moistness on the button that would let her fly. As she shuddered and tried to cry out, he covered her mouth with his own and rode her orgasm with her.

Rebecca moved as if to relax and land gently in Simm's arms as she had in the tent and days before in the hidden corner at Coffee Joe's. "Oh, My Lady," he whispered into her ear as he kissed it and teased it with his tongue, "I promised that you wouldn't end there." He ran his hands over the length of her body, playing for a moment with the hair in the wye between her hips, as he moved back again to pleasure her perfect breasts.

"Oh Lady, let us see where else you can go." Rebecca barely heard him, as he pinched and rolled the nipple of one breast between his fingers while sucking on the other. She wanted rest, to make him stop. She cried "no" and pushed at him, but he grabbed both her hands in his one larger and stronger free hand and held them over her head, while he firmly attacked her wanton breasts until she became aroused again, her nipples erect again under his skilled tutelage as if they had been following orders.

Rebecca's senses were heightened beyond anything she had even imagined. Simm, who had been kissing her mouth and breasts as he rebuilt her desire, moved downward to kiss and suck on her bellybutton, kissing and sticking his tongue in and out of it very suggestively. She wanted to giggle, but did not have the blood in her head to generate more than a growl and a grunt. Soon she understood that kissing and sucking on her belly had only been a warning. Before her mind could grasp what was happening, she felt his mouth and tongue between her legs. Now she wanted to fly, to scream with pleasure and push away from fear and pain, to float and drown in a million rivers. At the moment when her release came, she sensed Simm rise above her and enter her, deep and hard, insistent and rhythmic.

She sighed with perfect pleasure. She matched her rhythm to his. She was aware of moving together in a way that was so different from the pleasant minutes in the boat in the tent. Now she pushed forward to meet his thrusts, feeling his need deep inside her. This one night was sexual perfection, and she understood that John meant it to last her a lifetime. She pushed her hips forward to meet him, again and again until her own needs evaporated and it was not her, not him; they were truly one. Finally she shattered again as he thrashed with uneven rhythms into her and they lay entwined, spent.

Simm knew that what had just happened was not part of his life plan. There was no room for such passion in his life. He insisted on pleasant relationships. Maybe this explained why rakes should never take virgins. He knew it was not that simple. He let problems slide away for another time, as he ran his fingers through her soft, silky hair. He wanted to bring her to the edge of reason at least one more time before they had to sleep.

He lifted himself off of her but kept a commanding hand on her belly, holding her still. She tried to turn over to find some comfort in rest, but again he said, "My Lady, rest will come, let me show you how wonderful you are." He put a soothing hand between her legs and rubbed at her swollen and very sensitive petals, opening them with gentle encouragement, gently circled and massaged the round button and bringing her to ecstacy one more time. He kissed her passionately, losing himself for a moment in her smell, her hair and her open, willing body.

"Sleep now, Rebecca, My Lady. We will dance again before dawn." Simm wanted to be remote, the master of this situation. He wanted her to experience all the pleasure he could fit into one night. She had wanted to loose her virginity in her own way. And he hoped he was fulfilling her need. He had not expected to respond to her as strongly as he had – a good reason to try to sleep without too much interruption, and just let her walk away in the morning. He tossed and turned, trying to keep his thoughts away from speaking promises that were impossible to keep. Then, finally, he joined her in sleep.

Rebecca spooned against her lover, feigning sleep. As inexperienced as she was, she knew he had gotten carried away that last time, and hadn't meant to lose himself with her as he had. She resolved to make sure he was not hurt. She would leave him without looking back, as they had agreed. She would let this night stand alone, and never hunt for or request anything more from this god who fell to earth for her pleasure.

Although she had resolved not to let him, Simm woke Rebecca to temptation and pleasure two more times before dawn. After the second, in the deep cool of the night, she woke, still limp and spent, aware that Simm was moving in the room. He'd snuffed the stubs of the candles, and was returning to the bed unaware that Rebecca had woken. "John, I'm sorry, but do you have a nightshirt? Its hard to relax this way," he heard her shyly ask.

Simm looked at the exhausted blonde on the bed, lit now only by moonlight. He was tempted to say no; to make her stay naked and ready. He put that ridiculous thought away; he did not have the heart to deprive the girl of a simple comfort. He pulled a fresh shirt from his press and brought it over to the bed. Rebecca sat up, ready to take the shirt from him, but he did not relinquish control even of this simple thing. Instead of handing it to her, he put it over her head and helped her arms find their way into the oversized sleeves. Feeling vulnerable to his own needs, he gathered her into his arms and, holding her tight against him, let himself relax and sleep.

Not long after, Simm was aware of Rebecca awake and moving in the room. Years spent expecting a knife in the back during the night had made him a light sleeper. He watched her silhouetted in the moonlight as she pulled a hairbrush from her reticule. He lay still, mesmerized as she brushed and braided her hair into a loose plait. She tied the end with a soft leather ribbon that she pulled out of the bag as she put the brush back in. Silently, she returned to the bed, pulled the light blanket over the sleeping man, and snuggled down next to him.

This was not what Simm had in mind when he'd invited Rebecca back to his rooms for the night. He'd wanted to revel in her sensuous beauty, pleasure her to furious ecstasy, and gently let her walk away. He did not have time for human connections beyond the physical. When Rebecca gently pulled the blanket over him, checking to make sure he was evenly covered, Simm felt raw, as if a shell had dropped from a great height and cracked.

That shell, his protection, developed over many years, was a necessity for reading people and their landscapes. It was essential to his work. Success required that he must be charming, friendly, and shielded from the sharp eyes of others. He never drank to excess, and kept his socializing minimal. It was important that associates should observe only what he wanted them to see. He never let men interfere with his sharp intelligence – they might see too much. And he did not let women under his skin.

He enjoyed everything about women – their bodies and their company. He had never had any complaints about time spent with him, in bed or out. He insisted that he not take anything but pleasant memories from these assignations, and that he leave his partners feeling the same. He lay awake, staring out the window at the dark sky. Thoughts of women, cracked shells and his disaffected life ran though his head, until he again let Morpheus overtake his anxious mind.

Simm woke up with the first rays of daybreak, tired and desperately needing more sleep. The colors of dawn were not yet in the sky when he turned to wake Rebecca as he'd promised. She was neatly curled in his shirt. Her legs had escaped from the blanket, tantalizing him with their strength and perfection. The wanton beauty who had gone to bed naked, sweaty and awry, had appeared in the morning with her hair neatly plaited, flawlessly clothed for sleep in his starched linen shirt. The sleeves hung over her hands, making her look small, but the deep vee of the neckline showed a tantalizing amount of breast. Deep in his essence, he growled with desire.

This new desire was not one that would be slaked by simply taking her and bringing them both to sexual rapture.

No, this was a more earthy passion. This was something he had never felt before. This was as ancient as man himself. And Simm recognized it as a man's ancient need to possess, to own. Simm realized he had been right earlier when he'd wanted to leave something of himself branded on Rebecca, something she would know as his, know deep in her core. No matter who she lay with, or married, she was and always would be John FitzSimmon's lady, this woman who did not know his name, this woman he would never meet again.

Realizing quickly that the day was breaking, and he had nothing to leave but the power of his passion, he turned to her lying peacefully on the well-used bed. He did not try to wake her gently, or even consider her needs. Simm simply kissed her awake, pulling her against him, and running his hands under his fine linen shirt – one he was sure would never look as good on him.

She woke. Fully aroused, she turned to him. She deepened his kiss, pulling him into her. He rose and entered her and she moaned with pleasure.

His body demanded that he possess her, brand her as the sun brands the flowers, leaving no doubt who caused them to open. The lovers moved together, harder and deeper and more emotionally connected than before. Rebecca screamed as she thrashed under him, answering his movements as he drove her higher and higher into ecstacy. Finally spent, she drifted down, only to be taken again by Simm's final thrusting and orgasm.

Rebecca did not know what had happened. She could insist that this last coupling was the same as the others – wonderful and fulfilling. But that would be to insist on a lie. This last was not the same, not even close. This would require some thought, but she was sure she would have lots of time to think about this night, a night and man she would never, could never, forget, even if she wanted to.

Simm brought wash water, and they washed themselves in silence. He helped her on with multiple layers, tying the laces on her corset nice and tight. Her gown was in as good shape as it could be from the mud and sand of the shoreline. Happily, there was nothing amiss anyone would notice. Rebecca fixed her hair and plopped her bonnet on her head. She looked over at Simm, who had dressed, hat on and ready to leave.

"John," Rebecca hadn't spoken a work since she had screamed with pleasure not an hour before, "leave me at my mother's friend's home. It is just around the corner from here." Her voice showed that she was already resigned to her future. Simm could hear that acquiescence and rebelled. He wanted to tell her to fight for her future as she had fought to take control of this one slice. But that would have been unkind. He had nothing to offer but a ride on Artemis.

"Rebecca, my horse is nearby, we could ride. I would see you safe."

"No, John, I promised I would walk away. I promise you, I will be safe at my friend's house."

Rebecca could not let John see where she lived. If either knew the other, the temptation would be unbearable to meet again. Her aunt was nearby, on Chestnut Street, and her servants would be awake at this hour. It was a short walk.

Aunt Amalia's house was too close. The magic would evaporate too soon, as it must. Simm put her hand decorously on his arm, for all the world to see – they were a simple couple out for an early morning stroll. Rebecca stared ahead, trying not to cry. As they neared their destination, she looked up into his eyes, hoping everything that needed to remain unsaid could be read there. He read everything in her gray-blue eyes that he felt himself.

The gentle touch of her hand on his arm was tortuous, and yet he would have endured it happily for much longer. Sadly, the mansion was very near his rooms. Rebecca led the way around back to the servants' entrance, where a driver was polishing the brass on an elegant carriage. Samuel lifted an eye at seeing "Miss Rebecca" so early in the morning.

"Samuel," Rebecca went up to the older man, leaving Simm a few steps back, "I need a ride home, if you don't mind." She smiled at the kind fellow: "Could I bribe you with biscuits not to tell her?" She motioned toward the house with her head.

"Sure, Miss Rebecca and I'll expect those biscuits soon. I'll polish later. The lady ain't up yet anyway."

Simm stepped forward to hand Rebecca into the carriage. She almost refused his hand, but put hers into it. He kissed her hand good-bye, lingering just a moment too long over her knuckles and, looking into her storm gray eyes one last time, handed her into the magnificent carriage. He did not turn to watch the carriage with its four perfectly-matched horses carry his goddess away. He kept his eyes straight ahead, and when the hoofbeats passed, turned on his heels and walked back to his life.

Rebecca thanked Samuel and watched the carriage begin its return trip to town. She quickly put coffee on to boil and ran into the barn and did her chores, wanting to be finished before her father saw her. She'd poured fresh milk into the cool can and stored the eggs just as she heard her father's footsteps on the stairs. The sheep had spent the warm night out of their shed, so, with her work done, she quickly ran upstairs to hide the gown from her curious father.

She heard him pour his coffee and then go out the kitchen door into the farmyard. Her bedroom was over the kitchen, on the back stairs, so she slowly closed her curtains, hoping he had not noticed that they had been open. She took off her shoes and the pretty gown. Now she was confronted with a corset that had been properly tightened and knotted behind her shoulder blades. She tried to grab a string, but could not reach.

Realizing that she was going to have to walk to her brother's house in the tight corset if she could not figure out how to get out of it was a special motivation. She looked in the small mirror, imaging ways to make the corset looser so it could be turned. She thought of one way. Although it made her blush with memories of the previous night, she untied and loosened her shift and pulled her tender breasts from under the tight corset. With the tension supplied by her generous breasts released, she was able to turn the corset and work on the knots Simm had put in not two hours before.

As Rebecca was struggling with her garments, her father called up to her open window.

"Rebecca! Girl, where were you last night? I saw you get out of a fancy carriage this morning. I can't have you traipsing around like a floozy, coming home all hours."

"Da, that was Aunt Amalia's carriage." She answered in a childish whine. "So, obviously I spent the night in Philadelphia. And with who but her? Don't be so suspicious. Right now I am having lady problems and will be down soon."

"Lady problems" was the family code, used by Charlotte, Rebecca's mother and her daughters for their courses, and other things that made the men of the family cringe and run away. Rebecca really meant it for untying her corset, but when she returned to her room with warm water for a good wash, she noticed that indeed her monthly courses were just beginning. "Well, John, I guess I won't have anything to explain to father or Herodius Smith." She spoke quietly, sending the message to the ethers.

She scrubbed using lots of scented soap, hoping to erase the smell of amber oil that seemed to linger. She picked up her shift. It was her finest, with lace at the neck and sleeves. Rebecca lifted it to her nose. It wasn't ruined, and she could probably wash the heady smells out of it. Instead, she folded it neatly and placed it in her trousseau box, carefully hidden by pillowcases, sheets, dust rags and quilts.

She dressed for a day of farm work, and carried her buckets of wash water down through the kitchen to dump. "Da," Rebecca called out, after weeding her herb garden, finding herself easily tired. "I am walking to Jane and Hackett's to see the baby and have a cup of tea. I'll be back to cook us some dinner."

"Like you did yesterday? I think you are being loose, and I won't allow it, I won't!"

"Da, I told you I am not being loose, and right now I am going to see my new niece."

Rebecca almost blurted out that she was too tired to have that argument, but governed her tongue in time. It was thirty minutes to the other side of the long pasture, if she did not jump the stream. Hackett was capable of telling Jasper Willent that she had arrived muddy from a walk over the pasture, so she went the long way round, arriving at Jane's spotless kitchen just as she was putting baby Mary in her cradle.

She cooed for the baby a while, and paid proper homage to two-year-old Abby. When both children were deep into their naps, Jane brought a pot of coffee to the table and they sat to talk.

Jane observed her young sister-in-law carefully before she spoke, "Rebecca, you are a loving aunt, I know that. But I don't believe in spontaneous visits in the middle of a busy summer. What's happened?"

Rebecca related as much of her tale as she could, leaving out only the minute special details of the night. Jane listened carefully, hearing the exhaustion and hidden pleasure in Rebecca's telling. "Becky, this is all because of your father's crazy ideas about Herodius's land, isn't it?"

"Yes, that and Jefferson's Declaration and Thomas Paine's pamphlet. I don't know, I've felt so trapped, and there he was. I know it was wrong. But there won't be consequences, I already have my courses."

"Then I won't judge you. Herodius won't notice anything as delicate as a maidenhead. But even so, Becky, make your father postpone the wedding for a year or so. The world is so unsettled, maybe something truly wonderful will happen to you."

They heard a tiny wail from the back room, so Rebecca kissed her sister-in-law good-bye and let herself out. She enjoyed the long walk back, skirting the pasture, not relishing a return to her lonely room. Jane had suggested that something wonderful might happen. Rebecca did not believe in fairy tales, but more time was good idea.

Simm returned to his empty room. The aroma of scented oil and sex filled the air. The sheets were tossed and half on the floor. He roughly pulled the room back together and lay down to catch a nap, before Barrow came to straighten out the mess and help him dress for the day. Sleep would not come.

He tossed and turned, his mind consistently circling uncomfortably. He gave up and rose, ready to straighten the room himself. He stripped the bed, throwing the well- used sheets in the corner, found where the landlady kept the fresh ones, and made the bed with clean-laundered sheets. He put the oils and candles away where they belonged, straightening out little things as he moved around the room.

On a small table, away from his clothing and cases, protected from the general chaos and disorder, he noticed a neatly-folded linen shirt, stark white against the black table. It looked finger-pressed and ready to be worn again. Simm picked it up and held it to his nose. It still smelled newly washed, but also ever so powerfully of the sweet herbs of Rebecca's soap, the amber oil and sex. Carefully leaving the neat folds intact, he hid the fine shirt at the bottom of his valise.

Three days later, Major Lord John FitzSimmon made ready to leave the Town of Philadelphia, Province of Pennsylvania. As he packed, he sent his valet to collect the post at the front door. Barrow walked into the room whistling, holding a delicate leather band.

"Major, there weren't nothing posted for you. But, I found this downstairs where landlady puts the mail, thought it might be yours. Someone maybe drop it, Friday night?"

It was the band that Rebecca had used to hold her plaited hair while she slept. Simm took it, staring at the small item. He knew that Rebecca had not dropped it on Saturday morning. She had plopped a bonnet on her misbehaving hair. This was newly delivered, and left on the front table with various packages and mail. The same soft leather ribbon that had tied Rebecca's blond hair now tied stalks of rosemary, for remembrance. Simm held the needles to his nose and inhaled the sharp scent. When Barrow turned to other tasks, he put the gift deep in his valise, wrapped in a white gentleman's handkerchief, gently on top of his white shirt. Perhaps he was not the only one who wanted to be remembered.

Chapter 3

October 10, 1777.

Simm rode the horse as though he and Artemis were one. The filly came from his father's stables, a gift when he was assigned to this task – stop the Americans, and convince them to return to being good colonial subjects before more blood was spilled. So far, although many were loyal British subjects, most of the Americans he had met had no intention of ever being "good colonials," subservient to a King who ruled from thousands of miles away. Nor could they be patient with a Parliament that could barely govern its own small island.

The year had been a long one. While the army had won most of the battles that mattered, subduing the Pennsylvania countryside and moving into a defeated colonial capital in September, it was not easy for the regulars. The Americans had certain advantages the British would never overcome. They knew the countryside and they were willing to move far inland. The British and Hessian armies needed to stay nearer the coast. It might even be possible to hold all the major coastal cities and still lose this war.

The British had retaken Fort Ticonderoga on Lake Champlain, but since then, the New Englanders had been again outmaneuvering them. This seemed to happen whenever they moved inland. Simm wondered when his commanders would get the idea that an inland battle was best left to the Indians. That was what General John Burgoyne had done. But even if that brutal route was one they were willing to take, it might not work, especially since it sent neutral colonists fleeing to the American side.

Now Simm was heading to Saratoga to help with the surrender of the general's troops. It was hard to handle the logistics of office work when he was so far away from offices and couriers. Somehow these tasks always fell to him, and, as ready as he was, it was never fun. As he rode on, he thought that maybe if he had to stay in America, they should just let him have his bayonet back and let him fight – let him stop doing paperwork, let him stop trying to make everyone happy.

The trip north was along the east side of the Hudson River. Like most of America, this landscape enthralled him. The deep valley created by the path of the mighty river led to the mountains the Dutch had named the Catskills. He remembered hearing the stories about these very old mountains, left over from the Colonial Dutch settlers. There were some about flying ships, and a famous one about a man who fell asleep to the sound of nine-pins and slept for one hundred years. The mountains here did seem magical, and it was easy to believe that a man from a century ago could walk out of the woods.

Above Albany, where the river headed into the higher mountains of the Adirondacks, Simm stayed to the east. There the land became more open. It was still hilly, but wide fertile valleys replaced steep slopes and ancient rock slides. Nestled between the Green Mountains of Vermont – where, at the small town of Bennington, Hessian mercenary troops and Loyalists were crushed in August – and the larger Adirondacks to the west, lay Saratoga. Saratoga and the land around it was farmland worth fighting for, and colonials from all the New England states and New York had appeared to fight General Burgoyne, the British Army and their Indian allies.

Simm decided not to mention to William Howe that by keeping his army in New York and Pennsylvania, he had lost the battle for Gentleman Johnny. The Viscount would hear enough of that from Parliament later.

General Viscount William Howe had enough to deal with. Everyone agreed that every battle won makes a general a genius and a hero, and every battle lost makes him a lazy fool. No one expected so many American troops to arrive in time to fight, just as no one had predicted that the Americans would know their way through their woods.

On his journey north, Simm met with friends and foes of the Crown. There is nothing frightening about one man on a horse asking questions, even if he wears the bearing a British officer. He never flaunted his status, but he chose never to hide his identity outright. Better that, he thought, than to be hanged as a spy himself. Most people loved to talk to him. Simm found on this journey that he had already visited many of the posting inns and taverns before, during the time he was in New England.

East of the Hudson now, skirting the border of New York and New England, he rode along the Battenkill, a river that flowed south from the Vermont mountains. The land here was fertile and lovely, the farms prosperous with ample land and water. The small settlements, it seemed, had little connection with each other, as each had its own church, burying ground and school. Interestingly, the residents were fiercely independent, even from each other. Simm always found it hard to imagine these folks bowing to any King, not even one who ruled from nearby.

The inn yard at White Creek was nearly empty when Simm rode up. He was dressed in leathers for the long ride, as any colonial would be, but he never tried to hide his British accent when he spoke. His few years in America had convinced him that the regional accents of the continent were varied enough that most inlanders believed he was from coastal New England. On the other hand, most New Englanders pegged him for an Englishman, even when he'd tried to hide it.

The landlord was out, but the landlady and her daughters were in the tap room as he entered. There were a few travelers eating, and some local men were chatting among themselves as they drank the inn's fine ale. He ordered a pint for himself, and stretched his legs in front of the fire, listening to the chatter around him. There was nothing new being discussed, and nothing that surprised him.

Burgoyne had been outflanked and outfought. The tenacity of the Americans might shock Parliament, but both Generals Howe and Burgoyne knew that it would take more than a skilled army to defeat them. Had Howe's men reached Saratoga in time, or at all, they might have had one more battle on their side of the scorecard, but how much territory could an army control after the battle had ended? That had become the overriding question on Simm's team, and one on which the generals had varying opinions. King George III had his own ideas, as did Lord North, and those were what mattered, not an intelligent military or parliamentary strategy.

Simm was being eyed in an interesting way by the very pleasant-looking landlord's daughter, whenever her mother was out of the room. The year had changed him that way as well, and he was no longer surprised at himself when no offers interested him. At first, he had kicked himself for staying besotted by his short week in Philadelphia, particularly the long, luscious night with his goddess. He'd never ignored so many charming invitations before, and had always prided himself on leaving wives and daughters satisfied and happy, giving each whatever she wanted. Now, he thought, he would simply have to wait it out and let it fade away, as he was sure it invariably would. He flirted gently with the pretty girl, and retired to his room early, planning an early exit.

The trip lasted a few weeks more. He had collected what information he could on the way north, and at Saratoga he worked behind the scenes and got the prisoners situated as well as was possible in the vast land. While he traveled, he followed his pattern of listening, and learning what he could about the mood in the countryside. He found that most people wanted to be left alone to live their own lives. They wanted to do their best and raise their children free in this illimitable land. The one thing they all agreed on was that they did not feel the need to pay for what had all ready been bought, and that was the debt owed for the French and Indian Wars. Everyone who lived on this warpath between Canada and America knew they had payed, many times over.

Finally in New York, with Burgoyne on a ship bound for the theater season in London, and the fine soldiers of his army sentenced to working as field hands on various New England farms, Simm settled down to paperwork. In fact, he had come to think of grueling hours of dispatches and memos whenever he thought of the city of New York. There was a letter from his older brother Robert that caused some anxiety, but there was nothing to be done if the King sent his own factfinders to see what was happening in the colonies. He wouldn't be the only one not to trust the information coming from Parliament. But the problem, only hinted at in Robert's letter, was the damage someone like that could do. Simm knew Robert and Stephen, his brothers who sat in Parliament, were concerned that such a man might find a way to stir up his own trouble. It was known that the Howe brothers' desire for conciliation clashed with certain factions' desire for total subjugation or complete independence.

Robert and Stephen, as well as other members of their large family, believed that America was best served by becoming an independent young nation, with kindly trade and export policies. That way, Britain could continue to benefit from America's vast natural resources, but at a reasonable price. Of course, as someone engaged in the process of convincing the young nation to surrender, Simm did not indulge in political thoughts. Whenever he saw his family, he made a point of leaving political philosophy to them.

The final dispatches were his own orders to report to General Howe in Philadelphia at Amalia Willent's home on Chestnut Street. Thoughts of returning to Philadelphia found him anxious to return, and afraid at what a year of battles in the region had done to America's capital and its prettiest town. He vacillated between being joyous and deeply worried. Simm had lived in Boston between 1774 and 1776, during the British occupation and through Washington's siege. He was there when the British troops evacuated in March, 1776. He did not like seeing good people repressed by his actions. He recognized that General Thomas Gage had not wanted to destroy the town or its inhabitants. Still, that occupation was made bearable for him by Jason, his brother who had defected to a life at sea and had settled in Essex, on the north shore of Massachusetts. Jason had piloted a small ship into Boston harbor occasionally, to collect his brother for Sunday dinners. What Jason was doing with British, American and French flags on his small, fast ships – now that was strictly the business of Jason and his Marlborough privateers. Simm didn't know, didn't have to know, and rightly didn't want to know. What would his life be like in another occupied town, this time without the levity an older brother brought into his life?

Simm tried not to, but he could not help thinking that Philadelphia meant Rebecca. He knew in his gut that he could find her. He had nothing to go on, but he was very good at finding people, even those who wished to remain hidden. Should he try to find her? What if she were already married to the odious Herodius Smith, a man, however physically disgusting and spiritually bereft, of whom he would always be jealous? Would seeing him again make that union harder for Rebecca to bear? Maybe he was just the fleeting pleasure Rebecca had needed, and she was at least contented with her new life. And most of all, as he bumped down the rough post road of this New World, would he ever find someone else who filled his thoughts, and made him as uncomfortable in the saddle, as Rebecca no-name did?

Chapter 4

October 11, 1777, Philadelphia, Pennsylvania.

The best part of the horrible summer and fall of 1777 was that the battles had interrupted Rebecca's wedding plans. Rebecca had followed Jane's advice and put off the wedding as long as she was able, and the marriage had been planned for Sunday afternoon, September fourteenth. The Battle of Brandywine, the first major defeat Washington's Americans had suffered in Pennsylvania, was fought and lost three days before, on September eleventh. The battle occurred near adjacent farms, and the fighting had so upset Herodius that he had taken to drink and had been found out cold on the floor, at breakfast time, on the thirteenth, with his children crying and hungry. Upon finding his friend and neighbor so incapacitated, Jasper Willent had removed the children to Mrs. Gruenbaum's house, where they were found later that day making cookies with the good lady's daughter-in-law and grandchildren. Jasper dealt with Herodius by cancelling the marriage outright and forbidding Rebecca from ever marrying him.

"Rebecca," he had bellowed, "that man is drunk on his kitchen floor."

"What man, Da?" Rebecca asked, too thrilled by his tone to risk jinxing anything.

"Smith, that scoundrel, who else would I mean? Don't even think of getting dressed for that wedding."

"Sure, Da, I'll just go and tell Hackett and Jane that they needn't meet us at the church tomorrow. Do you mean, by the way" – Rebecca tried to slow down her speech to normal speed – "I am never to marry him?"

"That's what I've been saying! Don't be daft, girl, go on now. Tell your brother that *someone* dodged a bullet this fall."

Rebecca remembered that day. It had been, in fact, the best day of the autumn. The British had taken Philadelphia on September twenty sixth, and the final battle in the area had been at Germantown on October fourth. It had led Washington to move his troops twelve miles northwest to the town of Whitemarsh, where they set up a temporary camp.

Soon after the retreat to Whitemarsh, Rebecca found Nat in the barn early one morning as she went out to milk the cows.

"Hi, Becky. D'you have something to feed a hungry soldier?"

She flew into her brother's arms, delighted to find he had survived the battles when others had not. " 'Course. Finish the milking and I'll go and sneak something out of the kitchen."

After Nat had eaten, he climbed into the hayloft and pulled her up to talk privately. "Listen, Beck, I need your help. Well, not me – General Washington needs your help."

"Me? What can I do that Washington needs?" Rebecca asked, sure he was joking.

"Tell me, you are still a Patriot?" Nat suddenly sounded very serious.

Rebecca nodded her head. "Of course I am, Nat, but why?"

"There are people in Philadelphia who've been asked to collect and send information about troop movements and such to a fellow, we call him 'C.' But, Becky we need all the eyes and ears we can get. I don't want you to work for that fellow. I want you to work for me, and I will give anything important that you find to the General. We need any tidbits you can find.

We need to get a good picture of the town – who is in it and what they are doing.

"Washington says we need individuals who can mix as much as possible among the officers and Tories, visit the Coffee Houses and all the public places. The General is looking for people who live with the redcoats. We don't want you to steal their work, not ever! That would put you in too much danger, and it would draw attention to others if you were caught. But if you overhear soldiers talking, write it down and relate it to me."

"But, Nat, I don't live with any soldiers," Rebecca replied. "Those I see at the checkpoint when I go to visit the Gruenbaums, outside the limits, flirt with me, but they don't talk to me."

"Wait, that's what I have been saying. I had an idea and I spoke to Hackett last summer about a way for you to acquire a dowry. That if Da didn't force you to marry Smith, and the British ended up occupying Philadelphia and quartered in the city, they should allow you to landlady some of them in the house. The soldiers can pay rent – your dowry. The English are political enemies, but even I must admit the officers are not animals nor uncivilized. And, sweet little sister, it will put you in an advantageous situation to accidentally listen to your tenants."

Rebecca listened to Nat, stunned at the idea her brother had cooked up. It was a way out of her problems, but it certainly created nagging fears about living in a house with strange men.

She pulled herself out of her thoughts. Nat was still talking to her.

"Becky, do you still sketch at the docks?"

"Yes, some days." She was slow to answer, waiting for

Nat's disapproval.

"Good! We'll need you to do that more, at least on nice days when your presence would not seem out of the ordinary. Draw maps of where the soldiers are quartered, too. Tell us how many there are, how they get their food, if they are eating well, where they gamble, what coffee houses they have chosen as their favorites.

Rebecca was feeling more overwhelmed by the second, listening to Nat's careful plan, but she was sure she would do anything she could to help American Independence.

"Becky, I'm sure that Amalia will house William Howe if she gets her way. I'll visit her and see that she sets it up where you get Howe's top staff. Not only will they know how to keep their feet off mother's parlor furniture, but they will offer the best opportunity for you.

"Do you remember that field and the strange rock where we played Indians?" Rebecca nodded yes. Put your messages for me in that rock. There is room for about anything you can carry. The field is about five miles northwest from here."

"I understand, Nat. When should I leave them?

"Don't make it look like a pattern. You said you visit the Gruenbaums – what days do you go out there?"

"Most Fridays, maybe Sunday afternoon, or after marketing on Thursdays or Saturdays."

"Make it those days, and I will check for a thread or strand of hair hanging from a nearby branch."

"Okay, Nat. I will try to help. I'll make the first delivery one week from next Saturday. After that we'll see how often I need to come. I'm sure it would not be more than once per week."

Nat was pulling his blue waistcoat over his shirtsleeves and preparing to climb down.

"Hey, big brother, stay well and safe."

He jumped down and pulled her into his arms for a hug. He kissed her cheek, holding her tight and fighting his own fears for her safety.

"You too, Becky, and you know, when Da and Amalia suggest that you quarter and feed a group of officers. I think you should refuse, have a fit, and yell at them, even if they insist it was my idea."

"Am I usually so uncooperative? Is that how you all think I would normally behave?"

"Yes, little sister, you're stubborn." And with that, Nat slid out of the barn and was away before his Loyalist father could catch a glimpse of him.

Nat rode hard back to Whitemarsh, thinking what a problem it was to have a younger sister. Someone needed to take care of his favorite, but one parent was dead, and the other had lost interest in his brood three children ago. Rebecca, just two years younger, had always been his to care for, and from early childhood he had taken that responsibility seriously. Here was a chance for her to do something important for the cause of Independence, for her to help the man he admired most in the world.

Washington needed information on the occupied town, and Nat's family was in the perfect position to help. Amalia had been friendly with Howe since her childhood in London, and in fact was already housing him and his staff offices. When Rebecca took in four or five more, what would she find out? Would it be dangerous for her? Would she be good enough, careful enough to avoid detection? Would General Howe and his men find out she was spying for the Americans, and, if they did, would they hurt her?

Nat thought back to his last words before he left. He really did wish he could have avoided involving her with the others, but it seemed necessary that she know all. "Becky – there is a man, Joe, Coffee Joe they call him. He has a drinking hole the 'Liberty Coffee House,' used to be called the 'The Queen's Crown.' He's a good man, collects information at the Liberty. You could help him by stopping by to get his packages and bring them to me at that rock. That would help a lot. Help me a lot."

Rebecca realized that Nat had worked her into helping, whether or not she believed it was a good idea. She did want to help the cause of Independence. She also admired George Washington, and was greatly for America. Didn't she boycott tea? Wear her own homespun? Knit her own socks? Knit for the soldiers? These new actions felt dangerous and exciting. She had once been told she was brave. She decided to be brave.

The situation around Philadelphia had gone from bad to worse, but as the fall went on, news trickled in that there had been American successes in New York and Vermont. More than that, Gentleman Johnny – General John Burgoyne – had been soundly routed at Saratoga, and the man was heading home. All of this was indeed good news. But Rebecca's world was Philadelphia, and that city had been lost, and was now occupied by British soldiers who marched through the streets and were quartered in houses all over town. The Continental Congress had fled, moving the government west to York.

Now it seemed Nat's idea might actually come to pass. But what if Amalia never suggested her little niece take in boarders? Maybe no one would move into her house. But she swore that one part of her duties would be performed. The maps and sketches would find their way out to Nat.

Thinking this project through carefully and slowly, as she did most things, Rebecca realized that drawing paper would not fit nicely in a roast chicken, or fold small enough to fit inside suit buttons. If she were going to do this, she would need to construct a garment that would hide the documents she was carrying. With winter coming on, the easiest thing to make and wear would be a heavy cape with a double lining, one containing secret pockets.

She ventured into town the next morning to find the right wool for her new cape. Rebecca had heard about the punishment Boston took during its occupation just a few years before, so she was not prepared for the sight of new shops – shiny storefronts with new proprietors, London shopkeepers and other Loyalists hoping to take advantage of wealthy Englishmen stuck in winter quarters. She had no trouble finding what she wanted. She ended the short and successful trip with a stop at Coffee Joe's to see if she could practice the art of overhearing gossip. Rebecca listened to the chatter awhile, but heard nothing of interest, so a short time later she walked the few miles home to begin planning and making her new cape.

Rebecca was resolved that at least she would do something productive while living in the midst of the redcoats' occupation of her city. With the troops and civilians such an occupation brought, there were more crisp English voices mixed among the more common Pennsylvanian talk. She would turn and stare each time an aristocratic English voice caught her attention. She knew it was silly to expect to see John's face among the strangers who now occupied the streets – John whatever his name was, of her magic night, a year's worth of dreams and some interesting daydreams that intruded into her waking hours unbidden. She chastised herself that it was silly to expect a shipowner to make his way into such chaos.

She tried not to let the pier and the river remind her of that week, as she fell into the pattern of sketching ships and keeping troop counts carefully disguised as random squiggles in the borders of her artwork. She took care to sketch only the merchant ships. Then she would make notes on which Man-of-war was docked nearby. Drawing the beautiful two and three-masted ships brought memories of the man she promised to leave behind, memories that left her gasping with remembered pleasure. She would hear John's voice calling her name as she walked the alley past the coffee house; she felt his fingers on her back when she heard rain water, and even when bath-water ran down her spine. She had planned to hold the memory of that week – of that one night – carefully in her soul, as a bulwark against the future. Instead, the unexpected intensity of those memories kept her breathless.

Rebecca knew she had no right to try, and certainly there was no way to find him. Even with the additional English clerks and shopkeepers who had moved into town, there was no reason for him to be here, too. Her courses had flowed over a year's worth since their time together, so she had no need to find him. Besides, Rebecca regularly reminded herself, she knew nothing about him. Not a last name, not an address, not even if he cared a whit about her. She had only the name of a ship, *The Good Queen Bess*. And, who knew if that was truly his brother's ship to captain, with him as part owner? Even if she were his, Rebecca didn't even know the home port, or if that was all a farce.

Rebecca had reminded herself over and over that John, whoever he was, had simply been visiting America last summer and was gone. The beautiful man could be anywhere on God's earth by now. Rebecca tried desperately not to let her selfish memories, delicious as they were, interfere with the work before her. She admonished herself that John should stay a memory, stored for the dismal future.

Unexpectedly, she had found herself more changed by her short time with him than she had planned. She had not wanted to marry Herodius because he was old, smelly and his children were needy. Now, even with Herodius gone from her life, Rebecca found that she did not want any other man, even one who was young and childless. Getting over John was going to take more time, or maybe it would merely take a bright summer day and a different, dashing young man with sparkling blue eyes.

Chapter 5

On September 28, a warm Sunday afternoon, Rebecca was summoned to her Aunt's house "to pour for the glorious soldiers who were staying there." Aunt Amalia had always insisted that some of Rebecca's good clothes be kept in town, so she would have no excuse to appear a dusty mess in her drawing room. Rebecca arrived early, wearing a plain maroon gown and old bonnet. Amalia's maid rushed her up to her room, where she was hurriedly pushed into a fashionable day gown of browns and yellows, with a hint of pink in the embroidery.

"Tell Aunt to burn this gown after today. Why on earth did she think I could wear these colors?"

"I'll tell her, Becky, but I think you look pretty in the dress." And with that Annie began to pull Rebecca's reluctant hair into a semblance of order.

"Oh Annie, just put a cap on it. I'm not going out."

"Becky, she said she wants you looking your best to meet the General. Did you see him? He is sooo elegant!" Annie did her best imitation of Rebecca's aunt, and they both giggled.

A few minutes and many pins later, Rebecca's hair was tidy, and Annie pronounced her ready to go. "Annie, leave me for a minute. This is going to be a bit trying, and I need a minute to collect myself."

Annie was used to Rebecca's independent moments. She rolled her eyes at Rebecca, giggled again and walked out of the room, leaving Rebecca alone. The yellow room was familiar. It had been Rebecca's and Susannah's when they'd stayed with their aunt. As little girls, both of them had visited regularly. After Susannah had grown and married, Rebecca visited her aunt alone. She'd also stayed with her aunt when she'd been invited to Philadelphia parties that ended late. Those visits had ended with her mother's illness and death. Since then, Rebecca hadn't seen any good reason to stay in town. The bright room had been unused this past year.

Now, it wouldn't be the nieces's room. Rebecca saw a soldier's kit in the corner, and boxes of documents piled on the floor between the beds. Her room was being set up as an office for some of Howe's staff. Rebecca looked around the room at the fading blue-flowered wall paper and aging paint. The room had been so pretty and crisp when the girls were young, and now it was like the city itself, ignored, abandoned, and soon to be occupied by an intruder.

Rebecca eyed the documents and walked over to stare at some from above. She did not want to be caught opening boxes, but it might give her some idea of what was inside the crates if she at least read the titles. There was nothing revealing on the labels. They had come from New York, and were being delivered to a Major John FitzSimmon. She heard footsteps on the stairs and moved quickly to the other side of the room, where she opened the clothes press and looked at her gowns. Bringing them back to the farm would be a fool's task, but leaving them here to be touched by strange men, perhaps mauled by an enemy soldier, was too much. She would have Annie send them over when she had a chance.

Rebecca ducked out of the room, just as some workmen were bringing in a desk and filing boxes. She rushed to the back stairs and went down to the kitchen, "Annie, I need my gowns to be sent to my house, away from here. Frankly I would rather torch them on Pope's Day then let a redcoat touch one button."

"I'll have them sent right over, General Washington, your excellency. But you do know that most of them don't have any buttons, only pins and ties."

"You're right, Annie, just send them when you can." Rebecca laughed at the girl's literal take on her foolish request, but she was not sorry she had made it. Rebecca pushed her shoulders back and plastered a smile on her face, resolved to be a Patriot instead of a door mat this afternoon. She found her foe seated with teacups and scones, having what looked like a pleasant, civilized tea in Amalia's front parlor.

Her aunt was pouring while one of the young soldiers helped pass cakes. It looked, to Rebecca, not the least like a hanging, or a gathering of evil fiends, though she thought that might be easier to endure. General Viscount William Howe sat sipping at his tea, and smiling at Aunt Amalia like they were old friends. "Oh," thought Rebecca, "they probably are old friends – Amalia grew up in London and knew everyone, and the Howes, through their mother, were everyone. No wonder 'we' are so happy to be here today."

Rebecca hadn't drunk tea since the non-importation agreements that had led to the "tea parties" in 1773 and '74. Giving it up hadn't been a great sacrifice. She had only been fifteen, and only drank it with milk and more sugar than should have been legal. Now, she didn't allow her father to have any in the house, so it had never become a temptation. Still, she had learned to make a good cup of tea, even if she pouted and teased Amalia about her tastes for tea and English finery.

Holding her head high, with a pleasant smile pasted on her face, she walked aristocratically into the parlor.

"Oh, Becky, here at last. General, this is my niece on my American husband's side. A lovely gown, dear. Have you worn it before?" Amalia's voice had become strikingly British, and Rebecca was tempted to ask if she were seriously speaking that way. Living in Philadelphia for thirty years had flattened her Britishisms to an almost unnoticeable level – that was, until the commander of British forces in North America sat in her parlor drinking tea. Biting her tongue, and not bothering to answer her aunt's question, Rebecca smiled at the General and offered to pour. Carefully looking only at the tea tray, she spent the next hour engaged in pouring tea, light chatter, and the passing of tea cakes.

Rebecca feared that if she raised her eyes long enough to do more than be merely polite, she might glare at the occupying army, now munching cakes in her aunt's front parlor. So instead of attacking her enemy in her aunt's front room, she kept her eyes on the food and her mind on the complicated and engaging act of pouring very hot water into a pot with tea leaves and straining those same leaves, so they would not pour with the hot water into the cup. All of this was done at just the right moment and correct temperature. It was not a skill many Americans of her age and political tastes had acquired, but at the moment she was not sorry her aunt had made her learn to pour tea. The ritual kept her busy, and she was glad that she did not attract undue notice.

Amalia and her visiting neighbors carried the conversation, so that none of the younger officers, or Rebecca, who as usual found herself to be the youngest person in the room, were expected to do more than answer an occasional question. For her part, Rebecca had every expectation of leaving the room as soon as it was polite to do so.

Simm sat quietly in a corner of the same room. He was in the process of arranging his office in a pretty yellow room on the third floor when a fellow announced good cakes and hot tea. He had gone into the parlor for only a minute. The piles of paperwork in the new office demanded attention. Even during tea, he was interrupted to review the number of crates and the furniture that were being delivered to the house – the endless paperwork that war demanded. Summoned, he stepped into the hall to check on something and returned a moment later.

"Major," the General stopped him as he tried to reclaim his chair, "let me introduce you to our hostess. Amalia Willent, this is Major John FitzSimmon, my right hand when it comes to very complicated, ehem, things. Major, this is Mrs. Willent, a childhood friend of mine from London."

"Mrs. Willent, I am thoroughly charmed. Thank you for allowing me to stay here." Simm gave the older woman a half bow.

Amalia blushed prettily, revealing a slice of her younger self. "Major, it is lovely, always lovely to meet such a fine looking young man. But I am in the process of arranging housing that I believe will be more comfortable for you than living in your office."

"Thank you, Ma'am. I will avail myself of your advice when I return. Right now, the good General expects me to spend another week or so on the road. So if it is no bother, I will leave my things here until I return from my short journey."

Simm made his polite excuses and returned to his seat in the parlor. As he sat and picked up his tea, something caught his eye from across the room. He turned sharply and gasped.

He stared at Rebecca, who had turned to leave by the opposite door. He covered his gasp by pretending to have hit his elbow on the edge of the low table. He turned again, watching carefully while holding a stack of papers in front of his face. He was in dress uniform, which included a white wig. He knew that as long as she did not see his eyes, he was safe from her gaze – safer than she was from his. She spoke briefly to Mrs. Willent and placidly left the room. Simm put his papers down and finished his cooled tea, which was now being served by one of the General's clerks.

Simm grabbed his work and went back upstairs into the sweet yellow room that was now his office. He felt like he was violating someone's bedroom, though he knew Amalia Willent had no daughters living at home. Looking around the little room, he wanted to hit something, hard. What on earth was Rebecca doing here? And why was she wearing that horrible color? It made her look sallow.

If he could dress her she would wear – what would she wear? Who was he kidding, he mentally kicked himself, he would never have that chance. But why was she here? Was she a servant? Was that their alternative to her marrying the odious Herodius? How... why...? He simply could not put it together. He wanted to demand facts he had no right to know. Growling like the angry cur he wanted to become, he picked up his notes. Simm tried to read, but the words swam before him on the page, lost in memories of a warm, soft, willing body on a hot, windy summer night.

Simm closed his eyes more than five minutes to clear the past from his vision, and when he opened them, a new stack of memos had appeared on the desk. He threw himself into the task before him, opening each packet and reading just enough to be able to send it off to the right clerk in the right office.

The tedium of this daily, and endless, task had become the worst part of a long war far from home, but paperwork and tangled lives – that was his fate.

"Corporal!" Simm shouted a while later as miscellany continued to appear. He rose from his desk and went to the door of the room, "Roberts, where did this box come from?" Simm roared out of the door and down the hall. A young clerk in full-dress uniform ran into the room, breathless with his response.

"I don't really know, Major, it came down with the packet from New York."

"Thank you, Corporal, sorry I roared." Roberts left the room mumbling about trying to make sense of all the mail and memos and people's personal items, which were now his problem.

Simm examined the blank box, vaguely recognizing it as one packed with quills and powdered inks. He put the box in the corner and arranged his personal goods so that they would be ready to be moved to his next billet, whenever Mrs. Willent arranged it.

When he finished the must-do's, Simm checked his traveling kit for the short trip to Charleston. He had every intention of beginning the journey this afternoon. He'd found that even one night of good rest softened his resolve for another trip, and it was easier to stay on the road. Grabbing his things, he went down to the stable in the back of the small alley behind the house. He saddled Artemis and led her up the small hill and out onto the road. He turned to mount and stared down the alley behind the row of mansions. In his imagination, he added the greens of high summer and a lovely carriage that could easily belong to someone as rich as Amalia Willent. Yes, this was the alleyway where Rebecca had walked away from him.

"That girl at the tea really was her, but I don't think that gets me closer to unraveling the puzzle of why she was in Amalia Willent's front room, or who she is," Simm spoke to the horse as they rode away from the elegant houses and south, out of town.

Rebecca was in the kitchen, gossiping with the staff. "Annie, that was the most wasted afternoon I've ever spent. You know I couldn't even flirt with any of those handsome young men. Aargh, those damned red coats make every man a devil, even if they are the most civilized beings on the planet."

Amalia Willent came through the kitchen door, just catching a glimpse of Simm and Artemis as they rode off. "Becky darling," Amalia began, "I've cemented an idea while talking to the General just now. You know how you and your father have – umm – had discussions about your dowry and that .... " She trailed off as Rebecca began to glare, color rising in her cheeks. "Becky, listen to me, I think you should take in a few of these officers as boarders. They will all be well-behaved and gentlemenly. William will make sure, he promises me, and they will pay rent and stay with you in that farm house of yours – pay quite well, I'm assured. I'll make sure your father understands that it all goes to your dowry." She repeated herself nervously, knowing that she could suffer an angry tongue-lashing and would, at the very least, have a sullen refusal on her hands.

Rebecca let her eyes flash disbelief at her aunt. "Aunt Amalia, you are making very little sense. You are suggesting that I allow strange men, soldiers, to quarter in my house. You are telling me they will be well-mannered, and that they will not be ungentlemanly, on the word of General Howe." She rushed on, trying to stay shocked. "Furthermore, you insist that they will pay rent, and that you have gotten my father to agree that the rent money will go to my dowry?" Rebecca shook her finger at Amalia, "Have you really discussed this with my father?"

Amalia was visibly relieved Rebecca's reaction was a mild as it was."Why, yes dear, I did, yesterday. Jasper stopped by after breakfast to meet William. He said it would be no problem, and even promised that he would move to Hackett's so you would have more room."

"Did he? Did he mention who would replace him to do his chores at his farm? And did he mention anyone helping me with cleaning and cooking and caring for a house being trampled day and night by a group of soldiers with boots?"

"Oh, Becky, you are making too much of it, I'm sure you will be fine, such a competent young lady. We'll find you help, and the men are used to camp life."

Rebecca walked away from her smiling aunt, pleased with displaying just the right amount of reluctance. The autumn day was delightful – warm, but lacking the summer humidity and strong sun. The first fallen leaves were crisp on the ground and, high above, the thinning clouds foretold the winter. She relished the perfect afternoon, realizing that her life was about to change irreversibly. In response, she felt a chill of fear run over her, but she stomped it down. This was not a preposterous idea hatched by Amalia and Jasper – it was Nat's idea to help her uncover British secrets and raise money for her dowry. She walked the wagon path to the stone farmhouse, reminding herself that with changes occurring so quickly, she should tell Nat about the boarders, and she should get to work and finish that cape.

Chapter 6

The kitchen chimney puffed welcoming smoke as the stone farmhouse came into view. Rebecca always loved coming home from this side. The symmetry of the building gave it the appearance of solidity and safety. The outbuildings, the stable, and the semi-attached kitchen added to the feeling of order. "Unfortunately," she mused as she approached, "it had all become a chimera, as tangible as the chimney smoke."

Rebecca walked on the path through her herb garden. Her mother had helped her plan it when she was a young girl, wanting her last child to have something a little different from all the older children. It was perfectly designed, with each perennial and annual marked, so she knew whether to mulch in the fall or propagate by seed. She had already done most of her seed collecting for the year, with each species' seeds already wrapped in dry paper, and labeled. Filling her lungs with the mix of herbs in the fresh air, Rebecca walked into the house.

Jasper Willent sat in his chair at the kitchen fire smoking his pipe. "Becky love, you spoke with Amalia?" She nodded yes. "And don't you think it's all a wonderful solution?"

"Da," Rebecca responded, "solution to what?"

"Solution to all your problems. You hold on to the board, an' keep money them young soldiers'll give you, for your dowry. And when they leave, you'll have a bit to get going."

"Who will come and help me cook and clean, so that I won't have to hire someone – so I will have enough left over for a dowry? To say nothing of having the energy left for a marriage bed?"

Jasper ignored her pointed rudeness and simply looked a bit embarrassed. He just shrugged. "Amalia and I thought you could do it. That'd leave you enough for yourself."

"Oh. Of course." Rebecca walked out the kitchen to the back stairs, and went up one floor to her room. It was her favorite room in the house, built over the kitchen. It shared the chimney and collected all the smells and warmth of that room. Her mother had died in this room just last year. But, instead of making her sad, those memories served to make her feel safe and warm.

The room was warm from the kitchen chimney, too, but never over-warm, since there was a summer kitchen with a separate chimney they used in the warmer months. The room was painted a warm yellow with white trim. The drapes were made from leftover fabric from Aunt Amalia's best bedroom, blue and gold brocade with a white silk border. It was always bright in here, even when the rest of the world was dull. Life with soldiers in her house, and running packets through checkpoints for Nat – all the changes would be bearable as long as she had her room, her sanctuary from the world.

Rebecca woke that night to silence. She wasn't used to such emptiness. Grabbing a robe, she went down to the kitchen. The fire was cold, not banked, the coals nearly out. Her father's chair was empty, his pipe gone, the dog with him. The room did not feel as though he had simply gone to his bed. Rebecca wanted to run and check, letting the moonlight drifting through the windows guide the way. Instead, always practical, she knelt at the large hearth, gathering together the almost-dead coals. She put tow and kindling on the coals and blew gently. Once there was a stronger glow, she fed the fire with larger wood, and then banked it, covering the now-hot ashes with cold ash.

Satisfied that there would be hot coals for morning coffee, she lit a candle from the small fire, put a lanthorn over it, and went up the main stairs to see if anyone was in the house. If he had been nearby, Cromwell, her father's dog, would have pattered out to see who was in the hall. But the stairway was quiet, and no growls, snores or grunts greeted her from the front bedroom. Rebecca crept closer. She was right – the house was completely empty except for her. Jasper had just left her, had not touched the fire, had not thought to take the minute to tell her he was going.

Anger boiled up and, seeing no reason to resist, Rebecca screamed at the unfairness of fate. In time, she started to cry. Collapsing into the chair at the hall landing, she sobbed inconsolably. The candle was almost a stub when she numbly stood and took command of her life and the house. She did a quick assessment of the space the soldiers would need, and what she would need to do to get ready. Walking through the second floor of bedrooms, she counted beds. Finally, she walked through the room that connected to hers with one locking door between. The key was in the lock. She locked it from the main hall side, took the key, and went back to the kitchen. She climbed the narrow kitchen stairs to her own room, and pushed the bar lock into place. She then put the key to the door in her secret space under the window sill. Shivering from crying and cold, but fully resolved to hold herself together and do this thing, she climbed under the covers and slept.

Waking to first light, she remembered her resolve from the middle of the night. The first thing was to make that cloak. On her shopping trip earlier in the week, she had found the perfect wools for the two layers. The outside was to be thick and warm – a beautiful, shimmering, dark blue. The lining would be thinner, a weight meant for autumn and winter dresses. This second was blue-gray, the color of a hazy summer sky and her eyes when she was happy. The interior third layer, the pockets that no one would see, were to be silk – strong, slippery and thin. The two layers of wool should mask the movement of any rolled or flat documents stored in the hidden pockets. Pleased with the design, Rebecca set to work, completing the sewing by candlelight, late on the second day of work.

It was beautiful, with frog buttons holding the front together just at her neck. The hood was warm and lined with the blue-gray, and when it was down it fell gently across her back, showing off her blond hair, the two colors making her eyes sparkle. "Not that I want to sparkle," she said to her reflection in her small looking glass, "but maybe some of those lonely soldiers will look at my face and hair instead of my pockets."

She was vastly pleased with the way the interior pockets worked. They were accessible only from the warm pockets in the light wool lining. With her hands deep in the pockets, she could not find the openings to the secret pockets unless she pushed her hands forward past a false end, where there was a flap that opened, revealing the entrance to the lower pockets. She found some old sketches in a box. She rolled them and pushed them into the pockets. She walked around the house, delighted that she could not feel the sketches in the pocket, and nor did they make any difference to the flow of the garment as she walked.

Rebecca hung the blue cloak nonchalantly on a peg in the

summer kitchen, and turned her attention to the house. She started in the kitchen. She wanted to make certain that there were enough pewter and heavy stoneware plates and mugs. She didn't want to be pulling out her mother's fine china for soldiers rough from battle, even if they were all officers. She brought one of the neighbor girls over to help her turn the house out, and for two days the young women aired bedding, washed windows, and let the cold autumn winds blow through the house. On Wednesday, Rebecca declared it done. Windows were closed, and fires laid in the parlors and bedrooms. Amalia's staff came that day with sacks of flour, turnips and other basic provisions which were stacked and locked in the summer kitchen.

Later that morning, Rebecca walked into the back room that doubled as the summer kitchen, only to discover that her loom had been pushed into a corner, the legs loosened, and her weaving on the loom left in a mess. She carefully removed the legs from the loom, and tightened the warp to preserve the unfinished weaving as best she could. She took her raw materials – flax and wool she would not have time to spin and weave – and put them away in a box, hidden in the kitchen loft, before someone should decide to use them for kindling. She thought, as she packed the fibers away, that this is was a good metaphor for her life, all pushed and folded to the side. With that done, she sent word she was ready for her tenants.

Within a few days, Rebecca had collected sketches of ships and maps of the downtown area. For her first foray past the soldiers at the checkpoint, she wanted to carry things that were of no significance. She set off from the farm soon after lunchtime. She hoped that would seem like a normal time to be delivering eggs to some far-away neighbor. Eggs were a last-minute idea, but not one that would work when her house was full of grown men who would need large meals at least twice per day. But for today, the eggs did seem a good reason to be taking a walk past a checkpoint.

It was barely cold enough for a wool cloak, but there was enough of an east wind, and Rebecca decided she would be someone who was easily cold.

The spot Rebecca and Nat had chosen was just southwest of the farm, about a five mile walk on the roads. Though it was slightly shorter on the paths through the woods, they had agreed it would be best that the soldiers at the checkpoints get used to her comings and goings. Winter would leave the trails impassible, forcing her back through the manned checkpoint. The little rock cave was eleven miles from the American camp at Whitemarsh, a short ride for Nat and one that avoided all British-held areas. For Rebecca it would mean a ten mile round trip after a day of chores, and a week of walking into Philadelphia for visits, marketing and all the normal things she was expected to do. She wished her horse had not been stolen, but one could not rewrite history.

She was just contemplating new walking boots when she was stopped by a pleasant young soldier on patrol.

"Young lady, could you please state your business going in this direction, this afternoon."

Rebecca wanted to giggle. He probably had never stopped anyone before – easier, perhaps, to shoot, so she made herself serious. "Officer, I have a family friend who cares for foster children as well as her granddaughters, I am bringing them some eggs, since my hens have been laying well." She gave just a little swish to imply she knew what "laying well" meant, but not so much she looked easy. A little flirtation, she decided, was the way to get the soldiers to like her. And if they liked her, they would be pleased to see her when she walked up to their checkpoint.

"Well, Miss, that seems very nice of you. Do you have a pass to get back into town?"

"Oh, no. Will I need one?"

"No, Miss, it's not necessary since you live here, but it will be easier for you. Just a minute and I will have my commander write you one." The young man disappeared for a few minutes. His colleague waved a wagon with pumpkins and bags of milled corn past them, heading toward the town. Rebecca realized now that this checkpoint was not going to be as difficult a barrier as she had feared. The first soldier came back with a signed pass, which she carefully placed in the basket with the eggs.

She thanked the young soldier for his help and continued her walk. She realized that she had been holding her breath when she was finally out of sight of the little make-shift hut, and she let it out in a big whoosh. She sat for a minute on a stone wall that bordered the road to rest and catch her breath. She checked the pockets in her cape. All was well, and she pulled the pass out of the basket to look at it. It was written in a beautiful script, each line even and taking up only as much space on the paper as was required, and no more. It was dated today, and he had written that the pass was open and could be used whenever the carrier wished to go in and out of Philadelphia. It was signed "Maj. J. P. FitzSimmon." "Well," Rebecca thought, "wasn't it nice that Major J.P. was here today to solve all my problems!"

She spent the rest of the walk feeling quite airy, enjoying the beautiful autumn afternoon as does anyone who is aware of what happens after the lovely days of autumn. She found the rock without any difficulty. She hoped Nat would come soon enough to use the eggs before a racoon found them, but if that was the only risk of this enterprise, it seemed minor.

The next week, when she passed the checkpoint, she had her pass in her skirt pocket and fresh rolls for the soldiers. They smiled and thanked her for the bread, and waved her through, not even looking at the pass in more than a cursory manner. It got even easier as the weeks went by. Some weeks she brought fresh baked bread or tarts, and once or twice she brought chocolates or other sweets. Bringing the soldiers biscuits and sweets was easy enough, since she visited her aunt regularly anyway, and the shops in Amalia's neighborhood were tempting. Who was to know that the extra bag of goodies was for the sentries at a checkpoint leading west-southwest out of Philadelphia?

Times at the Liberty Coffee House were not as easy. Coffee Joe was a grubby man who never came out and said what he really meant. He gave Rebecca things to deliver to Nat, but none of them seemed of any importance. Most of what she read in Joe's scribbles was available to anyone who grew up in the area as Nat had. Rebecca hoped there was some code that made Joe's notes important, but she feared she was wasting her time.

In consequence, she kept a sharp eye whenever she was near the Liberty. There was one man she particularly did not like. Unfortunately, he was there often. He wore black and stared strangely at the visitors to the coffee house. The man in black, as she had come to call him, did not participate in discussions, and sat and drank alone. Rebecca often saw him talking to Coffee Joe, but he would stop when anyone looked in their direction, then he would sidle away and go back to his table. She had never heard him speak, so she could not tell where he was from, but his demeanor made him seem distinctly not local. More than that she could not ascertain. Of course, she did not know the others who left things with Joe for Nat, but she did not think the man in black was local enough to be helpful.

Chapter 7

Once the men moved onto the farm, Rebecca's life became so busy that her thoughts did not dwell on Coffee Joe or the discomfort she felt at his coffee house. Her busy household kept her away from the Liberty, and gave her plenty to send off to Nat. She found, happily, that she would only need to go into Philadelphia, and see Joe, no more often than twice a month.

It was one week after the capture of Philadelphia that the men arrived with all their gear. The five officers moved in throughout the afternoon on Tuesday, October seventh. They said they'd chosen to quarter on the farm because they wanted to live apart from the flurry of downtown activity. Each was a good horseman, delighted to live in the country and willing to ride the short distance each day to General Howe's headquarters.

They were a pleasant bunch who had been warned, by the General himself, to treat Rebecca like a little sister – a sister who happened to be an officer in the British Army. With that warning, Howe decided that Amalia's niece should be safe enough, and he sent his men off to the farm.

Rebecca greeted them cordially and showed each to his room. Two were assigned to share the largest room with two beds. And so a pattern developed right from the first week. Rebecca cooked and kept the shared spaces clean. The soldiers were responsible for their own rooms, serving their own meals, and bussing the dishes to the dining room mantle. Rebecca would retrieve the dishes and wash them in the kitchen. The men helped with fires, chopping wood and gathering kindling as needed.

On the whole, Rebecca did not find living with the men offensive. She had the kitchen to herself, and was able to continue sketching the town and the ships and complete her maps of quartered soldiers, including the five in her own house. One night a week she met friends for a knitting circle, where they knit stockings for Washington's men, or for widows and orphaned children, depending on who was doing the asking. It was after the evenings at her friend's knitting circle that Rebecca would walk to her Aunt's, stopping at the Liberty Coffee House to ask Joe if he had anything for her.

The light was fading earlier each day, and Rebecca noticed that the supply of soap and candles was getting low. At breakfast on the next warm autumn day, she made an unusual visit to the dining room while the men were eating breakfast.

"Good morning, gentlemen. Sorry to interrupt your breakfast."

The soldiers, most not quite in full uniform looked up and smiled at the pretty girl addressing them. "No problem, just tell us what is on your mind." "All right, young'un, what brings you in here this pretty morning?"

Rebecca looked at the assorted men, who had become almost brothers to her. "Gentlemen, we have to make soap, and if we have time, we need some tallow candles before winter comes."

"Rebecca, my love, this is a civilized town in a semi-civilized country."

The other men started laughing at this and Rebecca started to react when she realized it was all in fun. He continued:

"So, since we have all this civilization, why can't we just buy soap?"

"We can, of course." Rebecca responded, "but do you want army soap or that soft good- smelling soap you have been using the last few weeks?

"Aw, that's your soap? Never felt so smooth in all my years with the battalion."

"Someone tell the General we have to help on our Becky's farm today. But don't tell him we are making soap; that is children's work, did it with me mam when we were all wee ones."

"Cut the brogue, Sammy, you graduated from Harrow, you're just the second brother."

"Ah, 'tis true, Mistress, but I did make soap as a child."

Rebecca gasped at all the different responses coming at once. "Excellent, whoever can help, that will be fine, I will cut some meat for lunch; there will be fresh bread and apples. And if we can get the fire going by eight o'clock this morning, we should have it all done by mid-afternoon. And one other little request. If anyone has time, could he find some cranberries? I know they are native in England too, but they grow in New Jersey and may be available somewhere. I want to make us a good dinner next week."

It was almost her favorite time of year, when her Boston-raised mother would create the best meal of the year for a Thanksgiving. Most Philadelphians did not believe that the last Thursday in November was special, but Charlotte Willent had insisted on a roast turkey, potatoes and cranberries from the inland swamps of New Jersey, Indian pudding, and pumpkin pie.

Rebecca went back to the kitchen. She finished cleaning the breakfast things, and cut last night's roast into thin slices. She pulled a loaf of bread out of the brick oven, grabbed a small basket of apples, and put the food on the table, ready for the workers to eat when they were hungry. With things ready, she went outside to start what was always a long day.

"Sammy, since you have done this before, the ashes are in that shed next to the barn in an old barrel. Roll that out here, and we'll add some water for the lye."

By noon the lye was purified from the ashes, sheep fat with extra lanolin had been added, and the men were taking turns stirring and walking the large spoon around the cauldron in the barnyard. They took responsibility for keeping the fire up, and they were getting ready to pour into the molds.

"You might be ready to pour, but the mixture isn't yet. Keep going and I will find my herbal oils to make the soap smell good." Rebecca reminded the men to continue their "child's work."

She went into the summer kitchen, where her stock of herbs and oils was stored. Rummaging in the dark room behind some dried meats, she found the bayberry oil and lavender from a year ago. The thought of British redcoats smelling like French lavender made her laugh, but she put the bottle back on the shelf, bringing the bay out with her.

"Here, we go, gents. I'll just add this to this first big batch, and we can pour as soon as I get back from the garden."

She walked into her kitchen garden, frost-tipped but not fully killed. She pulled the hay off the thyme and rosemary. She crushed the leaves together and sniffed. Imagining herself faintly giving off that scent, she decided on rosemary and sage – powerful, but not masculine. That should help her through this winter. She carefully replaced the mulch, and tended to the few plants that had become exposed to the cold air. With that done, she went back to the barnyard and the cooking soap.

The texture was just perfect, and the bay very pleasant, so they began to pour the mixture into molds. The wooden molds had been carved by her grandfather many years ago. Each square had an elaborate W carved into the wood, so each bar of soap was imprinted with the letter. Just enough lanolin and bay oil had worked into the wood over the years to allow the soap to pop right out when it hardened.

The second, smaller pot was nearly ready as well, and Rebecca added the crushed rosemary and sage leaves. The herbs caused the mixture to turn a dark green color – just as well, as it would be easy to tell the soaps apart.

The day was getting late as the second mixture was ready to pour. By now, three of her four helpers had gone to Philadelphia, to headquarters, or off on their own business. There was only the pouring to do, and the work was over. Rebecca was pleased with all they had accomplished in this one day. All she had to do was get this pour finished and put her feet up. She yearned for a cup of hot cocoa, drunk in front of the fire with a good book. Sammy, her first and last helper with the soap, had excused himself for a moment, and Rebecca was stirring the soap just as it reached its peak.

"Sammy? We need to pour." The spoon was standing and the soap was perfect; another minute of cooking and it might not harden well. Knowing that she was perfectly able to do it alone, she set the molds on the ground near the pot. She scooped the liquid soap with a pitcher and poured it into the molds. There was only a small bit of soap on the bottom of the pot that could not be pushed into the pitcher. Rebecca picked up the pot to pour the rest when she was distracted by hoofbeats and voices near the barn.

One of the grooms ran up to her. "Mistress Willent, the General's sent word, there is another coming to stay here. A

Major. He needs a nice room."

"That will be mine, I suppose." She looked down at the ground, silently grinding her foot into the dirt. She took a deep breath and found a smile for the young man. "That's fine, don't look so concerned; let me finish the soap." The groom held the cauldron still so that Rebecca could reach the last of the precious soap. He then helped her clean the barnyard of all the soap- making equipment, and poured water on the outdoor fire.

"Miss," he asked when the obvious work in the yard was finished, and the trays of soap were stacked and hardening in the summer kitchen, "can I help you move your things? You said the Major would need your room. Where will you go?" He looked around the kitchen as though he expected her to sleep there, like a servant in a large manor or a character in a faery tale.

"Oh, really, I'll move into my old room at the top of the stairs. It's the attic, but it's quite nice. When will the Major – what's his name? – be moving in?" Rebecca spoke with a false enthusiasm that did not fool the groom.

"Name is John FitzSimmon. We don't know when he will be back, been away south to see about something, they don't let on what. But he should be back in a day or two. Why don't you take your special things upstairs and I'll help you with anything else in the morning."

By the time Rebecca was done with the evening milking, she was dead on her feet. She had carried all of her clothing up to her old room in the attic, as well as her hairbrushes, ribbons, and all other little sundries that make a person feel at home. She had hung the sheets from the yellow room, and aired the attic trundle bed as well. When the bread was ready to rest in until morning, she was more than ready to join it.

She climbed to her new room, looking somewhat forlornly at her old one on the way by. She burrowed into the narrow trundle she had used as a child, and slept the sleep of the truly exhausted, her good book and cocoa long forgotten.

The morning brought baggage and crates of all sorts, a beautiful writing desk, and a clothes press of curious elegance for an army man, but no Major. She had her larger things moved upstairs, along with the crate of her gowns that had finally been sent from Amalia's. She had the crated gowns put into a deep corner of the attic, to ignore until they were needed.

It wasn't until the Tuesday before Thanksgiving that Simm found himself back in Philadelphia. It had not been a bad trip. The scenery was beautiful, and he'd had some fruitful meetings with loyalist militias throughout the Carolinas. They were anxious to fight the rebel patriots, something that Major FitzSimmon was not authorized or prepared to let fly. He spent the night in his empty room at General Howe's headquarters, and was told early the next morning where he was to move.

Simm was in no hurry to meet the hostess with whom he would stay. He had visions of an elderly widow who knit and kept the house too warm and lived with cats. He rode the long way around and stopped for a minute at the crossroad checkpoint he had supervised at its founding to see how the soldiers there were doing.

"Major, good to see you again." A young lieutenant greeted him. "Come in sir, we have fresh bread and sweets. Honestly, Sir, the bread is day-old now, but still very good."

Simm sat and grabbed a piece of the fresh bread. It was

good, so he sat and enjoyed the company of the young men. "Where did you acquire such morsels, stuck here as you are? Have you taken to baking?"

"No, that sweet filly, one you once gave a pass to, she brings them on her way to visit her friend with all the children."

"Does the girl have a name?"

"Of course, but we don't really know it. We just refer to her as the girl in the blue cloak. The color brings out the blue in her eyes and she is so pretty, and brings sweets."

"Lieutenant, you are smitten. Careful you pay attention to what goes on here." Simm smiled at the younger man, which belied the warning he had spoken only slightly in jest. The lieutenant laughed and offered Simm the last of the sweets before he mounted and rode off.

Nearing the farm, he saw some of Howe's staff riding in the opposite direction.

"Hey," Simm called catching up with Captain Samuel Reding. "Sammy, where are you fellows off to? Can't be work from the direction you are heading."

"Major, long time getting home. No, we are off to find cranberries."

"Cranberries? Small tart berries, jellied and served with poultry and meats?"

"The very same. Our Becky, Little Sarge we call her, would like cranberries for our dinner on Thursday."

"Someone named 'Sarge' wants cranberries for a dinner, mid-week?" Simm looked baffled and thought maybe it was time to find his bed after all. It had been a long trip.

"Yes. But maybe you need explaining to. Becky Willent is our landlady, now yours too. She is making a fancy dinner for some Thanksgiving, like her mother made. And we like to eat, so we hope to bring home cranberries."

"Our landlady likes to be called 'Becky' at her age?"

Captain Reding laughed, "Simm, what age do you think that would be?"

"Like Amalia, I suppose, between forty and sixty."

Sammy looked around for the other riders. "Hey, Jack and Benji, Simm here supposes that Becky is between forty and sixty years old. Should we tell him or surprise him?"

They rode off laughing and Simm, who knew where there were good farms with cranberries just north of where they were, went with them. They all got back later in the afternoon. The men stabled their horses and went into the farmhouse by the front door.

"Make a good first impression, FitzSimmon, you're taking her bedroom," the Captain said as he handed Simm the basket of cranberries.

Simm spent a few minutes talking with the grooms, who found a stall and feed for Artemis while Simm curried his horse. When he was satisfied with her comfort, he headed to the house.

The other men had gone straight to the front door, so he supposed that he should, too. He wanted to take a minute to size up the person who kept up such a well-built stone farmhouse. It looked like it grew out of the surrounding countryside, and had clearly been here for many years. Maybe Mrs. Willent's husband had built it years before, when they were first married or had moved to the area.

He walked the long way around, past the sheep meadow dotted with the few sheep visible from the near side. He saw, nestled up to the house, a well-tended herb garden and what had been a flower garden before the hard frosts of the past month. He walked into the herbs, carefully staying on the small paths laid out between the plants. He stopped at a rosemary, as he always did now when he saw the plant. He took a few needles, crushed them on his hand, and let the smell bring him back to a small stem tied with a leather band, deep at the bottom of a valise he supposed was already delivered to his new room.

He jolted upright suddenly, realizing that he should not spend the afternoon in a daydream. A new room meant he must meet the landlady. He wasn't sure why, but the main door felt the wrong way around, so Simm headed toward the kitchen door at the other end of the herb garden. He realized he probably smelled of rosemary, but there was nothing to do about that. He caught a glimpse of a young blond elbow-deep in bread dough through the kitchen window. He thought that such sweet kitchen help could be a charming distraction during a long boring winter quartered in another strange city.

He knocked at the kitchen door.

"Anyone in a red uniform uses the front door. Didn't the others tell you?" Rebecca called over her shoulder, not really looking away from her kneading.

"I think I would rather use the kitchen door. I have cranberries." Simm was shocked. He wanted to take a minute to enjoy the speechlessness that this delightful surprise had brought. Becky Willent was not elderly. She was his Becky. She was not going to be happy to see him. He could bear that. He would bear anything just to see her again.

Simm had faced guns in April 1775, during the retreat through Menotomy, later at Charlestown during the battle called Bunker Hill, and in the attack in late August, 1776 on the Americans in Brooklyn, on Long Island; he had faced negotiators on ships and in back woods; but he dreaded hurting Rebecca more than he did cannon fire. He pulled up his courage and opened the door to the well-kept kitchen and stood, staring at her back, reveling in simply having found her.

He looked around the kitchen, taking it all in. He had imagined she lived in a faery castle, a garret, or a barn in an enchanted wood. But he should have guessed it would be a well-kept country kitchen in a stone farmhouse. Hanging on pegs near a back room were only women's things – a thick gray cloak, a woven shawl in a dusty rose, and a knitted sweater and, under them, neatly lined up, was a pair of wooden clogs and a few pairs of stiff, hearty shoes, at the ready for egg gathering and milking. He hadn't seen a cow in the barn, but there was a cooled milk can at the door, and a butter churn just in sight in the back room, so the cow was not far away.

"Lady Becky?" he spoke very softly. "Is that really you? I really do have the cranberries. The fellows had no idea where to buy some, so I offered my expertise." He had no doubts that it was the Rebecca of his summer dreams, and even if his eyes had doubts, his body did not. He was as aware of her as if he had seen her only that afternoon, not seventeen months before. He recognized her movements, her features and even her smell. It was as if she were a puzzle piece that simply fit. He could not speak. He just stared, completely delighted, but afraid to go on.

"Oh!" Rebecca felt caught. His sudden silence struck her as a kind of rejection. Here she was in the middle of kitchen chores, wearing a dull dress, her hair formed unceremoniously into a thin plait that hung down her back. She was sure she was covered with flour from the bread, red- faced, and dripping sweat from the oven's heat. Bravely she spoke, "I get it – John is Major John FitzSimmon. John, I mean Major, if

you give me a minute, I will show you your room." She
motioned to the door to the dining room, and Simm bowed
just slightly and left the kitchen. He hoped he had left her
with the dignity she deserved.

Tom Houghton's voice came in clearly. "Major, you here
too? Goin' ta be great fun! Let me introduce you to our
Becky."

"Thanks, Tom, I just met her. I think she will show me
around later. What have you fellows been up to since they
sent me south?"

Rebecca had wanted to turn and run to him the minute she
heard that voice at the door. She had looked at him when he
insisted on coming into her kitchen. She didn't suppose she
would get him to understand the boundaries, as the others did
– that it was her kitchen. It would not help that he had to use
the back stairs to get to his room. She pushed the dough into
a bowl to rise, covered it with an oiled cloth, and pushed it on
the edge of the hearth. She stood in front of the fireplace, not
feeling the heat of the flames but remembering his breath, his
arms, his strength merging into her. Just that second in the
kitchen had awakened what was supposed to be a happy and
distant memory, one meant to be pulled out when she was
alone and lonely, not a roaring need that growled deep inside
her that she was afraid she would never lose, and that she
knew now, with certainty, she could never lose.

Thoughts went spinning round her head. Had he been in
the army when they'd met? He must have been, to be a Major
now. He is valuable to Howe's staff, and Howe has been in
America for over two years. Did he plan this reunion? Was
that even possible? Could he have known her name from the

beginning? Did she dare ask him if it was a coincidence that he happened to be in her house? Was such a happenstance even possible?

"Major?" Rebecca had rinsed her face with cold water and pinned up her hair into something respectable, and now she stuck her head into the parlor to get his attention. "I can show you the upstairs now."

"The men tell me you had to give up your room for me. I'm sorry." Simm tried to made conversation as they climbed the stairs off the kitchen.

"The attic was my room when I was little; I don't mind. This whole year seems surreal to me, anyway. Nothing seems to matter very much."

Simm grabbed her hand that had made a motion, almost pulling her against him. He held her hand hard in his. "Becky, it has to matter – if only as comedy."

Rebecca had no reply. She led Simm to his room and told him to call if he needed anything. Before she left, she turned to the still-open door, "Major, comedy?"

"Miss Willent, I know we are not now what we were for that brief remarkable moment in time, friends. Please don't call me 'Major.' Call me John, or use Simm; it's what everyone else calls me. As for comedy – sometimes life is a farce not of our writing. For instance, you must wonder if I planned this – this move into your house."

Rebecca leaned back against the wall, waiting silently for the information he was about to give her.

"Rebecca, I may have to spend a lifetime convincing you that it was not of my planning. But it is not a coincidence, not completely. When I met you, I was in Philadelphia for General Howe, as I am now. Since I was traveling anyway, I took time to meet my brother's ship when and where he was expected to dock. So I remained here a while, waiting for Jason and the *Good Queen Bess*. And I was here with the *Bess* when you met me.

Rebecca wanted to ask if he was a spy. But now he was in his uniform. Was he spying while he was in Philadelphia in the summer of '76? He didn't seem interested in the government or politics; nothing else was happening there then. So maybe he was just visiting, waiting for his brother and getting to know America. Rebecca let the issue go. To get closer might mean she would reveal too much of her own life.

She smiled ruefully and turned to go back down to the kitchen. "Settle in, John. I ring a bell for dinner, which is served in the dining room." With that, feeling a little more balanced than she'd expected to feel, she went back to the kitchen.

Chapter 8

Simm settled into the pattern of life on the farm. With the other soldiers, he heartily enjoyed the traditional New England religious and harvest holiday called Thanksgiving. He recalled that the Great and General Court of Massachusetts had occasionally called Thanksgivings and Fasts, though not during the British occupation. It seemed a quaint Puritan tradition to the men, but they enjoyed the good food nonetheless.

Simm got in the habit of bringing wood in for the parlor fire, and for the kitchen if the wood box wasn't full. He made a point to stay out of the kitchen. But when he found himself there, while Rebecca was baking bread or stirring stew, he found himself lingering, just for a moment or two.

Those moments, when he watched Rebecca at her work, graceful and competent, became images in his dreams, often hitting him unexpectedly, early in the morning, as the heavenly smell of fresh baked bread wafted into his room through the shared chimney.

One morning after Simm had been at the farm a week or so, he was awakened by loud voices in the stable yard. He quietly pulled back the curtain to see Rebecca and two older men. She had already finished the milking and looked tired, but sensuous with her hair loose and a pale blue robe over her nightdress.

"Da, it is too early. I'm just starting chores. Let me dress. Come back later."

"Daughter, 'tis no way to speak to your father in front of

the neighbors. I heard you were off flirtin' and dancing with your so-called tenants last night."

"Father. It wasn't last night and it was Amalia's party." She took a long breath. "If I have men in the house, it is your fault."

"Well, Smith here don't like it, and he's spoken for you."

"It's too late to complain, unless YOU want to move in here and I'll go and stay at Hackett's. I would think Smith would no longer care. You called off the wedding, remember!" Rebecca was livid and outnumbered. Simm could tell she wanted to throw something at the men. He was impressed that she maintained any decorum at all.

"I might have spoken too soon. He has made a more than generous offer for you. You won't see the money you're collecting for your dowry unless you behave yourself." Jasper barely spit out the words.

"Da, you're complaining and making this up so you can steal my money. Leave me alone! I won't let you bully me in front of Mr. Smith."

Simm pulled back from the window as the men strode away from the yard. The chickens gabbled around them, pecking for food no one had yet thrown. He watched again as Rebecca, still in her robe, fed the chickens and let the sheep into the near meadow for the day. Simm wanted nothing more than to help her with these chores, especially if her father wanted to cheat her out of the rental money. Money and legal agreements – *that* he understood.

Dressing quickly, he assessed the situation. Handling Jasper Willent and Herodius Smith had to be easier than preventing armed rebellion or stopping a war once it was well begun. He brushed off his dress uniform, scattering the dust and ash from the previous night, before belting on his dress saber. Voices again came through the window.

"Rebecca, it's Mr. Smith you said you would marry. What about that now? That would stop all the talk."

"Father, we agreed I was not to. And the only talk is your talk. Besides, the war and occupation disrupted those plans. I am not even thinking of marriage till this war is over, independence is won, or we are all simply enslaved – then marriage will not matter."

Simm had forgotten that the date of the proposed marriage was supposed to have been this fall, six months or so after Rebecca's nineteenth birthday. The battles around Philadelphia certainly had delayed that union. Looking at Herodius Smith, he wasn't at all sorry that Rebecca had not been bullied into marriage, even if it had taken the slaughter at Brandywine and Germantown to prevent it.

Smith was well twice her age, with an ill-kept sense to him. His clothes were too big, as if he had been shrinking, and his face looked like he spent too much time being drunk and angry. His hair was graying, but more than that, he did not clean it. It hung uncombed and greasy, tied into a queue with a broken lace, hanging inelegantly down his back.

Simm sighed to himself, thinking that he didn't blame Herodius for wanting Rebecca. He couldn't blame any man for feeling that way. However, if Rebecca had so much as smiled in Herodius' direction, he probably would use the saber now strapped to his side. Taking control of himself, he walked down the stairs and into the kitchen yard.

"Good morning, gentlemen, a word with you, if I may?" Simm led the men into the garden at the side of the house. "Let me introduce myself. I am Major John FitzSimmon of the 23rd Regiment of Foot of His Majesty's Army. I am obviously one of the men living here under the care of – " he looked at Jasper Willent – "your daughter, sir, Rebecca Willent. Miss Willent is doing a wonderful job of caring for the house and the meals – as of course you have heard?" Simm inquired by glaring harshly, first in Jasper's direction, and then at Herodius Smith.

"Of course we have, haven't we, Jasper?" Herodius responded almost too quickly, to Simm's question.

"No doubt that." Jasper put in grudgingly. "It's not the caring, it's too much caring that I worry about."

"Sir – " Simm put on not only his official but his aristocratic air, and continued – "if something untoward was happening in this house, it would fall badly on the men within. Do you mean to imply that the behavior of the officers living here has been less than gentlemanly? If so, you really must tell me. Or General Howe, if you are more comfortable with that. You see, he gave direct orders that no one was to interfere with Miss Willent's person, if you get my point. I assure you that when the General gives an order, everyone within earshot gets *his* point. So if you know of something untoward happening here, you must speak up."

The two men shook their heads, harumphing about how sure they were sure that the men were behaving themselves just as they should. And it must all be a big misunderstanding about Rebecca. They would tell the neighbors not to jump to conclusions, and all that.

"Well, Mr. Willent, I am glad we are clear on that. Wouldn't want to get a man falsely hanged. We do take these things seriously, you know? But sir, while I have you here –"

The men had turned anxiously in an effort to leave the garden, but Simm held them with his gaze as he continued. "It seems that the rent we men have been paying over at headquarters is not getting where it ought to be getting, isn't that right?" Simm did not wait for a reply to his question, but continued. "So it seems to me, the solution is that we soldiers will pay our rent directly to our landlady. I'm sure the efficient landlady will not forget to buy food. I will personally see to the household provisions at headquarters." Simm finished by glaring at Jasper just a moment longer than he deemed absolutely necessary, nodded to the men, turned on his heel with military precision, walked around to the other side of the house and disappeared through the kitchen door.

Rebecca had seen her father and neighbor follow Simm toward her herb garden. The dead, frost-shriveled plants played the perfect background to the scene. Still in her nightrail and warm robe, she went into the dark summer kitchen, where she watched and listened through the window, carefully keeping the thin curtain closed. She viewed the scene with growing awe. She knew that Simm was a powerful man. A superior officer to many, he held his men's respect, but there was the other thing as well – the potency she had felt on the pier in the summer sunshine that magical morning; a manly power that may have come from inheritance, or education. Whatever it was, her father, who was a nasty and proud landowner, a man who bowed to no man, was completely mastered by Simm's few words. She could not see Herodius from her position, but the rent money had little to do with him, so she did not care.

Rebecca watched her father object, and then give in to Simm's suggestion that she had done nothing wrong, and then that the rent money be given to her directly. She supposed she would hear again from her father before that was settled, but she would tell him that one of the men was keeping it for her, and would give it to her at the end of their time in Philadelphia.

She practiced her speech – "Da, I have nothing to do with it," in her perfect daughter's whine. Laughing at her father's discomfiture, so nicely delivered and so richly deserved, she wheeled around. Still laughing, she continued into the kitchen, where she smiled openly at Simm for the first time that fall, caught herself, stopped, and skipped up to the attic to dress.

Simm's personal power, and this unexpected goodwill for her benefit, surprised her. She had never doubted that the man lusted for her. That was clear every time he walked through the kitchen, hard as he might try to hide it. What she did not expect was his effort to defend her name and protect her promised dowry. The incident was interesting because it was so clean, so legal; not what she had expected from a soldier in His Majesty's 23rd. She would have thought that if Simm were going to defend her from danger, it would have been both chivalrous and violent, with swords and fisticuffs.

But on Friday afternoons, from that week on, Rebecca found the rent money, correct to the penny, in her mother's fine porcelain soup tureen in the dining room china cabinet.

Simm spent the next days cautiously watching Rebecca. Early winter brought icy roads and sleet, so like the other men he simply went to headquarters during the mornings and returned to the farm early most afternoons. Rebecca was always cordial to him, but he could not help but feel she'd rather be brusque and rude. After that one guileless smile, he was hurt.

He could understand if she hated the British invasion and occupation of her town, but she did not seem to. On the contrary, she was friendly to all the men; they called her Sergeant Becky, and joked happily with her. Simm remembered she had read Thomas Paine and quoted the Declaration of Independence, but she did not seem to resent the inevitability of their living here. If she really hated the British, well, he had met plenty of people who truly hated having troops in their town. They glared at him, they cleared their throats, and spit after he walked by. In Boston, they had taunted the soldiers and spoken none too softly behind his back.

Simm would never blame townsfolk for not wanting an invading army in their midst. Philadelphia had changed under British occupation – changed in many ways since his visit the summer before. Not all of the changes could be blamed on the soldiers' occupation. The sense of excitement that had run through the streets after that "Declaration" had been signed had been palpable. Now there was no excitement, no happiness, no joy.

Rebecca wasn't like the angry patriots who, for whatever reason, had not left Philadelphia. She had her friends and was happy here at the farm, but she would not smile or talk to him. It seemed she could not forgive him for being here. And yet, at this moment, there was no place on earth he would rather be.

Simm would have accepted the same easy friendship she had with the other soldiers. But Rebecca would not allow it. When he tried to banter with her, she would turn abruptly away and talk to anyone else. If they were alone, as they often were, sharing the back staircase, she would just shake her head and leave the room. More than once he heard her angry crying from the attic. He had no grounds to ask if he could help, and certainly no right to give comfort.

Rebecca's memories and daydreams were always of John

FitzSimmon. And the more she worked to stay out of his way, the more aware of him she became. Because the trips to the rock cave needed to stay so secret, Rebecca planned the trips carefully around the men's schedules. She was particularly wary of being discovered by Simm; she never left when he was at the farm, and she tried mightily to return before meals needed to be started and the men had settled in for dinner.

To stay safe from Simm's sharp attentions, she had found she needed to create a barrier around herself. And to do that she needed to pretend to be angry or, better yet, ignore him. Hard as she tried to ignore the man who lived off her kitchen stair, she knew it remained pretense. He was always coming and going through the kitchen from his room to the dining room, or to the stable, because, typical of the caring man he was, he took care of his own horse. Avoiding him was impossible. She found that ignoring him was equally impossible. She might not look up and smile at him, but she was aware of his presence, even when he was silently in the room, just as she knew how long the smell of his soap lingered as he passed through the kitchen in the morning. And though she should have been delighted, the impersonal nod he returned to her stony silence nagged at her.

For his part, Simm tried to respect Rebecca's need to stay apart. His room on the back stair made total invisibility impossible, but he tried to minimize contact as much as he could. He found it hard to remain aloof, however, when even leaving his room meant walking right by her in the kitchen. Too often as he walked through, Rebecca was at her work table kneading bread dough. She might pointedly ignore him, but he could not help noticing how her hips moved as she kneaded the soft dough into the wonderful fresh bread she served each day. Sometimes he would stare silently, imagining that he was the dough. The best he could claim was that he said nothing.

But as the December chill pulled in closer, time spent in the same house without speaking or exchanging a polite nod had nearly driven him mad. The weeks between their Thanksgiving feast and Christmas had Rebecca baking almost constantly, and now sugary breads, pies, and cookies – what the Americans called biscuits – filled shelves and tins in the kitchen and spilled into the back room as well. Even though he tried to suppress the it, the vision of Rebecca while she rolled and kneaded the doughs merged with the heavenly smells coming from her kitchen. The shared chimney meant baking smells were the last thing he noticed before he blew out his candle and the first thing he noticed when he woke.

In his dreams, asleep and awake, Rebecca was kneading dough, their hips moving in rhythm as his arms around her held her against him rocking with the movement. Sometimes the dreams became so real he woke, hard and panting, only to smell rolls baking for the men's breakfast. He had always loved baked goods. His parents employed a chef just for desserts, especially for the children, but this, he had to admit, was different, as the wonderful smells wafting into his room each day had become a kind of delicious, sexual torture.

One day in the middle of December, Rebecca returned from town with a large number of small, carefully wrapped packages. The stores had not stocked some of the spices she usually associated with Christmas, but she was pleased that most had been available. She loved how the Christmas spices made the season smell different, special and exotic. Good smells wafted through the farmhouse, and most of the men had, at one time or another, peeked in the door and asked about the new aromas.

Rebecca enjoyed teaching the soldiers about the different family traditions practiced around Philadelphia, and she was pleased when they came into the kitchen to see the little ginger men and angels. Simm, too, had inquired about the trips to town and the new spices she was using in the biscuits. He was determined to use the change in her domestic patterns to ease the tension between them. As always, Rebecca resisted talking to him, but one morning after breakfast he wandered into the kitchen while she was pulling trays in and out of the oven, and was therefore trapped in place.

" Becky?" Simm was hesitant to use any other nickname – the other felt unnatural. He had not spoken a direct word to her in over a week. That conversation had been about her father's dog who had wandered over from Hackett's farm, and had lasted less than a full minute. He desperately wanted to find a way to connect with Rebecca. He knew it might be inappropriate, and anger the General as well. Worse, she might be more injured than helped by their friendship, but still he was determined to try, since neither of them was happy with the ways things were.

"Yes, Major?" Her voice was quiet, so cold and polite he wanted to scream.

"Rebecca, I was wondering about the shapes and smells, the spices you are using in the biscuits, things like orange peel and ginger. Are those recipes from Boston, from your mother?"

Rebecca cringed that John remembered that her mother was from Boston – that he remembered anything at all about her. She wished he did not, as she wished she could forget, or at least suppress, the memories of him as well, memories of warmth and gentle touching that rose up when they were most inconvenient. Right then, she wanted to do what she did so often, and simply walk away and leave him in the room, but the cookies would burn if she gave in to that whim. And just as it was wrong to leave the baking, leaving John just then felt unreasonably rude.

"Well, the molasses cookies are from Boston. But the others are from German neighbors here in Pennsylvania. The farm down the road is owned by Mrs. Gruenbaum and her son Friedrich. He is ... away. Mrs Gruenbaum taught me to bake them. She lives there with her daughters and a daughter-in-law and grandchildren. Marie, her daughter-in-law, taught me to decorate the windows with waxed paper shapes." Rebecca pointed to the kitchen windows which had been adorned with waxed angels, shepherds, snowflakes and candles. They were almost unnoticeable from inside the house in the morning sun, but would glow from the outside in the evenings when lit with fire or candlelight. Simm considered they might be the second most beautiful thing he had seen recently.

Rebecca realized that she had spoken more than a single word to Simm, and she was enjoying herself in his company. Abruptly, she stopped speaking and just stared, bewildered. It was so easy to talk to him, to tell him things that mattered, the tidbits and stories that made up her life. She bit her lip to stop herself from speaking. It would be far better for him to think her rude than for her to give away her secrets. She shrugged in frustration, took the cookies from the oven, and set them to cool on the racks. She was relieved when the last batch was set to cool. She pulled on her cloak and went outside for air.

Simm strode by her in the yard, heading for the stables. Rebecca was rounding the corner, wanting to kick something or someone, when she saw Artemis and her master gallop past her like a black streak.

On December the seventeenth a stranger rode into the

yard. Rebecca was taking advantage of a crisp, dry day, and had just hung bed sheets. She was starting on her own laundry when she looked up at the rider. The man had reddish brown hair and dark black eyes. He did not move like a soldier. He did not seem particularly comfortable on his horse, yet, from his bearing, he was a man who commanded men. Rebecca was aware that she now noticed such things. She found the stranger intriguing, so she went into the kitchen and quietly watched him from the window.

His clothes were good. He wore a tricorn, no wig, and made no effort to close his coat against the chilly December wind. Not a Pennsylvanian nor a Virginian, this man was used to wind and cold. She watched until one of the grooms took his horse and pointed to the front door at the other side of the house. It didn't take long for Rebecca to understand – the man moved like he would be better balanced standing on a rolling storm-tossed ship than walking on firm ground. Maybe he had just come from a ship and brought news of something interesting. He carried a satchel. If it were official, whatever he had would have been brought to Howe's offices, so it was not military. No, this had to be a personal visit.

By this time of day, the soldiers were all in powdered wigs. This made finding family resemblances difficult. The civilian must be connected to someone who was here. Rebecca felt she deserved some sort of change of pace, and this pleasant puzzle was as good as anything to break up her morning. She took off her apron and firmly tucked her restless hair under her cap using misshapen pins she had rebent a dozen times.

The pins always reminded her of John's hands inside her cap, playing with her hair. As always, she stuffed that memory firmly away, and walked into the front room to welcome the stranger, who was talking amiably to the men sitting there. Simm looked over as she came in. She carefully avoided his icy blue eyes, keeping her own straight ahead, looking at the handsome stranger.

"Mistress Willent, may it make known to you my brother Jason FitzSimmon, just arrived from Salem, Massachusetts on the *Good Queen Bess*."

Oh, he is a sailor – then maybe John really does own a part of that pretty ship, Rebecca thought, as she answered, "How do you do, Mr. FitzSimmon. And how does it come to pass that you find yourself in Philadelphia?" Rebecca was growing exceedingly tired of coincidences, and had developed a general distrust of them.

Another FitzSimmon. Rebecca's thoughts started to run in multiple directions. It could be no accident that Jason FitzSimmon found his brother at her farm just weeks after John was coincidently quartered there. Had Jason been looking for John and simply found him at home? She had papers to bring to the rock-cave, chores to do at the farm, and the blasted FitzSimmons were everywhere. No matter how hard she tried to ignore it, they were interfering with every thought and breath. Why couldn't she just be somewhere else? She wanted to stamp her foot and make them all disappear, and all her chores finished, the run to the rock cave over and unnoticed. How was she going to get away if Jason were here all day with John?

She stayed in the parlor with the men for a few minutes to be polite, realizing early and easily that he had no secrets to discover and carry off in the pockets of her blue cloak. She also admitted to herself that he had simply arrived for a visit with his younger brother since the *Good Queen Bess* sailed from London and had legal merchandise for shops and some goods expected by the army. His goods were probably slightly more than legal as well, from what John had told her. Certainly an interesting family – but she reigned in her thoughts, admonishing herself to be polite. After chatting with him a few minutes, just long enough not to seem too eager to run away, she excused herself and retreated to the kitchen.

"Jason, how about a short ride back to headquarters. The staff over there keeps the kitchen open all day, and we can talk in my office," John offered, seeing how anxious it made Rebecca to have his brother in her house.

Jason shrugged his agreement. The men got their coats and horses and quickly rode out of the yard. Rebecca watched them leave. She marveled that she had not noticed the family resemblance when she had first seen Jason dismount in the yard. John was the taller brother, but they had the same wide shoulders and long legs. And even with John's required wig in place, they had the same cheekbones, square chin, and laughing eyes. Maybe away from here, away from her, John laughed. She remembered hearing him laugh and seeing those dark blue eyes light with joy and fire. She pushed the memory away and went back to her baking.

"Oh, Johnny," Jason started, as soon as soon as the brothers were sitting at Simm's desk with a bottle of burgundy, two glasses, and a plate of fruits, cheeses, breads, and meats, "if I lived in Philadelphia you would have a run for your money over that one. What a delicious morsel," he ruminated aloud, as he popped a grape into his mouth and savored the juice.

"You're married, and anyway she is way off limits. General's orders." Simm almost growled at his brother.

"That seems to be working for the other men, and besides they're all scared of her. They think of her as no more than a friendly young sister, or the house maid.

"Scared of her? You're mad, Jason."

"Me mad? No, I am happily and well married, but you will be. I saw the way you looked at her, or should I say tried not to look at her. Your body reacts to her like a ship to changes in the wind. You don't know you're doing it, but you are warning the other men that she is your property. Hell, they probably don't know you're doing it either. It's the kind of thing we see at sea if there are passengers on board and the men start to look at the wife. Most of the time no words need to be said – the man announces his ownership just by standing there. She may be officially forbidden to all the men, but it is pretty clear that you don't believe that she should be off limits to you. You were getting angry in the two minutes we were in that front room because she was clearing away dishes and tidying books and such, and not looking at you while she did it. I know you, brother, you can't hide those things from me. But I don't know how she feels about you. Should I ask her for you?"

"No, it's more complicated than two people who may or may not want to speak to each other."

"Okay, brother, you haven't seen me in over a year. Lets see, we met here, in Philadelphia. It was hotter than hell. I couldn't wait to get back to sea. I recall you were looking very pleased with yourself, and in a very strange mood. Had those rooms near the dock and disappeared every evening till I sailed. And, as is so often the case, you wouldn't talk about it."

Simm did not answer. He just stared at the wine swirling in his glass, remembering licking warm brandy off of soft skin on a windy Pennsylvania night.

Jason stared at his brother while he filled his plate again.

"You really should eat something, Johnny, you are getting very thin."

"Nonsense. Becky feeds us like kings. I'm just worrying away, I guess."

"The girl? No, that worrying must be something more likely related to king and country. Now that I am a deserter from the cause, I won't ask any leading questions on that score. I really don't want to know – might mean my neck. Better off to stay neutral and stupid!"

"Much. Do you find yourself drifting to the other cause?" Simm spoke so softly that the crackle of the fire nearly drowned him out. "No! don't answer that. We will discuss that when we are old and gray. When none of it matters anymore."

"Good, back to the girl."

Simm groaned, knowing that when any of his brothers got into this mood, there was nothing to do to stop any one of them, and of the five of them, Jason was the worst. "All right, if you must."

"That look in your eyes when you remembered that summer. That was a girl. I know, it's always a girl. It was that girl? The same girl?" Simm nodded, still staring at the dark red wine. Jason continued his torment. "So from hot pleasure to ... and now she won't even meet your stare. Ouch!!" Jason got a gleam in his eye as he began to enjoy unraveling his brother's knots. "And you live in her house, where you and – what is it, ten other men? – are quartered for good King George.

"Its five others and two grooms who sleep in the stables, but may move in when the winter comes."

"Close enough to ten. My guess is that she is not too happy about all the visitors, especially you. Is she a Loyalist?"

"Her aunt and father are. Brother's on Washington's staff. I've met him in my work."

"Your work? In battle? No, that's a stupid question, I won't ask."

"Good, I won't tell."

"I knew that. But, is she a Loyalist, or does she want to slit your throats every night?"

"I don't think she wants to slit our throats, but I don't think she wants us there. Her father lost her dowry, and the only way she won't have to marry a rather repulsive fellow, whose lands touch her father's, is to raise some of her own money. This was the bargain we worked out."

"That's interesting – you said 'we'?"

"I overheard the father wanting to steal the rent money from her, so I intervened a little."

"Did you? In uniform? Wearing wig and saber? I'll bet you intervened quite a bit. You are rather imposing when all dressed up, Johnny, my dear brother."

"Thank you. I believe that was what the couturier had in mind."

"Well, brother. Back to the original problem."

Simm's head was heavy from thinking and the fine wine. He wanted to see his brother out and die on his couch, but Jason still had energy. "It must be the salty sea air he breathes all the time," Simm thought, just before he exclaimed, "Mercy, Jason! There is no fixing my problem. Surely, now that you know the truth, even you, you thick-headed sea monkey, must see that."

"What's the truth? That you, Major Lord John FitzSimmon want to, no more than want, need, to possess a woman who is 'off limits' to all the British soldiers in Philadelphia? And 'blimey', to quote my mates, lets assume she is more loyal to brother than father, and she doesn't want anything to do with a one of you blokes. But maybe, if we are more specific, she doesn't dare, or can't let herself get too close to one particular lobsterback.

"From what you haven't said about that week in Philadelphia, she might be a bit cautious about getting too close to you. See, it might be a bit obvious to the neighbors if she started growing abnormally large while living in a house of men. It might start rumors of a sort that's hard on a girl; so my Oona tells me. So your Becky avoids you the only way she knows how. Freezes you out till you run away. How'm I doing?'

"Sounds very close. What would you do about it?"

"First, keep your pants on, and I mean that quite literally. Don't let her run every time. Find ways to be close. I don't know what it'll be, but if you go on this way, John, you'll hurt yourself or her. And someone will get hanged, or at least court-martialed."

"Wine?" Simm had filled the glasses again. At least, Jason noted, the food on his plate was slowly disappearing between swallows. The brothers changed to easier subjects, like Jason's wife, Oona, their two young children, and the sea. As the night turned colder, and as the late autumn dawn drew near, John walked Jason toward the pier and his ship.

"John, come aboard a minute. Mother sent packages in case I should see you. Something about scouring London and Paris for hair pins. I don't understand why you told her you needed pins, but she sent hundreds, as far as I can tell, and some other stuff as well."

Simm, with his saddlebags full of small wooden boxes, arrived at the farm just after sunrise. He called a cheerful "good morning!" to a startled Rebecca, who just was on her way out of the barn with a basket of eggs and a bucket of milk. He handed the horse to the waiting groom and intercepted Rebecca on her way to the kitchen. He lifted the heavy bucket from her arm and carried it into the summer kitchen, the unheated room where the milk can was stored during the winter. He poured the milk into the can and carefully replaced the lid. He did not even look in Rebecca's direction, but climbed the stairs to his bed, where he collapsed until the bell rang for breakfast.

That evening, just after dinner, as the house settled into post-dinner bonhomie, Rebecca decided that since all the ginger and anise cookies had gone so well, she would use the time and bake Scottish shortbread. The oven was still hot from dinner, so it needed very little care. Her mother's father had been from Scotland. Charlotte had baked shortbread often, for they always reminded her of her father. Charlotte Bigelow Willent had taught her daughters that there were two tricks to good Scottish shortbread – the first was never to overcook the dough, and the second was good Scotch whisky.

Jasper usually had a bottle or two stored in the house, so Rebecca went to look. It did not take much hunting through kitchen cabinets and shelves to come up empty. Not expecting better success in the dining room, Rebecca went in to look anyway.

"Hi, Little Sarge. What are you looking for? Can we help?" Jimmy, a sweet clerk and a good and helpful friend to Rebecca, asked.

"Maybe, Jim. I'm looking for a bottle of Scotch whisky for shortbread." Rebecca continued opening closing cabinets and checking behind dishware and plates. "Do any of you have any good whisky? I only need a spoonful or two."

"Sorry, Becky. Only wine, ale, and sometimes weak rum. General's orders. He doesn't want us getting drunk and forgetting ourselves. Rumor is that's how the Hess lost Trenton."

Rebecca who made a point never to comment on Patriot losses or victories in front of the men, answered quickly, "Does no one have any whisky? All you Englishmen and no whisky?"

Jack spoke, "I don't suppose you'd ask him, cause you can't seem to stand the man. But I suspect FitzSimmon keeps a bottle upstairs – for medicinal use, I'm sure."

"Thanks, Jack. I'll swallow my pride for the sake of shortbread for all. Hey, why don't one of you go ask him?"

They all looked at her and sadly shook their heads, making it clear that disturbing the Major after dinner was unacceptable. She did hear a voice query the others as she retreated through the door to the kitchen. "Why is it, you suppose, that she won't even say 'morning' or 'evening' to the Major? He's not that much of an ogre. I've worked for him on and off for three years. Most of the girls hang on to him like limpets."

Rebecca pulled her ear away from the door. Well, that's what I get for eavesdropping. Did I expect the men to understand why I can't be friendly with him? Thoughts and fears aside, she checked the temperature of the ovens and made sure she had enough of the other ingredients before she made this uncomfortable journey. Taking a deep breath, she opened the door to the back stairs. She stood still until she was convinced that the importance of procuring the whisky outweighed her own fears. Rebecca climbed the stairs to the next landing and knocked.

"Hello! Come in, come in." John sounded groggy, and Rebecca realized that since he had gotten home at dawn, he might be sleeping. Too late to back out now, she opened the door. He was, in fact, lying on his bed. The room was warm, heated by the kitchen fires she had been keeping hot for her baking. It smelled of ginger, anise, tonight's dinner, and something distinctly male. His cravat was off and his shirt was unbuttoned. He looked absolutely magnificent, and Rebecca wanted to join him in that warm room, on that soft bed.

Simm saw her lick her lips and swallow hard. "Rebecca!" he almost shouted with laughter, but suppressed it so as not to embarrass her. "I don't suppose you came up here just to stare at me, as wonderful as it is to see you standing in my door way. Mistress Willent, what can I do to help you?"

Rebecca swallowed again. She was sure he could tell that she actually gulped, and she noticed that he was trying not to laugh. "Major, I need whisky, and the men all tell me that you are the only one here who has any. My father seems to have taken all the kitchen stock on his way out."

"May I inquire why you need my uncle's finest single malt?"

"Shortbread."

"Shortbread. You want to use the finest Scotch whisky currently to be found in the Americas for biscuits?"

"Yes. They're very good."

"So I should hope. You wouldn't steal any if I said no, would you?"

"No, John, I would never steal anything from you." Rebecca saw that this conversation was creating its own seriousness. She would have stopped it, but it was too late.

Simm sat up, bringing his legs over the side of the bed. He spoke solemnly. "You have already, Rebecca."

"No John. I wouldn't." Her discomfort began to make her voice louder and slightly shrill.

"Becky, you know you have used my Christian name twice. That's two times more than you have spoken it all year."

Rebecca was getting uncomfortable at this interrogation. It seemed petulant, as if John were picking a fight. But, as was so often the case when she was flustered, she spoke quickly without the careful planning she tried so hard to employ when she spoke to him. "John FitzSimmon, you said this year! How do you know how many times I said your name before you arrived here last month? Screamed it, in fact!"

"Oh, that's interesting." Simm stared at her, amazed at her honest intensity.

"And *John*, I haven't stolen anything. I am not a thief." She stopped herself from letting the shrieks out, lowering her voice, " I'm sorry I yelled. I meant nothing by that." Rebecca covered her face with her hands, embarrassed and flustered by his proximity and teasing tone. She was also afraid she knew what it was she had stolen. And, there was no way to give it back. She had worked all fall to harden her own heart. She could not take responsibility for another's. She raised her eyes off the safety of the floor. Simm was still lying there, looking delicious, but now he was holding out a bottle of amber liquid he had taken out of the box he kept under his bed.

He slurred his words just slightly, his voice deep from sleep or drink. "Take as much as you need, sweetheart. It's your reward for making a personal appearance in my dreams."

Rebecca gulped again. Sweetheart – he called her sweetheart? She stared back blankly. She walked hesitantly into the room to take the bottle from his outstretched hand. She murmured her thanks as she fled down the steps to the sanctuary of her kitchen.

Simm watched the door as Rebecca flew away. He'd felt

like he had gotten some wild thing to eat from his hand. He enjoyed the sensation as he drifted back to sleep in the warm, sweet-smelling room.

Later as Rebecca pulled heavenly-smelling shortbread from the oven, she was reminded that she had broken her self-imposed edict about never crossing the doorway into John FitzSimmon's room. She stored the cooled shortbread carefully in a closed tin, and hid it well away from her hungry borders. She prepared the room for breakfast, did her few chores and climbed the stairs. She carefully put the bottle of good whisky on the landing where Simm would see it and not knock it over. She waited a moment, staring at the door. She thought of the warm room on the other side of the door and the hard man lying so beautiful on the soft bed, tapped gently, and ran up to her cold, attic bedroom and its small hard bed.

Lying awake an hour later, she contemplated that she said she would do just about anything for good shortbread. Going into John's room – had that been a journey into hell or heaven? She threw her pillow across the room and then stamped around the small attic room after it, hoping to disturb someone, until finally she forced herself under the warm eiderdown.

Chapter 9

For the town of Philadelphia, the days before Christmas were busy ones. It seemed all the town wanted to host an event, maybe to prove their loyalty in the likely event the King's forces would win back the colonies. Amalia, who was doing her best to entertain the Commander of the King's forces who quartered in her house on Chestnut Street, had decided to host her event after the New Year on twelfth night, January 5, 1778.

Of course, all her friends and General Howe's entire staff were invited. The General made it clear that no one was allowed to refuse his invitation. For Rebecca, there wasn't even a possibility of refusing. Her Aunt knew she was friendly with many of the men, and she would be required to be junior hostess. Amalia had insisted on two trips to her favorite modiste for a new ball gown. "And you are such a good dancer," her aunt had reminded her more than once.

Real dancing wasn't something that Jasper Willent and his Puritan-raised wife were too thrilled about, but Amalia had insisted all the Willent children learn. Charlotte had pointed out to her husband that he should just give in to his sister-in-law, since he wanted his children to be in- line for his brother's money. Like most of Jasper's schemes, that one was foiled when Amalia gave her husband two sons, some twenty years ago. But of all of the children, Rebecca was the best and most natural dancer.

The trips to the dressmaker were not wasted, since Rebecca was able to combine those trips with short visits to the Liberty Coffee House. She would go to the Liberty before lunch, and spend only a minute to see if there was anything new she should know. But one day, Joe claimed he had important things she just had to carry. Most often she insisted she take a moment to memorize the information, which gave her the chance to write it down at home, and not risk walking through the streets with rolled papers in her pockets.

"Very well, Joe." Rebecca agreed reluctantly, "I will take them, but let me into the kitchen to fix my cloak. I'm having lunch with a relative." She turned the gray liner to the inside, carefully putting the documents deep in the hidden pockets. Once she was pleased with the way the cloak swung, she reentered the main room. She said good-bye to Joe in the almost empty room, noticing, not for the first time, the man dressed all in black, nursing an ale and a bowl of stew. The man caught her eyes for a mere second and tilted his head just slightly at her. For weeks she had seen him at Joe's. He was certainly a regular, but she had never seen him speaking to Joe, or to anyone else. She was curious about his identity, but she didn't want to spend more time at Joe's than she had to. So she walked up those seven steps that brought back so many memories, and went on to Amalia's house.

As usual, Amalia's gracious home on Chestnut Street spoke to the world of an elegant tranquility. But with General Howe's headquarters nestled there between hand-painted wallpapers, Rebecca knew the tranquility was gone. Tranquil or not, she knew that all her tenants worked in the offices here, and she was very curious about what her tenants did while they were at work. She wasn't sure if it was fear or good breeding, but she was too well-behaved to hunt them down during her visits to her Aunt.

She tapped at the kitchen door, and Annie rushed her

upstairs to her aunt who was waiting, reading a light novel in the morning sunlight. After lunch, they sat for a moment until Amalia reminded Rebecca they must go off to the dressmaker.

"She's just arrived from London, Rebecca dear, she knows all the latest styles." Amalia was adamant that Rebecca come with her for yet another fitting.

"More likely Liverpool, but at least she hasn't claimed to be Parisian."

"Rebecca, no wonder you are still single, you are always so difficult."

Simm was on the stairs, on his way down to the General's office, when he recognized Rebecca's voice and couldn't resist a moment of eavesdropping. He wasn't in a particular hurry. The Americans had finally moved away from Philadelphia, and had settled into winter quarters some thirty miles away. That made the information coming in from spies watching the Americans of less immediate import, since nothing new of a military nature was likely to happen until spring.

Simm hadn't meant to overhear his lovely hostesses in the parlor, but it was his nature to discover everything he could. And he had developed a certain habit of needing to defend his lady, even if she would not admit to being that.

He strode into the little parlor, grabbing a small sandwich off the table. He sat without being invited, suddenly filling the room with his presence. "Mrs. Willent," Simm began his lecture in a leisurely manner, "I don't believe that Rebecca is difficult. I think what you have here is a niece who will not lie for the sake of love. I admit that I don't know her very well, but I have lived in her home for a few weeks now, and I am a keen observer of people. So, I feel I speak with some authority." Simm gave Rebecca a half smile, bowed graciously to Amalia, and excused himself to resumed his errand. On the lower floor, he was greeted by Howe's clerk, his face a deep shade of purple, frantically searching through a stack of papers on his desk.

"Montgomery, what on earth is the matter? Nothing that happens during a lull at Christmastime is worthy of this anxiousness."

The man looked up and saw it was Simm. A look of relief crossed his face. "Major, I can't find a record of this one phantom that comes in and out unchallenged at a checkpoint on one of the western entry points. The men say she had a pass, signed months ago, giving her free access. She doesn't carry anything of interest, in or out. But someone higher up than us wants to know who is the 'girl in a blue cloak'? "

"First off, who signed the pass?" Simm was bemused, all this chaos over a girl who carried nothing of importance in or out of the town.

"You did, Major. At the end of September, just after we took the town."

"Well, then, it must be fairly harmless."

"I'm not sure, Major, but I think the fact that it was you who signed the pass is what makes this person interested in the girl."

"And what is my alleged connection to this 'girl in a blue cloak?" Simm wanted to find this a laughing matter, but something about it itched along the hairs on the back of his neck.

Montgomery just shrugged, expressing his ignorance.

"Montgomery, take a note and file it with the rest of this nonsense. 'I, Major Lord John P. FitzSimmon, signed the pass in question, on a lovely day in September that had very little traffic in or out of the town, for a girl who was carrying eggs to a neighbor who had moved a bit away. Not only was she only carrying eggs and biscuits, she shared the biscuits with the fellows in the guardhouse, who very kindly shared some with me.'

"Monty, you many write as much or as little of that as you wish to include. You may make up a flavor to include your favorite childhood treat. I need to see the General about my trip to New York. Clinton needs my expertise for some reason. By the way, do we know who requested the record of the pass?" Simm hoped that by adding that last nonchalantly, Montgomery might reveal something.

Lieutenant Montgomery shook his head, chagrined, and waved Simm into the General's office. Somewhat calmed, he went back to his work.

"FitzSimmon, all your work, all my work and Richard's is being ignored. Someone, it seems, is interfering with our dispatches. They are either being ignored or reinterpreted before we can clarify. Parliament fail utterly to grasp the fact that the colonies are no longer the simple plantations of their bloody imaginations. Honestly, look out the window. Do those lace curtains next door, or the carriage being drawn down by those matched white pacers, look simple to you? Somewhere in London, I suspect there is but an inkling of a grasp of the actual situation here, but the constant stubbornness, ignorance and utter lack of imagination combine to prevent those blockheads from understanding what we have been trying to do.

"You know I hate to lose you even for a few months, but I think you must leave for New York and see what you can do." The General, who was usually uninvolved with his paperwork, was frantically waving dispatches and letters that had only just arrived from London and New York. Simm felt his trip north had been confirmed, and quietly left the room. As he made his way out of the office, he motioned for Montgomery to go in to take his place.

Simm returned to the quiet of his own office, glad that he had over two weeks before he had to ride north. As he did whenever he felt contemplative, he stared at the pretty wallpaper, letting his mind wander. He often found that puzzles unraveled themselves if given the time. But, as happened so often in this room, the puzzle became the room and the wallpaper itself. The room was very feminine, yellow and blue – he could imagine a pretty blue flowered counterpane covering the bed and lace on the dresser that now held his papers and ink, sealing wax and other equipage of war. He was always struck by the room, empty except for his office things – a desk, a lamp, two desk chairs and a slightly more comfortable one, a dresser, a trunk and a small woven rug. But it was designed for someone special – the handmade French wallpaper spoke to that. He knew the Willents had two sons, both of whom lived in London. He didn't stop to waste time on this little domestic puzzle, but still, he liked pondering the missing girl or girls.

As he had when Jasper wanted to steal her money, Simm had jumped right in to defend her stubbornness. Rebecca could not get Simm's kind interference out of her mind. The family always teased her about her need to tell the truth. His voice echoed in her head – "I don't believe Rebecca is difficult ... she will not lie for love." That was the nicest thing anyone had ever said about her, and she desperately wanted time to think that through. It seemed the key to the whole thing must be honesty. Even if she could not tell Simm the truth, she would not lie to him. She would much rather stay silent.

"Rebecca, are you listening? I don't know where your head is!" Amalia was pretending to be insulted while inspecting the new dress from a chair in the modiste's shop. "You're right, you know, he really is delicious." She turned to the dressmaker. "That rose is lovely against the blue, Mrs. Andrews. You have done a magnificent job."

As the women chatted, Rebecca pushed her mind to considering the gown. It was indeed beautiful – deep rose silk damask with an open skirt and split sleeves, both showing dark blue silk. Mrs. Andrews had ordered new stays and made new petticoats. They agreed she would wear the gown over the linen shift, with lace edging on neck and cuffs.

"Rebecca, while we are here, let me order you a new cloak. I see you in that blue one all the time."

"Aunt, I made it only this past autumn. The wool is new and it is very warm. I don't need another. And don't be silly about the Major. I don't think he is delicious, just kind. That is such a rarity, it tends to shock me after growing up with Father and my brothers."

"That I don't believe. You don't stare at him because he is kind. How about a lighter cloak, to keep a longer gown clean? White wool, to be worn only on special occasions, like our party. And Rebecca, not all your brothers are unkind. Are you perhaps weary of Nat, too?"

"Aunt Amalia, you know I won't talk about family, and thank you so much for the new gown and cloak," Rebecca answered, amused by her aunt's demanding generosity. The women agreed on delivery terms, and Rebecca and her aunt left.

Rebecca walked with Amalia until they reached her house, and excused herself. She had suddenly remembered that she had Joe's documents in her cloak pockets and wanted to get to the rock while the sun was still up, quite a task during these short late-December days.

That afternoon, as Rebecca headed toward the guardhouse with fresh cinnamon rolls for the soldiers, she heard voices louder than usual coming from the little house. She hid in the wood a little off the road, behind a stone wall, just before the little house. She stayed hidden, carefully watching the road leading to the checkpoint. For a while, nothing changed. The loud argument continued, and there was no traffic on the road. Rebecca considered taking a shortcut through the damp woods, in spite of the encroaching darkness, but thought she would wait just another minute before she willingly soaked through her boots.

From her hiding place, she watched through some dead wildflowers that rose above the rock wall. She saw the man in black leave the guard house and walk back toward Philadelphia. When he was out of sight, the two soldiers came out and lit their pipes. They spoke angrily, reliving their interrogation and then began to relax and joke about the man who had seemed superior to them, but was not in uniform. Rebecca knew she was not supposed to have seen the man in both places that afternoon, but was scared that she was the person he was looking for at the checkpoint. She was shivering with fear as she exited her hiding place. She gave the men their treat, and went quickly and uneventfully to the cave and back home before it was too late to prepare the dinner.

While stirring the stew, Rebecca continued wondering. Who was the man in black? Joe's was a hotbed of Patriot rhetoric, even if someone didn't know about information-gathering. The man in black was there just this morning, staring hard at her, and maybe at everyone else. And then he was at the guard house, a place that obviously belongs to the British soldiers, where he seemed to have some authority, but at the same time he seemed to be resented by the young soldiers stationed there. Who was he? Rebecca tried to imagine how someone had the authority and the audacity to be in both places publicly. The only person smart enough, and with enough background, to unravel this mystery was the very person she could never ask. She served dinner, more frustrated and removed from Simm than ever. After the dishes were done and chores were completed, she went slamming upstairs again.

Simm had no idea what had set Rebecca against him again. He had tried to do everything his brother had suggested. He had helped her with chores, carried heavy buckets, and flirted gently whenever he got the chance – not that flirting wasn't fun. But he hoped to prove to her that the dislike was only one-sided. Again, in spite of his instinct to retreat or seek revenge, he determined to ignore her anger and continue his own mission to show her how much he cared. Simm's only frustration was that in a very few weeks, he was moving to New York for as long as four or five months. He didn't know if Rebecca would get into trouble while he was gone, but as Christmas drew near he was not happy with the orders that would separate him from these beguiling winter quarters.

For Simm, Christmas during wartime had become a habit, but he had never grown used to it. No matter where one was, there were always parties and dancing with officers' wives and the daughters of magistrates and potentates. He would have loved to spend the season decorating with green boughs and attending church at midnight, as he did growing up. But army life did not allow for personal extravagances such as those.

The staff was kept constantly busy with meetings and social affairs that kept him away from the farm until late most evenings. When he was home, it was almost never at regular hours, so he had not seen Rebecca often for weeks. The few minutes now and then that he was at the farm, and awake, he could not miss the pleasant, homemade greens and other decorations. He hoped Rebecca was doing some of the pretty decorating for him, and that she was missing him as he was her. He also prayed that her anger would dissipate if he were often gone.

Where Rebecca's home seemed to get warmer, with the pine boughs and holly now decking tabletops and mantles, Amalia had transformed hers completely. Even from the top floors, it was hard to miss the beautiful greens being brought in to decorate the house for Christmas. Simm supposed that even with farmland nearly completely surrounding the town, there was still enough woods left to satisfy Amalia's demands for ivy and mistletoe. And sure enough, in a few day's time, Amalia's main rooms were transformed from sheer elegance to Christmas magnificence.

Christmas morning foretold a chilly, rainy day. Rebecca left the household asleep as she finished the morning chores, changed, and walked the familiar path to her family church in the constant drizzle. As always, she was torn between her father's tradition of a joyous day with gifts and too much feasting, and her mother's solemn, New England approach to the day. Bostonians had banned special worship on Christmas during her mother's childhood. Cotton Mather had written that everyday belonged to Christ, not just the one day called his birthday. Still, even her mother had enjoyed the happiness and the decorations in the houses of her husband's family. Rebecca had even picked up the traditions of their German neighbors, and those brought even more joy indoors during the dark season.

Memories of her parents and her childhood swirled in her head as she trod through the muddy road toward the family's Presbyterian Church. Happy and wet people rushed in from carriages and on foot, shaking water onto the floor and shaking hands of greeting. Rebecca felt peaceful as she entered the empty family pew. That solitude was broken seconds later as she was surrounded by nieces and nephews, brothers, and sisters-in-law.

Simm's eyes followed Rebecca as she walked forward in the plain white church. He had risen early to find some solace and solitude in the day. This year, more than others, he found himself wanting more from Christmas than a series of fancy parties given out of meaningless duty, thousands of miles from home. The empty church was already illuminated and welcoming as he found a seat in the far back, away from the central aisle. The clear windows glowed with the flickering candlelight against the wet, gray morning sky.

The white clapboard church with its high-box pews brought back memories of Christmas in Boston. Although the Puritans had banned the holiday, it had become a day of fasting and feast by the time of the occupation. The soldiers quartered in the town had gathered what greens they could find to decorate their barracks, and the day was always spent with song and food. As Simm sat in the little church, watching the rain against the windows, he thought of another occupation of a very different sort of American town.

He remembered the High Anglican Mass celebrated at

King's Chapel with the other officers and wealthy loyalists who had migrated into the protected town. The beautiful stone church near the top of Queen Street stayed alive, in sharp contrast with the Brick or South Church, the Third Meetinghouse, that the first group of soldiers sent into Boston in 1774 had turned into a riding stable, to punish the town for destroying the tea. He looked around this church, holy with Christmas and joyous families, and mourned the destruction of the other.

Memories and thoughts of Christmas and family eddied as he sat there in the quiet back pew. The church filled with happy people enjoying the day and delighted to see their friends and family on Christmas morning. Simm made room for various newcomers, keeping his eyes over the top of the pew. He watched Rebecca enter an empty box near the front of the church. In seconds, he heard giggling and saw little feet flying down the aisle. Looking to his side he witnessed two small girls, the first no more than two years old, and the other around four, running down the center aisle, effectively dodging between the legs of the more sedate church goers singing "Bay-Ca, Bey-Ca," a song he could only assume meant Rebecca. The small girls were trailed by a number of adults and various older children, all of whom crowded into the box where Rebecca sat.

The service was lovely, and perhaps not long enough for a man so far from home. He sat in the pew, lost in thought as the congregation moved out into the rain behind him.

"John?"

He heard Rebecca's voice carrying over the happy voices of the crowd.

"Miss Willent," he answered "A lovely service, wasn't it?"

"Yes, Major, it was. Well, excuse me." Rebecca turned to

her family, who were watching her conversation with the unknown man.

"Well, Rebecca, aren't you going to introduce us?"

"Oh, Becky, don't bother, I'm Jane, the kids are Abby and Mary, the baby is Hackett, but he doesn't answer to anything yet." She pointed to a very small bundle currently being held by the larger Hackett. The rest of the herd just left, but if you're a friend of Becky's, why don't you follow us to our farm for some dinner. It's just family. We'll be eating around two o'clock."

" Jane, Hackett, family," Rebecca jumped in to try to stem the tide before more family was introduced, may I present Major John FitzSimmon, one of the men who has been quartered at the farm. Its lovely to see you, Major – yes, do come for dinner. Jane's mother stayed home to cook. That is, unless you have other dinner plans?" Rebecca almost added, "other than the cold ham, bread and Christmas biscuits I left on the side board?"

To have shown the reluctance Rebecca felt would have revealed too much to her family, and would have been outright rude to Simm. He noticed her squirm at Jane's invitation. He silently smiled encouragement that only she would notice, and made a silent promise that he would not stay past dinner. "No Mistress Willent, no particular plans, but I did promise the men I'd be back in the late afternoon." He answered both Jane and Rebecca.

Simm liked Jane Willent. She was a woman who did not let life's larger issues get in the way of raising her family. She continued the informal introductions, while trying to grab the hands of her daughters and push them into their cloaks. She kept up the commentary as they moved toward the exit, partially to marshal her large group out of the church and out into the rain, and, Simm was sure, to keep him from feeling left out.

They found the carriage and crowded into it. Simm was pushed in with the crowd and ended up sitting between Jane and her daughters. Abby clambered over one adult after another, trying out laps. Finally she turned and settled onto Simm, finding the thick wool of his cloak and the velvet of his fine suit just right. Soon the child was asleep on his shoulder. Jane made to reach for her sleeping daughter, but Simm waved her off. He adored his nieces and nephews, and missed them terribly. It felt very nice having such a trusting fellow human resting in the crook of his shoulder. The child smelled of fresh soap and that special sweet scent that children have.

Nat had followed the family to Hackett's farm on Metacommet. He laughed, enjoying the fact that the haughty FitzSimmon was stuck in the crowded coach with the babies. Simm and Nat had recognized each other immediately as the family had gathered in the church. They had become acquainted in the performance of military negotiations. The project was a private enterprise between the Continental Congress and Parliament, secret even from their own battalions. It was impossible to explain to the family that they had met before, many times, in various negotiations between the Howe brothers and the Adams cousins, and then finally with Washington and his staff.

The men had met first, two years ago in 1775, before Charlestown, and before it became clear that the war would need to be fought through to its ultimate finish. Nat found Simm efficient and organized. The Englishman always seemed to know what was expected of each meeting, as though he could see the outcome before the negotiations began. To the less experienced and worldly Nat Willent, all that efficiency was a form of British aristocratic arrogance. He did not understand that experience and careful observation led Simm to the see the outcome of each meeting only as it was unfolding.

Nat rode the bay into the barn as his brother, walking the team which was now harnessed to an empty coach, followed. "That FitzSimmon put up a fuss about being crowded in with a bunch of babies?"

"Na, seemed to settle right in. Carried Abby into the house just now. Like as not, good with kids. Likes 'em, far as I can tell. You have some sort of military problem eating with him here? Nat, it's Christmas." Hackett half reprimanded, and pleaded with, his younger brother to stay and behave like one of the family. "We are lucky that you are so close, you can get leave to come for dinner, really Nat, don't make me ask 'the stranger' to leave the table at Christmas." With that said, and the horses cared for, Hackett turned and went out the barn door into the rain, pulling the collar of his great coat over his head.

Nat contemplated leaving, but decided a warm kitchen and good food outweighed any personal animus he felt for John FitzSimmon.

Simm hadn't been at a family Christmas celebration since he left for the army when he was sixteen. He had visited his family many times, but had been away at the holidays most years. Now he sat at the roaring fire, waiting for a roast goose to be served. He could smell the dinner cooking three rooms away. He sat nearly motionless, enjoying the family chaos, but feeling very alone in an alien world.

Soon the children were seated in the kitchen, and mulled wines and ciders were served to the adults. People moved to the table to eat. The five-course dinner was extravagant for farmers in wartime – of that he was quiet sure – and he tried to eat sparingly so the family would enjoy more days of the wonderful, well-cooked meal.

Not feeling comfortable enough to enter into natural conversation, Simm sat watching the family interact. They were happy to be together. Even Jasper Willent was not the angry patriarch he was when he visited his home. Nat, at home on leave from his unit at Valley Forge, glared at Simm between eating as much of the good food as he could. Simm could not help noting the twist of fate that saw him living in Nat's house eating well each day, while Nat's army, the opposing army, was nearly starving not thirty miles away.

Hackett and Jane were devoted to home, family and each other. It was nice to be around such pleasant people, but he wanted to move to the children's table in the kitchen. He puzzled that, and realized that the last Christmas dinner he had attended had been spent at the children's table. He decided again to leave as soon as it would be polite to do so.

Rebecca, the youngest adult in the family and the only unmarried woman, was busy serving and helping the children in the kitchen as often as she sat down. It was she who allowed Jane and her mother to enjoy their dinner without hopping up to get the succeeding courses. As usual, Simm wanted to get up and help her, but that would have been seen as beyond bizarre, so he let the desire pass. He thought about his brother's advice, and started to consider how he could connect with her so as to prevent himself from falling into some form of insanity.

After dinner, drinks and desserts were served in the parlor so the table could be cleared. Simm sat for a minute, excused himself to go to the privy, then made his thanks and good-byes to his generous host and hostess instead of reclaiming his seat. The steady rain of the afternoon had turned to sleet and freezing drizzle. It made the road slick with bouncing ice balls, dancing as they hit the quickly-freezing ground. Simm chose the less slippery path, and made his way over the brown fields instead of the rutted road back to the stone farmhouse. Off the main road, his collar and hood over his head against the weather, he watched others riding and walking to and from their Christmas dinners. It all seemed so normal, calm and healthy. These thoughts were dragging him away from the tight focus he tried to maintain. Maudlin thinking had no place anywhere near a battlefield. Maybe seeing Nat Willent again had brought it home, but he felt done with the whole project. The months with hard-line Clinton in New York wouldn't make it any better, but it might just prove distracting.

Politically, he understood his brothers Robert and Stephen's support of the American cause, but he was also finding it harder, personally, to accept the majority position of Parliament. This was perhaps what came of living too close to real Philadelphians, or maybe because he also had read Mr. Paine's *Common Sense*. On top of his unease with politics, Simm could not get the image of Rebecca laughing with her nieces and nephews out of his mind; the sight of her holding tiny Hackett in her arms as she politely said her good-byes and Merry Christmases at the door, nearly had him breathless with desire. He could not want to destroy any of that, but so often war tore families apart.

The distance to the farm was short, and Simm was in the empty, cold kitchen too soon. The other men were out, and if any were here, they had let the fires go out. Simm set the kitchen fire and coaxed it back to life. Then he put a kettle over the flames, to boil water for tea.

He sat alone on a hard wooden chair, eating wondrous shortbread and thinking of soft skin and silky hair. So sweet, so beautiful. So, his Rebecca was Nat Willent's baby sister. Had Nat not known that Simm had been among the men living in the house with his sister? He couldn't like that. If it had been legal, he was sure the young lieutenant would have challenged him to a duel just for being at his family's Christmas dinner. Honestly, if either Anne or Janet had a strange man, known only as a military adversary, home for Christmas dinner, he might challenge him as well.

He finished his tea and another shortbread upstairs in his room, and then he replenished the wood and kindling in his and Rebecca's rooms. In time, a few of the other soldiers came back and sat in the parlor, telling maudlin stories and drinking brandy. Simm was tempted to go down and join the self-pity of soldiers far from their homes on Christmas evening. But his thoughts drifted to the future, something hopeful he could only dream about.

Lying on his back staring at the ceiling, he built a dream of a beautiful, caring, blond wife with smokey blue eyes and children, many happy bright-haired children, all of them living away from here, far away from war and things that would drag them back into war– maybe in Essex County, on the rugged coast of Massachusetts, near his brother Jason.

Simm had gotten a glimpse of his future in the front pews of the church. He could do what he needed to do to achieve it, or let it lie fallow and die. He went down to say Happy Christmas to the men, but made polite excuses and went back upstairs to write letters of explanation to his mother and father.

"Simm!" Ellerby called from the front room, "When will 'Becca get home tonight?" His voice was slightly slurred, and it was clear the men had not finished drinking.

"Not till late, Ellerby. I told her I'd do the milking and fires." John lied, but considered doing Rebecca's chores as a Christmas gift.

"Ish too bad, I have a preshent for her."

"Lets all do Christmas gifts tomorrow at dinner, Ellerby, when we're not in our cups."

"Dash a good idea."

"Happy Christmas, Ellerby."

"Happ' Chrishmas, FitzShimmon."

Ellerby went back to the others. Simm heard other voices call out in good cheer. Simm went to the barn to see if he remembered what the milkmaid said when she taught him how to milk a cow.

Somehow Rebecca made it through Christmas dinner. She found she would rather help than talk, so she stayed busy with serving and helping in the kitchen with the younger children. When she did sit, she did so silently, eating her dinner, intent on seeming engaged while ignoring Simm. She would not be rude. He was her tenant and, if she admitted it, her friend of sorts. Her family saw them as colleagues. Outright rudeness, she noticed, seemed to be Nat's job for the afternoon. But what ever daggers Nat threw, Simm smiled, and said something to ease the tension, and he was very good at calming tense words before anyone much noticed. Rebecca assumed Nat's rudeness was because John was a British officer. But even so, Nat should know not to be openly rude. Many of the men in town were officers, and it was not their doing where the King sent them.

But try as she might, the Major was hard to ignore. His velvet suit was as beautiful as anything Amalia owned, and she was sure those dark blue sparkly buttons were real sapphires. The ultra white of his cravat spoke of a trained valet, and she remembered a man called Barrows who was mentioned the summer before but had not appeared at the farm. Where, she wondered, was John keeping a servant? Rebecca had wanted, almost desperately, not to have Simm at her brother's Christmas dinner.

The family had a long tradition of inviting a stranger to share their bounty, and Hackett would have allowed no one to interfere with that, so she simply stayed busy and tried to pretend he was any other guest. By the time FitzSimmon left, she wanted him to stay. His presence at dinner had unnerved her, yes, but when he was there she felt anchored and safe, as though she truly did have a place in the world.

Rebecca was at the door to see him leave. He had thanked her brother and sister-in-law, and was making his way out when she was standing at the doorway with the fussy baby, hoping the cool air would calm him down. Rebecca didn't know why Simm was leaving early. She supposed he'd had enough of Nat's evil looks. And maybe she had been too obvious at the church about not inviting him for dinner. But he had had a remarkable way of finding well-meaning intent even in the rudest statements and, in spite of the way she thought she had treated him that evening, when she looked into his eyes and thanked him for coming, and he had politely repeated how much he had appreciated having a friendly home dinner for the holiday. He seemed to mean every sentiment. Then he reached for a hand she had not meant to offer, raised it and kissed it slowly, making her insides clench and her toes curl. It was the first time he had touched her since they had parted at Amalia's mews. Then the baby wailed; he gently touched her cheek, laughed, and took his exit.

Rebecca stood at the door and watched Simm cross the icy field, his head high, his stride strong and sure even in the bouncing ice. He had pulled the hood over his light hair, but even hidden and almost eclipsed by the fog she would have recognized him. Finally, the blast of cold did the trick and Hackett settled, so she backed away from the door and handed the little one to his mother.

It was later, when the two women were drying the last of the dishes, that Jane gave Rebecca a look that said it was time to talk. "Becky, what's wrong? You are so tightly wound I fear you will break. I've never seen you rush around so at a dinner. You know we all share the chores, there was no reason for such."

"Jane, dear, I know you're right, I am sorry. Nat and FitzSimmon were making me nervous, or rather Nat was. He sat there so stiff."

"He's still here, Becky – why don't you ask him why he was so angry? Maybe it was sharing bread with someone he sees as an enemy. You know, we are used to it here, having the soldiers all over the place, but maybe it is harder for him?"

Rebecca thought over Jane's words. She suspected it was deeper than that, but it would be interesting to hear what Nat had to say. She headed into the parlor, but stopped to listen to the men talking. After a few minutes, she decided that eavesdropping was a bad idea all around. All she had learned was that Nat had been involved with political missions that he was glad had failed. That barely answered her questions unless he and Simm had known each other through those negotiations. Unlikely as another coincidence would be, it would explain why they seemed to know one another.

Rebecca spent some time reading with the little girls whom she had barely seen since her life had become busy with running to the rock drop-off and her houseful of soldiers. When at last they were ready for sleep, she said her good-byes.

"Beck - you need someone to walk with you. It's very dark and late," her brother Nat said as she grabbed her cloak from the peg in the hall.

"Nat, you're as likely to land face down in the ice as not. I know you need to get a good night's sleep when you have a chance. Besides, you don't want to see the men at the farm. I'll find my way home, and I'll be fine – see, the moon is out." And indeed the storm had cleared to an icy, clean night with a nimbus moon.

Rebecca walked through the barn on her way into the house to see what chores she could put off till morning. She found the cows milked, sheep penned and chickens fed. Pleased and surprised, she walked into the kitchen to find the kitchen fire banked and the floors swept. She peeked into the parlor and sitting room, and found most of the men contentedly drowsy or asleep beside a dying fire. She quietly put a thick log on the coals, knowing that when house got too cold, the men would find their beds. Carrying her shoes, she tiptoed through the dining room and back through the kitchen.

Still carrying her shoes, she climbed the stairs to the first landing. Simm's door was ajar, and a lanthorn was lit. She could just make out that he was sitting at his desk, working. Quietly, Rebecca continued up to the attic. She lit a candle and covered it with the glass, carefully placing the light on the floor. She went to the large chest that took up most of the wall under the window. It was where she was storing most of her things since Simm had moved into the house in November.

She lifted the lid and rummaged inside the wooden chest until she found a package wrapped in flax homespun in a pile of cedar shavings. She pulled off the wrapping and examined the contents. Inside was a bolt of fabric, about the size of a small blanket she had woven the autumn and winter before. Last year everything had felt different, for although the war was on and her world was upside down, there had still been time to dye and spin. A year ago, there had been space to assemble her loom and sit and weave the tartan she was sure she would never look at again, and certainly never give away.

Rebecca refolded the soft wool, pushed her feet into a pair of warm shearling leather slippers and went down one flight.

"Knock, knock," Rebecca called hesitantly into the open door. "Major, may I disturb you a minute?"

"Yes, Miss Willent," Simm jumped at the unexpected and welcome interruption. "Yes. Of course, come in. Can I help you?" He looked up at saw Rebecca standing holding a blue and green piece of wool fabric.

"No, I don't need help. I'm sorry, I won't interrupt your work." She made as if to turn.

Simm felt desperate to stop her from leaving. Short of screaming, he simply barked an order. He tried to do it quietly."Stop, please. You're not bothering me. Let me start over. Miss Willent, to what do I owe this unexpected visit?"

"I'm afraid this – " she held out the limp wool – "It isn't what I would have chosen this year, but didn't make it ... recently, I didn't have time or I would have made something more ... more formal, a fine linen cravat or something." Suddenly feeling like she did want to run away and abandon this effort, she made herself finish a bit defiantly. "You had mentioned that your mother was a Douglass."

"Yes, her mother's father was a Scottish Douglass. The

clan is dissolved now."

"You see – " Rebecca took a deep breath and steeled herself to tell her story. "I started this that fall, you remember? I really didn't have any reason to think I'd ever give it to you. I think I made it for myself to remember you, while I wove it. Now, I think you should have it." Embarrassed, Rebecca turned away.

"Becky?" John spoke softly. She turned back to the room and handed John the soft wool weaving. He took it in his right hand, while with his left he reached behind him to grab something on a shelf. He handed her a four-inch by four-inch by four-inch wooden box that rattled as he moved it. "Similarly, I had no reason to write my mother about a girl that I had met. A girl who explained the entire geo-political industrial history of colonial America by explaining about 'pins,' but I did. My mother sent this last year. Jason brought it.

"A year ago September, I wrote her about my trip through America. I tried to keep all my stories bland and even. My thoughts are that I was not very bland. Mother and my niece, another Elizabeth, have gone hunting for pins of all sorts, throughout London and Paris. She told Jason to give me this box – you would want it. I assume mother was right?"

Rebecca reached for the box as Simm reached for the package. She sat on the floor in front of the warm fire, and slid open the lid of the little wooden box. Inside, there were long, thick straight pins for closing heavy coats and capes, and long thin ones for hats; there were curved decorative pins with dulled ends for hair, even a large set to be used for utilitarian things such as sewing and diapers.

As Rebecca was marveling at the variety of pins Simm's mother had found, Simm was examining the plaid fabric. He ran his hand over the soft wool and held it to his nose, noticing the fresh cedar smell and texture even before he looked at the fine weaving of the tartan. It was, in fact, a perfect blend of browns and blues, with white lines in the woof.

His mother's family had been English for so long he'd not thought of their tartan, but he had seen some cousins wear the kilt occasionally, and Rebecca had got it exactly right. More than that, she had woven it for a man she was certain she would never see again. Simm wanted to take her into his arms and turn the world around so there was no war, and she could be his. Instead, he steadied himself to deal with the matter before them.

"Becky, you did all of the work on this? I didn't know you wove. Where is your loom?"

"Well, I can't weave now. The loom is taken apart and stored in the summer kitchen. But before all this –" She made an all encompassing motion with her hands – "I wove as often as I could find time. My mother wove. She taught me, and when non-importation and homespun was all the rage, we wove as often as we had time."

She went on, happy to talk about this part of her life. "The wool is first wool from the lambs. I had to fight my father that summer to let me have it. I didn't know yet what I would make, but I think I knew I would need it. I do my own spinning and dyeing too. I grow dyestuffs, and some I find in the wild."

"Its beautiful, very beautiful, thank you." Simm, spoke almost reverently. He had seen the future in a split second in church that morning, and now had another vision. This one was more clear, of Rebecca with a baby, a child that was wrapped lovingly in the warm tartan.

Rebecca broke the spell with her delight over a box of pins. "Oh John, the pins! your mother is a genius! Thank you, thank you, I know you think this is silly, but it's really a terrible problem. I need to thank her, let me give you a letter to send her, I'll write tonight." Rebecca gushed.

"I have something else. This is truly from me, but I did not make it."

He handed her a large flat package wrapped in paper. She opened it and found loose, beautifully-made paper and German artists' pencils.

"I see you sketching so often, I thought you might have finished the ones we bought before and needed some more."

Rebecca could not believe the gift. Not only was it beautiful, it was very expensive, better even than the set he had purchased for her that summer. She immediately vowed never to sketch maps for Nat using Simm's colored pencils – that was a level of horrible she could not abide. Now, with the new set in hand, she wanted so much to draw with them – draw beautiful things, like John FitzSimmon lying in relaxed deshabille on his bed. Thinking too quickly of the recent things she had sketched and brought to the rock hiding place, she suddenly felt shy and deceitful, and wanted to run up to her attic hideout. She did not want John to think that she was rejecting his beautiful, thoughtful gift. So she kissed him gently and quickly on the cheek and stood there awkwardly saying, "Merry Christmas John FitzSimmon, good night."

When she was out of sight of his door, she ran the last steps into her room, closed the door as quietly as she could, and sat on her cold bed and burst into tears. She pulled the eiderdown over her shoulders and head, rocking with sobs. Alone in her attic bedroom she stared at a box of beautiful pins, and the set of lavish German kohls and fresh drawing paper. She could not see a way out of this loneliness. She sobbed, gasping for air between renewed tears. The situation was unbearable. John FitzSimmon was all things kind and generous. He was beautiful, and he was hers. He was also an officer with the King 23rd Regiment of Foot, and an aide for the hated General Viscount William Howe. Even if she could find a way to be with him again, she could not trust him with the truth of what she was. There was no nice way to slice it. They might be lovers, but she could not trust herself with him, she could not trust him. They were enemies in this war. It simply was not fair. She could find no way out of this maze, no way to set herself on a path that could include John in her future.

She was dozing, nearly asleep on top of her bed wrapped in the quilt, when Simm quietly walked into the room. She looked at him mutely and just shook her head.

Hoarsely she whispered, "I can't tell you. Please leave me alone. Don't ask me to explain."

Simm felt all his genteel formality slip away. "Becky, it's too cold in here, you need a fire." He got onto his knees and started to build a fire in the small fireplace. Talking into the fire as he coaxed it to life, he spoke softly. "I expect for one thing, you feel confused about Nat and me –" he shrugged – "the vagaries and secrets of war. I won't ask you to explain your crying any more than I will explain my work, but Becky, there is just one thing I want you to understand, about me, not about my work. May I speak?"

"Yes, of course." She sat up and opened the quilt as she began to feel the warmth radiate from the fire.

Simm sat on the floor in front of the fireplace, occasionally feeding the growing flames. Looking over at her, he began. "I have more understanding about the American cause than you think I do. I'm not the hard-hearted evil villain that you want to paint me. I have read Locke and Paine, Franklin and Voltaire. My family are Whigs in Parliament, supporters of the American Whigs. Lady Elizabeth FitzSimmon, Duchess of Chardon, the nice motherly lady who scouted Newcastle, Carlyle, Manchester, London and Paris with daughters and granddaughters like a banshee on a mission, hunting for pins for a girl she knew nothing about, because she decided that the first time I even mentioned a girl in a letter she would – must – become important to me, and therefore to her, is such a staunch pro-American Whig she insists her sons vote against North and the King whenever they can. She also writes on behalf of the Americans to the newspapers, as 'Queen Bess'."

John took a deep breath and waited, keeping his arms around his knees. He was pleased when she did not chase him away. Instead, she settled comfortably on her eiderdown, smiling sleepily at the man on the floor.

"John?"

"Yes, Becky. Do you mind terribly if I call you Becky? We were once Rebecca and John. Though most people call me Simm, my mother and siblings do call me John."

"Simm," she said hesitantly, trying it out. Can there be a someday, without there being a now?"

"Yes, most emphatically. There has to be. So I believe there will be."

He was quiet a moment, and continued.

"Becky, I have another question for you. This one's easy, answer yes or no."

"Okay."

"When I have a chance, and no one is home to notice, may I stay in the kitchen with you? Watch you bake? Even talk to you while you work?"

"I suppose so, but why?"

"Honestly?"

"If we don't have that, we will have nothing. Let us vow not to speak at all unless it be the truth." She began to preach in jest, getting more animated as she went on, "Let us agree that silence is absolutely allowable, as long as we announce that is what we are doing."

"I so vow." He spoke calmly, moving toward Rebecca. He pulled at the quilt until she slipped off the bed and onto his lap on the floor. He breathed in her scent, feeling whole for the first time in a very long while.

She looked him deep into his bright blue eyes, sparkling like the sapphires on the coat he'd worn earlier, and spoke clearly. "I, Rebecca Willent, vow never to lie, but agree that silence is an acceptable alternative."

Simm went back to his original question. "Well, since I have taken a vow of honesty, I will say that watching you knead dough, and by extension the smells of baking wafting into my bedroom, make my mouth dry and my heart beat faster."

"Is that all?"

"No, that's not all." He took Rebecca's hand and put it on top of his hardening shaft. "That's what the thought of you working flour and water, eggs and sugar together does to me. If I behave myself, may I watch?"

He nuzzled at Rebecca's neck, and she turned toward him and lifted her mouth to his and he covered it with his own. They sat on the attic floor, finding exquisite wholeness in this simple bonding. He kissed her eyes, so tired and red from crying. He pulled her hair free from its ribbons and let it fall free, he ran his hand through the straight blond silk, till cupping the back of her head, he deepened their kiss.

Rebecca put her arms around Simm, under his loose shirt. She felt his body tighten as she ran her hands slowly over the perfect, rigid muscles that lined his back. She moved her mouth away from his and began to nuzzle him, leaving a trail of kisses on his neck and down the open neck of the fine shirt. Simm moaned, and pulled Rebecca's mouth back to his own.

Thoughts of kneading bread, the rhythm of her hips working bread dough onto the flat table, had her own body on fire. Her breasts had minds of their own, erect and sensitive to his every touch. His hands ran the length of her needy body over the rough linsey-woolsey shift she had thrown on for warmth. She quivered with desire, letting her head fall back and away. Pulling her closer, he started kissing her neck, but stopped suddenly. He pulled the quilt over her again, wrapping it around her shoulders and pulling it closed in the front..

"Becky! We should stop."

Rebecca settled deep into the quilt and into Simm's lap.

"You're right," she whispered hoarsely, "the others would know. At least now we won't be lying if we say 'no we didn't.'"

Simm lifted Rebecca up, cradled in his arms, held her very close for a long moment, and then he gently placed her on her bed. "Listen, I think this was Jason's idea, so don't blame me if it fails. Take off your shift and lie on your stomach on the bed. I am going to give you a massage." He walked from the room and returned a few minutes later.

Simm went into his room and opened the small chest that was partially hidden behind his dresser. He generally had no use for the hedonism that oils unleashed during military life, but this might well prove to be an exception. He took a small bottle of amber-colored liquid and rubbed it between his hands. Almost as an afterthought, he took a bottle of brandy which he put in a pocket, and a goblet suitable for Christmas night. Then he turned down the lantern and left the gloomy room.

Rebecca's attic was warm now and firelit. He went straight to the fire and warmed the bottle of oil in the edges of the dancing flames. When the oil was just warmer than his wrist, he turned to the bed, and drank in the vision of Rebecca naked on the soft white quilt, her pink buttocks inviting touches, and her body enhanced by the shadows of the fire. Simm realized that had never seen her relaxed before. She had her head on her arm, looking at him with the hint of a smile dancing around her lips and eyes. If he was not holding to his vow of chastity, he would have thought the smile was an invitation of sorts.

Simm wanted nothing so much as to throw off his clothes and join her on the little bed, and show her that the games they had played in the summer heat were nothing compared to the burning desire that stirred within him now. But he didn't. Jason was right— they needed to get closer before they indulged in real carnal pleasure again. So instead of lifting her into his arms and showing her what her lovely body and passionate spirit did to him, he approached the beauty lying on the bed with warm oil, and fully clothed.

He sat next to Rebecca and put the bottle on a little table next to her head. Simm decided that destroying his best shirt with amber oil was not worth it, so he took off his shirt. Then he got off the bed and poured a glass of the fine cognac he had brought upstairs. He looked at the amber liquid in the golden goblet, a gift from his father when he left for the army. It had been in the FitzSimmon family since the Normans. It was no longer part of a set; the others had been melted down for cash centuries ago. He briefly wondered how this one survived the centuries. He swallowed a large mouthful of the good wine, and turned toward Rebecca. Simm approached his task like Odysseus exploring a dangerous, unknown world.

He arranged the pillows so that she could breathe and keep her head down, and then he took the warmed oil and poured a nice bit onto her shoulders. When he was satisfied that there was enough oil to work with, he pushed the oil into her tired muscles. When her shoulders were warm enough, he picked up the bottle of oil again. This time, he poured oil drop by warm drop down her spine from neck to buttocks. Slowly, he rubbed the oil into her back, working the tired muscles that any housekeeper and farmer must endure. Working back up toward her shoulders, he slowly worked each arm. Simm rubbed extra oil into dry elbows and hands, kneading each finger in turn. He worked muscles, returning up to her lovely back, and he repeated the pattern to the other arm and hand.

"Becky? A quick question?"

"Ummm." she groaned with pure pleasure. "Uh huh?"

"Do you mind, I mean, will you be embarrassed if I continue down your bottom and legs? Normally I wouldn't ask, but, well, there is nothing commonplace about our friendship."

Rebecca chuckled into her pillows, "finish, please." She was perfectly happy to have him stop right then, but it was obvious from his voice that he needed her to trust him to go on. But did she trust him? She knew she trusted him with her body and her life. Rebecca wanted to, but could not, trust him with the secrets that might make him hate her. That, then, was the crux of the problem. If he knew what she was doing for the Americans, he probably would not turn her in to Howe to be hanged, but would he still look at her with such yearning?

She could not take the chance, and nor could she stop helping the Americans.

She promised herself again to keep her mouth shut and let this strange friendship find its own course. Now his strong hands, oiled again, worked each thigh, calf, foot and toes in turn. As he touched delicate parts without doing more, she marveled at his control, especially since she had felt his desire quite plainly even before she was naked on the bed. Whatever he was feeling, Simm was leaving trails of heat as he worked oil into Rebecca's responsive body. He worked his hands back up to her neck, and with his hands wiped on a corner of the crisp sheet, worked his fingers through her hair and onto her scalp. He elicited feelings Rebecca had not known existed, driving her into a passive ecstasy, lost in rich smells and sensations. She was aware that Simm was kneading her tired muscles much as she kneaded bread. Maybe, she thought in a happy haze, there might be a connection she should care about ... later.

When he felt she had collapsed as far as she should go, he pulled back. Staring into the fire, he took a deep swallow of cognac, wondering, while he stoppered the small bottle of oil and collected his shirt, if Rebecca loosed as much frustration making bread dough as he had massaging her delectable body. He leaned over Rebecca, nearly asleep on the bed, and kissed her cheek. He pulled the sheet over her, making sure that the oil wouldn't spread to the more valuable blankets. Then he covered her so the cold night would not disturb her sleep.

He found a warm nightrail hanging on the back of the door, so he tucked it near her and whispered that if she woke she should put it on.

"Simm," she smiled as she sat up and stretched showing her breasts very un-self-consciously. She reached for the nightrail and pulled it over her head, never taking her eyes off the statue-like man standing at the door. "Thank you."

Simm carefully closed the door behind him and went to his room to finish the good cognac. He was pleased at his restraint, but thought he heard Rebecca speak softly to him as he left. Later, he swore it was the brandy, but he thought he heard her quote Shakespeare when she called to him through the door: "O, wilt thou leave me so unsatisfied?'"

Chapter 10

For days, Amalia's staff had been scouring the wood just beyond the town for the perfect greens. Amalia herself looked over each batch as they were brought to the house, consigning many to the fire and some to the servants' parlor. By the evening of January fifth, the entire house was perfect and Amalia was satisfied.

The candles hung on invisible strings, and the greens twinkled with candles hidden in glass bowls beneath them. The guests that evening did their best to match their surroundings. Simm, observing the magnificent decorations, thought how thoroughly foolish it was in a city under foreign occupation for the occupiers to celebrate with the occupied. He was sure, however, that the royalists among the guests were happy to be there, and those who considered themselves to be Patriots hid their motives and true feelings very well. In other words, even the American soldiers who attended were having a wonderful time.

Rebecca couldn't use her old room to change. The split skirt, and the rose and blue under-gown, were perfect; the dressmaker had done the wonderful job Aunt Amalia had predicted. Annie had put her hair up and covered it with the slightest of caps.

"It won't hold this slippery mass, Becky," Annie began the familiar trope.

"Annie, just let it start the evening up. I will grab it later–somehow. Maybe just stuff it all in the cap?"

"This pretty cap won't hold it. If only we had more pins to use. 'Miss, only use those made in America.' But your dress is not homespun, you know."

"I know it is not homespun, but I also know the fabric is smuggled French silk. I happen to have pins – a gift, so I don't really know where they are from. Hurry, I hear carriages, and I don't want to make an entrance."

Annie fixed Rebecca's hair, and stepped back to take a good look at Rebecca in the deep rose dress. The silk fell with a life of its own over the bright blue underskirt. Whether it was the dress or the magic of wearing it, no one who watched Rebecca enter Amalia Willent's perfectly-decorated ballroom would disagree that Rebecca glowed.

The soldiers, both British and American, vied to dance with Rebecca, and since she had promised her aunt she would have a wonderful time, she barely sat down. Simm watched her as she moved through lines and squares of the reels. She looked so happy, smiling in turn at each of her partners, that he tried to stay out of her way and allow her to smile. He did his best to dance each dance as well, always staying in other lines away from Rebecca. There was no reason to publicize what they were.

Toward midnight, as he was sitting at a table having a drink, he saw a man in elegant black evening dress approach Rebecca. Simm recognized E. P. Manning. The man went by no other name. He was on King George's staff, independent of all military units in America. This made the Howes, both the General and the Admiral, nervous. But there was nothing they could officially do about this. The man, it was well known, opposed any sort of conciliation with the Americans, preferring total subjugation to diplomacy, or any strategy that would give the Americans any control over their lands or government, even as loyal Englishmen. Simm conceded that Manning had been in Philadelphia long before the army had moved in, maybe a year or more. Had he somehow insinuated himself into Amalia Willent's household? That could compromise more than kind Mrs. Willent would realize.

The man sidled over to Rebecca and spoke without a formal introduction. "Mistress Rebecca Willent, I believe we have met previously, but let me introduce myself. Manning, E.P. Manning, British representative in America." Manning lifted her hand and kissed her knuckles.

"You have the advantage, Mr. Manning – where have we met?" She felt smothered by his closeness, and moved slightly back, rubbing her hand on her skirt as she did.

"Why, we were introduced by your aunt, just about a year ago, last summer. But I am afraid your head was in the clouds that day. Later I saw you at the Queen's Crown, the one they have prematurely renamed the 'Liberty.' You met a young man, if I remember correctly. Maybe he was the reason you don't remember me?"

"Well, Mr. Manning, please accept my apologies for being so rude. I am sure I will never forget you again."

Mr. E.P. Manning made Rebecca uneasy. Surely it was not her imagination. There was nothing at all trustworthy about him. She tried to move away as she finished speaking, but he was not finished.

"Mistress, I did mention that I was a British representative here in America?"

"Yes, sir, you did. What exactly does that entail?" Rebecca wanted to be polite, but the man gave her a terrible feeling, like cold snakes climbing up and sliding down her back.

"It means, Miss Willent, that I do not listen to what our generous General Howe has to say about how to treat you

Americans. And it means I can watch whom I want, and do what I want to the miscreant – with the King's protection, in fact. And, Miss Willent, it means that I have been watching your friend –" he nodded subtly in Simm's direction – "for some time, and for reasons probably not known to the Major, and I will be watching out for you. You won't mind – a little protection by an old friend of your aunt's should be welcome in such dangerous times, I should think."

Did he know about the cloak, or was it because he worried about Amalia's niece in such perilous times, and why was he watching John? The Major had nothing whatsoever to do with her efforts on behalf of the Americans. Such puzzles, and again, the one person with answers was the one person she would not burden or trust with her secrets.

Rebecca wanted nothing more than to run from the man out of the room and far away, but to the rest of the guests the night was still young, and the music and dancing, gaming and drinking were still in full swing. She bowed politely to E.P. Manning and backed away into the crowd, where she joined the next set. She did not stop dancing until the musicians took a break some time later.

Simm tried not to watch too closely. He knew that any obvious contact he had with Rebecca in Manning's presence would put her at risk. He did not understand what interest Manning had in Rebecca, but was certain it was due to his position on Howe's staff.

He watched Manning leave the ballroom, perhaps in search of easier prey. He needed to reassure himself that Rebecca was uninjured. He walked to the dance floor, and for the first time joined the same line as Rebecca so that they would partner on the next set.

Rebecca watched Manning leave the room. Simm joined

the dance, his nearness making her feel safer, and perhaps a little dizzy. She smiled at him with genuine pleasure as he took her waist for a turn. His touch warmed the cold snake feeling that had lingered from the encounter with Manning.

"Did he frighten you? You looked like ice was being poured down your back."

"Well, as a matter of fact, I was thinking cold snakes."

"Were you? Well, he does do that to people."

"He seems to know you very well. He watched us at The Queen's Crown."

"Did he? The lech. I thought I saw him around there. He is annoying. But I don't think he can get too close to me. He has never liked me. It does seem personal, but I don't know why. He hates the Howes, you see, but can't touch them because they are too close to the King. I guess he takes it out on their staffs. I am truly sorry if he scared you."

"Thank you, John." Rebecca would have loved to be able to tell him about Manning at the Liberty and then again at the guard house before Christmas, his interest in her having nothing to do with Simm, but she could not. Those three short words were all she could say, but they were said with heartfelt simplicity and such human connection that Simm nearly gasped when he heard them. As the dance ended and the musicians headed to the refreshment table, he drew Rebecca into the small hallway that lead up the stairs to his office.

"I shouldn't be surprised, since you work in this house, but this hallway is so hidden from the main rooms, I didn't know you knew about it. I remember once Amalia telling me she fought with the carpenters over the design." Rebecca spoke very quietly, making sure her voice did not carry into the ballroom beyond.

"It leads to my office. Do you want to come up and see my

messy desk? It's very different from the military precision of my room at the farm."

"Is that safe?" She lifted her eyebrows with the question.

"Probably not. I'm sure I can control myself, if I really must." Simm let his eyes tease her back.

"Is your office the little yellow room?"

"Yes. I love being in there. It is lovely in the late afternoon when the sun comes in from the west over the town. Makes me think of the world beyond, not paperwork, or war. I was wondering if you know why your aunt has such a feminine room up here when she had two sons? I hate a mystery, but thought it might be rude to ask her, in case something horrible had happened."

"Nothing horrible. It was mine. Maybe Susannah was horrible a bit. But no. That's unkind, Susannah is my sister. Amalia made it up for my sister, Susannah, and me. Amalia wasn't sure she would have children when Susannah was first old enough to visit. And then I came along, really quite awhile after her sons, but she'd wanted daughters too, you see.

"Amalia has been sort of our town mother. She made sure we had lovely gowns," Rebecca motioned to her own lovely rose. " She made sure we had dancing lessons and music lessons. That's why I can play the harpsichord and sing. She also made sure we would eat with the right fork and could maintain dinner table conversation.

"Mother, the real one, taught us real things, like how to be kind to people, to care about family, to knit, weave and cook. My herb garden was her idea, and she taught me to make medicines from herbs in the garden and from wild plants. She taught me how to find the plant and what season to harvest it." Suddenly the bright energy that usually shone from Rebecca faded and she looked tragic, sad tears welled in her eyes.

There was nothing more she could say. "John, I'm sorry, I can't talk about it yet." She turned toward the door and moved as if to leave the little yellow office.

Simm thought he would try to distract her, when what he wanted to do was pull her into his arms. "See?" he lit a candle to show her his work space. The desk was covered with papers, but each was in some sort of neat pile, clearly sorted by a method known only to the user.

"That is not a mess, John." Rebecca sniffled, trying not to sound like she wanted to cry.

"Not a mess, but it is a bit disorganized." He looked at her very seriously. He took her shoulders in his hands. "Becky, I wanted to let you know that on Thursday I ride to New York for a new assignment."

"You're leaving? This week? When did you find out? No – I'm sorry. Don't answer that last one."

"You're right. I can't discuss orders with civilians, but I have known about a week. I will try to visit at least once before I return to this assignment in the spring. I don't know when I'll get back. Expect me some time around the beginning of March.

"Becky, I needed to tell you about that. But that is not what I brought you up here for."

"Oh, what then? Rebecca asked, just on the polite side of taunting.

Simm held her soft blue- gray eyes in his deep blue gaze. His hands were still on her shoulders. He tightened them as Rebecca took two steps toward him. In one, he moved toward her and pulled her against his chest. He nearly growled with possession, and in that same motion he covered her mouth with his own. Simm deepened the kiss as he held her against him, feeling her heart beat into :s. He ran his hands over her back, wanting to feel skin, wanting to take her as his body grew hard and ready.

Rebecca looked at Simm. Each kiss they shared was as if it was the first. This time, however they had agreed to honesty. There had been no pretense. She had openly admitted that there were things she could not tell him, as there were things she was not allowed to hear. But between them, as man and woman, this, she was sure, was honesty. She opened her mouth and body to his as he pulled her against him, and deep into the protection of his arms. She heard the rustle of the silk damask as he played with the fabric along her back.

Too soon, he pulled away the micro-inch that broke the connection without severing it. He breathed deeply and made motions that it would be prudent for her to return to the party. He looked back at Rebecca, who was just fixing the skirt of the gown. He sat at his chair, which was pushed away from the desk.

"Come here." He hadn't meant to issue an order, just as he hadn't meant to growl audibly this time.

Rebecca stopped playing with the layers of skirt and walked to Simm sitting in his chair. Her eyes were held by his as she moved. Entranced, she followed his command and was pulled into his lap. He leaned her back onto his desk, his neat piles shifting and falling onto the floor. He blew hot air on the line above her breasts along the low neckline and followed with kisses that left a trail of heat. Gently, and without loosening or stretching her gown, he plucked first one breast and then the other from inside the tight corset. "I do love the new low styles," he murmured into her ear as his tongue teased her neck. He put his lips on her right nipple, kissing and sucking until her hips began to react, and her body arched for his.

Simm withdrew just long enough to tease and kiss her left breast, leaving her breathless and him uncomfortably but happily aroused. Rebecca wanted to feel his body against hers, to undo the months of aching for him while she threw pillows and slammed around her room. She put her hands against the fine linen of his shirt, remembering the night she slept close to him, in a very similar shirt. She lifted her lips to his, and Simm put his head down to hers again, kissing her long and hard. He ran his hands through her silky hair, loosening pins as the kiss deepened.

He reached below her skirt and ran his hand up her leg while his lips teased and suckled her breasts. He opened the delicate lips hidden between her legs, and played in the moisture there, making her hips writhe with pleasure. Rebecca moaned, trying to at least silence her response. Suddenly, Simm pulled his hand away. She started, feeling abandoned, but instead of lifting her to her feet and sending them both back to the ball, Simm sat her on the desk. He gently pushed her backward, so that she was lying on piles of papers that were falling over themselves in chaos.

Simm ignored his paperwork and ran greedy fingers over pale pink breasts, each with a rosy nipple crowning it. While his lips stayed entranced with her breasts, his fingers returned to where she truly ached. He built her intensity toward orgasm, enjoying watching her hips dance on his desk. She begged for him to fill her, but he could not risk a child. If there was more time he would have happily lain with her and been happy to claim her again and again by exploding in her, even pulling out to decrease risk, but this was not the time or place. Even in her own delirious ecstacy, Rebecca understood that.

When she had flown, floated and crashed, Simm pulled her

back onto his lap, holding her tight and safe within his arms. He pulled her corset over her breasts and made sure they were carefully covered and safe in her shift and gown. He lifted each leg and pulled up her stockings, carefully tying garters, fixing them so carefully that the best trained lady's maid could not tell the difference.

When she was demurely covered and ready to return to the crowded ballroom, he kissed her. It was a kiss unlike the others. It did not whisper of further enchantments or pleasures. No, it was simpler than that. It was a kiss that promised that Simm would return to Philadelphia, and when he did, she would never be alone again.

Simm was surprised by how much he needed to hold Rebecca in his lap, feeling her close and safe. As he had their first night together, he needed to make her his. But unlike that night, he had no doubt that she felt the same way.

She certainly had made the desk hers. He looked at it over her shoulder, dreading the extra hours he was foreseeing working at putting the chaos back in order before he left for New York. And then she looked into his eyes with her silent, trusting soft grayish ones, and he kissed her – the kiss that promised the world.

They stood, trying to find separate space. Simm let a finger mark an invisible line along the nape of her neck. "Rebecca, on my word – unless I am dead, I will return. Expect short notes now and then. Ellerby will bring something to the farm. I'm afraid they will be a bit restrained." He laughed at the word restrained.

" John, we should go down." Rebecca caught her breath, "I will miss you." She ran her hand over his neck, playing gently with the soft hair that had escaped from his queue. Then she started moving quickly around the room, collecting pins scattered now on the desk and floor. She pulled the soft mass of hair up into some semblance of its former design. "Dammit." She stabbed at her head. "You better go down first. No one would presume that Major FitzSimmon was rude enough to precede a lady into a room."

She smiled, hoping to make him laugh, and was rewarded with a wry smile. She spoke directly to his back as he opened the door of the office and prepared to leave the room, by checking the hall. "Simm, I will be fine. Please don't worry about me." Then he was out the door. He turned, looking back into the room, and gave a final bow, with a look in his dark blue eyes that was reminiscent of an eagle or other bird of prey. Rebecca felt marked as his in a way she had never noticed before, though it seemed not to be an entirely new feeling.

It took Rebecca a few more minutes to compose herself. She checked her skirts and hair again in the mirror, and when she was ready, she stuffed her sorrow deep inside, prepared to return as a chaste niece to Amalia's party. She would miss Simm for the weeks he was gone, but she was certain that when it was practicable, he would be hers and so, as sad as she was, she was sad as well to have to remain silent. When she could tell him the full truth, all would be well.

Rebecca descended the front stairs as if she had merely taken a moment to herself in the ladies' retiring room. She reentered the dance and flirted charmingly with all the dancers. She was sure she was pleasing her Aunt tremendously. Much later in the evening, when she saw Simm again, he was at a gaming table, hard-faced and calculating, ready for any hand. Major John FitzSimmon was well settled in for the night. As she walked by, he raised his head and caught her eye, nodding a glancing familiarity as any member of her household soldiers might.

On the nineteenth of December the Americans, with General George Washington in command, had moved into winter quarters at Valley Forge, about twenty miles as the crow flies from the Willent farm. Rebecca knew this by Christmas, when she had learned of it from her brother, but she pretended to be surprised when she heard about the move at the Liberty on January thirteenth. The coffee house was as crowded and dark as ever with a mixed group of normal strangers and Coffee Joe's regulars milling about, drinking and discussing the day's news.

By now, the crowd at the Liberty had sorted itself out to include active Patriots and quiet supporters of the American cause, just as the newly-renamed Crowned Lion, up the street, now served Tories and red-coats. The two coffee houses were only blocks apart, but times had dictated the separation of clienteles and the old friends who presided over them.

With the town completely occupied by the British army, there were not many patrons left to sit in Joe's seats, but the Patriots that were left in town, and farmers and tradesmen who did not feel comfortable at the Lion, needed a friendly place to go. The Liberty was it. Rebecca could not help but notice that the Liberty was always crowded, and people there were always drinking. This was remarkable since times were tough for the locals, especially those who were outwardly Patriot.

This afternoon, as usual, she was one of the few women in the tavern. The crowd had grown to know each other through the fall and winter, and to some extent they were all friends. The room was heated by one large stove in the center of the room, and on this cold January afternoon people were sitting as close to it as they could. Rebecca had maps and documents in her pockets, and the chill of the room gave her a great excuse to keep her cloak on.

Joe had again insisted that she carry other people's work on her journey. She tried to explain that it increased the danger, but he was stubborn and used her brother's name whenever she complained, making her feel guilty. Joe always gave her the materials in the tavern's kitchen, out of view of even the Patriots and real spies that frequented the place. That at least gave her a minute to hide the items and check the flow of the cloak. But it meant that the cloak was blue side out while she was in town, and that made her worried. Even so, once she was satisfied with the movement, she had returned to her seat at the table with some friends of Nat's from school days.

"Becky, I hear you have a house of soldiers quartering at your farm. Do you feel safe?"

"Ez, they have orders to treat me like a sister, and they are better behaved than my brothers. They help get the wood for the fires, clean their own rooms and sweep the parlor fireplace."

"Think they would object if a fellow came by for a visit of sorts?" Ezra sounded more hopeful than Rebecca would have liked.

"I don't think you would be comfortable in a house with seven British soldiers. There are only five officers there now, but usually two grooms sleep in the hayloft or the parlor. But you can drop by if you want a cup of tea." She purposefully teased him with the offer of tea. Everyone knew that real Patriots drank only coffee, chocolate or roots and such, never tea – hadn't had any for years.

"You're right, Becky. Perhaps I'll wait till they pull out of town in the spring. You won't mind then, will you Beck?

Rebecca thought that she would not mind in the least if Ezra did not call till spring. She had always liked him fine. If only he had had the nerve to ask her father if he might call for her before he went away to William and Mary College in Virginia – then she wouldn't be in a quandary over Simm discovering that she was watching and listening for Washington.

She talked with the men, always with a thought for the documents in her pockets. And always in the corner of her mind she wondered where Simm was now and whether he was safe. He had ridden Artemis to New York, leaving Philadelphia on the eighth. He would have arrived on the eleventh if the roads were dry and he had not pushed Artemis too hard. Today was the thirteenth – she wondered what he was doing now. Was he missing her in some New York tavern as much as she was missing him?

Rebecca pulled her mind back to the people around her. The young men were a charming diversion. She could not imagine that any of them were involved with Coffee Joe's network of spies. It was never clear if anyone drinking in the tavern had given Joe the documents she put in the cloak. She had to assume that the others knew who she was. She knew she would be less conspicuous if she were a regular at the Liberty. But it simply was not possible to come into Philadelphia more often, with her charges needing food, and the farm needing care.

The Liberty had been busy all that afternoon, so she finished her coffee and went to have a word with Joe, carrying her cup back to the kitchen.

"Joe, think this will be it for the week, or should I come sooner?"

"Bec, I think a couple of days." He had his hands in soapy dishwater and turned to speak to her. "So what day you bringing the stuff to the woods, you could come that day?"

Joe had never asked her what day she made her trips. She answered in what she hoped was her normal tone. "Joe, I never know, depends on the weather and stuff."

Joe's question triggered a sick feeling in the pit of her stomach. He knew better than to ask. It had been impressed on all of them that only she and Nat were to know the pattern. And not only that, she was to switch it every week and start fresh at the beginning of every month. All the couriers were to keep their identities, schedules and routes a secret. Nat had stressed that above all. Lying to Joe felt much safer than giving him a whiff of the truth.

"So, I'll come by Friday afternoon? I need to be in town anyway." She was sure Aunt Amalia and Annie would love to have her over for tea on Friday. She nodded good-bye to Joe, waved at Nat's friends who were still sitting at their table, and walked up the stairs into the weak sun of a January afternoon.

Rebecca inhaled the bitterly cold air, glad to be out of the smoky coffee house. She hurried along the road. The weather and the late hour meant that there were only a few people still out. Those who had braved the day had a ready market, selling to the British quartermaster and to the few private ships at the port. Now the empty wagons were heading back to the country after selling their produce.

The farmers' trips in and out of the town kept it fairly busy, but the town under occupation was a pale version of what it had been before. Rebecca held her head up, proud that she was able to do something to make this place whole again. She danced with the wind as it tried to whip her cloak around her. Her pace quickened as she neared home, sure of work, but equally assured of a kitchen fire and a warm sitting room.

The farmhouse was empty when she returned that afternoon. She had the rare extravagance of being alone in the house. She laid fires and started water for the vegetables. The stew was almost done, the farm chores finished, and the sun nearly set when Rebecca pulled her cloak on, grabbed her knitting basket and headed through the dining room into the parlor.

"Gentlemen, I have set the food on the side-board as usual. The plates are out and the bread is cut. Help yourselves. I need to go to my knitting bee."

"Becky," Sergeant Tom piped up, "knit me some socks, will you?"

"If I can Tom, if I can." Rebecca countered good-naturedly.

Rebecca took her knitting basket and hid it in the barn. Then, turning west, she headed toward the hollow rock. She had not made the trip since before Christmas, but now it seemed important. She never knew exactly what was in the others' papers. She'd always felt that she didn't want to know, but her own were full of maps and sketches of streets, streams, bridges and houses. More recently, she had begun to mark the houses on the maps where soldiers were quartered, as Nat had asked her to do.

The guards at the checkpoint were alone this time, and gladly accepted the loaf of fresh bread she offered. Just over an hour later, Rebecca arrived at the hollow rock in the wood. As always, the trip required knowing roads, fields and woodland paths. Happily, by following all those turnoffs, she made sure that she had not been followed. Rebecca was always pleased, proud that she and Nat had picked a spot that only they would know. She knew that someone other than her brother might be retrieving the documents, but she was certain that she was the only one leaving them.

The nice thing about large rocks, she thought, as she walked around to the hollow back, was that they don't move or change their minds. Reaching in, she found a note that Nat had left for her. She removed the paper and made sure the space was dry and empty, making room for the unusual number of documents Joe had given her to carry. She arranged the scrolls so that nothing showed from any angle, and turned away relieved, as she always was, when the pockets of her cloak were empty.

She was well away from the clearing before she lit some tow to look at the note. Across the fold was her name written in Nat's distinct hand, so she slipped it into her pocket to read at home. The moon had come up as the sun set, and the light on the snow made it a bright night. Things had gone well, and Rebecca was pleased as always with her little adventure.

She entered the kitchen tired, but ready to do battle with a houseful of chores. Dirty dinner dishes were neatly stacked on the kitchen table, ready to be washed, so she rolled up her sleeves and finished the clean-up. While washing and rinsing the plates and cups, she mused that children in the house would be more work than these men, because at least these "little strangers" swept the floor and scraped their plates. Help with chores made her mind drift as it often did to Simm, though she really didn't need a trigger to think of him. She dreamed for a while about his helping with the farm and the household tasks, not only missing his help, but the warm feeling of safety she felt when he was near.

Of all the soldiers quartered here, Simm had been at the farm the least. But their friendship had grown so that she did not feel at home unless he was in the stone farmhouse. It was interesting, now that she had weeks to think about it, how quickly she had gotten used to him, even when they were barely exchanging "hellos." When this new feeling had crept up on her and what it was, she was not sure.

With the kitchen straightened, it was now time to devote herself to Nat's note. She sat in her father's big kitchen chair near the fire to read.

Had a meeting with J. He thinks we need to be more specific about where the Brits are housed. Could you connect names with the houses you place on the map?

J? The first glance confused her. What J did he mean? She knew more than one. She read it again. The J must stand for Joe – it must be Coffee Joe. She reread it carefully. Joe wants to know. What military reason could there be for knowing names of the troops? And since when did Joe make demands? Rebecca let her thoughts run untrammeled.

Puzzles! Again, she would have loved to hand off all these puzzles to John for him to solve. But he was hundreds of miles away, and one of the people who must never know of Rebecca's secret mission. She threw the note on the fire and watched it turn to ash before she turned away from the hearth. It was hard, sometimes, to sit and wait for the notes to disintegrate completely before she left the room. Nat had insisted that all correspondence be completely destroyed, and so far they had.

She pulled the flour bin away from the wall and scooped enough for tomorrow's loaves, adding enough water and butter to create the dough. She mixed the ingredients into bread dough, and had started to knead it into the bread board just as Ellerby stuck his head in, waving an envelope at her direction.

"Note for you from the Major. And the Sarge says you're knitting him socks."

"I said I would if I could, and tonight I got no knitting finished in any case. The cat was having kittens and we all stopped to help." Rebecca hated lying, but that was the sort of thing that was impossible to check - cats were always having kittens.

"How many kittens?"

That was specific, Rebecca needed to stop this before she found herself in a lie she could not get out of. Thinking as fast as she could, she answered the question. "Three before I left, after that I don't know. At least four. Ellerby, give me that note. Did you read it?"

"Nah, probably too hearts and flowers for my taste. You two give romance a bad name."

"Romance? Ellerby, why is that?" Rebecca had not been aware the men had noticed anything between them.

"Taking so long." He dodged the next question by putting the note on a side table and backing quickly out of the room. Rebecca went back to the big chair in front of the fire. This time she did not dread the intent of the note, and was only sorry that it had to be as brief as it was.

Mistress of mine – The trip to NY was uneventful. Artemis made the journey without a problem. The cold weather made riding easy, but necessitated stopping often.

The offices here are even busier than in Ph. and the food and scenery not nearly as enlightening or arousing. Needless to say, I remain as unsatisfied as you would predict.

It does look like I will make an interim visit at the end of February or beginning of March.

I remain truly – your servant in all things. JP FS.

Rebecca blushed at the phrasing in the note, finding it more arousing and stimulating then she would have expected. As she baked, she was now too aware of the motion her hips made while she mixed and kneaded the doughs. She went back to her bread dough, oiled it and covered it with a damp cloth.

Rebecca found that Wednesday night, the twenty first of January, set the tone for the weeks that were to follow. Each week she visited her Aunt for tea, and a juicy gossip with Annie and cook in the kitchen. While she was in town she ducked into the Liberty Coffee House to catch up with friends and collect the local news. While she was at the coffee house, Joe gave her the materials – maps, notes and documents – that he expected her bring to her drop-off spot.

Rebecca always left the Liberty with the rolled and neatly-hidden documents and maps in the seams of the secret pockets of her cloak. These were dutifully brought to the rock in the wood on the day of the week the plan with Nat dictated. Usually, the soldiers at the checkpoint waved her through. Whether this was because she always brought them a baked treat, she did not dare risk discovering.

It was obvious that they were not going to ignore her, the pretty blond who came by more weeks than not. She needed the men to remember her as a harmless, friendly local, and not associate her with any information that spies on the other side found coming out of Philadelphia. She decided she would rather appear harmless than interesting. She achieved that with the sweet bribe of baked treats, always explaining that she was bringing similar treats to the children who lived in the farm down the road. Why, she would have asked, should those children have treats, and the soldiers, so far from home, get none?

Men never argue with logic that feeds them, so they were always happy to see her. She hoped that she looked harmless as well, her hair in a simple cap, her hood off her face, and the cape open to reveal the clothes of a smiling, friendly, simple farm girl. Rebecca considered making extra trips on days without any hidden messages, wearing her new green cloak, but she was too tired from the trips she did make. She could only hope they saw the soft gray as often as the bright blue.

With personal safeguards in place to prevent the guards from sensing any threat from her, she trod out to the wooded hiding place each week in whatever weather the fates threw down. Since winter weather was not as predictable as prearranged dates, she made her trips on roads and trails covered with mud, snow and ice, and through freezing rain. The winter of 1777-78 was not as cold as some, but the messy weather held hard and would not let up.

Chapter 11

Rebecca altered the day of the week she went out to the woods, but she found it was easier to keep the trips into Philadelphia consistent. She had started fulfilling Joe's request that she put troop numbers with each of the quarters on her maps. She balked, however, at his second request that she include the soldiers' names with the house maps. Rebecca did not believe that there was a good reason to do that and so increase the danger to herself. As it was, just being in town drawing maps was garnering her more attention than she had before. In the fall, and through the first part of the winter, her sketching had been innocuous. Those first maps were of the city itself, and drawn for someone who did not know the town. Those maps showed the streets, bridges, docks and neighborhoods.

In the early months, people had grown used to seeing her with sketch pad in hand, observing the town and docks; and sketching them. The new and extra work requested by Joe had her sketching in places of limited interest, where there were few people during the day. Being in such places, sketch pad in hand, always made her uncomfortable. If she were to complete Joe's project, she needed to ask questions of residents and the soldiers living in a certain part of town. In order to look inconspicuous, she needed her subjects to see her as what she was – an artist who lived just on the outskirts of the town.

As a consequence, over the weeks of the late winter, she

became known as Rebecca, the blond girl in the blue cloak. Soldiers in their bright red coats waved as she walked by with her sketch book. Most of them had heard of the good food and the fun they were having at her farmhouse full of British officers. Tories, shop keepers and tradespeople smiled at her as well. These were people who knew her aunt, Mrs. Willent. They knew also that General Howe was Rebecca's protector in the town.

Laborers and matrons with their children smiled as well, but most of them were unsure why Rebecca was so often near their homes . They were, she was afraid, increasingly distrustful of the intense scrutiny she was giving the various neighborhoods of Philadelphia. This, in turn, made Rebecca fearful that she might soon run into a frightening situation.

The increasing distrust her sketching was causing among the normally placid townsfolk was not the whole problem. Rebecca could not help but notice that there were rumblings against her friendship with her Aunt's friends among the patrons at the Liberty. It was obvious that some of Joe's regulars thought that she might not be completely honest, or entirely committed to the Patriot cause. They resented Rebecca's good luck at having all the food she wanted. They resented her wealthy aunt, and the pretty dresses she wore to visit her. Joe's ring knew she wouldn't show them, and they never asked directly why she refused to show Joe her sketches and maps, but they were clearly bothered by her secrecy toward them. The subtle accusations did not bother her; she knew that the work was asked for by Nat, for General Washington, so only he would get them.

As for her supposed good luck, Rebecca wanted to scream at these people that each of these bits of good luck, these alleged advantages, and the good luck that benefitted her, were not things that helped her, but things that she endured – things she suffered for, in fact, with tired legs, bleeding hands, an aching back and a broken heart.

They could not know that she fed "her" men and pretended to approve of them being in America because she was poor and had no dowry. Or that she smiled at her Aunt Amalia and drank tea, because anything she overheard in the public spaces of the house she considered fair game for notes in her pockets. Anyway, Joe's folks probably wouldn't approve of the code that stopped her from eavesdropping at keyholes, or ruffling through papers in empty offices.

And unknown to any of them, she suffered because she had spent the last months living in the house with a man she wanted desperately but could not have. War and duty to the cause they each served made it impossible. That war made missing him nearly unbearable, and speaking freely to him when he returned impossible and hopeless.

Truly, she thought later as she kicked a frozen ice chunk down the road, she would enjoy being involved in something so important if it hadn't taken so much work. She had done everything Nat had asked her to do, and nearly everything Joe wanted. It wasn't work she liked. It made her tired, lonely and sad, and the few people who knew what she was doing resented her anyway.

Joe promised to keep her identity as a courier secret, but it was clear he hadn't. She knew she would be happier, and probably safer, if he had.

Without Simm in the house to distract her to other longings, she had discovered more problems with Joe's requests. Why was it important for the Americans to know where in Philadelphia the individual quartering houses were? Washington's Army was not going to go house-to-house rooting out the British Army. She did not mind obliging the request for information, and did not object to supplying troop numbers neighborhood-by-neighborhood. But she drew the line at naming the men who lived in the houses and the landlords who owned them. Blaming people for being poor, or for being forced to quarter troops in their homes during war, was mean-spirited.

What Joe wanted was information for local gossip and enforcement by his Committee of Safety, not for General Washington. But local people always knew who quartered soldiers in their houses. And the Committee didn't need the names of the soldiers. Why would they? The real question was, she thought later as she pulled her eiderdown and warm wool blankets over her and reviewed the day – if maps with the names of quartered soldiers were not for General Washington, or for Nat and his colleagues – and, as seemed obvious to her, such knowledge was unnecessary for military intelligence – who needed it? If it was Coffee Joe, why would he need this information? If Joe was not the intended recipient of the detailed maps enhanced with names, who was?

Rebecca shivered, and not from the cold of the room. She was afraid she knew the answer to her question. The essence of the question remained the same – who was E.P. Manning, and why was the King's emissary as comfortable at the Liberty as in Aunt Amalia's drawing room?

As usual, New York in winter was unappealing. Simm spent his free time, when there was any, musing on how it was that during the dead of winter, while the world had ostensibly ceased dying, it refused to be reborn any time soon. Not only were the days short, and the icy snow gray and brown, he hadn't kissed her good-bye. Yes, he had watched as she floated back into the ballroom after their brief assignation in the yellow office. Then he had seen her dancing till the very end of the ball, while he tortured himself with the searing memory of her smell, the feel of her soft pink skin, and the taste of her lips.

All evening he had watched her smiling at every partner except E.P. Manning. Had Manning's grim affect given him the excuse to grab her, and torture himself by eliciting the reaction he knew he would get from his ambrosian baker? Not surprisingly, she had been as responsive to him in his office, as she had been that summer – in that heavenly little room near the docks. Almost lost in memories of cool air on hot bodies, something wagged at him from the edges of his mind.

Her secrets stayed hers, no matter how close they became physically, or how kind and helpful he was. He was happy to show her that he truly did care, but at the farm she never spoke to him. Oh, sometimes she almost did, then clamped shut, stopping lighthearted banter as well as deeper thoughts. Something was bothering her, scaring her. Simm knew he could help her with her troubles. That's what he did. But it was clear to him by now that she would not come to him for help. Simm could not figure out why not.

At the Twelfth Night ball, she had said she felt cold snakes when Manning spoke to her. Then she moved unhesitatingly into his arms. If there were another man she ran off to find each week, would she have kissed him like that? If he knew nothing else, he knew her body told truths she never uttered. But her edict to tell the truth or stay silent rattled in his empty rooms. Like the cold west wind blowing over the Hudson, it had no substance.

Simm tried to convince himself he was glad to be hundreds of miles away from her imposing silence. But in a quirk of fate, his New York rooms were across the alley from a bakery. The baker and his fat wife were nothing to look at, but they were very skilled, and the delectable smells of fresh bread came wafting over the alley. Each morning, as he fought his reaction, he concluded that it really wasn't fair that he had become so delightfully conditioned to associate those smells with Rebecca's shapely haunches. Lately, he thought they had been swaying just a bit more than was necessary for the bread.

He lay in his empty New York bed dreaming often of grabbing those hips from behind and moving with her as she worked the dough; of running his hands over her beautiful body, cupping her full, beautiful breasts, and rubbing rosy nipples till she moaned. Each morning, the wonderful smell of baking bread brought back the dream in an agonizing perfection – doubly agonizing, because he couldn't accentuate the torture by descending the back stairs to her welcoming smile, and then watch as it suddenly went out when he returned it.

He understood her request that they not speak of anything important. They both knew he was not free to speak of his work. Too often, that left him with little or nothing to say. That was partly because he did not want to speak of his family when she was uncomfortable speaking of hers. As for why Rebecca withheld so much from him, he supposed it was frustration with war, with family, and, he had to admit, even with himself. Perhaps she realized that if she started talking, she might never stop. He was a very good listener. She seemed to house so much sorrow and anger. Simm did not blame her for her silence; he only wished it were not so.

He walked the short distance from his rooms to General Clinton's headquarters. It was in yet another gracious mansion in another occupied American city, his third, and still the work dragged on, going nowhere. Here, no one was particularly interested in the Howe Brothers's proposal to bring British diplomats and the Americans together to see if any progress could be made to avoid further war. Clinton himself agreed with the King, and disapproved of all diplomatic attempts. He probably agreed that the Howes's work should be kept from Parliament. Simm never broached the subject, and the General never brought it up.

Simm could not be sure what the King's approach might be to stop the project, but was afraid there might be one. Piles of dispatches arrived daily from Philadelphia and Rhode Island. He helped his local colleagues with as much as he could, not really sure why he was in New York, until a particular problem caught his attention. The prison ships holding American prisoners were fast becoming another reason for the colonists to resent the British government. Again, Simm felt frustration with his King and country. "If we, the capturing force, could not treat prisoners with simple decency," he thought, "how could we expect to bring the Americans willingly back to the English bosom? Did General Clinton and his ilk expect to hold the entire continent by force? Did those idiots believe that forced stability in large coastal towns would lead to any sort of peace?"

If there was one thing he had learned during his travels, talks with Americans, and work with the Howes, it was that holding the big towns and cities would never lead to obedience in the interior. He knew William Howe expected him to try to convince the New York contingent of the truth of that, but after seeing the condition of the town, and then what he saw during his tour of the prison ships, he thought talking sense into these people was impossible.

Lord North wanted a treaty with the Americans that would

avoid French involvement. In spite of the Prime Minister's desire, a treaty between the Americans and the French was expected at any time this winter. Suggestions from Englishmen stationed in America had been ignored for years by North and his friends in Parliament. Now, they floated notions, through back channels, of getting rid of the tax on tea and restrictions on trade. To the Americans, this was too little, too late, and would not postpone the expected treaty with the French.

Simm grimaced privately after reading another foolish request for information that had been supplied hundreds of times. His mother, Elizabeth FitzSimmon, the Duchess of Chardon, could have told them that the Americans had outgrown caring about tea taxes. She had lectured her family about the growing sentiment for independence in America a number of years ago, as had her cousin, the one who had married John Burgoyne.

Alone in New York, with no interest in the local entertainment, Simm had time to think. His brother Jason had just about officially declared he was an American, even though his privateer flew whichever flag would expedite his voyage. Over the weeks, Simm's ideas about America were beginning to gel. He had always been intrigued by the boldness of this hundred- year experiment, conducted two thousand miles from home across the Atlantic Ocean. That should have been something that all men who called themselves English found exhilarating.

Simm found that he did not feel the disdain that most of his fellow soldiers felt for these people. He realized, while working in New York with people who disagreed with such sentiments, that his feelings had evolved over the past few years. He had lost whatever disdain for Americans he may have had. But rather than developing a hatred for things British, he had felt, lately, a yearning to be a part of this American project. He was sure that his feelings for Rebecca were part of it, but it was bigger than even that. He believed what Jefferson had written in the Declaration. That a nation might be founded on the ideals of the enlightenment was breathtaking to him. He tried to ignore his growing animosity toward the stubborn soldiers around him, and focus on anything he could do for one group of Americans who could use some help.

Over the next weeks he gathered what information he could about the condition of the prison ships and the prisoners. The suppliers bringing in food and bedding were, as expected, stealing as much as they distributed. Unfortunately, the Loyalist who was in charge of the prisons was husband to a close friend of General Howe. Simm did what he could about supplies, and documented the misuses as much as possible. Since he was unable to effect change while in America and in uniform, he sent off information about the treatment of prisoners disguised as letters home to his mother and his brothers in England.

He had last written home just after Christmas, sending on the note Rebecca had left on his bed. She had disappeared to her attic, but there was the letter to his mother, placed neatly in the center of his bed, unsealed so he could glance at it. It was a sweet thank-you, about pins and his mother's kindness in a time of chaos and confusion. Considering the pain she had been in – the wracking sobs he hoped he'd calmed with that massage – the note was plainly true. He had enclosed a quick missive of his own, and dispatched them both to London.

These days he wrote mostly of mundane things – that he

was now in New York, working in yet another office. Deep in the letter, he included the information he knew his mother would find useful. To his brothers he wrote about the importance of removing shipping and trade restrictions, and the tax on tea, things Parliament already knew had to be done. His mother was an inveterate letter-writer to all the British newspapers – she continued to sign her letters "Queen Bess," except when she signed them "Athena." She, even more than his political brothers, might be able to construct some outrage. Right now, all he could do was send information to her. He had never felt so useless.

The days in New York were spent reading dispatches from places where he would rather have been. He concerned himself with notes and observations from around the outskirts of Philadelphia. The area, he was pleased to find, was mostly quiet, with a few American forces creating the occasional skirmish, bent on keeping the King's forces from foraging in the countryside, and the farmers too intimidated to bring goods in. This was nothing he had not already known, although it might make it risky to take his regular route down through New Jersey. He supposed he could go down by ship. It was as well that Artemis never minded a day or two on the water.

Work, which had always kept his mind clear and his thoughts focused, no longer required the intense focus it had before. As always, his desk was stacked high with dispatches from London – from the war office, the Prime Minister's office, and, oddly, from some friends who were close to the King. The letters were guarded, but all of them were now warning Simm that the royal gossip reported that he was the target of something, but no one knew precisely what.

That his name was part of the gossip mill surprised him. He had never been close to military or political decisions. The generals always assumed that a duke's son was more useful corresponding with diplomats and lawmakers than dissecting maps and reading terrains. That might be true, and Simm was sure it was, but being unable to do anything useful with his diplomatic skills rankled him now more than it ever had before.

His interactions with his current landlady, and with various tavern owners in the busy town, reminded him of how kind Rebecca was to all the soldiers who lived at the farm, no matter how tired or how hurt she was about her fate or that of her city. That kindness was not replicated everywhere he went, which had him retiring to his rooms most afternoons. And that gave him too much time to think.

Contemplating the direction of his life had become a common pastime during his weeks in New York, but one afternoon on his way home after another fruitless day at work, he was delighted to find that the sun was still above the horizon. He realized that he had not looked at the calendar for days. Was February passing more quickly than even he had wished? Feeling somewhat optimistic, he continued his walk uptown, back to his rooms.

At the corner of his street, his musings were interrupted by an unpleasantly familiar voice. He looked up, and found himself staring into the colorless eyes of E.P. Manning.

"Major FitzSimmon?" The voice perfectly matched the dark of his clothes and probably his soul. Simm was reminded of the cold snakes Rebecca had described.

Simm sat on his urge to cut the man and walk in another direction. "Yes."

"Or, should I say, Lord John." The man was wasting time

with disagreeable pleasantries.

"No, Major will do, thank you. Please keep it brief, I'm not in the mood for verbal fencing. Manning, what do you want?" Simm had been having a enjoyable walk back to his rooms, and now Manning was in the way of getting back to his thoughts.

"Major, I didn't plan this meeting, if that's what you think. But what would I want?" The man actually stroked his chin pretending to think. "You – away from North America. That's a simple desire. FitzSimmon, I think you enable these treasonous rebels with your ridiculous diplomacy. God knows what trouble you have been able to stir up here in New York." Manning dragged out the words like he was cleaning the privy.

"Manning, thank you for being so candid. But we both know that the diplomacy you are so disdainful of has been Parliament's work, slow as they were to start it."

"Yes, those foolish Whigs," Manning replied, "always trying to increase their power and limit the power of the righteous monarch."

"Fine, Manning, you've proven yourself loyal to absolute monarchies. Why are you here wasting my evening?"

"I saw you across the street and couldn't resist a chance just to say hello. I know you must miss living at the Willent farm. Nice girl running the place, very pretty. You must miss her. She a friend of yours?"

"No," John tried to sound nonchalant, "Live there, eat there, barely know the chit."

"See that stays true, for both of your sakes. I don't trust you, don't trust your work with Howe. And I don't trust the girl, think she's a sneaky one. Make sure, Lord Major, that I don't get wind of anyone seeing you together – might make me call for a noose or, better yet, two of them."

Simm was more than angered by the threat. He wanted nothing more than to kill Manning on the spot, but that was treason and for that he would hang. He swallowed his anger and walked away from the man in black, forcing one foot in front of the other. There must be a reason for Manning to harbor that much anger against him, but what did it have to do with Rebecca? Could Manning know about his feelings toward the girl? He barely understood them himself.

By the time Simm returned to his rooms, he had decided that in order to keep Rebecca safe, he needed to move off the farm when he returned to Philadelphia. He was afraid for her, and had no idea how far Manning would go to hurt her in order to punish him. It would be nice to know why Manning hated him, but even without knowing, he would keep Rebecca safe. He lay awake each remaining night of his stay in New York, already missing her, again. For over a year she'd figured in his dreams, but living in her house had changed that, and she had become the air he breathed or the bread she made so well – a necessary part of life.

Chapter 12

Many years in Philadelphia had made Amalia Willent American enough for ten o'clock coffee, just as growing up in London had made four o'clock tea a requirement. Rebecca arrived at her downtown mansion at precisely nine fifty-eight.

"Why, Becky!" Annie gushed as she ushered Rebecca into the parlor where Amalia was sitting down to a newspaper and a cup of coffee. "Have you come to see the officers? They are in an uproar – the General keeps shouting something about the French and a treaty; the others keep shouting back 'that Parliament was warned and waited too long.'"

" I wouldn't want have to sign that dispatch they're sending to Parliament, but Annie, I came to see Aunt Amalia and find out if there was any news, but I suppose a treaty should be considered news?"

Annie went to get a cup for Rebecca and she joined her aunt at the table.

"Aunt Amalia," Rebecca began, "you are sitting here calmly reading about the latest hairstyles and bustles, and meanwhile the yelling is getting louder. Aren't you at least curious?"

"Your American parents, young lady should have taught you the subtle art of listening while seeming to ignore all. It is an excellent skill."

"So tell me," Rebecca moved in closer for a conspiratorial

listen, "what is going on?"

"Well of course, I don't know anything, but is sounds to me like the Americans are about to sign an alliance with the French against Great Britain. There is hope they have not signed yet, but some contingent or other is about to head to New York and another to Rhode Island, or so I gather."

Rebecca had a jolt. This was information that had to be given to Nat. He would know about the treaty, of course, but not that so many officers were leaving Philadelphia. "Leave? How are they traveling?"

"Oh, they are taking horses, mostly to New York, I suspect. Shouldn't take more than a week or two. I bet the foolish Americans sign the completed agreement with the frogs by the end of the week. You'd think they'd remember that the French were the enemies in the last war, and be careful about such an alliance. But war makes strange alliances."

"What do you base that on, Amalia, divine guidance?"

"Oh, Becky, you have so little faith in my abilities. Divinity has nothing to do with it. I have a better memory than your dear Americans. And dear William, who got the information only this morning, is now sending his men north to try to head off the agreement. You know, just recently Parliament sent word that they are willing to remove the silly navigation acts. Now, you see the French came in before the Americans had a chance to listen to their own government, by which I mean the Parliament, but we all fear it is too late."

Now Rebecca had more information than she expected – more than she needed to explain the chaos and quick packing at the mansion and, she supposed, at her own house as well. She finished her cup of coffee, peeking over Amalia's shoulder to look at the latest hairstyles from London and

Paris, and the advertising from the London stylists who'd arrived with the flotilla to coif Philadelphia.

Before she knew it the day was half gone, so she said her good-byes and set off for the Liberty Coffee House to collect what Joe had for her.

"Rebecca," Joe asked her as soon as she arrived, "what was going on over on Chestnut Street this morning? Your Aunt's house was popping, people running in and out, lots of noise."

Rebecca looked at Joe and the others interested in what she had to say. She also noticed the man in black deep in the dark shadows of the corner of the dark room watching her. "You are right, Joe, lots of noise, but no one gave any indication of what they were about. Sorry I can't help."

Joe glared. Clearly, he did not believe her.

Rebecca stood her ground. She'd made her decision – her final decision, in fact. The information she found would go to the American camp, no longer to nosy Philadelphians. This might be the Committee of Correspondence, but she had signed on to be a courier, not a correspondent.

"Joe, you have those stew vegetables you said you'd save for me?" Rebecca headed into the kitchen to collect whatever materials Joe had collected for her to deliver to the hollow rock. He gave her a few things which she carefully hid in the pockets of the cloak. She checked the swirl to make sure it flowed evenly around her. Once that was completed, and before E.P. Manning moved toward her to utter one of his not-so-veiled threats, she left.

At home, she stored the materials in an empty grain bin in the summer kitchen. So far, none of the men had even ventured into the extra room, cluttered with all manner of family artifacts. It was here her spinning wheel and loom were stored, now pushed even further back into the room than at Christmastime. Suddenly, Rebecca was overtaken with a burst of restless energy made up of fear, anger and frustration. She began moving bins and furniture around until the clutter made a bit of sense. She moved the men's empty trunks to one side, the empty food bins to another. In one corner she found furniture broken by having been at the bottom of the clutter. She pulled out the pieces and put them in the woodpile. At least, she thought, the old chair will be more use burning than left in broken pieces.

Exhausted, but pleased with a bit of restored order, she went through the dining room into the parlor to find the main part of the house as empty as she had expected. She sliced cold meats and bread and put the plates in the dining room, did the farm chores, ate her own dinner, and climbed up to her attic.

Rebecca was awakened the next morning by men's voices, loud footsteps, and horses being saddled and walked out of the barn. She looked out her window into the farmyard to see ten soldiers, three of them her tenants, mounted, in full uniform and fully wigged – far more elegant and imposing than they generally looked for the morning. She would have loved to ask what was happening, but it was obviously a military move, and she was not going to be told.

The house was empty, or nearly empty. There were one or two of her quartered soldiers remaining behind. She wondered if she could ask them to eat at Amalia's so she could have some time to herself, but they were paying. She would have to discover how many had stayed in town, and adjust accordingly.

Rebecca sat with paper and pen, trying to remember everything Amalia had said yesterday. She had said they were riding to New York, desperate to stop an agreement with the French. An agreement would make it much harder to beat the

Americans – Rebecca smiled at that – and it would also renew hostilities between Britain and its traditional enemy, the French, and in time the Spanish might join in against the British as well.

Rebecca finished the morning chores and waited for the few men in the house to head into Philadelphia for their day. Then she went to the empty grain bin to check the materials Joe had given her the day before. Nothing in them had anything to do with the British movement or the American agreement with the French. It was curious that nowhere else in town had anyone picked up information on what was happening.

She finished her notes for Nat, telling him what Amalia had heard and what she had seen. None of this would surprise Nat. She remembered that he had seemed to know Simm and his work, whatever that was, when they had met at Christmas.

Simm met the Philadelphia contingent on their arrival in New York. They had ridden hard, and made New York late on the second day. They fell into command headquarters just as Simm was about to leave for the day. He turned around and let the men catch their breath before they headed to the pier where the dinghies were tied up, with Simm leading the way. From lower Manhattan, the men were rowed to Admiral Howe's ship for deliberations. The talking went on and on. Simm knew in his bones that the British had waited too long.

As long ago as September 1776, he had met with the American statesmen, John Adams and Samuel Adams. At that time, it was already clear that with the Navigation Acts still in place, the British Parliament had waited too long to repeal them. For over a year, he had told anyone who would listen that they had a limited time span in which to act to convince the Americans they were not the enemies they were presumed to be. Now it was too late – too late to generate good will, and too late to prevent the kind of war the Howes had not wanted to wage.

Word of the French alliance reached Simm's office from Rhode Island, even before it got to Philadelphia. The alliance was confirmed by the third week of February. Many of the British soldiers and the Loyalists in New York were delighted with this new combination of enemies – the rebels and their historic enemy, the French. French aid would make the Americans harder to defeat, but for many it also made the war worth fighting, in a way that putting down a Patriot rebellion had not.

This alliance had different meanings for Simm. Its signing meant the dead-end of a great deal of work. There was little left for him to do. His skills as a negotiator, and whatever influence he might have had as the son of a duke, were, quite simply, no longer needed. Maybe they would be years from now, when the warring sides sat down to hammer out the new peace, but he had no interest in waiting that long to be needed.

He had also discovered over the last few weeks, while staring at his ceiling, that he had no stomach for working on another general's staff, where he would be tasked with effecting yet another winning strategy for destroying the American line. When he could clear his desk of whatever work General Clinton needed from him, he would head back to Philadelphia and wrap up his work for General Howe, clear out his office, and resign his commission. In fact, he wouldn't be surprised if William Howe wasn't thinking along the same lines. It was very likely the general and his staff would be reassigned before the winter season ended.

Simm felt that his time in the British Army was over. His work was complete, and any good he could have done for country and King was at an end. It only needed the General to agree to his resignation, a requirement in time of war. After what had transpired these past weeks, Simm thought obtaining that agreement would not be very difficult.

Simm left New York, ready to confront the changes in his life that the alliance between the Americans and their French allies dictated. After crossing to Staten Island and then to the Amboys in New Jersey, he rode south slowly, letting the horse find her footing on the muddy roads. Taking advantage of the bad weather, he stopped often to visit people he had met during previous travels. These were people who knew him from his work, and also knew that no matter the outcome or which side their allegiance, Simm was a good man, one who held American and British interests foremost in mind throughout all of his negotiations and factfinding. Simm was happy at least that no matter what was to come, these friendships were true.

The trip south took longer than it needed to, but Simm needed the time to iron out his feelings about the emerging Nation and his own work. He did not arrive in Philadelphia until the last day of February.

He rode directly to Amalia Willent's home, and went in to find General Howe. Their talk went far into the night, so Simm let Artemis sleep after the long last leg of the trip. Simm grabbed his bedroll from his saddlebag and bedded down in his office. His couch was not particularly uncomfortable, but being so near the farm, and almost close enough to Rebecca to feel her breath on him, did prevent a good night's sleep.

She was not expecting him on any particular day, so he did not worry about her anxiety, but he had plenty of his own. He had stomped down thoughts of her during those last days in New York, occupied as he'd been with important policies. Now, with many things no longer his responsibility, and others decided definitively, his thoughts were filled with his reticent beauty. She was never reserved with her eyes, and he could recall how she opened to him in voluptuous silence. He prayed that now with his own life taking a new track, she would at last talk to him about hers. Time would tell, but Simm desperately wanted to know her mind as well as he knew her delectable body.

Rebecca knew that the men would return within a few days. And she had used the time alone to collect medicinal and edible plants that were available in the late winter and early spring. Not needing to bake and cook for her large group had meant she'd had room in the kitchen to prepare the plants for drying or fermenting. She left the house early most mornings to collect, just after the cow was milked.

The days were fresher now, even with the heavy frost that settled each night, and she enjoyed walking into the woods in the bright sunshine. Today, March first, would be the last day; she had collected almost more plant matter than she had room or time for.

Simm grabbed a piece of toast and a quick cup of coffee in the kitchen before the household awoke.

"Major, I wonder if I could send a request along to Becky, since you'll be heading out that way."

"Of course, Cook, what can I do for you?"

"Well, Becky brought me some fiddleheads from her wilding – that's collecting wild plants and such – and I thought if she should find a few more, she could bring them in to me. I'd pay her a bit from the kitchen accounts."

Simm nodded to Cook that he would indeed let Rebecca know. He walked out the kitchen door to get his horse. Artemis had been walked by the busy grooms, and had just started her feed. Simm never liked to interrupt a friend's breakfast, so he wandered along the mews looking at the horses, tackle and carriages until he felt he could interrupt the filly's breakfast. He had turned to head back down the mews to Amalia Willent's stable when he became aware of E.P. Manning coming his way.

"Been home yet from your futile journey, Major?"

"No, Mister Manning, not yet this morning, came right from Jersey. Thank you so very much for your concern." Simm was as sarcastic as he felt he could get away with. This man always made him want to commit a violent act, one that would unfortunately be construed as the murder of the King's friend.

"It's too bad, really, that you're not there."

Simm said nothing, but listened carefully, wondering where Manning was headed. This much talk was unusual from the man.

"Those woods of hers, that chit you said means so little to you, deep woods like those here around Philadelphia, have such good places to hide things and people. Shame you had to leave her so many weeks, alone and exposed to strangers and such. You know, I would never let a *friend* of yours fall into harm's way. But I had to put those boys somewhere, I'm sure you understand."

Simm felt a cold shadow pass over him. He hoped it was only the cold snakes, but more than ever he wanted to pummel the slimy man. He turned on his heal with as much aplomb as he could muster and whistled for Artemis, who lifted her head from her last apple and trotted over. Simm moved toward the horse, as she moved toward him, and mounted and rode off, in what looked like a single being in motion.

Simm dismounted in the stable yard, without reining in the horse, and ran into the house. The farmhouse was empty. Various plants, roots, and new green leaves lay in neat piles, ready to be processed into foods and medicines. He quickly checked the kettle on the hearth. It held heat, so Rebecca had not been gone over long. Simm went to the barn to see if anyone was about. There was one groom raking out the stalls, taking advantage of the empty farm to clean the muck.

"Mick, Do you know where Miss Willent went this morning?" Simm asked, to slow his words and his thoughts.

"Looking for yur lady?"

Simm was a bit shocked at the question, but was forced by time to nod yes.

"Wal, s'far as I could tell, she was going wilding."

"So I heard. Do you happen to know what direction she went this morning?"

"Last few days she's been heading that a'way." He pointed with a dirty thumb. "Probably did again – she's been finding lots of good things, she showed me. New tincture for the horses' salve as well. Going ta be nice. She has a way with the plants, like my ma did."

Simm felt he should have known that about Rebecca. Had she mentioned it? He had not paid too close attention. Now he rode as fast as the muddy, rutted fields would allow. He left the open land and rode into the wood, in the direction Mick had pointed. He wondered what Cook did with fiddleheads, whatever they were. He wished he had time to wonder what plants Rebecca collected.

Winter was truly loosening its grip on the area, and the

early spring meant that certain flowers, stems and roots had sap moving and were ripe for collecting. Having seen Rebecca's stores drying in the kitchen, and hanging from the rafters in the barn and the summer kitchen, he was not surprised that she steadily needed to replenish her supply of plants for medicinal teas and tinctures, as well as the plant matter he recognized as being used for dyeing.

He rode a few miles in the direction Mick had directed, hoping that he was more or less heading the right way, and listening for any sounds that might give Manning's ruffians away. He could only pray that they had not found Rebecca, and that he would.

Ahead he saw a bush at the edge of the path covered with yellow blossoms. Branches of the bush had been carefully cut and lay on the ground. Simm reined in Artemis and listened. He thought he heard voices just beyond, so he carefully and silently dismounted, dropping the reins. He signaled the horse to stay ready. He pulled his pistol out of the saddlebag and checked his saber. He hitched the sword close, so it would not rattle as he walked.

Simm followed the path that looked like someone had been dragged along it, but not simply dragged – that person purposefully left a trail that could be discovered. By breaking twigs and dragging her heels in the soft mud of the rough woodland path, Rebecca had left behind a perfectly-marked trail to follow. His heart in his mouth, he walked toward the sound of the voices. As he approached, they got louder and angrier. He stayed in the cover of the wood, walking toward the sounds.

"Damn you! Stop!" Rebecca never swore, Simm froze, every nerve poised for action.

Rebecca had been cutting witch hazel when she heard men's voices near her. At first she thought they were friends – her soldiers she had come to see as the men who lived in her house. But these voices sounded rougher, and when their words were close enough to understand, it was clear the soldiers were not "hers."

"Must be around here. He said picked she flowers in these woods."

"Yeah, but it's been all week, I'm tired of waiting."

"We have our orders to wait until we see her alone. Those popinjays living in that farm house are having too good a time with the filly; it should be our turn. That's what E.P. said, anyway."

"Shhh, don't use his name, someone might be near."

Rebecca tried to sneak deeper into the wood and away after hearing the men's conversation. Whatever they were up to, she knew she was better off away. Her foot snapped a twig and she stood stock still hoping the men would resume their talking. They did not.

"Ooh! Look who's here." The skinny one talked at her.

"Yes, ahem, good morning, I was just on my way to meet my brother." She tried to continue to walk in the direction she had been heading.

"There ain't no body around here, I a-ready looked." The big fat one called back at his friend while he blocked Rebecca's path of retreat.

"Oh – she breathed in sharply trying to think of what to do next – "He's meeting me, he'll be right here ... soon." Her words became feeble as the two men began to circle her like dogs starting to tree a bear or racoon.

The thin man grabbed at her and pulled her to him, forcing a rough kiss onto her lips. She spit and tried to push him away. "My pretty, we heard you like a good time. We just want a good time, too."

"I'm afraid you heard wrong, its not like that at all." Rebecca's words came out cold and angry. She was trying so hard not to show the fear she felt.

"Not what we were told, blondie." She looked at the men, both were tall, but one was much fatter than the other. Their hair was dirty and their clothes were torn. At first glance, she could not tell anything about them from their clothing, but as they moved in closer and slowed down, she noticed that the clothing looked like the uniforms of the British Army without their jackets. Their pants were dirty white wool and their shirts, though missing the ruffles and collar, were from one of the units staying in the area.

"Why you dirty, filthy lobsterbacks! You don't even have the decency to wear your ugly red jackets, do you! Go away, damn you!"

The thinner one looked at her like she was a stew bone and he was a mangy dog.

"No, please, leave me alone."

"Can't, Miss, we were promised you'd cooperate with us, just like you do with the other boys."

"What!" Rebecca couldn't make sense of what he was saying.

"Blondie, we were told you'd be around here and available, so here we are and here you are. Don't pretend you don't like it." He reached out and grabbed at her, ripping the sleeve from her bodice as she tried to run.

Rebecca screamed, "Damn it, stop!" as she tried to get away. The fat man grabbed her. He pulled her into him and ran his hands over her body. He tried to kiss her, and roughly put his tongue into her mouth. Rebecca bit him, making him yowl in pain.

The fat man yelled "bitch!" He pushed her hard onto the cold, muddy ground. He pulled out a knife and put it against her throat. "You won't squirm any more, bitch, or I will cut you and you'll be bleeding in more places than you'd like. Oh, that's right, the other won't bleed again, will it? You think you can share with the boys at your house and not with us?" He nicked her throat with the knife. He cut the drawstring of her shift and the strings of the old fashioned bodice she had worn for a morning of work. While waiting for his friend to hand him a gag, he pushed the bodice and shift, and sat at her head with her hands held tightly in his, ogling her breasts. He put one tentative hand out to fondle her, pinching her nipples. "Hurry up, will ya?" Hand me a gag and a tie for her hands. These titties are making me very hard."

Rebecca squirmed against the heavy man's weight. Every time she growled that she was going to kill him as soon as she could, he pushed his knife at her throat just a little bit. She could feel warm blood dripping down her neck, while the other man removed her shoes and threw them across the clearing. He took off her stockings and handed them to the fat man, who shoved one in her mouth and used the other to tie her hands. Now he was able to use his full strength to hold her down.

"Why do you look so scared, blondie? We heard you liked the boys."

Rebecca looked up at the fat man holding her, pleading with her eyes that he let her go.

"You get to go first. I'll hold her, but don't forget my turn." He licked his lips while his friend unbuttoned his pants and pushed up Rebecca's skirts. The first man pinched and twisted her nipples, holding a knife close to her throat. "Oh, and she wants you to hurry too, she's pleading with her eyes for me to do it."

Both men laughed as she struggled, twisting her hips hard to get away from the man holding her legs.

Rebecca wanted to swear using all the words her brothers had taught her but never let her use. Her head was full of words, but her mouth could not work. If she could have, she would have bitten the men holding her down.

As the thin man touched her thighs, he started to coo at her, which made her even angrier than being called a "bitch." She would much rather have been a rabid dog than a helpless female. His words made her blood boil.

"Ooh, my pretty, such a soft thing. You shouldn't be so far out here, away from mommy and daddy. But you'll like it, I know you will, all the girls like me."

Rebecca used his arousal for a chance to get an advantage. She twisted away and kicked at the thin man with all her might. The fat man let go of her breasts, and put the knife hard on her throat. "Stop thrashing, bitch, or you'll end up dead. I'll just hold you till my friend finishes. Then, if you're a good girl, I'll show you how sweet it can be. Just you put up with him for a bit. Though watching you move like that is a bit of a party."

Rebecca was livid now, no longer as scared as she had been. Mostly she wanted to kill these bastards who cooed at her while raping her. The thin one pulled her skirts over her head again, and she could feel his hard penis touch her. As the thin man pushed to enter her, she heard a familiar voice call for the men's attention. She heard the voice order the men to stand up. Then in the same harsh voice she was ordered to stand and walk back to the path. Thinking only that her feet and breasts were cold, she did.

Simm saw the two ruffians in the clearing. One man was thin and dirty, the other was big. Both men wore faded, worn red uniforms. Simm took in the scene. He stayed motionless, hidden in the undergrowth which was thicker at his side of the clearing. The older man was leaning over Rebecca, whose skirts were pushed up nearly over her head. He couldn't see her face, which was facing away from him, half under her skirt. Now the only cries he could hear from her were indistinct and scared.

The big man was near Rebecca's head, holding her down with a knife to her throat. Her bodice was cut open, showing white skin and exposed breasts; he could see thin lines of blood dripping onto her white skin where the blade had cut as she had struggled. Simm had a moment of sheer, possessive rage. He wanted to destroy the men who were torturing his Rebecca. He had been in battles of all sorts since he was a boy, and never had he felt so enraged, so full of animalistic fury.

He allowed himself only that single self-indulgent second before the skilled tactician emerged. As much as he wanted to roar into action and shoot at the men, he had only one single shot pistol with him. It was possible he could kill one, and the other would run away. But it was just as likely one of them would try to kill Rebecca rather than face him. He had to move so that he could at least try to guarantee Rebecca's safety.

"Gentlemen, cease your actions." Simm shouted at the men, hoping he sounded more like a commanding officer than he felt. The men looked over at Simm, slowly registering that there was another man in the clearing.

"Hi, Officer, want to go next? I'm sure you won't mind waiting, we got here first."

Simm walked into the small clearing holding his pistol in his right hand. "Which one of you vermin wants to die first?" He spit out the words, waiting for either one to make a move. The fat man took his knife off Rebecca's throat and turned toward Simm, holding the knife in an aggressive stance. Simm gauged the men were shocked enough for Rebecca to get out of the way. Using the same authoritarian voice he had used to get the men to move away from the girl, he spoke slowly and loudly at her. "Rebecca Willent, get up and move behind me." He eased out of his uniform coat by slowly transferring his pistol briefly to his left hand, and slowly threw the coat to Rebecca who grabbed it to herself and slid onto the muddy ground at the edge of the clearing.

Holding Simm's coat like a shield, Rebecca moved into the brush. She spit out her gag, but could do nothing about the knot that held her hands. Relieved, she was able to wiggle enough to fix her skirts. She sat on the ground, leaning against a grey rock, pulling Simm's warm coat to her front, wishing for her warm stockings and shoes.

She watched as Simm drew his sword from the scabbard. He circled in front of the two men, a pistol in one hand, his sword in the other. He was so angry that he would have had no trouble running through both of them where they stood. Why even waste a pistol ball? But he needed to confirm that Manning had suggested they come to this wood and find Rebecca. He was sure they would not know why Manning would make such a proposal, but he would have the name.

"So, gentlemen, tell me why I should not kill both of you right here on the spot and save your regiment from shooting you – either as deserters or rapists?"

The men turned white, all the blood draining from their faces. The fat one spoke first. "Didn't hurt the girl, just warming her up I was."

"Oh, soldier, that was the wrong answer. I'll ask again – why shouldn't I kill one or both of you?"

Simm addressed his question to the thin man, while out of the corner of his eye he saw the fat man pull a pistol and fire at him. He felt the ball rip into his thigh, as he turned to the man and with a single motion fired at him. The ball went straight into the man's chest, dropping him hard on the ground, pistol still in his own hand. Simm dropped his pistol and transferred his sword to his right hand. Rebecca saw the fat man move toward his bag and pull out his pistol.

" Simm!" She bit her fist to stop herself from distracting her avenging angel, realizing, as she bit, that her hands were still tied together.

Simm turned to the second man, sidling over to his bag and tidily lifting his pistol off the ground with his sword and tossing it into the wood, never taking his eyes from the man. "'Tis a pity he died so quickly – is there anything you would like to tell me that might make me not kill you? No?" He waited a minute staring at the man who was now wielding his knife, trying to fend Simm off. "How about first, soldier, who told you about these woods? Who said this was a good place to find a girl? And don't say what you are about to say – about luck."

"A man told us to stay here, said we'd be safe. No one would find us, and might be a sweet girl using the woods for some plants or something. He said if we found her, we could try her."

Simm's blood froze in his veins. "Who told you these things?" He was sure he knew the answer – the real question was, did the man know?

"Don't know the man's name, sorry, mate." The deserter

turned to walk away from the clearing.

Rebecca had been watching and listening to the interchange. "Simm! I heard them say a name, he knows!"

Simm nodded acknowledgment, keeping his eyes and sword pointed at the man. "We'll try again – who was the man who told you to come here?"

The man was not going to tell. Simm was impressed with his loyalty, but not his manners. "I think you know, and I think you will tell me before you die, soldier, because you will die."

"How were we to know the girl was yours?" Simm moved closer, his sword teasing at the man's coat buttons. "Black, he wore a lot of black, more than most people who wear black. Black shirt, pants, cape, hat. Everything. And he talked in a rich man's whiney drawl." The man took the satisfaction in Simm's face as an omen, and he lunged with his knife, making a deep wound in Simm's right shoulder, just as Simm ran him through the neck with his sword. In seconds the heart of the heartless stopped beating.

Rebecca hid her face in her bound hands, not wanting to see the final moments of the cruel man's life. She was sure Simm had enough information to know that E.P. Manning had told the men to come here and to wait for her. How was she to explain Manning's interest in her activities without telling Simm too much?

But then there was only Simm. He limped to her spot on the cold ground, cut the stocking that bound her hands, and helped her on with his coat so it covered her torn clothing. He pulled her against him, so they were both on the wet ground and held her very hard and long enough that he felt his wounds stiffening.

"Becky ... tell me I wasn't too late to help you."

Rebecca buried her head against his chest, never wanting to lift her head ever again. She'd started to shiver with the cold and relief, realizing that it was now truly over.

"J'John, I'm fine, he didn't touch me, not in, not really, almost, but you came. H'how did you find me?"

"Mick the groom, he said you'd gone wilding." Simm ran his hand through her hair, holding her close, needing to hold her to make up for the protection he was too late to offer.

"You knew what 'wilding was?'

"Cook told me. She wanted you to find more fiddleheads, whatever they are." Simm looked into Rebecca's soft gray eyes, thinking he had never seen anything more beautiful and important. "I ran into E.P. Manning this morning, too – he said something about my being gone a long time, and hinted about you needing protection Howe and his men were not providing. I guess I know when to be scared, and Artemis did the rest.

"Becky, I don't want to move you before you have the strength, but I'm afraid I am pretty badly hurt."

Rebecca could not believe she had been so selfish and oblivious. "John, where did they hurt you? I confess I was too scared to watch."

"If I have to do an assessment, I'd say I have a lead ball in my left thigh and a rather painful knife wound in my right arm."

Rebecca stood and ran over to her shoes and pulled them on. "John, where is Artemis?" She asked, trying to take charge before she was further overwhelmed by the day. Simm whistled, and she heard the wonderful sound of a trot through the woods. "Can you mount?"

"I think I can, from the right. You will have to come up and hold me, I might fall asleep from the c'cold." He pulled himself up on the left side of the horse, put his right leg in the stirrup and swung his injured left over. Rebecca stood on the right of the horse and let Simm help her with his good arm. Once seated, he clucked and Artemis, sensing a problem, walked at a steady but even pace back in the direction of the farm.

Simm found that Rebecca's heat from behind, with her arms tight around him, and the warm horse under him, kept him from the worst of the shock that was threatening to overwhelm him. His head dropped now and then, but he was able to hold the reins and keep his feet in the stirrups. They passed bunches of cut stalks with bright yellow flowers thrown aside on the ground. "Becky?" Simm pulled himself out of his daze, "if you want to dismount and collect those, I think I can still help you back up."

She ran through the area quickly gathering the witch hazel, stalks and roots, that she had collected that morning. The day had started out sunny with such promise. Now the day had turned; the weather had, as well, turning to rain and cold. She let Simm help her back onto the horse, holding the plants in one arm, her other around Simm holding him against her. She let Artemis walk them patiently back to the farm and her warm stable.

Chapter 13

Although Rebecca's mind was flying through possible tasks that would need doing, her body reacted on its own, and by the time they arrived at the farm she was shaking from shock and cold. Simm was grateful for Mick's coming right out to take the horse. The groom's gaze went from Rebecca to Simm; he gave the pair a deeply sympathetic look as he followed Rebecca, with Simm leaning heavily and limping, into the kitchen.

"Miss Rebecca?" Mick stood in the door, waiting for an order of some sort. "Is there something you need me to do?" He was quite insistent, and Rebecca was glad to shake her mind out of its tumblings.

"Yes, Mick, of course." She wanted a warm bath and a bed, but the fates once again had put real problems ahead of her own. " Help me get the Major into this chair while I run to get things. We need light and fire." Rebecca fairly flew up the stairs, and within minutes she and Mick were helping Simm onto Rebecca's soft mattress that had been laid on the kitchen floor in front of the hearth. Mick collected all the candles and lanthorns from the dining room and parlor. He lit them, creating a wall of light around the wounded man. Rebecca slid out of the room into the summer kitchen, where she collected her medical tools, bandages, and salves. She tossed the tools into a pot of boiling water on the hearth, and addressed the groom.

"Mick, I think I can take care of the Major, but you should

ride for help. We'll need a doctor – get General Howe's physician if he is there, and tell any of Simm's staff they should come." The groom left with deliberate speed, and Rebecca heard hoofbeats galloping toward town a minute later.

She pulled her knives and tweezers out of the hot water, and threw them into cold. They hissed, and Simm who, trying not to lose consciousness from the pain, hissed back. "Becky, do what you have to, I don't need to wait for someone to hold me down." The girl was amazing him again, but he didn't have time to puzzle it out. She seemed to know what she was doing – how or why, he did not have a clue. He lay back and gave in to the pain. His whole body felt done in.

"Don't be silly, John, you won't need holding down. I do need to ask, before you fall asleep – are you hurt anywhere but the right arm and the left leg?" He shook his head and mouthed "bruises," and lay back.

Rebecca propped up his head and helped him drink a strong mixture of brandy and her poppy tea. While she waited for him to fall asleep, she cut gauze, and melted strained lard and beeswax in a pot. When the ingredients were completely melted together, she stirred the pot and spread the mixture onto clean linen gauze, leaving it near the warm hearth to stay soft.

Rebecca took a clean bread towel and rolled it tight. She put it where she would remember to put it, between Simm's teeth, when she went in for the pistol ball. With her equipment ready, she carefully assessed the state of the patient. She needed access to his right arm and the upper part of his left thigh. As she cut away the sleeve of his beautiful shirt and ripped open his britches to expose the wounds, she thought, with an amused sigh, that as many times as they had been intimate, she had never before undressed him. Almost laughing at what a ridiculous notion that was at this moment, she set to work.

It looked to Rebecca that the knife wound was the dirtiest of the two, and she wanted to clean it first. She poured distilled witch hazel sap over both wounds before she looked more deeply into the arm. The knife had not been sharp, and it had lacerated the flesh fairly far into the muscle. Rebecca poured the distilled witch hazel into the wound until the only thing rinsing out was fresh blood and the clear liquid. She brought a lanthorn closer to his arm for a clearer look. She reached for her sewing box and took out needle and thread. She found what she needed – a needle fit for the finest embroidery. Her English needles and threads were one of her great indulgences. She threaded the fine needle with silk thread, glad that her hands were calm and steady, though it had certainly been a nerve-wracking day.

She used seventeen tiny stitches to hold muscle and blood vessel together. By the time she was ready to dress the wound in her green balm and cover it with gauze smothered in simple ointment, the bleeding had slowed. She covered the entire wound in a soft gauze dressing and left it open. She knew the doctor would want to review her work, and she or he would complete the dressing later.

She washed her hands to remove the wax and lard the gauze had left on them, and prepared to take out the pistol ball. The leg around the entry point was getting increasingly red and swollen, sure signs they should not wait, so Rebecca moved as quickly as she could. She forced more of the poppy tea into Simm's mouth, even though he had not yet even squeaked in discomfort. She looked at the roll of towel, and decided to forgo using it until he showed he needed it.

Following the angle of the wound, Rebecca pushed her long tweezers deep into his leg to feel for the hard metal ball. It had not hit the bone, and she was able to pull it out on her first try. She held the light over Simm's leg, checking for any foreign object, clothing or debris that might have been pushed into the wound by the ball. Finding only a bits of linen pant leg, she pulled out as many of the threads she could find.

Again, she poured the distilled witch hazel into the wound. It did not bleed overmuch, and soon cleaned itself out. She put clean gauze over it until it was dry. She drew the raw edges of the pistol wound gently together with her fingers until they touched, and pushed the sticky gauze into place, wrapping it around the leg to hold the wound. She covered it with dry cloths until the bleeding eased. Then she dressed the wound, as she had the other.

She sat at the little table to collect her thoughts and sip on chamomile tea. After a while, she cleaned her tools and herbal jars, carefully washing everything that was stained with blood and replacing anything she had used. She made careful notes for anything she needed to buy for her medicine kit, and put away the needle and red silk thread.

After another hour, during which Rebecca threw stew bones, carrots and an onion into a pot of water to make a broth, sitting by Simm's sleeping body, occasionally feeling his forehead for fever, hoofbeats woke her from a light doze. The doctor led a group of four into the yard from the stable. Rebecca met them at the front door and motioned to Simm's men, her friends now, to wait in the parlor – she would be right back.

She walked the doctor into the kitchen and, in as much detail as she could, explained the wounds and what she had done. She showed the doctor the ointments and gauzes and left him with the patient. She returned to the parlor ready to drop. "Men, I won't try to make this nice. There are two dead men –" Eyebrows were raised across the room. Rebecca went on – "North-northwest of here. They need to be hidden, burned or eaten by wild dogs. Honestly, I don't care which." The eyebrows changed to looks of real concern. Although everyone tried to talk at once, only one voice was clear enough to answer.

"Becky, what happened? Where is FitzSimmon?"

"Second question is easy. The Major is on the floor in the kitchen. He will have to be there about a week, unless the doctor tells me different. I couldn't move him before I stitched up his arm and took out the pistol ball, so he'll have to stay there for now. We can't risk opening the wounds to more bleeding. He has lost too much blood already.

"As for what happened, two men attacked me in the wood this morning." She swallowed hard, remembering these were all friends. "The fates must be kind, because Simm found us before they could really injure me. The attackers are dead. I think the thing is to find out who they were. Simm was trying to find out where they came from. I'm afraid I did not hear very much. If he is awake before you are ready to go, he might have a word for you. I don't know." Rebecca tried to smile at the men to allay their worries. At that moment, she wanted nothing more than to lay down next to Simm on the kitchen floor and sleep.

That was not to be, so with as much energy as she could muster, she turned and went back into the kitchen. She fully expected, and was prepared for, the doctor to chastise her and tell her that women had no right or ability to deal with wounds. Girls, he would say, should leave these things to the medically- trained; they should stick to caring for childhood fevers and swollen ankles. In fact, those were her father's precise words when her mother slipped and fell onto the barn rake when she was cleaning the muck.

The doctor looked up from Simm. He stood, stretching his back from kneeling near the mattress on the floor. "Tell me about the knife wound. How deep is it?"

"The knife was ragged, but it did not get to the bone. He must have moved sideways, because it went off at an angle and up." She demonstrated gesturing with her hands.

"How many stitches did you do?"

"There are seventeen very small knots. As you can see, I left threads to be pulled out later." Rebecca pulled over a decorated pocket covered with tiny crosses on it to show the doctor. "Similar to these."

"You say you washed the wounds with a distilled root?" The doctor nodded his head, interested. "Well, young lady – " Rebecca braced herself, remembering she had done her best and infection might well have moved in if she had waited for help. The doctor went on – "you have done fine work. I like the plasters, and the balm seems quite a good one. Reminds me of something the groom has been using on my prize stallion recently," He winked at Rebecca. "Leave him here, and I mean DON'T move that arm or that leg for four days – not from now, from tomorrow morning. Then, you may change the dressings.

"When you're in there, cut the silk threads as close as you can without reopening anything. Having some tiny embroidery in there won't hurt him. I notice you used good British Army red." He winked again, enjoying having a pretty young girl to talk to, even if she looked nearly done in. "Keep him fed, keep the wounds clean, and don't change anything for four days!!! And I mean it. Three or four days after those first four – we'll take him over to your aunt's for full recovery, let you get some sleep. I promise, after a week of nursing a full grown invalid in your kitchen, you'll need it."

Simm, who had heard the doctor quite clearly, smiled weakly at Rebecca. She was beaming like a torch. He had no idea why, but in spite of the rottenness of her day, and the pains in arm and leg, he was happy that she looked so happy. He watched as Rebecca walked the doctor to the door, and was a little bit jealous as the still fine-looking older man kissed her on the cheek, congratulating her again on doing a fine job.

Rebecca watched the doctor leave in Aunt Amalia's coach, Mick who had just arrived in the fine coach, rode the doctor's stallion back to town in the rain. Rebecca reflected on Simm's status, since the doctor was willing to ride out so quickly on his horse in the rain for him. Still, she was glad the work was finished within that first hour. Of course, she was also glad the nice doctor had approved of all she had done.

Rebecca went back into the kitchen and knelt to feel Simm's head. He reached for her wrist with his good hand, holding it hard. He pulled her hand to his mouth, and breathing hard against it, he kissed it. "Becky, take a minute for yourself, I need to talk to the men I hear in the other room. Please send them in. I hate to give you orders, but I have a bruise on my chest, and I'm afraid I cannot shout."

Rebecca realized that she had not inspected the rest of her patient for lacerations and bruises, something she would have to do as soon as he was through with his men.

"I'll send them right in." She smiled down at him, and went into the parlor to tell the men to go into the kitchen. She grabbed an old cloak off a peg and went out the front to get some air, walk in the garden, and see if anything was sprouting yet.

The men sat on the floor around Simm. They waited until he started, respectfully not asking him to speak until he was ready. Simm felt a bit like a potentate of old, his petitioners arranged around him on their knees. "Gentlemen, I guess Rebecca told you that she was attacked and nearly raped this morning. I was less than a minute away from being able to prevent that crime, but she was hurt, for which I hold myself responsible. But be that as it may, the miscreants are dead.

"I have an idea how they happened to be in the Willent wood, but not why. It seems the deserters, and unfortunately they are ours, were told by E.P. Manning that these woods were available." The men listened to the story carefully, used to following complicated trails laid down by John FitzSimmon and used to, as well, those trails leading to important discoveries.

"Very strangely, Manning told these men that Rebecca, or rather a girl he described as one who was frolicking with a household of men, would be in the wood collecting wild plants for her medicines. He might have been implying that she was a witch, but I would like to interject right now, that I am glad she knows about those plants. Now, back to the narrative. Manning knew she would be there because he heard Amalia Willent's cook go on about the fiddleheads that Rebecca found in these woods. Men! Men, don't look so confused, I think it is a fern before it opens. A north American spring delicacy. Maybe Cook will make you some.

"So the real question is not who sicced those bastards on Becky, but why would Manning do that?

"I've had a few thoughts. We know he hates our work. Perhaps he wanted to disrupt our little household out here, and send us a message that we are not safe. From what the men said, they were told that the woods out this way were a good place to stay, with a girl for them. Now I think I believe the connection between Cook and Manning is simply that she would have no reason to guard her speech with the King's agent. But why would he send those men out there to ambush Rebecca? That specifically– that's what we have to find out, if we can!" Simm lay back on his pillow wearily, letting the men digest this information.

"Ho, Simm, I'll kill him!" Captain Smith shouted, above the roaring of the others.

"Manning has been looking to bring the Howes's project down, and us as well, but remember – he works for the King, and any move against him is treason. All we can do is guard ourselves and, by extension, Rebecca. So lets get rid of those bodies, find out about those men, and see what Manning is really up to."

The men left as a swirling mass of red uniforms and black cloaks, expressing good wishes for quick healing and promises to stay away for all meals, and to return to make sure the house was full and safe at night. Rebecca thanked them from the bottom of her heart, and watched them ride off, across the field and into the woods – the King's finest fighting force setting off to avenge her, she thought; how odd.

Simm dozed off, exhausted from talking to the men so soon after his surgeries. Rebecca gazed longingly at the sleeping man. She had done nothing about her own injuries and cuts. Stopping finally after the intense few hours with Simm's deepest wounds, she confronted her own condition. She needed a bath, clean clothes, food, and some of her green salve for where that horrible fat man cut her neck and breasts. She hauled fresh water and placed it on the fire to heat for her bath.

Waiting for the water to heat, she wheeled in the big tub and filled it with the warm water, throwing in lavender blossoms. She arranged her soaps, towels, and an herbal mixture for her rinse water. Checking that Simm's eyes were still closed and his breathing even, she stripped out of her clothes and climbed into the hot, fragrant water. She washed her cuts and scrubbed parts that felt peculiarly dirty. Then she washed her hair and rinsed it with a cool tea of rosemary and chamomile.

Simm felt delightfully sinful. He was still dozing in and out of consciousness from pain and the wonderful tea that Rebecca had given him. Sometime, when he was sure he was awake, he dreamed he saw Rebecca take off all her clothes and climb into a primitive tub full of hot water. He watched her delicious back and glorious hair as she washed and rinsed. He must have slept again, because the next time he looked up, the tub was gone and Rebecca was sitting in front of the fire brushing her hair, wearing warm nightclothes and a woolen robe. He had felt connected to this beautiful woman since he had greeted her that bright summer morning on the dock, and possessive of her since he had held her in his arms on that strange, windy night, but now he knew that he would kill hundreds just to keep her looking as she did at this very minute, her hair glowing as it caught the light from the fire, an expression of relaxed contentment on her face.

Later, full of fresh bread soaked in beef broth, Simm slept more deeply. It was only very late at night, with the heat from the fire gone, that he woke to discover Rebecca sound asleep on a pallet next to him. He wanted nothing so much as to pull her closer, but an injured right arm and left leg made that a logistical impossibility.

Rebecca hardly slept, suffering through the whole night.

She found she needed to be held and comforted because of her ordeal. The one person who might hold her was not allowed to move from his frozen spot on the floor. It was like so much else. That same person who could help her unravel the knots and puzzles that were holding her back was the one person to whom she couldn't bring her problems, or trust with her secrets. It had become a pattern. She mused wryly how much she needed John FitzSimmon, and how many and large the barriers were between them.

The next morning, Rebecca woke before sunrise to finish her chores before she was needed in the sickroom/ kitchen. She served a small breakfast in the front room and smilingly explained that, yes, Simm had spent a comfortable night. The men did not need to know that he had moaned in pain and mumbled all sorts of things she probably should not have heard. She carefully paid no attention to Simm's semi-incoherent muttering that might have included something about General Clinton, Admiral Howe, prisoners and tavern names, somewhere. Rebecca was wise enough to leave Simm's puzzles alone.

With the house finally empty, she decided it was a good time to bathe her patient, as well as assess his bruises. She set water on to heat and went upstairs to find something comfortable for Simm to wear. Her father was a much fatter man, so Rebecca looked to see if he had any breeches that would be large on Simm. She found the perfect pair in the back of his closet, folded neatly and packed with clean herbs. A moment of sadness overcame her. This careful cleanliness was certainly her mother's work.

She grabbed the breeches and found a short nightshirt of her father's as well. These would do for a few days; then the man could wear his own clothing. She returned to the kitchen and set up for washing her patient.

"John! Wake up." She whispered loudly while gently nudging his good arm.

"I'm awake, I think. What happened, why am I in the kitchen?" Simm looked around, confused until he remembered the day before.

"Morning! You are getting a bath." Rebecca licked her lips in an exaggerated motion, making him smile.

"Am I a kitten?" He smiled at her, laughing lasciviously.

"You wish, you naughty man. I have wash water, soap and clean clothes. Honestly! And I need to look at your other bruises and cuts to see if there is anything more I should do before too much time goes by."

"Wash away." Simm opened his one arm in a grand gesture.

Rebecca held a large pair of scissors. "I don't want to stress your wounds by pulling your tight uniform over the bandages." She carefully cut the well-made uniform shirt and britches along the seams so they could be repaired. It was unlikely that Simm would wear darned clothing, but there was no reason to let them go to waste. When she had finished, she lifted the clothing carefully away from the injuries, and looked Simm over to see what else was hurt.

She inhaled sharply and Simm looked down at his own chest, a montage of purple bruises and small cuts. She showed him how to hold his right arm close to his body while she helped him sit up. His back was not quite as bad, but there was a large purple laceration that looked like he had been struck by a small log. Rebecca was sickened at how much pain he must be in. She did not remember watching him get this badly hurt. And she could not let go that he had incurred all these injuries for her. She had already deeply cared for and appreciated how he protected her in so many ways. Now she had the care of her hero, no matter their secrets.

While he sat, she washed and patted dry his back, using the softest, oldest cloths she could find. She gently spread her green balm over the cut and bruised skin, covering it with soft, dry gauze. As she helped him back into his pillows, Simm gave her a wicked grin, pulling her into him for a kiss. He cringed with pain. "Ouch, but you're worth it, pretty nurse."

"Stop it, Simm." She sat away from him, trying not to laugh at his antics, which had succeeded in lightening the moment. You'll just hurt yourself, and vain though I may be, even I am not worth re-opening wounds that will heal soon enough."

"How soon?" He grabbed the hand holding a towel and brought it slowly and seductively to his lips.

"The doctor said four days immobile on this bed; then I think you can sit up, but not climb stairs or ride with that leg. After a week or so, I think you can walk around with a cane – sorry, elegant, ebony and ivory-handled walking stick. The arm will take longer, but inconvenience you less."

"Depends on what I need to catch."

"Stop being so wicked. I need to wash and dress these bruises. Wait till you see the oversize clothes I found for you." She set to work washing and rubbing the healing balm into the cuts and bruises on his chest, enjoying every minute she could spend touching and looking at the work of art that was Simm's wonderful chest and legs. He was sculpted like a marble statue of a god, even with the uneven line of painful bruises. He was beautiful. Incredibly beautiful. She wanted to ignore his pain and enjoy the sensation of running her hands down his sculpted muscles and stop ever so slightly at his tempting nipples, so strong and flat. She wanted to follow the vee of hair and muscle down to his waist, where she had not yet started to wash. Of course, she would never cause him unnecessary pain. She finished dressing the bruises that would benefit from the green balm, and brought the gauze from his back to the front, where she tied it off.

She helped him on with her father's old nightshirt, laughing at how ridiculous such a well- made man looked in it. She did not want to embarrass him, nor start anything she could not finish by washing too close to his male parts, but he needed to be clean and checked for cuts that could cause infections. She shrugged and pulled off the blankets, ready to confront the inevitable. She soaped up her washcloth, completely ignoring the fact that he was pleasantly aroused.

"Simm, there is nothing I can do to cure THAT without hurting the deep wound on your leg."

"I know. It's fine. Just wash. I can't help it. Happens when I look at you fully clothed. Imagine how hard ... it is to cope with you rubbing me all over with soap and soft, sweet-smelling, soothing balm." He smiled angelically and lay back on his soft cushions, letting Rebecca wash and dry his most intimate parts.

Rebecca found washing those parts of Simm caused an equivalent reaction in herself. She wanted nothing so much as to "cure" that throbbing deep inside herself that started as she let her mind roam with the soapy cloth over Simm's legs and well-made feet. Now those were parts of a man that even lovers rarely explored. She carefully washed between each toe and rubbed the balm onto them, just to soften and heal feet that spent too many hours covered in stiff boots. As soon as she helped him into the warm, dry britches and pulled the warm, soft quilts over him, he was asleep. He slept comfortably for the rest of the day and most of the night, waking only to drink some broth and exchange a polite word or two.

Simm was awakened early the next morning by arguing voices – Rebecca's and a man's. As always, his first instinct was to go to her rescue, but his body told him different this time, and from the sounds she was not in physical danger. There was a bucket of milk in the corner and a basket of eggs on the table that he could see from his mattress, so it was not so early, and her farm chores were done. He tried to collect other clues as to the situation, but this was difficult while glued to the floor.

Bit by bit, as his ears became attuned to the sounds from outside, he recognized the man as Nathaniel Willent, Rebecca's brother. He'd missed the first part of their argument, but now Rebecca was trying to explain about her attack.

"Nat, I don't know how or why, but that friend of Joe's, that man who wears black and says he works for the King, sent men into the woods to attack me. If not for John FitzSimmon I would probably be dead, certainly raped."

"I've heard about that man – why do you think he is a friend of Joe's?" Nat sounded more concerned about Joe's reputation than Simm thought was justified.

"Well, he is at the Liberty whenever I stop by, and Joe does not throw him out!" Rebecca knew her instincts were right in this, but there was no proof. She would have thought that her brother would understand.

"He is creepy, but I don't think he could be evil if Joe accepts him at the Liberty." Nat gave a nod to say that the subject was closed.

Rebecca fairly hissed with frustration. "Nat, listen to me

– the men said that the man in black told them there would be a girl coming into the wood. I heard them. They named him." She whispered the last, not wanting to relive that morning.

"Beck, I'm sorry they scared you, are you hurt?"

"Scared!! Major FitzSimmon is on the floor of the kitchen and cannot move. He was slashed in the arm, beaten on the back, and took a pistol ball in the thigh. And if I hadn't been as skilled as I am with healing and needle, he would probably be dead now."

Nat was ready with a sneer, "Oh, the mighty British Army could not send a doctor to care for one of their own? Becky, you know doctors are more skilled than you are. Da went over and over it two years ago."

"Yes, I know, and Mama died. Da and the doctor did such a good job keeping me away."

She ran into the kitchen, grabbed a loaf of bread and a few slices of last night's roast ham, ran back out the door and handed them to her brother, who stood confused about what had upset her so. "It's a good thing you are a soldier and not a lawyer or something that takes brains, Nat, because you are dumber than dirt. Take these and go, just go. I have real work to do."

"Becky, I'm sorry I hurt your feelings. What happened?"

"Nothing, Nathaniel, I am fine. I will be in touch in a week or two. Now go!"

Rebecca went back into the kitchen, with as much grace as she could muster. "Sorry to have woken you, Major. It won't happen again." She started to run to the back stairs to cry alone in the attic when a stentorian voice penetrated her sobs.

"Rebecca, get back here, now!"

Rebecca turned back down the stairs and stood dutifully at the door, a little surprised to be ordered around, "Yes,

Major?"

"At this point, calling me Major sounds like a dirty bed game. Maybe someday when all this is cleared up we can play it." His blue eyes twinkled kindness at her. Meanwhile, you have two choices, and you know them. Come here and sit with me."

Rebecca sat obediently on the floor at Simm's left side, facing him. "Becky," he started gently, reaching over and cradling her face with his left hand, "tell me the story of your mother's death. It weighs on you, let me help."

Rebecca still cried, but wiped her eyes with the edge of the sheet and sniffled. "She died the year before I met you. That's when my father used the dowry money she had saved for me to buy the land. Then he gave her things to my brother's wife. I like Janey, I do, but Mama and I were very close."

Simm nodded sympathetically. He waited for her to tell the story that mattered. "It was the fall. My mother liked to get the stalls clean before it got too cold to do a good mucking out. So she and I were in the barn cleaning stalls. We had more animals then – ten cows, goats, sheep, chickens and a pig. I don't know exactly when it happened, but Mama slipped on some wet hay or something and fell on the rake she was using. The wound was not deep, and it would have been fine, but my father would not let me clean it or care for her. It got infected, and she died about a eight days later.

Simm almost couldn't breathe with the grief of what had happened to her and her mother. "Did he not at least call a doctor?"

"Yes, but it was a day later; when she developed a fever, it was too late. He washed it with a little cold water, and put some old bread on it." Rebecca took a deep breath, preparing to say out loud what she had never allowed herself to think. "I think the worst part was that she was the one who taught me what I know about choosing and preparing herbals. None of it is magic, and my father knew it. He just didn't want me to do it. If my brother had known anything about cleaning and caring for such a wound, she would still be alive. But Da did not believe that a mere girl should be doing those things. Maybe he thought I would be accused of witchcraft."

"Becky –" Simm spoke slowly and carefully, not wanting to break the spell. This was the first time Rebecca had told him anything important about her mother, or her sorrow. "I think you are wonderful. I was hurt only one day ago, and I know my wounds were deep, dirty wounds. I have never felt so good so soon after being hurt. I'm sure you noticed more than a few scars from old wounds. Most were minor, but a few scared a doctor or two. None healed as painlessly or as soon as the ones you are caring for.

"And Becky - I heard what Doctor Geralds said to you. I saw you glow from his simple praise. You deserved it."

"Simm, thank you, you are so very kind to me." Rebecca felt shy after revealing so much of her soul, even to Simm, who seemed to know nearly everything.

"Thank me? Don't be silly, you saved my life, girl."

"Have you forgotten, dear man?" Rebecca curled into him, carefully avoiding his bandaged leg and bruised ribs. "You saved mine first." She leaned over and kissed his cheek, resting there for a while, relaxed and happy.

The days went by without further interruptions or intrigue. Rebecca was able to keep up the farm chores without having to tell her family there was a crisis. And Simm dutifully stayed still, letting his body heal, even while his mind chafed at that same stillness. Whenever he threatened to get up and run around the farm, Rebecca threatened to make him drink poppy and fall sleep. So far, that had calmed him each time.

Simm's men buried or hid the bodies in the wood, and were working to discover the inner workings of E.P. Manning's mind, but his motivation remained unclear, and then General Howe ordered them not to stir up more trouble since, as he said, Rebecca was basically unharmed, and Manning wasn't present at the crime. It was at least pleasant to know that the General believed that Manning had been behind that attack.

The night before Simm was to move out of the farmhouse kitchen to a comfortable bed with plenty of help around to carry him up and down the stairs at Amalia Willent's mansion, he knew he had to say to Rebecca all the things he had planned to tell her during those weeks in New York. Now circumstances required he reveal the complete story. He would allow her to do with the information what she would, and he would accept her decision. His leaving early the next day would give her time to decide how she felt about him, without the pressure of caring for him or seeing him every day.

It was late in the evening, but neither of them was particularly tired, having spent too much time these past days indoors. Rebecca sat in front of the kitchen fire, knitting a pair of socks. The needles flew seemingly of their own volition; there were two loaves of bread baking in the ovens; water boiling on the hearth for tea and washing. She looked over at Simm, so much more comfortable now that the superficial wounds had changed from purple to a light red, and the deep ones were cool and soft.

It was the last night, with just the two of them alone in the kitchen. Simm was to leave in the morning, and she knew she would miss the intimacy of caring for him terribly, especially those wonderful baths. She smiled at the thought. The day before, Simm had started sitting for an hour or two in the big kitchen chair. He sat there now, his wounded leg on a box. "Becky, I have a long tale for you." She turned to look at him, curious at how much he would tell her about himself, thinking back to how little she knew, and how little she had told him.

"Becky, my stay in New York allowed me to assess my past and current state in a way that war rarely supplies. If any of this is going to make sense to you, I need to start at the very beginning. I apologize ahead of time if I bore you.

"I know you won't believe me, but the Howe brothers did not want to fight the Americans. They were three brothers, all of them here in America during the Seven Years War, your French and Indian War. They fought with and admired the Americans. The oldest brother, General George Howe, died here at the hands of the French. They only undertook this enterprise as a favor for their cousin the King. They agreed to come to America in order to affect conciliation and bring Americans back to the British fold – something about which Richard and William, the living Howe brothers who sit in Parliament, feel very strongly. The Howes know and admire my brothers, who also sit in Parliament. They are all members of the Whig Party.

"It was because of my brothers that I was plucked from my original regiment and set to work for William Howe. The feeling was that with my education and family, I would be more valuable behind a desk and at the negotiation table than holding a musket. It was also my work for the Howes that sent me off on my wanderings around America. Not as what we would call a spy, I was not looking for military secrets. What I was sent off to discover was who Americans were; was the idea of conciliation ever going to be possible? I discovered in my wanderings that British Whigs and American Whigs had become so different there would be no conciliation. Simply – and this won't surprise you – Whigs in Britain want to include the King as part of Parliament. Over the last century or so, Britons moved from accepting the King as the head of Parliament to his being a part of Parliament. On this side of the Atlantic, Whigs want no King and no part of a monarchy. They see each mini-Parliament of their colonies as equal to the one in London, not subservient to it. I grew to see no room for compromise.

"William Howe wanted to confirm what we had learned. That was why I was in Philadelphia in the summer of 1776, while your Congress was signing the Declaration of Independence, and where I met my brother and his ship. Jason now calls himself an American and lives in Salem, Massachusetts. When I am done with war, I will move there. There is an incredible beauty there; it reminds me of home.

"Now Jason you've met. Sometimes he runs legitimate cargo, but he has a ship's hold full of colors that will get him past anyone's Man-o-War. That, sweet girl" – he looked at her with deep eyes – "was how I met you, and why I have friendships with good people up and down the Atlantic, in each one of your colonies.

"Because of the Howes, I work the attempted negotiations, and I've worked on a conference that has met on and off the last few years. That is why, I know you wondered at Christmas, your brother Nat and I know each other. We were part of one such conference that met until last fall. It was while we were having that last meeting, that my mother's favorite cousin, John Burgoyne, was making stupid bargains with the Indians that made it impossible to get the Americans to agree to anything. I left the conference after his army in upper New York lost so spectacularly at Saratoga. I was sent north to quietly take care of his army in surrender. That's why I arrived here later than the other men and interrupted your sleeping arrangements. I am sorry about that." Rebecca shrugged at that – the anger at losing her room had been overtaken at the joy of having him nearby.

"The British loss at Saratoga began to convince the French that they should aid America against their oldest enemy, Britain. When it looked like that agreement was imminent last month, I was sent back to New York to try to make as good a deal between the British and the Americans as we could hammer out, before they could sign with the French. I feel, as does everyone involved – all Englishmen, at least – that France will prove a fickle friend to the Americans. The Americans are more hopeful about the French intentions.

"But already it seems long past. When that last treaty between the Americans and the French was signed a month ago, I decided my skills are not needed here anymore. And, as I no longer wish to control the lives of men at war, I don't have a future with the British Army in America. Becky - there is no doubt that Howe will be recalled by the time we leave Philadelphia. I don't wish to be reassigned."

Rebecca had been listening in stunned silence. She knew the men did office work, but had no idea what it had involved. She'd assumed it had to do with destroying the American Army, but to discover that efforts had been made to avert or minimize this war was astounding. That John and Nat had sat across a table and nothing had come of it, that was sad. She looked at Simm with a new admiration and cringed at her own dishonesty. She promised herself she would end her trips for Nat, cutting off the horrible Joe, as soon as she was able. Until she was free of the promises to them, she had nothing to offer Simm in return for his honesty. She wondered what he would do after General Howe left and he was no longer part of the army, but was afraid to ask.

Simm continued talking. After a minute, her mind wandering through her own life, she was jolted back to Simm's story with the mention of a name - Manning. "There are more questions about Manning than answers, but you of all people deserve to know what I know. After the bloodless evacuation of Boston, the Crown got very angry at the way the Howes lost the town. The King knows that William Howe is a brilliant strategist, but he got into his head that Howe could not be trusted, so he, the King, sent his agent, E.P. Manning, to America to keep an eye out– specifically, to watch the Howes's activities.

"That is really all I know about Manning. We know he has been seen near Amalia's, and we believe he and Cook share a cup of tea now and then in her kitchen. The man has been seen at some drinking spots in Philadelphia as well. We don't know what information he is gathering or who his staff, or his compatriots, are. None of us can figure why he would send those men to attack you. I don't suppose you have any idea? No, that's insulting, I won't even ask. The man is mad. He has taken such a dislike to me and my staff, or to the General or to Amalia, that he would punish you. For some reason he wanted you hurt in order to punish someone." Simm steered the conversation to lighter subjects, and soon they fell back into companionable silence.

Rebecca wanted to crawl into a hole in the ground. John was taking the responsibility for her attack. She was sure he was wrong, and equally sure Manning's hatred had something to do with the Liberty Coffee House and Joe's friendship with the evil man. She was frustrated that she could not understand enough of the relationships between the players to put those pieces together. It was possible that her bits and pieces of information compiled with Simm's would help him complete the puzzle; but she could not help him. It was not that she did not trust him – she knew she could trust him with her life – but she could not ask him to ignore what, to the British, was her treason. She gently kissed him good-night, and spent a few minutes resting at his side before she set her pallet next to his mattress for sleeping.

Chapter 14

The next morning Simm was taken to Amalia Willent's home to enjoy the elegant caretaking given to a prize invalid in a grand house. He appreciated the efforts made on his behalf, but he desperately missed his small mattress laid out in the corner of a plain Pennsylvania farmhouse kitchen. His clothes and things were taken to the pretty yellow office at the top of the stairs, but he was seated on a chaise in the front parlor. The move to headquarters meant an end to the relaxed healing he had been allowed to indulge in for the last ten days. Now, with his left leg propped up, his right arm in a sling, and help whenever he requested it, work was plopped by the wagonload in front of him, and he was expected to digest and condense all of the dispatches and letters that had arrived since he was hurt.

Rebecca to returned to work as well. It was hard leaving the house those first few days, but she quickly got back in the habit of shopping, and making meals for her household. She found that she sat with the men more often, missing the conversations she had over the days with Simm. The men were anxious to see that she had gotten over her ordeal, so she put on a bright smile and it convinced even herself that she was happy enough.

Rebecca planned on one last visit to Joe's and her boulder. She applied herself to finishing the maps of streets, bridges and buildings in the town, sector by sector. She patently ignored the requests, made during the winter, that she supply information on individual American landowners and the British soldiers quartered with them.

After staying away from Amalia's house for a week of exploring and sketching, Rebecca dressed one morning to visit her Aunt. She was let in the front door and entered by the main stairs. She walked into the familiar front parlor. Her heart jumped unexpectedly when she spotted Simm hunched over a small desk with enough work on it to cover a much larger table. His eyes caught hers and his face lit up. He motioned for her to come in and close the door.

She sat next to him on a small chair, fighting the instinct to climb onto his lap and devour him. Instead, she accepted a cup of tea and a light kiss on her cheek. Simm spoke softly, so that the various people walking in and out of the parlor would not overhear. "So, my goddess has descended from the heavens for a visit with us mortals? Rebecca, my quiet goddess, it is so nice to see you, and while I have you here – will you marry me, when I can walk again?" He seemed serious about that question, but she balked at marrying before she could tell him the truth of her work. Simm went on, "I should be walking again within the week. Doctor Geralds wants me to take it easy for as long as I can before I'm ordered up and about."

Rebecca didn't want to put him off by being flip. Yes, she would marry him, a million times yes, but how to put him off without denying her deepest wish? "John I know you want to move on with your life, but marry? Truly, that's unexpected."

"Not that unexpected. We did anticipate it by some time." He grinned at her, " I know you think I'm teasing. But Becky, I am completely serious. We know we belong together, we are good together, good to each other. I adore you." He made a growl deep in his throat that only she could hear. That sound and the expression in his icy eyes, far more than his pleading, had her ready to scream – that, and hunt for a minister, and then drag him off to the quiet room upstairs. Simm had continued to talk. Rebecca heard only the last bit, "So, marry me. I'll be a whole man soon, you know that."

Rebecca blushed, remembering some interesting baths when he wasn't technically a "whole man." "I'm going to say yes. But John, please, don't tell Amalia or the General that you asked me to marry you, not yet! Please. There are going to be too many people at tea this afternoon, and I don't want to explain to each of them how we met while you were quartered in my house. It sounds more sordid than the strange truth it is. Let's tell her when it's closer, when it's time to plan the wedding." Rebecca looked happy at the prospect of marriage, but frightened of something. As usual, she gave no clue what might be wrong. Frustrated by his inability to help her, he stuffed his questions deep, and soon others entered the parlor for tea, so Simm let it go.

In seconds, the sounds of men's voices drifted down, announcing the arrival of William Howe's staff, in time for Amalia's weekly high tea. Amalia Willent had had little choice about letting Howe and his staff move into and take over her mansion, yet she managed to live her life as though she was a grand dame entertaining invited guests. As always, tea was as pleasant as Amalia Willent could make it for anyone who attended. The officers who were there that day were aggrieved with thoughts of their failed project, and the warfare to come. These were men who did not believe that any Englishmen – in this case, the Americans – intent on forming their own government could be easily defeated. They understood that these adversaries would not easily be brought back into the fold of empire, even in defeat.

On this afternoon, Amalia had invited her closest neighbors to join the men for tea. Amalia's neighbors and friends who had stayed at the center of the town were staunchly Tory. In fact, most of the local Tories were stauncher supporters of the King than many of Howe's staff, something that continued to rankle the Crown and factions in Parliament. Neither the soldiers nor the local people were pleased with the price that would soon be paid, but the locals held faith that the rebels, so intent on destroying their way of life, would soon be defeated.

Rebecca showed her happy face to the world. It was one she had learned to paste on in order to convince her housemates that the attack no longer bothered her. But the attack in the woods, orchestrated by E.P. Manning, had thoroughly frightened her, far more her than she would readily admit or could outwardly display. That afternoon, sitting in Amalia's parlor, she let her mind go over the final work she had completed for Nat. She had found that staying busy and focused on her work, the charts and maps she'd wanted done and finished, kept her fears at bay. But when she was most safe, as she was now, comfortably surrounded by nice people talking about general things, her mind drifted back to E.P. Manning and the attack.

Manning saw her often at the Liberty Coffee House. It could be no secret to him that she met with Joe, walked in the kitchen, and left without staying long. She'd seen him there as well, each of those times, sitting in his darkened corner – watching. Joe had to know him, and why he was sitting there in his corner. This week, maybe today after she left Amalia's tea, she would go right to the Liberty and announce that she was finished with errands for Joe. She would sever all connection with Joe and the coffee house. Then, hopefully, she would never see Joe, or E.P. Manning, again.

Rebecca needed some air away from the polite chatter in the parlor. She found Simm's eyes and rolled hers toward the ceiling, motioning that she needed air. He nodded, and made a sad face at his leg. She excused herself and went to the kitchen to find Annie, who was in the back, collecting the hanging sheets in the windy afternoon.

"Hi, Annie, how's it with you?" Rebecca sing-songed in her happy voice, showing her hale and hearty attitude.

"Becky, it's fine. We heard you had some scare in the woods. Did those horrible men hurt you? I heard they was chased off."

"Well, they were chased off. They scared me enough. I won't go out there alone anymore." If this conversation was to work its way back to Manning, Annie was as good a gossip as anyone.

"Oh, that'll be better, I think you do too much."

Rebecca was sure that Simm would not have talked about the attack below stairs, nor would his men. Yet, Annie seemed to know a lot about what had happened, and that seemed a curious thing for a maid who had never ventured toward the Willent farms. To say that Rebecca "did too much"? Rebecca realized that she needed to find out more.

"Annie, who told you I do too much? Certainly not my Aunt or General Howe?"

"Oh no, not them, they don't talk. Friend of Cook's. Called Ezra or Eli or something, says to Cook, and I listened. Normally I'm not the sort to listen at keyholes or the like, but I'm your friend, so when I heard your name, I listened. Anyway, he says that he's seen you shopping, and running all sorts of errands. He asked where you lived so's he could help if he were ever out that way. Seemed odd to me, him being a stranger to the city and all. He's not the one who hurt you, is he? He sat right in this kitchen drinking Cook's stash of tea and brandy." Rebecca shook her head "no." "Asked Cook all about you, child and young lady. She bragged about all the medicines you make from the plants out there. He seemed very interested."

"He probably wants to see if he can hang me as a witch," Rebecca thought. She felt those cold snakes on her back again. But she only answered happily, "No, Annie. I don't know anyone named Eli or Ezra – what did you say his name was? I'm sure he was just making sweet to Cook."

The maid finished her laundry and headed into the house. Rebecca followed her, and excused herself, "Annie, I've got to go up, back to Aunt's tea. I'll see you soon." She waved at her old friend and went back to the gathering. Interesting, Rebecca thought on her way upstairs. Annie, it would seem, was an unexpected font of information. In less than ten minutes of her considerable chatter, she confirmed everything that Simm had found out about the man's interest. Remarkable. Now to find out about Joe's connection with the man in black, but that could wait for another day.

She ventured back upstairs, but Simm had already left; helped to his office on the third floor. The light went out of the room, and she stayed only as long as politeness dictated. Now, Rebecca was sure, he was ready to ask the General for permission to resign his commission. Rebecca did not want to intrude on Simm's work by remaining in the house, so she decided to walk home. It was still light at six o'clock on the early spring day, a perfect time to prove to herself that she could go out alone in the evening and be perfectly safe.

Pleased that she had not bowed to fear after only days of being on her own again, Rebecca began to walk toward home.

She had no interest in going by Joe's to collect the week's worth of materials. There were still days before she needed deliver them to the cave. Easy enough; she would come back.

She had turned onto the country road that led out of the town and toward the farm, when she became aware of a shadow matching her steps. She wanted to break into a hard run, but instead turned to see who had matched her pace. "Mr. Manning, we meet again, how unpleasant for me." Rebecca kept her voice as low and as polite as possible.

"Miss Willent, how are you today? I'm afraid my associates may have gotten the wrong idea about your wood, I do apologize." His voice slithered with false sincerity. Although Rebecca quickened her pace, Manning moved along side of her.

"Do you? Well thank you and good day! At least we can hope your associates will not get any more wrong ideas." She finished quicky and hastened her steps, walking as rapidly as she could without breaking into a run, hoping he would leave.

"Miss Willent – 'dear Becky' as Cook calls you" – Manning's voice got even more tinged with sarcasm and the overtones of threats – "everyone loves you so. They don't know the duplicitous you, do they? I don't know what you do in that house, Miss Willent, but whatever it is I know you can't get away with it for long. And soon, I know, it is going to get you and all your friends into some interesting knots."

Rebecca wanted desperately to figure out what Manning knew. Whatever he thought was probably incorrect, because nothing happened in her house. But there was too much that happened at Joe's and in the wood to relax at his blunder. "I have so few friends still in town, Mr. Manning. So many have fled. I don't know of whom you speak." She hurried on, again trying to move faster than the blasted man. Did he mean the crowd at the Liberty Coffee House?

"I'm speaking of the men at your house, my dear. Joe and I feel they are *too good* friends for a young girl to have. A pretty young girl at that. Living with men that way, you know others may get the wrong idea about you."

Rebecca's head wanted to burst. Joe? Did he say "Joe" and mean "Coffee Joe"? They were really *friends*? He was admitting it? Rebecca needed to make sure? "Mr. Manning – " she squeezed the words through a shocked smile – did you mention my one real friend here in town at the moment, Joe, at the Liberty Coffee House? I'm surprised you speak to him, a man like that, a bit gruff and unbathed for an elegant man such as yourself, isn't he?"

"Why, thank you, dear Becky." he paused thinking for a moment. "Joe, well I hardly know him, of course, sorry even to have mentioned him. But a last word, Miss Willent. I have spoken to your *very good* friend, a Major FitzSimmon." The man's voice now oozed false honey. "I told him that he should not trust you. I hope I made it very clear that *I* should not like to see the two of you together. I do think you should know that it would be very bad for you.

"Yes, you see, I'm afraid I even broadly hinted to the Major, that *if I* were to see the two of you in the same room, city, colony or continent, I might have to charge you both with treason. And that would make me very sad." Manning got mournful sounding as he continued. "You have such a pretty neck, so much else it could be used for." He stared baldly at Rebecca's neck, lifting a limp pale hand and almost reaching over to caress it.

She felt his eyes roam up and down her body – definitely cold snakes. "Well, as I said, it would be a shame, but you both would hang." He finished quite resolutely, and with that he turned and walked back toward town. Rebecca stumbled home, shocked by Manning's words, and the full knowledge that he could have her killed, could have John killed, for nothing – in an instant.

Rebecca barely left the farm for the next few days. She approached her chores with renewed vigor. She reminded the grooms to use the temporary good weather to muck the stables, while she polished windows and household artifacts, from andirons to her mother's silver, throughout the house. On Thursday, she went into Philadelphia to collect at Coffee Joe's. This would be the last evening she would make a delivery of the memos and maps to the wood, the last visit to Nat at the cave. It was a scheduled drop-off, and she was intent on ending this project, no matter the wind or rain.

She had suspected the weather would turn. The morning was merely cloudy, but since then the storm pelted the early spring day with rain and wet snow. Rebecca needed to finish this task. She waited as long as she could for the storm to let up, rebelling at the thought of having to once again endure soaking shoes and clothes for Nat and Joe. She almost gave in to her desire to curl in front of the fire with a good book. But the promise to herself that this would truly be the last time soon had her rising and walking out the door.

She left the house in the late morning, braving the wind, rain and wet snow. "Oh Nat, just this last time, my feet are wet!" Rebecca cursed her wet feet, and said unkind things to her brother as she walked the familiar road into town. She arrived at her Aunt's in time for a very brief ten o'clock coffee. Making apologies about leaving early because of the weather, and the need to buy new, dry stockings, she walked down Chestnut Street, pulling the blue wool cloak tight around her against the icy rain. She moved as fast as the slippery paving stones would allow, jumping now and then to wake up frozen feet and avoid half-frozen puddles. But as terrible as the day was, Rebecca was delighted to be out in the active town, happier than she had been in a very long time because this, her last trip to the Liberty, her last walk to the hollow rock, meant that she could say a truthful "yes" to Simm. She was smiling at the thought of being married to plain John FitzSimmon when she saw Joe.

Coffee Joe was standing near the kitchen door of the nearly-empty restaurant when she walked in. She shook the rain off her cloak and stamped her feet against the cold. She was tired of this place and Joe's unceasing demands. Now, she wanted to stand in front of the roaring fire, but walked over to Joe instead.

"Rebecca, you finished your lists for me?"

"Joe, I'm here to get stuff out to Nat, not give you anything."

"Becky," he snarled at her, reminding her of a rabid dog, "you were to get me the lists of who lives in which house, I thought you were aware. Nat said he told you."

"He may have, and I may have given him some information, but I am not giving you any of it. You are too good friends with Manning." She let that drop, waiting to see how he would react.

"How do you know that, little weasel?" Joe grabbed for her arm, but she twisted away before he could get a hold.

"Joe, you've just confirmed my suspicions, but why you two are allies I can not figure out. And Joe, I don't care. Just give me the materials. This will be the last time I come for them.

"Give me a minute, I want you to have that list of names

I want you to find."

Rebecca knew that fighting with Joe over the lists was a waste of time. She determined to take the lists home and simply destroy them. Burning them would be much easier than raising Joe's ire further.

A few minutes later, Rebecca sat drinking a cup of something that was thankfully hot, even if it was not good coffee. She was unsurprised to see Manning sneak into the room and move toward the back. Without turning toward him, she walked into the kitchen, grabbed the material Joe was just finishing, and walked out the kitchen door.

"Joe, your friend just arrived," Rebecca snapped back at him as she left.

The freezing rain had not let up at all. She had nearly gotten warm and dry from the hot stove. Now she was sorry she had dressed for Amalia's. Standing still to catch her bearings for just a moment, she was aware that her feet, even in her heavy shoes, were frozen and thoroughly soaked. Quickly, she stuffed the scrolled documents through the hidden pockets into the seams, and once again the bulk of the rolled paper was hidden in the movements of the cloak. She hoped, without much faith, that Joe's lists would be dry enough to burn.

Rebecca turned away from the town and headed toward the farm. At the edge that marked the shift from town to open fields, she was hit by icy gusts that nearly knocked her down. She lowered her head against the blasts as sleet bit her face and hands, and the ice accumulating under her feet made walking harder with every step. She resisted the urge to sit on the side of the road, to cry and pray for a quick death. Instead, she stubbornly put one foot in front of the other while the wind and ice pelted her, and cold seeped through her feet up into her legs. Falling into the wind, Rebecca continued homeward singing a song of "just one more damn time," and using her anger for fuel as her frozen feet trod through the wet snow and rivers of frozen rain.

It was still early afternoon when a frozen and dripping Rebecca slipped into the kitchen. Sanity returned when she saw the men had left hot, banked coals, and plenty of dry wood in the box. It was too early to worry about their dinner. It would be a stew, and everything was ready to be thrown into a pot later in the afternoon. This sort of in-between freedom was a rarity for her, and she was delighted to take advantage of it. The first thing to do was stoke the fire. Most days during the early afternoon, she let the fire burn low in order to save firewood. But today she needed heat, a hot cup of chocolate, and fire.

Rebecca threw her dripping cloak over a chair in front of the fire to dry. She took off her sopping shoes and peeled her stockings from her cold legs and feet. She reached into the pockets of the cloak and pulled the rolls of documents she'd collected, pulling Joe's lists apart from the other materials. She put them on the hearth under a cold pot. She walked barefoot over the cold, stone floor into the summer kitchen to collect more dry wood from the indoor woodpile to make sure the lists would completely burn. While she was in the summer kitchen, she gathered her own work and rolled it into the cloak pockets. She winced as she stepped on a twig in her bare feet, reminding her that she needed dry socks and shoes.

She added a bit of wood to the fire, plopped the rest in the box, and went up to the attic to put on warm, dry clothes and fresh shoes. Rebecca could still hear her mother's voice with its comforting Boston whine, reminding her always to avoid being cold and wet. New Englanders, she'd always said, know that warm socks mean life, and that cold, wet socks mean sickness and death. She'd imparted that wisdom while teaching Rebecca to knit when she was very young. Even boys had learned to knit, she'd reminded her daughter – everyone needs socks.

She pulled a wool dress over a dry shift and stays. The spruce green gown was in an old style, with lacing up the front. She'd always liked that gown. It was warm wool with sleeves past the elbows. The spruce color made her eyes a flashing green gray instead of their normal blue. The warm, woodland-green dress was perfect for such a dreary day. And now, with dry stockings and warm deerskin slippers, she was ready to go back to the kitchen and burn the infernal lists that Joe had foisted on her. She tied her hair back with a simple ribbon that perfectly matched the color of the dress, while she walked quietly down the stairs to the kitchen.

She opened the door from the stairs to find Simm sitting at the table with the lists in one pile and all the maps and telling documents open on the table in front of him.

"Your work is very good." Simm's voice was cold and his eyes, when they turned to her, were blue steel. "So this is what you do when you leave here? The men said knitting."

Speechless, Rebecca swallowed hard, hoping he had not yet read the lists. His name was the only one she had recognized. He would think, no, he would *know*, that she was a traitor, perhaps that she was an assassin – worst, that she had betrayed him. She looked at the pot on the stone hearth. Underneath was empty space. She listened to the wind and ice rattle and attack the windows. Rebecca held her breath, feeling her heart pound with fear in her chest. There was no other sound in the room.

Simm had missed her at Amalia's coffee. She had left so quickly. He had meant to tell her that the doctor said he was healed enough to ride. He had finished the small pile of dispatches that had appeared on his desk during the morning and had ridden out, anxious to see her. He'd walked in and found Rebecca's beautiful, blue and very wet cloak fallen to the floor. He'd picked it up, meaning to hang it back on its peg, when he heard a rustle of paper in the pockets. Surprised that anything was dry when the cloak was so wet, Simm assumed that the paper was something Rebecca had forgotten about, and went to pull it out.

The exterior pockets contained nothing, but the rustle continued as he swung the heavy wet garment. Finally, he had put on the cloak; finding the interior pockets, he'd pulled the rolled documents from the double seams. There were ink stains on the lining; it was clear that this was not the first time the cloak had been used to carry things. The girl in the blue cloak who playfully bribed the men in the guard house with baked goods? His baked goods, kneaded at this table, baked at this hearth! Well, he supposed he had found her. One mystery solved.

He remembered how often she left the farm when no one was home, and came back rushing with the cloak pulled tight against her, when an old great coat would have been more practical on a farm during this cold, wet winter. No wonder she would not let him tell Amalia or the General they would marry. At least in that she was honest. There was no doubt that she was drawn to him, but only he had ever professed anything more than lust. He had seen the qualities of strength and intelligence as well as beauty, and had fallen for her deeply. Was all of it a planned deception?

Simm felt as though cold water had been poured over his

head. He had been deceived by a spy of the first order, by a beautiful woman, and spied on in his own house. Maybe his arrival and being quartered here had not been an accident. Maybe Rebecca was working with Manning to destroy a chance for reconciliation with the colonies. There were Americans who wished for a total, and brutal, separation of mother country and colonies.

Simm's thoughts of Rebecca's duplicitous nature swirled round in his head, making him dizzy. He could not calm them. He thought he would make some tea, and perhaps that would help calm the storm and allow him to think straight. He was wrong.

Simm went to swing the kettle over the now roaring flames, when white squares of paper stuck under a pot caught his eye. His eye was especially caught when he spotted his own name near the top of the second list. 'Maj. John FitzSimmon' was not only written there on the list, but underlined with the words, "where is he!! Becky?" Under the list someone had written "stop stalling," in dark, purposeful writing.

For Simm, time just stood still. He was so angry, so shocked, he could barely breathe. He had exposed more of himself to this fiend than he ever had to anyone in his life. What had it gotten him? Wet feet and aching balls, that's what. Enraged, he looked up for the first time, only to see Rebecca standing there shocked and speechless. She looked so lovely, beautiful in fact, like the maiden in a child's tale. Usually her hair was braided or pinned under a work cap, out of the way of dirt and fire.

Now she wore it down her back drying, and tied in a simple ribbon; one he wanted very much to untie. How he wanted to run his hands through that fine, silky hair! His gaze moved downward over her clothing. The dress was not one he had seen before – prettier by far than anything she wore around the farm; a style more mature, older and simpler than anything she wore at her aunt's. He wanted to forget about all the papers strewn across the table, tell her she was beautiful, tell her and show her, his body nearly aching with the agony of finding her false. He forced himself back to the maps and lists.

Back to his anger. The one thing he would not do was force himself on her, but desire combined with anger was making the possibility of doing just that frightening.

"As I already said, your work is very good. I notice you've used no color." Simm 's voice was tight, barely containing his rage.

"Thank you. John, I couldn't use colors. Couldn't use your kohls." Rebecca whispered thinking that Simm would never want to see her or hear her speak, ever again. If he didn't charge her with espionage, she would leave here and stay at Hackett's, and send someone else to take care of this place the next few months. John would leave later in the spring. Nothing else would matter. She wouldn't cry. Looking at him blankly, she let him continue without speaking.

"Rebecca, before I ask all the other questions that are running races in my head, I need an honest answer to just one question. I believe our pact still holds?" Simm paused then, waiting for a nod of her head. After she moved her head the slightest nod, he continued, "Are you working with Manning? Truth only, Rebecca! I'm afraid of what I might do if I catch you in a lie?" He held clenched his fists at his sides, and slowly forced them to open. With hands held sternly but gently in front of him, he waited with an icy rage that matched the sleet beating against the windows.

Rebecca was stunned at the question. "No, John. I am not working with Manning."

"Talk, Mistress Willent! What is all this?" He hissed the "s," motioning to her scrolls and lists on the table.

Simm's tone told her that she was not his beloved, and might never be that again. Major FitzSimmon, the officer who hanged spies and shot rapists, who was absolutely honest and hated lies and semi-truths, was standing before her, and was not going to say another word until she offered some coherent explanation for the damning materials strewn over the table. Rebecca stood facing him, her hands folded in front, forcing herself to look right in his eyes, and began. She deeply understood that this was not a declaration of love or even passion. This speech was a fight for her life.

"Manning. He keeps popping up, doesn't he? You believed the rape, the attack on me, was a message to you, possibly your staff, or Amalia's household. You thought Manning sent those men here, to prove to you that you were unable to control the American theater, as you say. To show you that it would require a heavier hand than yours to keep your ladies safe. I believed there was something else as well, and that Manning may have planted the idea – that if American civilians thought British ruffians were behind every rock, waiting to attack, then he could get even loyal Tories to oppose British occupation. I believe he suggested this to Coffee Joe, who is the proprietor of the Liberty Coffee house.

"Joe insinuated to me that people here in Philadelphia needed tangible evidence to convince them not to be so friendly to Howe's troops. Joe believes strongly in dressing plainly in homespun, and is equally opposed to parties. And there is something else; Joe may believe that I deserved the attack as punishment. I have not been doing as he asks, and he believes, as do many others, that I cavort with your men in here, behind the closed curtains." She had trouble saying this last thing, turning nearly pink from embarrassment.

Simm groaned silently, thinking how untrue that was, and what a blasted waste of decorum he may have shown.

Rebecca continued looking Simm directly in the eyes. She spoke as clearly as she could through a very tight throat. "I believe that Manning knows I might be doing something for the Americans, walking around Philadelphia and getting information to Washington's camp. He knows I go to the Liberty, but doesn't see me leave with things, so he doesn't know precisely what I do, or when I do it. So I offer yet another theory for the attack. I wonder if the attack was set up by him to show *me* that I could not be safe, even in my own woods.

Simm spoke quietly. "I don't believe that E.P. knows what you have been doing. He has insinuated to me that you are up to something, and that I might be at risk because of it. I assumed he was wrong, but obviously he was not. Please go on." Simm wanted to be wrong. He wanted Rebecca to have an innocent reason to have lists of men, some of whom had been mysteriously killed. He could not see how she could be an innocent. He did not want to drag her down to her own Aunt's house to be tried, and then hanged in front of Independence Hall. The image of that horror, the thought of even losing Rebecca Willent, was terrifying. He forced his mind back to the present.

Rebecca was ringing her pretty green ribbon in her hands while she spoke. "John, I've wanted to tell you since Christmas, but it was too dangerous for me to tell you. Maybe I am a coward. I promise that I wanted to ask you about Manning, to tell you what I knew, so that we could work together and figure it out. Now I can, because the whole thing is over. I am done with maps and charts, done with the Liberty and horrible Coffee Joe.

"John, I'm sorry if its too late for us. You have been so honest with me, and I have not been honest with you. But I don't want you to think I'm telling you now because you caught me." She tried to smile at him. "Well, you did catch me." Simm nodded in sympathetic understanding. He felt his anger subsiding, and a small kernel of hope beginning to grow.

"Before I go further, I need to explain those lists. Those lists you are holding." She pointed at the papers bunched in Simm's hand. "They are from Coffee Joe. He forced them on me this morning at the coffee house. He was angry because he had been trying to give me lists of men for weeks, and I refused to take them, and I refused to help him find the men on the lists. Today, I was tired of fighting with him over the dratted things, so I brought them home to burn.

"I was just about to throw them onto the fire, but my feet were cold. I never even read them. I did not want to read them."

She rushed on, "Now I will tell my story. I have no guilt about my real work, I will tell you everything. Then if you think I should hang for what I did, I will, with pride."

Simm wanted to take her in his arms and promise that he would move mountains and walk through oceans to prevent her from hanging, but not yet. "Before you go on I need to dwell a moment more on the lists. You say that Joe at the Liberty gave them to you? And that Manning planted ideas, so that people there heard them? Does Joe know E.P. Manning well?"

"I think he must. I've seen Manning sitting there regularly.

Joe doesn't have to let him spend so much time at the Liberty. He could throw the man out. He's thrown out others, but I've never seen Manning and Joe with their heads together, either."

Simm explained, "I'm afraid Manning is not above assassination, especially if he can make it look like it was done by someone else – someone he wants to discredit. That's what those lists are for.

" Truly, Becky, I cannot tell you how enormously relieved I am that you are not working for Manning." He sighed, letting out air from his lungs he had been holding since he'd found the wet cloak.

"Now, tell me everything about your perfect maps and sketches. Whatever you've done for George Washington, since you haven't killed any of us in our sleep, is entirely up to you. Frankly, I can't say I wouldn't have done the same if it was my town, my country.

"And to change the subject for yet another minute – one professional to another – the design of your cloak is absolutely genius." Simm poised to separate the compliment from the demand. "But *Milady*, your story please. He spoke the last in a tone Rebecca recognized as the demanding voice he used when he insisted she not calm herself with her own hands on that hot night, so long ago.

This was a different sort of demand, but the outcome might be the same. Rebecca felt a warmth tingle over her body. She looked deep into Simm's eyes. She wanted to see the ice melting into the sexual hunger that was always lurking when he looked at her. It was not there, but there was a small smile edging in around the cold steel. Trusting that her tale would not lead to further disdain, she looked down at the old, well-used kitchen table. She sat down in the chair across from him, carefully spreading the green ribbon on the table. She smoothed it with both hands. With a deep relaxing breath, she began her tale.

"It's all very simple, really. Last fall, before the fall of Philadelphia, before you all came to live here, Nat came to ask that if the town did fall, would I help General Washington by counting troop arrivals and sketching warships, drawing maps of the area – anything to give them an idea of what life was like in the town." She continued her story until she felt she had unearthed all the hidden ends. She laid all her work in front of him, waiting for him to declare her a traitor, or not.

Simm had listened carefully, waiting for the treason to emerge. "Tell me, you are the girl who bribed guards with baked goods?"

"Yes. And a gentle smile, and I listened to their stories. They liked that. They are very nice boys."

"You know half the staff was crazy wondering what the 'girl in the blue cloak' was up to?" Simm found he was also relieved that she found the guards were little boys in need of sweet biscuits. He felt the knots in his chest begin to loosen. "Rebecca, did you ever come into our rooms and plant, steal or copy documents?" He spoke carefully, willing himself to listen, though he was afraid of the answer. They had all left so much around, so tempting to someone working as a spy.

Rebecca held herself very straight in her chair. "No. Joe and Nat wanted me to. They said they would protect me. I explained over and over that it wasn't protection I was worried about. I wouldn't betray my family, and you, all of you, had become my family. I made that clear to them, as clear as I could. No, John I did not plant, steal or copy anything here or at Amalia's. I never even considered it.

"On the other hand, taking materials to the cave was fun

and easy. At least it was until Joe got involved near Christmas, late in the fall. He asked me to gather and deliver things from other people as part of my deliveries. That's when I created the cloak, so I could carry it all without being noticed.

"Lately though, it hasn't been fun at all. Joe wanted more. He wanted soldiers' names, and owner's names on the maps that showed the houses where troops were quartered. I told him the number of troops quartered in a house was one thing, but knowing names was different. No one could explain why the Continental Army needed to know a man's name. But, I could think of why someone like Joe might want them.

"Joe really wanted me to fill in the maps, and he wasn't beneath emotional blackmail. About a month ago, that fiend asked Nat to order me to find the names to place on the maps. You heard us fight when you were on the mattress in the kitchen. I refused to do it. It did not matter to me who was asking, I wasn't going to do it – it is wrong."

Simm looked at Rebecca with a new admiration. She had tread a line between alienating her spy masters and committing treason against a formidable might. She had insisted on doing only what she thought was acceptable, and avoided what she believed was militarily unnecessary, even as Joe and her favorite brother were trying to pressure her. He wished he could have supported her more, but realized, ruefully, how impossible that would have been.

"Rebecca Willent, you are a marvel – go on."

"So then, I was away from the Liberty for weeks, first because of your injuries, and then because of my reluctance. This morning, I finally went back, and right away Joe insisted I take those lists and fill out the information he wanted. Those lists." She pointed to the papers stacked neatly in front of

Simm. " Those lists I intended to burn."

"Don't burn them. I'll keep them, I want to give them to Howe, if that is all right with you?"

Rebecca nodded her consent. "Please take them if they will help you. But I'd rather dear William does not know where you got them."

Simm laughed, at last. "I'll tell him they fell into my hands. Bosses don't ask spies how they come by their information.

"Becky, I don't think the lists have anything to do with the American cause. I think Manning wants Nat, or maybe this Joe fellow, to act for him - against us. The men on those lists are all William Howe's personal staff. And two of those men – good men, men with real interest in creating good relations between Britain and America – have disappeared in the last few weeks. Now, I think the worst. And I think Manning is behind their disappearance."

"Oh." Rebecca inhaled sharply, relieved and sad that her assumption was correct. This kind of personal war was harsher than anything she had considered. She knew men died in war. As horrible as the battles around Philadelphia had been, at Brandywine, at Germantown – war was not supposed to be about assassinations. She sat still, listening to the ice-cold rain rattle the windows, and the warm crackle of the logs on the fire.

She waited for the energy in the room to shift away from her and her story. She watched Simm, waiting to see a final lessening of the tension on his face. Finally, he stood, walked to the door, and put the lists in his saddlebag. He re-rolled the maps and documents and put them on the side of the room, near the drying cloaks.

Rebecca felt shy, watching him move about the quiet

room. "John, You always listen to me. You know, I wanted to tell you, to ask you so many questions I could not ask anyone. That's why cried at night. But you have always believed in me; taken me at my word. And you've saved me – from my father, from those men, from my fears and sorrows. No one has ever been so good a friend to me. I'm sorry if I've disappointed you. John, you have owned my heart, and my body, since that morning at the dock." Rebecca got very quiet, speaking barely over the noise from the windows and the fireplace.

Simm remembered watching Rebecca walk down the mews away from him, to the old dark-skinned driver sitting on the carriage. He relived the feeling he'd had at that moment, that the gods had torn his heart from his chest; the purest fear, that he would never hold, never taste, never see this woman again. And last fall, when he had spied her over the tops of the billowing sheets, he thought that perhaps the gods were not so cruel.

Simm stared at her now, marveling at her beauty and bravery, letting the knots in his chest and stomach melt away. He looked her over, as a man looks at a beautiful woman who is willingly his.

She wore that unusual gown accentuating her beauty with every move of rustling petticoats, and a faint hint of a flowery perfume that delightfully belied the housekeeper she had been all fall and winter, and harkened back to the entrancing young woman he had known the year before.

"Disappoint me?" He spoke the words dismissing them. At the same time, he moved toward her across the room. Simm pulled her into his arms and covered her mouth with his, claiming her and dispelling any doubts that may have lingered about his feelings.

Rebecca ran her hands through his hair, pulling it out of its queue and letting it hang onto his shoulders. She felt him deepen the kiss and she grew into him, melding that kiss until there was no distance between them. She let her head fall back in rapture, knowing that this time their kiss was not the finale, but a glorious beginning.

Rebecca's hands were still working their way through Simm's hair, claiming him as he had so often claimed her. She looked at him then, realizing that she'd had few opportunities to watch his ecstacy as he had hers. Taking a moment to stare at his beautiful face, relaxed and expectant, she saw a vulnerability in his eyes she had never seen before, even when he was shot and bleeding on this very floor. She saw, in that minute, that his fear that she was a traitor and an assassin was greater than hers of trial and hanging. "Oh Simm, I am so sorry. To put you in that position even for a second, breaks my heart." She put her lips against his, pulling him down into her for a kiss even more intense than the last. Simm felt his body stiffen and his fears flee in the face of the soft beauty pulling his lips to hers, as her luscious body pushed against his. "Mmmm, ambrosia, you are food for the gods." Simm nibbled her lips as he sat down in the hard kitchen chair with Rebecca neatly in his lap. He pushed her back over the table, untying and easing her bodice down to expose the breasts that had been taunting him all afternoon in that enchanting green gown. He kissed and suckled them while Rebecca groaned and mewed. She lay half on the table where he had watched her knead bread and cut onions. How many times he had wanted to take her as she worked her bread dough, how many times had he wished he were that bread? Now Rebecca's soft song, and his murmurs, added delightful additions to the noise of the storm in the late afternoon light of the dying kitchen fire. He moved his leg between hers and he raised her skirts, pulling her hard onto his leg, catching her rhythms and pushing her harder.

Rebecca accepted that Simm needed to return to familiar patterns, something he recognized and could control. What had passed between them, even though they would marry soon, was too close to the bone even for admitted lovers. She let herself float on the sensations Simm was producing in her body, becoming desperate to go upstairs and forget she had to deliver the papers to the hollow rock. "You know, Becky?" He pulled her back up from the table into his lap, fixing and retying the bodice. "I'll go and saddle Artemis. We'll ride. You take the reins, you know the way."

Simm grabbed his damp cloak and went out the door; then he turned, smiling, "Maybe while we're there, I'll ask Nat for your hand – it might be fun to watch him react, since he has bested me at all our previous negotiations."

Rebecca looked at him with eyes that pleaded for more. "Lady," Simm teased as he closed the door to keep the heat in and the rain out, calling as he left, "tis your task, not mine, and we must leave." In the barn a few minutes later, Rebecca was ready with warm layers of clothes, and the documents again hidden in her cloak. Simm threw her on the horse and mounted gracefully behind, wrapping his arms around her, and pulling her into his arms and his larger, warmer cloak.

Simm was pleased to have Rebecca in front of him on the familiar horse. He ran his hand slowly over her hip inside the warm wool, relishing the shape of her body next to his. Not far from the farm, the path turned off the well-used road. Simm was sure that even in bright daylight he would never find this trail again. He analyzed his feelings; he would have thought he would be angry at discovering Rebecca was a spy, but instead of feeling betrayed or bested by such an efficient enemy to the King's cause, he was delighted that he would have such a careful and intelligent wife.

"Rebecca?" Simm spoke in low tones, below the rain, rather than announcing their presence by screaming above it. "Would it be presumptuous to assume that you would give the care and protection to our home and children that you have given the preparation and delivery of your manuscripts and maps?"

In response, Rebecca fell back into him just a little, letting her body lean against his, as answer his question.

In a short while they arrived at an opening in the wood. Simm took in the scene. There was a rock outcropping on the right, no doubt where the "cave" was. In front of them was a natural meadow, the new grass apparent, even through the ice that covered the ground. The rain had finally stopped, so though the ground was cold and covered with rough, crunchy sleet, the clouds were racing away, leaving late afternoon gloom and a weak sun in their wake.

"Becky, how was it we did not go by the guard house where you plied the young men with sweets?"

"Plied? Humph. We turned off the road and went into the wood sooner than I would if I were walking. It's shorter, but if someone had noticed me taking a path that bypassed the soldiers, I would have looked suspicious. The rain made it easy today. I often come home that way if it's dark, but not pitch dark. I don't know, but I didn't think you'd want to explain your presence to the guards. You did sign my first pass, did you know?"

"Actually I did know. It was brought to my attention when the general's staff was busily hunting for the 'girl in the blue cloak.' I had to confess I'd not actually laid eyes on her. "

"Did you get into trouble for signing the pass?"

"No, Majors don't get reamed out for that, needs to be something interesting, like having the woman you live with commit treason, and not notice."

"Or if you helped her?"

"That! Lets get this over with, there is something else I want to accomplish this evening."

Simm dismounted and reached up to help Rebecca down. He pulled her against him, telling her again, with his greedy hands on her body, exactly what else he had planned for the evening. Rebecca turned and smiled at him, "Simm, stay here in the scrub; let me do this. I hear a horse coming from the direction of the Forge. I'll be done soon, and we can leave." She motioned for him to stay behind the growth, while she continued on the path toward the rock.

Chapter 15

Simm walked Artemis away from the clearing. He dropped the horse's reins, letting her graze on the new grass. He stood hidden, watching Rebecca put the rolls of paper in the protected rock and wait for the rider. Simm gazed across the meadow in the clearing afternoon. He could just make out the rolling hills and valleys that made the area so pleasant. It was a lovely place, he thought, and must be magical in the summer with the rocks and the dappled shade of the trees. Simm could see why the young Willent children would have delighted in finding this place and playing here.

In a few minutes he heard the sound of hoof beats, and saw a man in the uniform of the Continental Army ride into the clearing. Nat waved to Rebecca and quickly dismounted. Running over, he picked up his little sister for a hug and spun her around. They chatted quietly for a few minutes before Rebecca took Nat's hand while they talked.

Simm enjoyed the ease with which they greeted each other, thinking how jealous he would have been by this only a day ago. He was pleased was that Rebecca had such family, even though he had every intention of taking her far away from Philadelphia. The dripping from the trees died down as the wind let up, and he could hear Nat and Rebecca speak over the steady drip of water from the trees.

"Rebecca, you can't stop now – we've come to rely on your maps and charts!" Nat commented with military command.

Simm was again impressed as Rebecca withstood even that kind of pressure from her brother. "I don't really believe you. Nat. You know where all the streams, bridges and houses are as well as I do. Anyway, I'm done. I've said it, and it's final. I've sketched every boat in the harbor, made a map of every street and every house. I've put a little 'x' on the spots where soldiers are quartered, with a general number showing the number of bedrooms in each billet.

Nat was pleading now. "Joe says that you could do so much more to help us understand what is going on in Philadelphia."

"Joe says? Nat! Nothing special is going on in Philadelphia. People live there, they do the best they can, the army stays as quiet in the houses as they can. They muster and march around the parks, exactly as you'd think." Rebecca's voice got so quiet Simm had to strain to hear her. "Nat, I thought Joe worked for you. Does he give you orders now? Do your superiors know? Does General Washington know?"

At Rebecca's accusations, Nat looked flustered, but after a short moment of silence he pulled himself together. "Joe does not give me orders, but he has some good ideas, and we listen to him."

"Well you shouldn't!" Rebecca bit her tongue, wanting to tell her brother he was being manipulated by the King's man. Instead, she took a deep breath, prepared to ask one final question. "Nat, if I am making these crazy, dangerous journeys in mud and ice, past soldiers and marching sentries, to get these maps and documents to you, how is it you see Joe often enough to get ideas from him?"

"Just words in the street or some drinking at his place. He couldn't hand us anything without being seen, I promise, Bec.

But really, we could use your work if you'd continue. There is really so much more to know."

Simm couldn't hear Nat as the younger man continued wearing at his sister, praying on her loyalties to her big brother and the American cause. He watched Rebecca go from angry to forgiving, ready to give her dear brother anything to keep him happy, he figured. As a member of a large and interwoven family, he knew precisely what she was experiencing. But Simm knew there was no longer any choice in this matter. Rebecca needed to be finished with this project before a harder heart than his caught wind of it. On top of Rebecca's involvement, it was apparent to Simm that this Joe was either working for Manning directly and knowingly, or was naive and being manipulated by him. Simm was not sure if they should trust Willent with the bits of information they had gathered concerning Manning, or simply get Rebecca out of it and leave here. Simm was sure that the final answers concerning the man in black would not be uncovered in this round.

Listening for a good jump-in point, Simm listened to Nat plead and Rebecca resist, until she said,

"Oh Nat, I can't, you just can't ask me. Please!"

Simm had had enough. She was weakening, and the "what ifs" of her discovery almost paralyzed him with fear. He stepped out of the brush where he had stayed hidden, and into the misty clearing. He pushed back the black cloak off his face and open just enough to show his bright red officer's uniform and very clearly spoke, "No, Becky."

Nat spun and looked at man he knew slightly and probably didn't want to know at all. "FitzSimmon! Why are you here interfering?" And for the first time he saw the black horse loose in the meadow, prancing in the mist.

"Willent," Simm began, "I will be as quick as I can be, so we can all go back to our houses out of the damp. Well, not our houses, I respect that I am in yours, or at least your father's, but still out of the rain and cold." He continued trying to be as conversational as he could. "For a number of reasons associated with an ongoing investigation, it has become very dangerous for Rebecca to continue. We were sent a message, one I gather you did not fully understand. Rebecca was attacked, and very nearly badly hurt, by some men known to a colleague of your man Coffee Joe. In fact, this man sent those deserters to your wood. I have no doubt he would send others, either to stop Rebecca or to try frightening her friends away.

"I'd rather not elaborate further, but Joe is being watched and perhaps manipulated. Rebecca has come to this other person's attention. Right now he knows nothing substantial about her, but he is concerned, and has made it clear in many ways that he does not trust her, and is watching her. That distrust can only grow. She must stop her trips here."

"FitzSimmon! You, still haven't explained why *you* are here. With Becky!" Nat was becoming visibly angry; protective and increasingly possessive of his little sister. He looked like he wanted to beat this man who got to spend time with his treasure, his Becky, while he was living in a subhuman hut in the mud, learning a manual of arms that had been translated from German to French to English, earlier the same morning.

Rebecca saw the anger, even hatred and jealousy, in her brother's face. She turned to him and took his arm, leading him away just a step or two.

"Nat, things have changed. John is here because he wanted to save me having to walk ten miles in the freezing rain. Right now, I think he is the only person alive who cares if my feet are frozen or not. He has been a true friend to me all winter, and I don't want to lose him."

Nat jumped. "You're not following his regiment. I'll tie you up till he's gone."

"No, I'm not, We'll leave. We can't live here. Joe has polluted too many people about me. Think of that, all my wet tired feet and Joe and his cronies think I am a traitor."

"Maybe that's because you've gotten so close to the redcoats who live in YOUR house!" Nat nearly spit the words out, his anger now directed at his sister.

Rebecca wasn't shy about telling her big brother what she thought, "Nat! Whose idea was it that I allow the men to quarter in the house? If I recall, you conspired with Da and Amalia to let me get a dowry that way. Should I have poisoned the men and been hanged for murder instead of taking care of the household and Da's farm?"

Nat knew when he was defeated. "Okay, Rebecca. I guess I am glad you did not turn on us and help the British instead. I am sure with you they would win in an instant."

Simm laughed, "Willent, on that we can certainly agree. You do understand that my intentions are to marry your sister?" And with that, Simm took Nat's arm and led him away from Rebecca and out of earshot.

Rebecca wondered what they were talking about. She saw their heads together in brotherhood and their eyes flash warnings at each other. Eventually they walked back into earshot. They had been discussing the promise of America and Rebecca overheard Simm's last remark:

"It's the possibilities, the potential, that draws one in. Of course, getting Rebecca makes it a done deal. I doubt she would do well in a small, old medieval English village, and there is no good reason for me to go back."

Nat looked satisfied with the situation. Rebecca walked over to the men and linked her arms between them. "Friends? At least someday, please, Nat?" She turned to her brother, "I'm sure you've realized that John is not unsympathetic." Nat nodded and put out a hand to shake Simm's. That required Simm to drop Rebecca's arm; he did so, and shook Nat's hand with pleasure.

"Now Rebecca, give your brother what he really came here for, and let us return before we are missed." His voice was a shade heavier than it had been, and Rebecca was again aware of the danger that hovered just over them. She motioned to the rock. They walked over, and she pulled the rolled papers out of the dry cave and handed them to her brother. She kissed Nat good-bye, and waited for Simm to whistle for the horse.

The men had been so busy creating a friendship in the space of only minutes, and Rebecca had been distracted waiting for her brother and Simm to come to blows, that none of them had noticed the horses. In the far end of the small clearing and into the woods, Metacommet and Artemis had been busy, too. The two horses had met and seemed fond at the farm the few times they had been stabled together. If horses could have a romance, these two appeared to.

On the far side of the small clearing, they were nuzzling and making noises that were most unseemly. Rebecca recalled the signs Simm had obviously ignored, showing that Artemis was in season. But it was clear now that Metacommet, the resplendent bay stallion with Appaloosa blood that their Uncle had brought back from voyageuring in the Michigan territories, had smelled her as soon as he cantered over.

"Simm, would you consider changing Artemis's name if she is no longer the virgin hunter?" Simm did not immediately turn toward the horses. So, to grab his attention, Rebecca spoke a bit louder, "I think Simm, Artemis may need to change her name to Hera." Simm looked at the horses trotting around the clearing, with Artemis showing a certain well-earned contempt for the beautiful stallion. "Well, I guess we are all finished here," Simm chuckled, "The only time I have ever seen a lady look at a man that way, she had already got what she wanted. If there is a colt, though, he or she is going to be magnificent."

Nat made a quiet snapping noise with his fingers, and Metacommet came over. He reached up and patted the bay's pretty head. "Simm, I should think you would owe me some sort of stud fee. But you can owe me till we see the outcome." Suddenly the situation was either comic or tragic, so he pulled his little sister to him for a last hug and loud kiss, mounted the stallion and, sitting high and easy in the saddle, waved to Simm and Rebecca and rode back to Valley Forge, without looking back, and without another word.

"Simm, I know about farm animals and work horses. I really don't know about such beautiful horses" – she patted Artemis's neck – "but can she take you the whole of the journey?"

"For the next three or four months easily, and as far as New York, yes. Then I think we'll get us passage on a ship up to Massachusetts. I'll stable her at my brother's near Salem, until I'm settled. That colt might be very valuable." Simm gave his low whistle, and Artemis trotted over. She stood patiently while Simm re-saddled her. He helped Rebecca onto the horse, and quickly mounted behind.

They rode a while in silence, listening to their own thoughts. The stream water was running, trees were dripping, and sleet was crunching under the horse's hooves as they made their way down the faint trail back toward the road. Simm broke the silence. "Will you miss your adventures?"

"Honestly," Rebecca answered after thinking for a brief moment, "I probably will. I have felt very important, part of something so much bigger than myself. But I won't miss the wet feet." She wiggled them in the stirrups, making the metal jingle.

As they approached the open road, the mist of the storm finally gave way to a bright sunset. Even though the air was significantly cooler than it had been, the wind was dry and promising. Simm was able to push Artemis to a faster pace, and they were back at the farm before full dark.

Rebecca ran into the kitchen to stoke the fires and heat the stew that she'd set before they left for her last adventure. Simm dried and fed the horse, and did the few chores left on the nearly-empty farm. He was nearly done with the milking when Rebecca came in to see how he was doing.

"Simm, if we have to separate, how will I find you? Manning found me today, and walked me part of the way home. He was very sure of himself – told me never to be seen with you. I didn't tell you earlier. It was a problem for the future, and we were busy dealing with the past and present." She let the rest of the explanation hanging, unsaid.

"Go to Massachusetts. Can you start in Boston, with your mother's family?" Rebecca nodded. " Good then, you won't need to find me. Settle north of Boston by late summer, into Salem, Beverly, or any of the towns on the coast in Essex County, and I will find you. The towns are small, and I know people in the area." Simm spoke with such quiet passion and certainty that Rebecca had no doubt that he would find her. "Love, I don't know how long my own journey north will take, but I will be there before autumn." She looked into his ice blue eyes. He nodded, and then carefully put the bucket with the chicken feed back on its hook, away from the pecking birds.

He slowly pulled Rebecca into his arms, telling her, without words, that he would be there, that he would never abandon her. He let her go so she could get the meal served and his staff out of his way.

"Move aside, the cook needs to get there first!" Rebecca shouted into the farmyard as the men headed toward the house for their dinner. They had, to a one, waited out the storm in Philadelphia, and were all arriving later than usual, but "Sarge, you're late, too!" the men bantered back, with the same good humor with which they had always greeted their "little sergeant."

Later, after farm and kitchen were tidy, and Simm's staff were busy with cards, books and music in their rooms, Simm strode into the kitchen to find Rebecca tending the fire and setting the doughs for morning. He waited until she was finished with the simple tasks, breathing evenly, aware of every movement she made. He watched her finish and turn to him. He walked to her, and lifted her effortlessly into his arms. He carried her to the narrow back stairs. Leaning down to open the door, he kicked it shut behind him, and climbed to his room on the next floor. A fire had already been set, and the room had lost the chill of the stormy afternoon.

Simm set Rebecca on her feet and turned to close the door to the stairs. He turned to look at Rebecca, who stood framed by fire light. He saw no reason to move quickly. He just stood still, enjoying the moment, relaxed and very happy to have Rebecca's secrets fully revealed and the beautiful blonde in his room.

She looked him over, head to toe. "I'm going to paint you." She spoke while studying him.

"Do you paint?" Simm was no longer shocked at the things Rebecca knew how to do, but was always curious when he might know them all.

"I do, but all my things are locked away. Father didn't like me to do it, and there is no room at Amalia's. She paid for lessons when I was younger, and took me to Europe for a year when I was fifteen. I studied with James Peale until he left to fight last January. Maybe someday I'll paint again."

"We'll make sure you paint again, Becky; I'd love to have you paint me."

Rebecca moved closer to Simm and moved her hand like a paint brush over his clothes. He let the sensation of being touched overwhelm him, but then he picked Rebecca up by her elbows and put her a foot away from him. She leaned backwards and sat on the bed, falling back into the soft feathers. She let her legs fly over her head, showing petticoats, shift and a quick view of silky pink thighs.

Simm felt like the most noble of men when he asked, "Rebecca, we are marrying as soon as we can speak to a minister about a ceremony. Do you want to wait?"

"Aargh! What? Wait?" She nearly shrieked. "John, not only do I not want to wait, I want at those beautiful silver buttons on that uniform, now, one at a time, very, very slowly." While speaking, she had climbed off the bed and walked over to where Simm was still standing. She crooked a finger in his waistcoat. Slowly, she guided him back to the bed and pushed him down on it. She sat next to him, leaning over to unbutton the first button of the uniform. It was polished silver over pewter. She had heard that the enlisted men's were pewter only. The jacket was only buttoned with two buttons, so Rebecca slowly pulled it off of one of Simm's arms and then the other. The waistcoat offered many more buttons. Running her hands teasingly over his chest till he stiffened in response and moaned a deep growl, Rebecca unbuttoned one button from the top and then one from the bottom, slowly teasing the space between, as he had done so often to her. She worked her way from the ends to the middle. Finally, when the last button was done, she pulled it off his shoulders and dropped it gently to the floor. And then, it was on to his beautiful white shirt.

Rebecca had seen Simm dressed in his full uniform nearly every day since he'd arrived. She had never seen a thread out of place, a tarnished button, or anything other than crisp white linen, perfectly-pressed buff breeches, and cardinal red wool. She admired his perfection. Now he was hers to undo, and the crisp white shirt needed to come off. Simm's cravat was tied over the shirt, and Rebecca had a wicked desire to see his bare chest with the cravat still tied. Rebecca put her hands under his shirt. She pulled the white linen over his head. He sat up to oblige, and then put his head back on the pillow.

"There." She fixed the cravat with the ruffles just so. Leaning back on her heels to examine him, as an artist would a subject; moving forward, she kissed his lovely chest. Rebecca ran her tongue over a small hard nipple, biting and sucking until her own body began to react to what she was doing to the lovely man in front of her. Pulling herself back into the moment, she moved to the other nipple, teasing him until he moaned and shifted his hips. She sighed "no," and pulled off the cravat in one motion. "I think tonight has no need of a frilly cravat," she proclaimed, as she ceremoniously dropped it to the floor with the other uniform parts.

"Well, Rebecca, how will you deal with the boots? I fear

they must be next." Simm was nearly in a state of full arousal, but he was still going to enjoy Rebecca's next task thoroughly, and he fairly twinkled with glee at the thought of Rebecca dealing with his form-fitting riding boots.

"Just wait a minute." Rebecca ran from the room.

"In retreat?" He shouted after her. "So soon in the battle?"

"Retreat? Never, sir, never!" Rebecca shouted over her shoulder, reappearing just a half minute later with her voluminous kitchen apron. She put the apron on over the green wool dress, tying the strings in the back. She pushed Simm back down onto the bed.

Simm had had enough teasing foolishness for the moment. He grabbed for her, and in one motion had her under him. Rebecca lay back and let his kisses pull her toward ecstacy, his tongue following the line of her neck to the swells of her pale pink bosom. He made no move to undress her or reveal any more of her delicious body. He rained kisses on her, one hand on her thighs; over her dress and petticoats, he drew trails of the sensations to come. His other hand was on the back of her neck, playing with the soft, silky hair that had escaped from cap and pins. After a moment, he pulled back; turning to the side, he put his boots straight out, daring Rebecca to pull.

It took a few minutes for Rebecca to regain enough composure to sit up, let alone attempt a difficult task. Her first attempt was futile. She stood in front of Simm facing him. Taking the first boot in two hands, she pulled. Simm nearly came off the bed, but the boot did not budge. She stood back and assessed the angle of the boots and the legs. She pushed him till he was under her facing the ceiling. Grabbing his right foot, she put the boot right between her legs on the big apron and pulled. In a short time the boot came off and Rebecca and boot flew to the other side of the room, landing on her backside against the door. She held the shiny riding boot over her head as a trophy. She put down the boot, scrambled back up, and grabbed the other foot, repeating the operation, again landing on her bottom against the door.

They held their breath and waited for some shouts of reaction from the men elsewhere in the house, but the only sound they heard was the front door closing and hoofbeats as someone left for the evening.

Placing her gaze firmly back where it was before she went flying, Rebecca stood back up and addressed Simm. "Ah, yes," she crooned biting her lip, as she untied the apron strings. She threw the big apron onto the growing pile on the floor, and walked back to Simm, who was waiting expectantly on the bed. " Breeches and stockings."

Simm was enjoying Rebecca's pleasure as she undressed him. But it was taking longer than he would have liked, and his desire was already apparent. It certainly would be once she had those breeches off, he thought as he floated back in sensation, and Rebecca began pushing his stockings off and rubbing his toes and calves.

Rebecca knelt on the floor in front of Simm. Gently she grabbed his left leg and slowly unbuckled the garter, pulling the silk stocking slowly down over his calf and foot. She worked with her mouth and hands down his leg, messaging each with hard, small circular motions. She repeated this with the other garter and foot. Finally, she readdressed his feet and legs with kisses and licks, sucking each toe and working her hands and lips up his legs until she reached his breeches.

Simm lay back across the bed, lost in an ocean of sensation. Every nerve ending in his body was alive and in motion as he fell deeper into the trance of touch. Finally,

Rebecca started to unbutton the last buttons of his trouser pants. Then his body tightened, and he pulled her hands away.

"Becky, not so much too soon, or you'll spoil the fun. I don't advertise it, but I have not been with anyone for quite a time."

Rebecca was curious and a little shy at that. "How long?"

John almost whispered it, not sure if she would feel proud or horribly guilty. "Not since a hot night in the summer of 'seventy six."

"Oh." Even the unflappable Rebecca was stunned. Before she could utter a word, she felt strong arms pull her down on to the bed. Gently and slowly, Simm removed the light wool fichu that was still slightly tucked into the bodice of the green wool gown. He leaned over her, and put his mouth over hers. He held her close to him, deepening the kiss that seemed to last forever with lips, tongues and eyes each doing their own steps to the perfectly-choreographed minuet. Slowly, he moved a hand to her dress and started to untie the dirndl, rubbing his hands over the soft wool and heavenly mounds beneath.

Rebecca's breath quickened and deepened. Her body began to ache with a deep, clenching need. She took a deep breath to be able to speak. "Don't get too distracted, my lord, you are well ahead of me, and there is so far to go." Rebecca motioned to his near-naked state and her own fully clothed one; her gown, with all its intricate layers.

It was not a modern complicated affair. Rebecca wore no hoops and only simple stays, since she had been ready to ride and had dressed herself, so Simm found no trouble undoing all the lacing on the green gown. It came off, and was carefully set aside on the chest, but the stays joined the growing pile of linens on the floor.

Simm pushed Rebecca gently back onto the bed and lay next to her. He ran his hand over her, slowly over the soft linen of her shift. Such fine linen – he had not seen her wear anything so lovely as day wear before this. Although he did not need it, her undergarment proved that she had told the truth when she said that this afternoon, she was going to tell him all. The patterns on the bodice were unusual, even for a fine garment. He lifted and turned Rebecca toward the firelight so he could see the pattern better, expressing surprise and delight as he did so.

He should have already accepted that Rebecca was never what was expected, but he really did not know that sweet young farm-girls had such garments. The bodice was made of cutwork lace with the negative pattern filled in by skin. Into the bodice were worked two beautiful lush roses, and perfectly centered in the petals of each rose was the nipple of a perfect breast.

Simm let out a whoop of joy and fell on her, murmuring continued delight and seeming to devour the roses; first one pink flower and then the other. While his mouth was busy suckling dew from the roses, his hands found their way lower. Staying always on top of the shift, he ran his hand over the length of her hips, only occasionally teasing closer to her inner thighs and the sweet spot between her legs.

Rebecca moaned and tried to get him to increase the pressure, to release the tension that was becoming unbearable. She moved her body under him, and tried to pull her shift over her hips. She was not surprised when he stopped her by increasing the suckling and gentle petting. As before, she wanted to hurry him up, but the weight he was putting on her body was so comforting, she lay back and floated, letting him pleasure her at his own speed.

As Rebecca began to shudder with approaching orgasm, Simm pulled the damp shift over her head. He leaned back on his heels next to her, looking at her, burning with the need to fill, to possess, this woman. This was the end of the frustration that had started that night so long ago. He leaned over her and kissed her, possessing her mouth deeply and fully. He ran his hands over her hips, teasing open the petals deep between her legs. She started and purred, moving her body toward his. Nearly moaning with need, he rose over her, not releasing her mouth from his own. Her open legs pulled him in, and he found himself enclosed in the damp heat of his love's body.

Rebecca woke hours later, naked and chill with damp, but sated and enormously happy. She lay in the dark stillness, listening to Simm breathe. This time, she thought, it is finally the beginning. This time, whatever may befall us, befalls us, not only me and not only him. Relieved to belong to him at last, to plan the future together, she reached up and kissed Simm out of his deep slumber.

Simm left the next morning to find a minister who would marry them on May first, just one month away, in Amalia's living room. They decided they were happy to have banns read, but only in a church where no one knew either one of them.

Reverend Reed was a gentle man. His church was toward the south of town, away from Rebecca's friends and family. "Young man, I know you are far from home, but has the young girl no family? No banns in her home church? Surely there is some time before you leave town?"

"Reverend, Rebecca and I would be pleased if you feel you can read the banns in your own church. But please understand that it would not be safe in these troubled times to make this union too public."

The minister insisted that the couple come to church the following Sunday, when he would quietly read the banns to his congregation, a small Methodist group. The couple needn't stay to claim the good wishes of the congregation. Nor would he insist they attend services again before the wedding. He would meet them, and their friends and family, at Mrs. Willent's on May first, in the early afternoon.

Simm quietly made other arrangements throughout the town. He bought a ring, and left money at a mantua maker, a shoe maker and a haberdasher for Rebecca's use if she needed to remain in town after he left. Either here or in New York, she would need traveling gowns made and some clothes for her new life. Even with Rebecca, he went into only as much detail as was necessary. As the planner of major enterprises and operations, Simm had found that it was usually best to plan as carefully as possible, and then leave room for inevitable contingencies. He thought, with the wry smile that accompanied such phrases, of the total messes that perfectly-planned battles became.

Simm did not tell the general or Rebecca's aunt about the ceremony that would take place in the parlor. He said pn;y that he and Rebecca would attend tea at four o'clock on his last day, May the first. He did not mention any need for special cakes or visitors, but he did stop by Hackett's farm on his way home one evening to extend an invitation to Hackett, Jane and their children if they would like to see him off. Simm even invited old Jasper Willent, but he fervently hoped the man had not heard.

Rebecca and Simm spent every available minute together over the next few weeks, this time anticipating not the wedding, but the honeymoon. One morning, Simm followed Rebecca up to the attic. He hadn't been in the little room since Christmas night. This morning, the room was bright with sunlight streaming through the two miniature windows into the room. Simm sat on Rebecca's small trundle bed, looking around the room.

"Becky, how long has this been up here?" Simm pointed to a large wooden crate that sat in the corner.

"I don't know, I think it was accidentally moved here from Amalia's when I asked for my clothes."

"It's mine."

"Really? What a strange coincidence."

"Turns out. How smart of the workmen to save me the trouble."

"What trouble? I was simply going to send it back to Amalia's when you fellows were ready to pack up and leave."

"Not real trouble, but look at this." Simm moved over to the wooden box and pried open the lid. He reached in and pulled out an old shirt or two, putting them, neatly folded, on the floor. Next he pulled out purple and blue silk velvet breeches, and a dark blue waistcoat with purple stitching and gold, jeweled buttons.

Rebecca gasped at the luxury contained in that one suit of clothes, realizing that it must have been worn at court at least once. The sumptuousness of the fabric and the excellence of the workmanship left Rebecca breathless. She had thought, that hot morning at the dock and again in his rooms, that this man was truly out of her league. Well, it was too late for him to run now. She could tell the purple was not what John was looking for, but she needed to say something about the luxury and the status it portrayed.

"You wore that to court or something; it is truly most

beautiful." Rebecca had not taken her eyes off of Simm or his unpacking. She thought out loud while he looked through his things. "I'm scared for us to leave together ... he won't let us, will he? I feel like we have wasted so much time, this whole winter we could have spent together ... Oh, John, what else could we have done?" Rebecca sniffed and wiped her eyes, stopping her tears before they started.

Simm picked through the trunk. He saw her eye the silk waistcoat and purple breeches. He returned her look and saw his woman in a well-made, simple, dated gown, her feet bare, her silky blond hair loose over her slender shoulders, catching the bright morning light that made its way through the small attic windows.

"No, Becky, that suit is for show, and has come in handy as a costume now and again, but it is not the most beautiful thing." He let his words hang as he looked at her. "You are. You take my breath away."

Simm walked back to the sweet trundle bed covered with the eiderdown and a coverlet of an unusual and intricate candlewick pattern. He knelt next to the bed and picked up the corner of the blanket. The handwork was beautiful, each item was clearly made with care by loving hands. He ran his hands over the two blankets and could feel the love that was part of their making. It reminded him of his mother, and her care for each of her children – wherever they roamed. He thought of his mother's weaving, and then of the tartan Rebecca had started at a time she was sure she would never see him again. He got up, pulled back the coverlets, and sat on the little bed, itself made for a child by a father or grandfather.

"Rebecca?" His voice was husky with emotion.

"Yes, John." Rebecca hadn't moved, watching him connect the blue silk suit and the home- made candlewicking, feeling like the poor relation, until Simm spoke.

"Come here."

"Yes, sir." She took the few steps to the trundle and deep into his arms. He brushed her hair from her face and played with the silky strands as they tangled around his fingers. He drew her to him, and put his lips to hers, losing himself in the wonder of their kiss.

He sighed, leaning back and relaxed against the pillow, Rebecca lying next to him with an arm and a leg over his in order to fit on the little bed. She playfully handled the buttons on his vest, contemplating seducing him right there on the child's bed. Instead, she pulled a hairbrush from her bedside table and fixed the tangles in her hair, before she pulled Simm to make him sit, and began to play with his thick dark hair.

"John?" She spoke in rhythm with her brushing.

"Mm..., yes 'm, I mean." Simm felt like a child or kitten being groomed, and he liked it.

"John, I think you should burn your wig and never wear it again. Will you wear your uniform till New York or Nova Scotia?

"Neither. Civilian clothing and no wig. I'm glad I don't shave my head."

"Me, too." She ran her fingers through his hair, pulling out his queue again, and then worked her fingers back down his back.

"Unquenchable wench." Simm lifted her so she was on her back on the little bed. "Have I told you today how much I want you?"

"Maybe you did, a little." These were the last intelligible words Rebecca uttered until it was nearly time to start the fires for dinner. Simm dressed himself while Rebecca watched. He went over to the heavy crate again. This time he pulled an old army uniform from the bottom of the chest. He shook it out and held it for Rebecca to look at it.

"Why is that important? I see them all over town, and, frankly, I am damn tired of them."

Simm laughed. "Becky, look. This is my second best uniform. I wear it when I might get into a bit of trouble. Sticky places and situations that are trickier than I'd like.

"How sticky?" Rebecca ran her hands over the buttons of the second best uniform.

Simm laughed, turning the jacket inside out." You'll appreciate this – it has a false lining. The pockets are sewn shut to hide money. Right now, what's inside them are all Bank of England pound notes." Rebecca looked shocked, but Simm rushed on, needing to get in the whole before they had to part, even for a few hours.

" But more important for you, when the specie runs out, the buttons are actually solid gold under cheap pewter. I don't know when you will need them, but just in case – when it is safe, have them melted down by a goldsmith. Have him make something usable out of them, coins or bars. Also–" Simm picked up the suit and held a button away from the jacket and, shaking it, made a small rattle – "some of the buttons have gems in them. Not all, mind, but if you shake and listen, you can find one. Mostly small diamonds, but there are a few sapphires and emeralds." Rebecca inhaled sharply, marveling at the riches hidden in front of her.

"Becky," Simm pulled on his boots, his glowing blue eyes saying so much more than his words. He continued, "we cannot predict the future, but money, gold and gems always seem to make the future brighter. This jacket will get you to Essex County. That's the county north of Boston on the coast. The value will help you find a place to stay safe. Wait until I can find you, if we cannot travel together, and I think you may be right – he won't let us." The significance of the suit was clear. She must be ready to travel alone. Rebecca absorbed his tangible answer to the question she had asked.

Simm continued, rushing through everything he needed to tell her while there was still a chance. "In Essex, avoid Jason and Oona, his wife. The association might endanger them. I think Manning knows of him. The man has people everywhere. Send word to Jason and Oona 'from a neighbor or friend,' or – Simm smiled – 'from some brother of a soldier risking his life for King and country.' They will look out for you, even if you aren't aware of it. And most important, I will get there.

Simm rushed on, trying to tell Rebecca everything he had thought of to keep her safe over the next months. "Becky, I am leaving you maps and names. They are in the hollow windowsill in your yellow room at Amalia's. The names are of friends who will help you travel through the Jerseys. Ship whatever you want up to Salem, before you leave. Look for Pierson and Taylor – their offices are near where we met, and Jason's people in Salem will store your crates until you are able to claim them. Ship crates as they are full, one at a time. You can start tomorrow if you like, and no one will notice that you intend to leave.

"Becky, if we avoid Manning and leave together none of this planning matters. But if we need to separate ..." Simm looked down at the floor, not wanting to leave without Rebecca at his side. "Becky, don't plan on traveling right away. There is no reason to hurry, you are not traveling that far. To confuse people who might recognize you, order new gowns in colors you haven't worn before. I happen to know you look ravishing in certain greens, deep raspberries, rusts if they are deep enough and gray. Don't be shy about experimenting, and Manning won't spot you in a crowd if you are not wearing lavenders, blues and such. I have already left money with your mantua maker, cobbler and haberdasher. Order what you will need, and then ship as it is finished, you understand?" Rebecca nodded. She was not happy at the need for such care, but she was ready to do what was needed. "Spend the notes and the small coins of your dowry money first; save the gold buttons for later. It will require someone who would never trust E.P. Manning. Don't do it here or near New York. I trust no one.

"Don't leave Philadelphia before the men start to move out. When the town is busy with packing and moving, slip into the crowd and head north on boat or stage. Don't say good-bye at Amalia's house; leave her a note. I'm worried about Cook and her infatuation with E.P. Manning. I know I don't need to say it, but please be careful." Simm finished, relieved that he had finally given her enough information to keep her safe.

"Sweetheart, I've taken the day. Please forgive me; like a bad school marm, I lectured and ran, but I was supposed to be in at Howe's doorstop hours ago." He kissed the top of her head and headed down the stairs and away. In a very short time, Rebecca heard Artemis's hoof beats.

It was clear to Rebecca that marriage to John FitzSimmon was the correct thing to do. Not only did they have a great passion, but they cared about each other's safety. And she was sure that in time, maybe when things slowed down, and maybe when she felt safely away from the enemy army, she would identify the fluttering she felt when he was near. Now, at least, he would keep her safe and take care to help her escape from Coffee Joe, E.P. Manning, and whatever spy hunter was still looking for the girl in the blue cloak.

Chapter 16

Friday, May 1, 1778 was clear, with bright sunshine and fluffy clouds. The wind was shifting to the southeast, bringing warm, moist air, but no storm lurked, and Rebecca had no problem wearing her new blue silk gown. It was cut for a summer day, but with the light silk shawl she felt she should be quite comfortable. Unlike her other clothes, this was in the latest Parisian style. The gown was not overly complicated and, lucky for Rebecca, it was half-done in the dressmaker's shop, awaiting a second payment that had never come, when Rebecca went in to discuss her entirely new wardrobe.

After the dressmaker's, she'd spent the rest of the day ordering new corsets, shoes and bonnets. All of these were from merchants she had not frequented before, and in colors and styles that would be unusual for her. Simm's advice made good sense. In different colors, someone scanning the crowd would not notice her. Lately, she had seen Manning near Amalia's house too many times to feel comfortable in the town.

She decided she would not wear the new clothes here in Philadelphia, but would begin to wear them, instead, after she left. She had walking and traveling gowns made up for her journey. Summer clothes would be shipped to her mother's cousin in Boston, and anything too warm to be needed in the next few months she shipped to the FitzSimmon storehouse in Salem.

Simm had looked magnificent when he left for

headquarters that morning. If it were possible, his uniform was brighter, and the shirt whiter, than they had ever been. Her only request, since she had to marry a man in a red-coat, was that he not wear his wig. What the General would say she couldn't guess, but Simm was leaving this afternoon, right after the ceremony; in fact, that was the excuse he had given for planning this gathering. If things worked perfectly, she would grab her reticule and meet him on the ship, but that was very unlikely with Manning hovering around Cook. His threats hung heavily over the pretty day, but Rebecca pushed them away, dwelling on the future instead.

Rebecca walked the few miles from the farm into town. As she walked, dirt roads gave way to cobblestones and, finally, to the paving bricks of Amalia's pretty neighborhood. Her mind drifted happily through the past few weeks, the most wonderful time she might ever know. She and Simm had lived together as man and wife, enjoying each other's company and bodies. The men in the house had more than figured out what was going on. She was surprised to find that they were all delighted, since they had suffered with the lovers' anger and frustration, as much, if not more, than Simm and Rebecca had. The men had heartily drunk to their Major and his little Sarge's happiness, knowing the pair would separate, but not the extent of it – not Manning, not the other things. At least – she thought it through, kicking a small stone down the street – the secrets were no longer hers alone.

Simm stared out the front window at the lovely spring day. The breeze floated in, soft and warm with promises of summer and growing crops. He spotted her down the street, walking toward the house. Rebecca was a vision in that blue silk gown. Her beauty always pleased him. Today, it nearly took his breath away. The gown was the loveliest he had yet seen in America, made with layers of translucent silk, each a lighter shade of blue than the one under. The simple cut only underscored the beauty of the glowing fabric.

Simm stopped and stared at the woman who, in mere moments, would become his wife, and then he would abandon her again before the afternoon was over to keep her safe – again, perhaps this time for months. He supposed there might just be a chance he could find a way to postpone his trip and take her with him, or slip her on the ship unnoticed. Her clothes were being shipped north as soon as they were finished; she could travel in anything, as if he cared. He held out that hope while he went over the work of the past months.

For all the joy he felt at marrying and moving on, his recent memories felt like a list of failures and regrets. He was sorry to have to leave Philadelphia so soon – sorry too, that their project had been ended by the American treaty with France. Simm had given Coffee Joe's lists to General Howe. He had heard nothing more, but from then on, no one from their group had gone missing. In his line of work, that had to be enough. He was sorry to leave his men before the billet was broken up. They had grown very close over the months at the farm. Families were always hard to leave. He had taken the time to tell them so.

The minister arrived just before tea was served. Simm jumped right up from his seat to welcome Reverend Reed and explain to Amalia that he had invited the pastor to tea. Amalia graciously welcomed the minister, giving Simm a questioning look. Tea was served, and though the Reverend refused a cup, preferring plain hot water, Simm's staff came down to join the growing well-wishers.   By now Amalia Willent was thoroughly baffled.

Rebecca spoke to her aunt. "Amalia, Hackett and Jane will be here very soon, and we can begin."

"Begin what, Rebecca dear?"

"My wedding. I didn't want you to miss it."

"Your what? Oh, that is why you are wearing that delightful frock."

Just then Annie opened the door, announcing the arrival of the Hackett/Willent family, accompanied by Jasper who, Rebecca was happy to see, had cleaned up for the occasion. "I heard he had money." Rebecca overheard her father speaking to General Howe. She would have liked to eavesdrop on the General's reply, but it was time to stand up with Simm before their families, new and old, and take their vows. Never had she meant anything more deeply than she did those vows.

She felt especially connected to the part about "no man tearing asunder," and made a separate, silent prayer that Manning be remembered. Rebecca wanted to tell all the guests how real the possibility of death was, how long they might need to be apart. But their happy friends only heard the traditional words they were accustomed to hearing at wedding ceremonies. That was as it should be.

Rebecca kissed her sister-in-law, brother and their children good-bye as Simm paid the minister and thanked him for his time and discretion. Simm walked the man out and caught up with Rebecca, who was watching her family leave in their carriage, waving them down the street. He came over to her. He put his arm around her and pulled her close, murmuring and nuzzling her ear. He ran his hand down her back, feeling the soft silk, and creating silken waves of yearning down Rebecca's spine.

His message was very clear, but Rebecca knew that the tide was rising and his ship was sailing at eight this evening

– not enough time to go anywhere and still get back to the dock on time.

"We could go up to the yellow room. It's obvious, but we are married now." Rebecca knew there wasn't time. Sea captains liked everyone on board long before the anchor was pulled, especially if an animal needed to be secured.

"No sign of Manning. Do you want to walk me to the ship? Artemis is stabled down there waiting for me." He continued, whispering very quietly. "If we don't see him between now and the docks, come with me now, and we'll send for your clothes from New York." Knowing it was wishful thinking did not make the desire less.

Rebecca smiled up at him wryly. "Of course, let me get my shawl and reticule, and kiss Amalia good bye and thank you. She was amazing; a lesser woman would have fainted."

Simm mumbled, "but not Amalia Willent nor her niece. Brave women in this family!"

"Thank you!" Rebecca replied quietly, thinking how true that was of her mother. She darted into the house to collect her things.

Rebecca and Simm walked toward the ship. The clocks chimed six. The sun was low in the sky, the evening light brightening the sky in the west. They did not speak; instead, they savored the stillness of the early evening, enveloped in their moment of perfect peace.

Their reverie was interrupted when Simm felt cold steel against his neck. He turned to confront Manning, who was holding a knife to his throat, rolling his eyes at Rebecca as he turned. At the same time, a movement at his side caught his attention. Rebecca was being dragged away from him. She called, and she saw Manning's knife being held at Simm's throat. So she did not call for help. Instead, she lifted her head away from her captors and smiled hard at her new husband. As he looked at her, she mouthed one word, telling him to meet her in Essex County, the coastal towns in Massachusetts where he had friends and could find her. Simm nodded to her, pushed Manning away, and turned back to the ship waiting to take him and his horse on board.

Rebecca felt the pistol digging into her side as she was forced away from the pier and down the hill. She heard voices behind her. The first was Simm calling her name, loudly, just once. Then she heard Manning's slimy voice addressing him. She was being pulled away as she looked back at Simm, willing him to let her handle whatever was next, because she knew that if he came to help, Manning would kill him. Then she heard the click of a pistol.

There was another voice, the man pulling and pushing her down the street while holding his pistol into her side. This new voice was gruffer, and he said horrible things about her, as he pushed her down the street. She nearly tripped on rough paving stones, and was caught and held upright by the angry person pulling at her new gown.

Rebecca was pulled along till they came to a deserted square. She almost laughed aloud, realizing that this was the one place in the town without a British patrol, and this was the first time in her life she wanted to see one. In the center of the square was a fire with a barrel of tar being warmed over a fire. A small gang seemed to be responsible for keeping the fire going and heating the barrel. Then there was another bunch holding a young girl in a clear state of advanced pregnancy.

She was crying and begging for help while the laughing group painted warm tar on her. Rebecca wanted to run to the girl and pull her away before the smell of singed hair and flesh got any worse. Then the mob let the girl go, and as she ran away, they poured a bucket of white feathers over the tar, making her look like a hysterical, drunken swan. Rebecca heard the mob yell after the girl, telling her to stay away from lobsterbacks from then on. It was then that it dawned on Rebecca that she was next.

Rebecca was being held very tightly, so running after the girl was impossible, as was escape. She recognized many in the group, but knew no one by name. These were the other spies. Many of them knew of her activities, or knew as well as any of them knew about another. She decided to keep her mouth closed until she knew who was in charge. Then Coffee Joe stepped forward, his big belly nearly popping of his waistcoat and his grizzled beard badly in need of a trim. He wore a crooked tricorn and a smelly, heavy wool jacket. But all complaints about his appearance faded when she smelled his breath. Rum and decay. This was the man meting out justice? This man, damnable Coffee Joe, the man who had asked a young girl he barely knew to put her life in danger for a "larger cause." He was condemning that girl to punishment because she would not do his errands. Or could this be Manning again?

Joe's nasty whine broke into her thoughts. "Now, little Becky Willent, you see what happens to girls who don't act as they should? I asked you for yer help, and you decided to make decisions for yerself. We can't have that sort of insubordination in our group. So much as I hate to burn your pretty body with tar, I really got to set an example."

The others in the group looked expectantly at Joe, waiting – maybe for some sort of signal to start, or maybe for a better reason than simple insubordination to hurt their compatriot. She looked around. These people all knew her, knew that she was the one who did the carrying and the drawing. As she met their eyes, they looked down and away, pretending not to know her. No one said anything.

Joe was droning on about the importance of group cohesion, and the large group was looking at him, shielding their eyes from her. Rebecca did not know if they agreed with Joe's threats or were merely scared of him – too scared to move. She noticed that the man holding her had let his grip lessen just a little bit. Luckily no one had thought to tie her to the end of a rope.

Joe's talking was building in intensity, gathering the anxious crowd's rapt attention. "Now Becky, you understand," he addressed her while looking away from her, to the crowd, "we need you to go back there and collect a bit more data for us. We need to know where are the soldiers are staying. We told you over and over, we need maps with names. So far, my dear, we have given you time and you have not complied. "

"You need?" Rebecca turned to the crowd. "Does General Washington need those names? What information do you and *your* friends need, that the Continental Army does not need?" Joe knew Rebecca had her own contacts, people he did not know. He had no response to her questions, but continued to talk to the mob gathered around him.

Finally Rebecca knew that this event had nothing to do with her so called insubordination. Joe had never attempted to be the head of a group. He wanted to punish her for her success, for her survival in this time of occupation and war. It would prove to his master that he had made Rebecca Willent suffer. Joe probably didn't even know why she needed to suffer. But Manning knew. He would be proud of Joe, and Joe would be pleased by that pride.

She watched the mesmerized crowd listen to Joe's speech. They did not care what she had done to help the Americans. They needed to do something out of the ordinary; they wanted to make someone scream and cry, to make someone pay for the occupation of their city. Joe turned and stared directly at her. He looked at the beautiful blue silk gown, now without fichu or shawl. He leered at her, ogling the low-cut bodice and the skin it exposed. Rebecca felt the power of hatred and disgusting lust in that leer. She shivered at the combination of hatred and lecherousness emanating from the foul smelling, unkempt man.

She was dragged forward toward the crowd. Rebecca shut her mind to the pain and vowed not to give them the satisfaction of her tears. She smelled the tar and the burning feathers as they singed in the heat. She felt it drip down her arms, but they had forgotten to reheat the black goo and it did not burn. To make sure they did not recognize their mistake, she started to cry and tried to pull away.

Soon they let her go. The tar dripped from her hair and the tattered layers of the blue silk gown. Rebecca's arms and face were covered with sticky feathers, but she was sure that she was not burned anywhere. She ran as fast as she could away from the mob, taking the back roads and paths through pastures and woods to her brother's farm.

The girls were chasing the chickens in the yard when Rebecca came running into the yard.

"BeyCaa? Why you crying?" The little ones ran to her, to hug and comfort their aunt.

"Get your mommy, Abby! Please." Rebecca jumped out of the way so the girls would not get sticky tar on their clean clothing.

Jane found her a few minutes later. "Gad, Becky, I don't

know if I should laugh or cry!"

"Laugh, I think. They forgot to make the tar hot, so I'm a mess, but not hurt. Except the dress." She motioned to her body and gown. "The poor gown. I'll give it to you. It's magnificent silk. Cut it down for the girls." Rebecca walked toward the kitchen garden. "Janey, I feel like one of your chickens. Do you think we can get this stuff off of me?" Rebecca swallowed hysteria that was trying hard to break out. She breathed hard for a moment, then allowed herself a few minutes of sheer rage, hysterical laughter and tears of anger. "Shakespearian comedy I think, Jane." She mumbled as Jane pulled her into the kitchen.

They heated water to soften the tar just enough to peel it off. As the water heated, Jane found Hackett, who brought in some turpentine to break some of the heaviest tar. He carefully refrained from passing any sort of judgement about the trouble Rebecca had brought on herself. He kept his thoughts to himself and his mouth carefully closed. Rebecca was glad. Finally, the tar was just soft enough to be removed, and Jane combed warm water through Rebecca's hair.

Most of Rebecca's hair was fine and came clean very easily, but the almost-hot tar, combined with the solvents they used to soften it, had singed and frizzled the ends of her blond hair, and it had to be cut. Jane trimmed, grabbed a clean shift for her sister-in-law, and by nightfall Rebecca was pronounced finished. Her arms and face were pink with having been irritated, but not badly burned. Her hair was four inches shorter, but not so different that it would be noticed, and not unfashionable.

"Jane, you know I can't go on as I have been. I have been thinking it over while sitting here."

"Becky, John will take care of you, why worry now?" As

always, Jane saw the happiest and most practical solution.

"Janey, he's gone. We are to meet in a few months. I would tell you where, but I can't. I will write when it is safe."

"Becky?"

"Nat knows enough of the story. You can ask him about it when I am gone. And speaking of being gone, I think it best to turn the farm over to Hackett and you. I will tell the men to move anywhere else they can find room. I will move to Amalia's until summer, and then I am taking a ship south."

Leaving her sister-in-law a bit stunned at the news, Rebecca went to kiss her precious nieces and nephew good-bye, perhaps for so long they would not remember her. She needed to talk to Hackett about the animals and moving into the other farm. That took only a minute more. She kissed her brother good-bye, waved at her father who had appeared from the sheep shed, and walked home in a clean shift, a shawl covering her shoulders and an old skirt of Jane's.

Back at her own farm, it took no time at all to explain what had happened after the ceremony, and her decision to move to headquarters. After a cold dinner, the men went off to make plans for their moves, and Rebecca went upstairs to pack.

South. Rebecca thought that maybe she wasn't lying to Jane. "I could take a ship south and be let off at the end of the river, then make my way north, back through New Jersey. That would make a good beginning, setting off in the wrong direction." With that strong plan in mind, Rebecca packed old clothes, suitable for traveling on land. At the bottom of the bag she would carry with her was Simm's second-best uniform coat. Carrying the sack, she went downstairs and through the kitchen into the dining room. She carried her sack to the sideboard with her mother's large soup tureen. In it was the money the men had paid her for their rent. They had agreed that all the money would be hers, and that food and firewood as it was needed would come from regiment accounts. She had never checked it, since the money was partly a gift from the men that had stayed at the house. Inside the tureen she found gold crowns and pound notes – more than she could ever have imagined. This would more than pay for new clothes and whatever the trip north might throw at her.

She packed the paper money, a few of the gold pieces and all of the coins in her sack. The rest she distributed between the two crates she had packed to go to the FitzSimmon warehouse in Salem. They contained winter clothing, towels, pillowcases, sheets, and the quilts and lace-edged nightgowns she had made for her trousseau. Rebecca hid the money deep inside the crates, and, with that done, she went into the summer kitchen to pack the seeds she would need for her new herb garden. It was sad; some of the plants would only grow from shoots, and she would have to start then afresh. She took what she could, sure that starting from scratch would not be all bad.

On the kitchen table she left notes for the distribution of her mother's things that were to go to the grandchildren – the little bed to Abby, and the blankets made by their grandmother to be shared between the little girls. She also wrote her good-byes to her family, asking that the loom and dyed wools be shipped to her as soon as she sent her whereabouts. She was sure Jane and Hackett's growing family would be pleased to send off the large, useless loom. So, with the crates packed, ready to be shipped, Rebecca grabbed her small rucksack and walked to her Aunt's.

She got to the end of the dirt road. Realizing that she

would have no better opportunity to write to Nat, she turned around and went back to the farm. She lit one candle in the kitchen, pulled paper from her rucksack, and wrote one last note.

Dearest Nat,

So much has gone on in the past few weeks. First you must know that Simm and I are married. We had the ceremony at Amalia's. Hackett and Jane and Da came. The minister came to Amalia's tea. I would have tried to find you, but General Howe stood up for Simm; I thought you might be a wee bit uncomfortable. (Lord William is leaving for London, by the twelfth of May).

Simm has sailed, and I will leave Philadelphia by summer. I would love to tell you that these plans had been agreed upon weeks ago, but Simm was commandeered by E.P. Manning and forced away from me, with a knife pressed to his throat in case he wanted to come to my aid. At the same time, one of Coffee Joe's henchmen dragged me, with a pistol in my side, all the way down Spruce to Grays Ferry, down by the Schuylkill. They were tarring and feathering a very pregnant girl when I arrived. I wonder if they wanted to warn her not to get pregnant by the enemy again? She was sobbing and fairly badly burnt, as far as I could tell.

I was next. Nat, Joe was very mad at me. I'm not really sure why, but the incident was coordinated with Manning – he was there. Luckily for me, the tar was not too hot, but they destroyed a magnificent blue silk gown that Simm had bought for me, and they took a good four inches off my hair. The rest of me will heal in time.

I am afraid of Joe and Manning, and so I can not stay here at the farm. I have told Hackett to take the animals and move here whenever he will. The men are finding other billets. I am leaving. I told Jane I was to head south. That will have to do for you, too. I am sorry that is all the information I can give you.

I would love to see you before I leave, but it is too dangerous. I will stay at Amalia's until I sail. And that will be by the end of spring. If the fates are kind, I will see you and all the family at the end of this war, and I pray God that I do.

With love- R.

Rebecca folded and sealed the note with a bit of wax, using the seal she had carved when she was eight. She put the note in the sack with her other things and set off toward the field. The night was dark. The moon was not up yet, but the stars were bright on the pretty spring night as Rebecca moved silently over the dirt road. As soon as it was possible, she took the trail away from the road, continuing to make as little noise as possible. She left the note for Nat in the hollow boulder.

Not knowing if Nat was still checking the cave, she tied her blue silk hair ribbon, the last bit from her wedding gown, to a branch of a blooming dogwood – the only symbol she had that she'd been there.

She made the walk back to the main road quickly and without incident. As she neared Philadelphia, she heard hoofbeats on the road behind her. She dodged to the side of the road to get out of the way of the rider, but the horse was reined to a stop right next to her.

"Becky!"

"Nat! I certainly didn't expect to see you so soon. Did you read the letter?"

"Yes, I wanted to catch you before you got to Amalia's." Nat grabbed his little sister for a big hug. "Oh Becky, married! I suppose that's just as well, the way that man ate you with his eyes."

"Nathaniel!" She slapped him on the shoulder. "Don't make lascivious comments about your little sister."

"Becky, will you really leave?"

"I have to. Simm has already sailed to resign his commission in New York. I will meet up with him later in the summer, or the fall."

"South? The war is bound to head further south. We're sure the British have given up on the north. Have a care, Becky. Don't go into the heart of the anger again."

Rebecca said nothing – just looked at her brother, who stared back at her, a worried expression on his face. Finally she spoke. "Nat, you'll have to trust me that I won't. I just can't tell anyone here where we are meeting. I promise that I will write you, when both Simm and I are safe from – " she mouthed the last word – "Manning. I do not when that will be, that's the problem. I do know that the General made him let Simm leave, and his men will keep me safe as long as I am in town. But that will only be till he leaves. And he will leave."

Nat mounted Metacommet and pulled Rebecca up behind him. He rode as far as he dared on Chestnut Street, stopping the stallion on the far side of the square near Amalia's house. "Little Sister, this has to be good-bye. This war has caused so much separation and death, but stay strong. What you've done" – Nat paused, letting the enormity of his thanks for her help sink in – "far outweighs anything those idiots could do or say. But Becky, keep safe. You travel alone?"

Rebecca nodded. She pushed down her tears, knowing there was nothing Nat could do to keep her safe on her journey. She wanted to tell him she was planning on meeting Boston cousins, but that would expose her direction.

"Here." Nat handed Rebecca a small rolled parchment.

"What is it?"

"Clearance from Washington, a note giving you permission to travel as you need to."

Rebecca started to laugh. Her brother smiled and started to ask what was funny. "I have the same note from William Howe. Simm got it for me last week when we agreed that I'd need to flee separately. Thank you for this. Now whomsoever I run into will have to let me pass. I think I will save them, and one day frame them side by side, in my parlor."

Nat smiled ruefully, Rebecca put the scroll in her rucksack and kissed her brother on the cheek. She put her hand up to pat his face, noting how much more grizzle he had compared to the young boy he'd been when he had left to join Washington's forces back in 1776. She looked into his familiar face, memorizing it. Then she turned to go into the British command headquarters in Philadelphia, with a note in her rucksack declaring her allegiance to, and the hard work she had invested in, the American cause.

"Annie! It's me, Rebecca. Let me in." She tapped lightly at the kitchen door, knowing that it was still early enough for Annie to be sitting below stairs, having a last cup of tea.

Chapter 17

Simm got Artemis safely on board the ship, and slipped into his own cabin. His mind knew Rebecca was well able to take care of herself, but in his gut he wanted to run after her. Simply, he wanted to kill Manning and Coffee Joe, two traitors to the cause of English liberties and human decency. But all he could do was worry that they had hurt Rebecca. Simm could barely breathe with that fear. He sent an errand boy to headquarters, to let him know the minute Rebecca got to her Aunt's safely. The nagging worry would not end till he heard good news, and feeling helpless was not something John FitzSimmon did well. He paced his cabin like a trapped animal, knowing that any attempt to thwart Manning would have the man in black calling for the hangman's noose.

It was after midnight when the ship slowly left its mooring at the town, and it was nearly an hour later, when still moving slowly down the tidal river, the boy returned, having used every half-penny that Simm had given him, and every drop of his energy – running, hiring a rider to carry him on a horse, and the ferryman to carry him out to the ship in mid-river, with the message that Rebecca was safely in the kitchen at Amalia's Chestnut Street mansion.

Simm was relieved that Rebecca was safe on Chestnut Street. He sincerely hoped the kitchen was a safe as it sounded. He gave to the boy twice what he had offered for the errand, and sent him off to sleep. Finally, after a day that had been as nerve-wracking as any battle he had planned or fought, he found his own bed.

Spending the night alone, in a small cabin, in a small bed, on board a ship heading away from his new wife, was not what Simm would have planned for his wedding night. Instead, he tossed and turned, worried about Cook and her unhealthy infatuation with E.P. Manning. Dreams, when they finally came, were full of Rebecca running away from her attackers, and coming to him with passion in her eyes and longing in her smile, only to be torn from his arms by Coffee Joe. He woke before daybreak, breathless, his heart beating hard. He rose with the first bells, and went to stand on the deck and watch the sun rise over the vast Atlantic, sailors beginning their work around him in the early light.

The trip took two days, including stops for passengers, and for picking up and dropping off mail downriver from Philadelphia and then along the coast as they headed north. It was early evening when they finally docked at Bowling Green on lower Manhattan. This was the site of New Amsterdam's first fort and cattle market. As always, Simm tried to imagine the area open, with fewer buildings. The park was still marked by the vandalism wreaked on it two years before. Fence parts still lay strewn about the trampled site, unchanged since the day the locals tore down the statue of King George III and melted it into bullets. Simm, who was no longer a fan of the King, could not help but sympathize with the anger the colonists felt toward the overbearing monarch.

Simm collected his bag and made arrangements for his crated goods to be delivered to his office at regimental headquarters. He rode Artemis north through the streets of the town. Even in the dying light, it was clear that New York was a defeated city. The spark that was the town's essence, so clear each time Simm had visited before the battles of 1776 on Long Island and Manhattan, was long gone. The colonists' attempt to burn the town in retreat had left a blight that no one since had cared to mend. The hustle and bustle that should have been the backbone of such a major port was not the movement of commerce – only the comings and goings of the

British Army and Navy.

Adding to the ominous shadow that hung over the city were the two large prison ships anchored in the harbor, ignored and festering. The condition of the formerly-thriving town demonstrated too clearly the way the British felt about their regimental headquarters. New York, the only town in British America not founded by Englishmen, was too important to abandon, and too rebellious to care for.

Simm stabled the horse near his rooms. He changed into civilian clothing in an empty stall. His landlady had never seen him in his uniform, and having lived in her house for three years, there was no reason to give her information she didn't need.

Simm's work had required the keeping of many secrets. There never had been a clear line between friend and foe. So many Patriots wanted full- out war, and there were Tories who wanted conciliation. He'd had no reason to let the kind lady know what he did when he was in New York, especially since those days were quickly passing. He knocked on the front door, and walked into her parlor wearing a blue waistcoat and buff-colored breeches. She knew, after all this time, not to ask where he had been these past months. They exchanged pleasantries, and Simm retired to his room to rest and pack the few belongings he kept in the house.

In general, he had tried to create as little an impression on the town and her people as was possible. The landlady's pretty daughter knocked a few minutes later with warm wash water. She eyed him pointedly, staring openly at his deshabille, his fine linen shirt with no cravat or waistcoat. She licked her lips and smiled. Simm was interested in his own reaction and waited, watching himself as though he was observing a stranger. What he saw was that he did not care.

The girl was absolutely, fantastically lovely, and still it made no difference. Simm thanked her for the water, grabbed her shoulders, and gently but firmly steered her out the door, carefully locking it behind her.

The next morning, as he rode Artemis to regimental headquarters, he bade the town a quiet farewell. There were no knots in New York that needed unraveling, just as there were no longer people there whom he wanted to know. The paperwork to sell-out took an hour. He transferred some of that account to his friend and former valet, Lieutenant Barrow. Before the day was done, he had shipped his crated goods to his brother's warehouse in Salem, Massachusetts, and with saddlebags of food and clothing, he and Artemis set off to follow.

The mare was pleased to see the open road and have the sea spray in her face, so they raced along the coast, through Connecticut and southern Rhode Island. Simm knew to avoid Newport, with the French fleet circling to help the Americans. He might be a declared American, but the cardinal-red uniform in his saddlebag would tell another story. He was done with the war, and wanted desperately to keep it that way.

He rode well inland, avoiding the large coastal towns of Providence and Boston. He followed a northern route inland from the coast, through the colony of Rhode Island and Providence Plantations, then through what he had known as Massachusetts Province. When he recognized the towns of Cape Anne, he headed straight east. It had taken three weeks of careful riding and, at the end of it, Simm and Artemis were in Beverly, surrounded by his brother's family. The colors of spring had changed as he headed north. Summer was nearly full green and the fruit trees in full bloom in Pennsylvania and nearly so in New York, but as he headed north, it was like riding back in time. Days later, on the coast of Massachusetts, leaves were only bright spring green, and the apple trees were showing only the merest hint of their flowers.

Simm stayed with his sister-in-law Oona, and the two children, Martha and Jason Jr., known as J. J., for a few days before he set off for the north. He had a pressing need for Manning's people to see him leave from Halifax, Nova Scotia and sail to England.

He left Artemis stabled with Oona, and hired a small ship to sail out to the channel and wait with him till they rendezvoused with the British frigate *Hampshire*, on its way to Canada. Simm boarded, pulling his uniform out of his bag before the first mate had a chance to press him into service in the British Navy. Simm explained in detail that he was a member of General William Howe's staff, and was urgently needed in Halifax.

Only one day later, Simm was seen in fine wool, linen and silk waiting among the Loyalist evacuees in the salons of Nova Scotia. He wanted to be noted among these people, each one sure that he or she had seen the Major. To that end, he played cards with the men and flirted with the women. Everyone saw him, and everyone knew he was in the town. He made sure to be seen, so that one day when he wasn't – and the ship to Bristol was boarded and launched – no one would have the slightest reason to believe he wasn't already onboard resting in his cabin, and would appear at the captain's table as planned.

The ship sailed, and the one after. So many people were ready to tell his mother they had seen him, and to assure her that he would visit as soon as his business in London was finished, that Simm felt he needed to write to Lady Chardon as soon as possible. It might soon be necessary to let her know what had really happened. He would tell her as soon as he had a completed tale to tell. Meanwhile, she would take the information given as incomplete, and know that her John was up to something again.

Simm left Halifax glad that Artemis was safely stabled in Massachusetts. The terrain was rocky and uneven. It was hard on him, but it would have been even harder on the horse. After three days of walking, he'd reached the western shore of Nova Scotia, and stood staring across the bay at New Brunswick and the Massachusetts territory of Maine. In Conway township, he hired a doryman to row him over to Maine at the next low tide. Meanwhile, he watched the highest tides in the world fill the Bay of Fundy.

While he waited out the tide, he went to explore the little town. He found a general store that outfitted fishermen and woodsmen. He purchased coarse linen and wool undergarments, wool shirts, and breeches, a waxed cotton coat, deerskin singlet and breeches, a leather apron and a leather sac.

Simm took his fine clothing and his best uniform and tied them up with hemp twine. He climbed the hills to a cliff high above the sea to watch as the bay waters rushed out to join the churning North Atlantic. As the water pulled away, he threw the roll containing his fine London clothes, his elegant cravats and bright red uniform – symbols of a life in which he no longer had any interest – out into the fast-rushing waters. As they disappeared from sight, he threw his white wig and best hat after. Simm enjoyed watching the wind fill and tease the head-ware, until they, too, disappeared into the fog and mist.

Eastport, Maine, was a rough town. It consisted of a few

fishermen's shacks near the shore, and inland a few families had built farms in the almost futile attempt to work the rocky soil. Beyond the farms, the beauty of the land overcame Simm's first impression of roughness, as the rocky coast gave way to acres of wild blueberry bushes as far as the eye could see. Just beyond the blueberry barrens was deep forest where extraordinarily tall pine trees grew. It was there, on a tidal river close to the sea and the forest, that he found Rhys Jones's shop, and met the Welshman and master ship builder.

Simm stayed with Mr. Jones in June and through July. During that time, he learned to spot the best white pines for masts, and where and how the other valuable species grew. Many of these he had seen on his journey through the American colonies. He felt comfortable discussing those trips with the taciturn man. It was clear that Jones's skill outdistanced the ships he was now building in his little yard; he would not go into detail as to why. Simm did not ask, leaving the man to his reasons.

Here, between the edge of Canada and the sea, Jones built only ships and boats needed by fishermen in the fishing villages of the northern Maine Territories. Simm learned the craft of the shipwright, coming to understand what a master looked for, and how the designs he had worked on his whole life might come into being. He was not arrogant enough to believe that he would be a master in a month, but Simm was now sure he had the skill to hire the right one, and the assistants that shipwright would need.

By late summer, Simm was ready to journey south to Essex County and his new home. He prayed that Rebecca had found her way north as easily as he was finding it headed south, but he knew that she, even more than he, would have Manning on her trail.

May 1778.

Rebecca moved into her old room at her Aunt Amalia's without a problem. Her Aunt did not ask why she had broken up her household, and Rebecca did not volunteer the information. The servants were clearly curious, but Rebecca knew better than to take any one of them into her confidence. Her silence was rewarded one morning when she walked into the kitchen to ask for milk with her coffee. She had stopped outside the door when she found E.P. Manning sitting at the table, enjoying some of Cook's cake and a steaming mug of chocolate.

Although she preferred listen to their chatter, she knew she must. She stood behind the door, in the corridor, and listened to Manning try to get information from the cook.

"Oh, Sheila, this is truly the best breakfast I have had in America," Manning oozed in between bites of cake.

"Mr. Manning" – Cook was truly taken– "How sweet you are." She returned to her preparations for lunch and he to his chocolate.

"Sheila?" He began after a few minutes. "Why is your dear Rebecca here? Shouldn't she be at her farm?"

"Well, Mr. Manning," Cook settled into her chair for a nice gossip, "I don't rightly know precisely. I know that I made a nice tea, frosted cakes just like Rebecca asked. The Mistress had quite a few for tea that day, the General, and all his staff, and all sorts of others. Then they all left without a word to me. Rebecca, she fairly disappeared, that Major Fitzsomething hasn't been here since that day; not to eat, at least. Our Becky moved in here that very night, late it was. Annie said she carried just one bag, and never said a word why. She's been here ever since, won't say a word about it to any of us. Not one word, quite put out I am, too."

Rebecca moved silently back to the main part of the house, satisfied that she had done the right thing. It was likely that even Annie was untrustworthy in this, but she was needed as company and as potential diversion.

To that end Rebecca kept her busy. The first week, Annie accompanied Rebecca to the shops where Simm had left accounts for her new clothes. Rebecca always spoke to the artisans quietly out of earshot of even Annie. It felt unkind to keep her ideas of style and color from her old friend, but she knew she must. Annie must not know about the new colors – the risk of blabbing at the kitchen table over a cup of tea was too high. At the tailor, Rebecca ordered new cloaks – a winter one of a deep rose with a lavender lining, the other for summer to fall, which was of a lighter wool, in a deep green with blue-green lining. She discussed the coming need she would have for traveling with all her possessions and money. Together, they designed the dark green cloak with hidden pockets that would hold paper and coin within reach, but out of sight and hearing. The colors and new styles pleased her very much, and Rebecca was sad that her new clothes needed to be hidden away until her journey began.

The mantua maker had wonderful ideas for gowns, and created a new wardrobe that spoke not at all of a young farm girl from just outside Philadelphia. Rebecca chose well-made fabrics and deceptively plain styles, so that she would not seem to be of a high estate, except to those who had some knowledge of style and cloth. It was at the second fitting for her gowns that a comment by the dressmaker made Rebecca realize that she had better move to New England sooner than she had originally planned.

"Rebecca," Emiline Roth began as she pinned a simple gown for a fit, "you have changed size since you were last here. Is your aunt feeding you too much?"

Rebecca took a moment to answer, "No, Emiline, in fact I haven't been feeling at all well, hardly like eating at all."

"Oh?" Emiline eyed her knowingly. "I will make you some extra gowns for the late summer and fall. 'Tis lovely – you'll be proud to have such nice clothes. I'll pack some scraps you can sew into things for the baby."

Rebecca nearly jumped. "Baby?" she whispered, not wanting Annie to overhear.

Emiline smiled and patted her. "Oh yes, my tape measure never lies. I remember your man when he came last month. Lovely man. Cares about you very much."

"Yes, he does." Rebecca had made a habit of staying silent about when she would see Simm again. It made her sad, but it was better so.

The women finished the fitting in a pleasant silence, and Rebecca gave Emiline money for the extra work on maternity shifts and gowns, while Annie looked at sample patterns and read the latest penny papers from London.

Rebecca had taken to wearing her best linen gowns as daily wear at Amalia's house. She was sure she was watched by Manning himself, or his people. She never even bothered to look for them. For safety's sake she assumed that they were always there. So, she made sure they always saw her in blue. It was easy to wear only blue, since nearly all the gowns that Amalia had ordered for her over the years were blue. Some were outdated, but in the house and around the neighborhood, she never wore any other color.

"Your new clothing has all arrived, Becky, let's look at it, shall we? It's so much fun, boxes and boxes it is." Annie came barreling into the parlor one afternoon ten days after the last fittings.

"Annie" – Rebecca looked up calmly from her needlework – "have it brought up to the yellow room at the top of the stairs. I'll need to check it out before I sign for it." Rebecca waited until all the packages were delivered to her now-overcrowded room. It made her smile, for not too long ago this room had been full of John's dispatches and memos, long treatises, scribbled notes that covered the tables, books about Hannibal and Alexander the Great and letters of all sorts, and now it was full of linen and lace, ladies' shoes and bonnets, silk stockings, and lace neckcloths. She began to open the beautifully-wrapped shipments when Annie came into the room.

"Becky, you've changed colors, nothing in here is blue!"

Rebecca wished that Annie had not noticed. But she had learned to deal with life as you met it.

"Annie, that has to be our secret. I want to surprise Aunt with all sorts of new colors and styles next week after the General has left. Let's just leave them packed till then."

Annie, who loved a good surprise, especially when sprung on her mistress, agreed with a grin. Rebecca knew she would miss Annie. She had known her for years. She was as much a part of the Chestnut Street house as was her aunt. And now she was not only lying to her, but leaving without a good-bye. She put her best hat aside to leave for Annie. She wrote a quick note, and left the hat where the maid would find it when she came in to clean the empty room.

Toward the end of May, as the chaos of packing the headquarters took over, she had crates of her new clothing removed to Pierson and Taylor, ready to be shipped to Boston and Salem. She planned to sail just after her crates left town. Simm had stressed using the same general chaos in order to leave Philadelphia unnoticed. Rebecca heard the great hubbub of General Clinton's arrival as she packed.

She stayed in a state of perpetual anxiety while the regiments packed and moved out of town, while others came in. General Howe's staff moved house at the same time, and Amalia hosted good-bye parties for all the top officers. She wanted to be seen everywhere, so that when she was not there it would be assumed she was nearby. It wasn't until Rebecca was on board a ship heading south that she finally took a deep breath. She pulled her writing paper from the small bag she had with her and began.

Dear Amalia,

I am sorry to leave you without even a kiss good-bye, but things in Philadelphia are too unsafe for anyone to know where I have gone. Just know that I am safe. I will always be grateful to you for all your caring, and I love you beyond words. You are the Best Aunt a niece could ever have. I will write with real information when we are all safe.

Yours with love and enormous appreciation, Rebecca.

Chapter 18

Rebecca boarded a southbound ship, buying passage to Charleston without incident. She did not settle into her cabin, but sought a mate who, for a small number of her coins, agreed to put her off with the mail downriver. It was mid afternoon when they arrived at Chester, Delaware, and Rebecca was carefully let overboard into a small boat. The ship sailed on, while Rebecca and the ferryman waited for the wake to clear and interested eyes to sail out of sight. When she was satisfied with privacy, she let the ferryman row her across the still-narrow river, pleased at the control a little money could buy.

"Miss, don't mind my asking, but do you know what you are doing? Its pretty desolate down here on the Jersey side. You running from somebody?"

"Yes, my father. He wants me to marry someone I'd rather not. My lover waits for me just north of here." She reasoned that a half-truth would come out better than a complete fabrication.

"I reckon that you'll be a'right then. The sailor who put ya off, left these for ya." He handed her a tin of ship biscuits. "You goin' ta need them?"

"Yes, thank you, I believe I am." Rebecca was so tired of pretending that she had not been nauseated by the smells from Cook's kitchen, and now, the motion of the ship, that she leaned over the side of the small boat and allowed herself to spit up into the salty river. Then, to settle her stomach, she opened the tin the sailor had the kindness to send over, and ate one of the biscuits. She offered one to the ferryman once her stomach stopped churning.

"Good Luck! Ma'am, hope you find that fellow soon," the ferryman called after her as she walked up the bank to the road that would take her to the small town of Mount Royal, the first town on Simm's maps of the area. The main road, called King's Highway, was well-used and paved with stones. Rebecca stayed to the far side, away from working carts filled with fish from the ocean, and meat and cheese from the farms. It was getting toward dinner time, and the locals were hurrying up the road toward their homes.

Rebecca walked east away from the river, as the sun hung low over Pennsylvania behind her. She already felt that home was a world away from the flat, sandy soil she now trod. The five miles to town took every bit of the energy that remained in her. Hoping that William Eldridge and *The Death of the Fox Inn* would not be hard to find, she approached a woman calling her children home for their dinner.

"Excuse me, Ma'am, I'm looking for *The Death of the Fox Inn*?" Rebecca felt hesitant, but spoke with her bravest, most polite voice.

"Young girl traveling alone – I don't care for that, I don't, Missy."

"The inn, please?" Rebecca wanted to cry with exhaustion and nausea, but held herself tall.

At that moment a gangly boy of around fifteen came out of the kitchen through the garden door. He'd clearly been in the process of washing for dinner. His shirt was untucked, and his breeches were untied. "Ma!" He turned to his mother, "stop telling everyone what to do." He turned to Rebecca. "You want to keep going that way" – he pointed the way she was going – "at the next crossroads. It's right there; you take a right and you'll see it." The boy turned to go back to the house. He walked a few steps, and looked over his shoulder. "Ma, you coming in to feed the younguns?"

Rebecca was pleased that she had not been required to argue with the woman. She didn't think much of traveling alone either, and if she had been given any sort of reasonable alternative, she would have taken it. She must be a good mother, though – the children looked clean and happy, the yard was swept, and the kitchen garden was laid out and ready for the first summer harvest in a few weeks. The lettuce looked good, and the beans were already nice and tall.

It was a pretty town, although flatter than the world she was used to. The sandy soil probably required some work to get things to grow, but these were industrious people, and their gardens and farms proved it. The inn that, Rebecca noted quite happily, was only another quarter mile from the place where she had stopped, was a stone building, symmetrical with small windows and a sign over the door. The sign said *Eldridge Tavern*, but Rebecca figured that the name must have been changed. Simm's note said she was to look for William Eldridge, however, so that was a good sign.

Bill Eldridge was fortyish and vibrant, with reddish brown hair and all his own teeth. He had the bearing of a soldier, and Rebecca was sure he had been one. The wooden leg that had replaced his own did not slow him down or make him a less genial host. He was helping a young matron, who was probably his wife, serve a table near the door, as Rebecca watched, leaning against the wall, waiting for her eyes to adjust to the darker room and for the world to stop spinning.

Eldridge walked over and addressed his wife. "Suzy, this one looks done in. Set a place up near the fire where we can keep an eye on her."

Suzy Eldridge steered Rebecca to a seat in front of the blazing hearth. She had not known how chilled and tired she was until she finally sat. Now she was not sure she would ever get up again. Eldridge placed a big bowl of stew in front of her. Rebecca started to turn away from the robust smells coming off of it, but she bit right into it when she saw the buttermilk biscuit crust. Gratefully, the stew was just right. and the nausea and exhaustion fell off her while she sat by the fire and enjoyed Bill Eldridge's near-beer and fine food.

Later in the evening, when the locals had left and most of the travelers had found their rooms, Eldridge looked up from the clearing the tables. "So, Mistress, you don't look like you have anywhere you'd rather be." Rebecca shrugged and smiled. The man smiled back at her. "Give me a minute to settle the rest of the travelers, and Suzy and I'll be right back." It was clear that war and chaos had also required flexibility among inn hosts, as it had for herself, Rebecca thought, as she watched the couple clean the tables.

In a few minutes, the Eldridges sat down with her, and Rebecca pulled out Simm's letter to his friends, as well as her own notes and itinerary. Carefully leaning into the glass-covered candle, and using the light from the fire, they read the letter and notes.

"So, you're Simm's wife? Thought he was a little anxious to get back to Philly last winter." The host laughed at his absent friend. "Becky, getting you on the right road won't be a problem. But I think the next battle might be off Jersey by summer. When those two armies come out of their winter dens, it's gonna be loud and bad. Odds are they're goin' to meet about halfway between New York and Philadelphia. That puts them between Middlesex and Monmouth."

"Bill," Suzy interrupted her husband, "I think right now Rebecca needs a good night's sleep and a few days rest, and then she'll be ready to move on. I can tell this has been a long day for her." Suzy Eldridge took Rebecca by the shoulders and brought her upstairs to an unoccupied guest room. She left her to undress, and went to get some warm washing water. "You're traveling light; give me your shift, and I'll just put it in with the kitchen linens which I wash every night. It'll be nice and fresh in the morning." Suzy left, taking the laundry with her.

Rebecca stripped and washed her entire body, ending by standing in the wash water on her aching feet. Then she pulled one of the extra shifts from her sac, pulled it over her head, climbed between the cool sheets of a late spring night, and slept.

A while later, as Suzy brushed out her hair in front of her mirror, she spoke quietly of the day to Eldridge. "Bill, that girl is not telling us everything. Not that it is our business, but I think the way she has her trip planned has her walking too much. Something about that route says she is running from somebody, and I think she is in an *interesting* condition. She can't spend days going up the Hudson to Dobbs Ferry and back down to the Sound. We should find her a boat from Monmouth County right up to Boston. My brother's wife's uncle's boys make that run. You remember him, the one who gave us the Irish crystal candlesticks for our wedding?"

"Smart woman," murmured her husband, already in the bed with the blankets thrown back, "come here. Let's see if I can get you into an interesting condition too." He blew out the candle as she moved into his arms.

Rebecca deemed it unfair that she needed a week to

recover from one day's traveling. But that was the way she felt. It worked out for the best, really, because that way she did not need to find her own way to the next town, as she'd been afraid she would. The Eldridges were due to make a shopping run to the larger town of Mount Holly on Wednesday, so Suzy convinced Rebecca that she might as well stay with them till then. Rebecca's only concern was that she be able to pay these nice folks, but they laughed it off and told her to smile at the customers – it would make the men stay longer and buy more beer.

It was a pleasant few days, but by the end of it, Rebecca was anxious to get on with her travels. Not the least of it was that there was a crate of wonderful new gowns and hats waiting for her in Boston, and here she was, still in southern New Jersey, with one gown and three shifts. But her sac still contained what money she would need for now, and her cloak held what she would need later.

She left a crown for the girl who would come and clean the room, and went down to the great-room to wait for her kind hosts. Suzy was to stay at the tavern, so she waited in the public room to thank her for her kindness and wisdom. Rebecca left the inn and climbed into the wagon with Bill, and they headed the thirty miles or so to Mount Holly, the county seat of Burlington County. The market square was crowded with all sorts of goods, legal and less-so, offered for sale. There were the tables of early vegetables, live animals, and meat ready for the dinner table. Rebecca, who thought of herself as a city-dweller even though she knew about cows, sheep and chickens, enjoyed the afternoon at the market. Bill headed home after pointing out the widow who ran the *Bridetown Tavern* on Church Street, not far from the central marketplace.

"I don't need to introduce you. She's not too fond of me since Suzy and I got hitched, so I'll just let those nice letters and yourself do the job. You okay, girl?"

Rebecca nodded. Bill kissed the top of her head and went off to load the wagon and head home. Rebecca called after him as he road away, thanking him and wishing him and Suzy a good life.

That first visit and trip set the pattern for the entire journey, and it was six weeks later, on June twentieth, when she found herself walking down another road called the King's Highway toward the ocean. She hoped it had been named for some king other than George III. The highway hurt her feet and, between the war and Manning, the King didn't please her very much either. Rebecca trudged on.

After two hours, the day turned to dusk, and the soil turned to sand as dunes rose up around her. She was on her second pair of shoes, having tossed the first pair two weeks, and many miles, before. The sand was warm from the afternoon sun, so she unbuckled the shoes and carried them in her free hand. The wind was picking up, blowing off the cool ocean and urging her thin blond hair to escape the ugly dark-blue bonnet she had bought to protect herself from the sun and men's leers. She sat for a minute. She took off the bonnet, while she put the shoes into her sac. The wind caught the bonnet, carrying it away over the dunes. Rebecca enjoyed the antics of the blue hat, and let it fly away and out of sight.

Rebecca did not know where the road through the dunes would take her, or when she would see the ocean. The brisk salt air, and the note in her pocket from Suzy Eldridge to her cousin, gave her a sense of optimism. There had been no sign of Manning anywhere in New Jersey. When the ship was spotted offshore, and if the men would take her on board, this journey would have been worth it.

Rebecca leaned into a dune facing the sandy beach. While she waited for the dark, and the low tide the smugglers used to keep the revenuers at sea and away from their small, shallow- bottomed ships, she pulled out her letter-book to record her thoughts and tales of the journey for Simm.

Dear F-S- I am safe, waiting out the daylight in the tall dunes near The Sandy Hooke in Northern New Jersey. At dark we will be met by a small ship that can come in close at the shallows during the low tide. It has been a hot journey, made worse by slow journeying under a black blanket in a wagon being pulled by a slow ox. But my feet thanked my hot head. Thanks to your many friends, I have jumped from market town to market town, with inn keepers and their neighbors, in carts rather than by foot. Most everyone has been tremendously kind. I will tell you tales of the road when, some time in the future, you need entertaining.

Around midnight the tide reached its lowest point, and Rebecca heard people start to shout the muffled cries of smugglers. She waded out to talk to the captain. She showed the man Suzie's note, and used the first of the gold crowns to secure passage, with a promise of more when she arrived in Boston. Captain Fanning laughed. If he wanted all her coin, he reminded her, he would just take it.

The *Papillon* was a fast frigate built by the French navy and captured by the British in 1768. Rebecca did not ask how she came to be in the hands of her current crew, but was pleased with the accommodations. As the only long-distance passenger, she was given the nicest state room, probably one that had been built for a visiting admiral or other dignitary. It was not near a map room or the ship's stores, and as it was not desirable for any crew member, but it was perfect for her. She spent the days in her cabin, avoiding the crew and their not-too-subtle leering, using the time to rest and read the books that someone had left on board. In the evenings, she dined with the captain and walked the deck, watching the setting sun and darkening sky.

The few hundred miles from Sandy Hook to Boston took nearly three weeks to cross because of the number of nights they waited offshore in the dark for packages and people, but by late June they were heading northeast around Martha's Vineyard and the Nantucket shoals. The captain and crew of the little *Papillon* were all in a fine mood, the hold was full with goods, and they had already sold considerable quantities of goods at the stops along the south coast of Long Island.

It was getting foggy as they sailed due west into the Massachusetts Bay and Boston Harbor. Rebecca gasped in awe at the lovely islands that dotted the deep harbor, sitting like green and gray cakes, floating on the gray-blue water. They sailed in the direction of the town, but it was entirely blocked by a thick fog. The ship anchored in a cove near Bird Island, on the northeast edge of the harbor, to wait for the fog to lift. That night, a driving rain pushed them hard on the anchor. The sails were already down, so the captain decided to wait out the storm where they were.

I am continuing my letter from some weeks ago. We are now three days anchored in Boston Harbor. We should be easily in sight of the town, and a short sail from where we are at Bird Island. Unfortunately a storm affectionately called a Nor'easter has us "socked in" with fog and drizzle. The captain says there is no way to predict how long the wind will blow this way. He tells me to be patient and that we are lucky it is not snow. Someone mentioned that a late winter storm like this is what drove William Howe out of Boston. I am not surprised.

I am, as always, yours in all things-
R'b.

On July third, the *Papillon* finally pulled anchor and headed into Boston. Rebecca noticed the wood and brick town pushed close to the water by tall hills. The ship docked at Long Wharf, the easternmost end of State Street, the busiest street in the town, formerly called King Street. Ah, she thought, at least here someone had the good sense to change the street's name. Rebecca collected her few things, paid Captain Fanning the rest of her fare, and walked down the plank onto the wharf.

Long Wharf was lined with wooden warehouses, rough stores and taverns. The buildings did not touch, leaving a small space between them, and water was visible to the right and the left, behind the low rows of wharf structures, for a quarter mile. Water was everywhere. Rebecca was used to Philadelphia with its river harbors, but she had traveled, and like others she had seen, this was a real harbor – deep and long. Wharfs jutted in all direction, wherever one could be fit, each with boats tied up or moored near-by. Big and small counting houses, taverns and family homes were jumbled together as close to the waterfront as their owners could get them. This was clearly a town that earned its living from, and relied on, its harbor. No wonder closing the harbor had caused such distress in the town.

Rebecca saw big ships, ferries that carried folks between the harbor islands, lobster boats and fishing vessels. Near all the active ships were shipyards where men were building and repairing them. Further along she noticed thin buildings, each a quarter-mile long, where rope was twisted into the enormous tarred rope and netting used on the ships. It was as though all the shore had been condensed into one harbor. She could only imagine that all the coast here was built up the same way.

In front of her now, with the harbor at her back, she saw newer three and four-storied homes and businesses. Straight ahead was the Town House, where the governor had his offices and the General Court sat. Around the old building were new, elegant brick buildings, interspersed with wooden structures that appeared relatively ancient. Rebecca passed Dock Square, with muddy water and old warehouses left behind by a newer, brick market building called Faneuil Hall that sat right at the harbor. This place had already become famous as the site of the meetings that led to the destruction of the tea. Rebecca's legs were unsure of land, and she was not really sure where she was heading but, following her mother's old notes, she crossed Cornhill Street and walked one more block, up the hill to Tremont. Here she turned left, and soon found the new mansions being built in the woods on the Beacon Hill.

Most of the larger buildings in the shabby town were brick, but the oldest homes and some of the very new ones had escaped fire and the local ordinance. Her cousin's lovely house was stone and wood. With enough stone to satisfy the fire inspectors, it also had enough wood to satisfy the esthetics of Josephine and Michael Daggette. It stood three stories high, flat, with large windows facing Sentry Street like unseeing eyes.

Like many Bostonians who had been in shipping and trade before the British occupation, Michael had become far richer using his ships to outrun British blockades than he had been while engaging in legal (and taxed) trade before the occupation and siege of Boston. One of the unfortunate aspects of war, he was known to pontificate, was that goods were scarce, and therefore available goods were dear. It was his good fortune to be able to help supply the worthy citizens of the town with what they wanted.

Rebecca hadn't written to her mother's cousin that she was coming to Boston this spring. Such a letter could have been intercepted, and that would have destroyed all her carefully-laid plans. Now she was nervous about her arrival and greeting. Rebecca's mother and Josephine had been close as girls, but she was she unexpected and relatively unknown – and, she thought, as she walked over Beacon Hill to Sentry Street, she was also dirty, and smelled from her three-week voyage.

Rebecca knocked at the kitchen door at nine o'clock on the busy morning. She hoped that breakfast was finished. She wanted to speak to Cousin Josie, get cleaned up, and dress in her new clothes before she needed to see Michael Daggette, a fearsome man, according to her mother, who knew him growing up.

The kitchen maid answered the door. Rebecca steeled herself for outright rejection.

"Hello, I'm sorry to disturb your work." Rebecca spoke loudly so the carefully-listening kitchen staff, and whichever upstairs servants and grooms were having breakfast at this hour, could hear her. "My name is Rebecca Willent, now FitzSimmon. Charlotte Selby, my mother, was Josephine Selby's – Ms. Daggette's – cousin. I've come to see her."

The maid turned to the crowd in the kitchen and spoke so that all could hear. "It's that cousin the mistress has been waiting for." She turned to Rebecca. "Getting right worried, she was. Let's get you up to a nice bath, and into clean clothes. Your boxes arrived two weeks ago, you see, so we were all told to be on the lookout for you." The girl winked at that. She pulled a slightly-stunned Rebecca into the cozy kitchen, and led the way up the back stairs to a small but well-decorated room. The walls were whitewashed, there were yellow curtains at the windows, and stencils of birds and flowers ringed the room high near the ceiling and around the door. Rebecca was immediately drawn to the simple, painted walls.

There, in the center of the room, were Rebecca's two large shipping crates, and a chest that had been opened and emptied into the armoire in the corner. She had never been so happy to see a box.

Rebecca put her sac down. She felt so dirty that she didn't want to touch anything or sit on anything. She pulled off her shoes and stockings as a large tub was brought into the room, followed by various maids with buckets of warm water. The staff was unusually helpful in order to take a look at the owner of such a collection of clothes and sundries.

The kitchen maid helped Rebecca take off her dress and shift, and then, while she sank gratefully into the clean, warm water, she tactfully took the filthy clothes out of the room.

"I hope you intend to burn them." Rebecca said as the young women came back into the room.

"No, ma'am, we'll clean then up and give them to the poor. There's plenty of people in Boston who would be glad of any clothes newer than the ones on their backs."

"It's been that bad here, then?"

"It's been bad for the poor since before the occupation, but there is still little work. It has gotten better, but the blockade keeps prices high. But you don't want to hear all our problems, Miss Rebecca. I'm Jenny Warren. My uncle was Dr. Joseph Warren, who was killed at Bunker's Hill. I'm afraid politics is in every Bostonian's blood. Shall I wash your hair?"

Rebecca was not used to forthright talk, especially not from a young girl, but was not opposed. In fact, she thought she might grow used to this sort of honest speech. "Yes, please!"

More pitchers of water were brought in and poured over her head. Jenny took a soft soap and then poured what smelled like lemons over her hair. Once washed and rinsed, Rebecca's hair was wrapped in clean linen towels. Jenny left her, then, to dry herself and find her clothes in the large crates.

"Miss, I'll tell Mrs. Daggette that you are upstairs. I need to straighten the dining room, then I'll be right back to help you dress."

Rebecca was so comfortably clean, warm and content that she smiled and mumbled "thank you" to Jenny, as the young girl went off to finish her chores.

Later that morning, dressed in a fresh gown for the first time in a month, Rebecca sat drinking chicory and chatting with her cousin. "I know you must wonder why I have arrived so dirty and late. You see, circumstances dictated that I follow a rather circuitous route."

The older woman looked serious for a few moments before she spoke. "Rebecca, in the last decade, Bostonians have learned that many things happen of which we are better off knowing little. If your journey falls into that category, I understand and am not offended if you would rather not explain. In fact, I would rather you not. I think I will enjoy your company, and just help you on your way from here. You sent many clothes, but none for winter. Am I correct in assuming that you are not staying here, in Boston?"

"Yes, Cousin Josephine. That was a good guess. I will be near here, I think. Beverly, Salem, or one of the towns near there is to be my destination. I am to be met there by my husband John as he comes south, if all has gone well with his journey."

"Oh, that is good news. Salem is near, only half a day by ship, or a morning ride by carriage along the coast. Michael has family up that way. Perhaps they can help."

Rebecca was subdued by this generous effort. Having such a family would give her local roots. It was more than she had anticipated. She had felt so alone since Coffee Joe's henchman had dragged her away from Simm. And here, an unknown cousin was truly taking her in and finding connections for her.

"Cousin, I think I should go next week or the one after. I'd like to settle into a place before my location is discovered by, well, the person I was avoiding. This man" – she pulled out a sketch she had done of the man in black – "Josephine, I know naivete is pleasant, but let me tell you his name in case you need to avoid him." Josephine nodded her consent. " His name is E.P. Manning. He works for King George. And although it sounds so fanciful I hardly believe it myself, his goal seems to be to find my John and to create an even harsher war than will naturally happen, so the colonies can be trounced and the King can claim total victory. I don't know what he wants with John, but he will be hunting for me. And he will find me, but we want it to be in Essex County when he does. John and I agree that I should be established, and know my neighbors, before he interferes with my life again."

"Rebecca, let Michael find you a place with his sister-in-law. She is a widow with a growing son, and takes in tenants. I don't believe she has one right now. I will write her this very afternoon. The room is very small, but there is a workshop at the front; it opens to the street. You could use it for your things, I suppose. She rents that as well, so it may be available." Josephine Daggette drifted into thought, looking, Rebecca noticed, very much like her mother.

"Josephine, please write her that I have the rent money. And, yes, I would like the workshop, if it is available. I think I will spend some time and paint."

"Paint what, dear?" Josephine was opening the drawers of her delicate desk, taking out her writing things.

"Ships and people. I don't want to hide. I need John to find me and know I am fine, and I need Manning to climb out of his sewer and into the light of day."

Josephine was paying closer attention than Rebecca thought, and she was surprised when she blurted, "And who might this John be? I heard of no marriage."

"John FitzSimmon, Josephine. We met a few years ago, and married May first, but right now, I don't know where he is. Manning caused us to separate. I just hope Manning does not find me before John does." Rebecca sent a silent prayer that the last statement be true.

"I will talk to them presently. Let me start right away and write Michael's sister, Claire, immediately. Rebecca, I'm sure you need to run errands." She called out "Jenny!" and then resumed speaking to Rebecca. "The girl will love a day off to show you around, introduce you to anyone you need to find, and help you find the shops. We are not Philadelphia, but we do pretty well." She looked knowingly at Rebecca, and turned to her desk to begin her correspondence.

Jenny danced into the room, already sensing that there would be a change in the day's activities. "Yes 'm?"

"Jenny dear" – Josephine did not look up from her writing– "take Rebecca to see anyone you think could help her. I think she will need painting supplies, brushes and such, and she will tell you what else. Now off with you; I want to get this letter on the first packet we can find."

The young women left the room. Rebecca felt like she had when her sister lived at home, and her mother had asked the girls to leave her to her weaving. It was a nice break from responsibility, but she did not want to spend too much time reverting to childhood.

She started speaking as soon as they were out of earshot of any who might want to listen.

"Jenny, I need a silver and gold smith."

"Why, are you having something made?"

Rebecca pulled a few of Simm's buttons from her pocket. "I need to get the pewter off of these."

"Why, what's under 'em?"

"Gold and a few gems. But look closely – they are a British soldier's buttons, gold and coated with dull pewter, so as not to look too good. I want to make sure the smith will not ask how I got them. I need someone who doesn't want to know. All I can say is that the buttons were not stolen, but I can't tell anyone who the soldier was who gave them to me."

"Right, then, we are off to the North End."

"Why? Where's that?"

"North a few streets, to North Square."

Rebecca followed dutifully as Jenny lead her over a narrow bit of soggy road, wet from the same rain that had kept the *Papillon* anchored at Bird Island for three days. They passed a large number of taverns, and Jenny pointed out where they would buy paint brushes, and the chemist's where, Jenny knew, Gilbert Stuart bought his tints. To their right was the Long Wharf, where Rebecca had entered the town only a few hours ago. She thought she should be more tired, but she was excited now. The days at sea and at anchor had renewed her tired body, so that much of the nausea was gone. It bothered her only in the mornings and when she got too hungry. But better than even that, the bath at the Daggettes's, and walking with Jenny Warren through the busy town, was renewing her spirit.

Boston was a warren of narrow streets. Newer lanes built near the common on the hills were much wider. But the contrast between the new and old was stark. Where they were now, in the North End, the roads were so narrow that the houses seemed to hang over the street and greet each other in the middle. It reminded Rebecca of the tour she and Amalia had made through Italy. And here at North Square was the oldest house on the block, even older than the ones around it.

The house was three stories high and bordered by a yard with a small stable in the back. There were children running in and out of the courtyard, and Jenny called a little girl by name to ask if her daddy was home. Told to go on back to the workshop, they passed through the small stableyard, and entered an out-building with an older man at work. He was making something out of steel. On the shelves behind him were silver watches and fobs, belt and shoe buckles, silver and pewter tea pots, and dinnerwear in for repair. The man looked up and smiled at the two young girls. He had a round face with a square jaw. His eyes shone a sharp intelligence, a kind of all-knowingness mixed with a ready mirth and obvious kindness.

"Well, young misses, what can I do for you?" He clearly

recognized Jenny. Rebecca understood this sort of secret recognition after her months with Joe and Nat, so she did not say anything until she was introduced.

"Rebecca Willent FitzSimmon, let me make known to you Mister Paul Revere, our local smith of all metals and expert horseback rider. You met his horse a few minutes ago in the courtyard, but that is not the brown stallion of April '75. Mister Revere, I make known to you Mistress Rebecca FitzSimmon of Philadelphia. Rebecca arrived in Boston this very morning, being anchored in the fog on the ship *Papillon* at Bird Island for three days. Mistress FitzSimmon has a small project that I do not need to know anything more about. I will be visiting Mistress Revere in the kitchen." And with that, Jenny Warren left Rebecca with the now very curious Paul Revere.

"I did not know the *Papillon* took on passengers." He asked the question by way of a simple statement, waiting patiently for Rebecca to respond.

"Not usually." Rebecca left him to work that into what knowledge he already had about the privateers' vessel.

He said nothing further, simply raising an eyebrow in the fashion of Aunt Amalia, and Rebecca began her tale as she pulled the first of the thirty dull-pewter buttons from her pocket. Revere picked up a few, looked at them closely, and shook them gently.

"Do we just take these apart for the treasures inside, or is there more to the game?" He was practically grinning with anticipation, while he waited for Rebecca.

"Mr. Revere you are right, they contain treasures. And yes, there is more. The buttons need to be melted down and converted. She got very quiet and began to speak softly so the sound of the children in the courtyard almost drowned out her voice, "English crowns, Dutch or Spanish, whatever you are able to make."

"Under this terrible pewter is gold?"

Rebecca nodded.

"Pure gold, or nearly so, pure enough for ducats, guilders or doubloons. And inside them - gems. My friend, who gave me his waistcoat, said that he used the coat for when he attended to important negotiations, in case something *more* was required."

Mr. Revere looked carefully at the buttons, noting the emblem embossed on each, and contemplating what sort of man wore that waistcoat.

"Now I need to use them, so they should not attract too much attention. Can you do that?"

"I'm afraid a beautiful young girl with gold will always attract some sort of attention." The man was certainly a skilled flirt, but the workmanship evident in the items around her gave her hope. "Yes, I understand your friend. I also have such friends and, as it happens, colonial scrip is not of much value. So some of my own friends have asked me to convert some of their jewelry and finer household objects into similar coin.

"From you, I will take one button and whatever is inside as payment, we'll gamble on that, shall we?"

Rebecca pulled out the other twenty nine buttons from her pocket, and put them on the table in front of the silversmith. Revere picked up one button from the table and shook it. It made a rattle, and he put it aside. "This one, this will be my payment for the work. You know that I will never tell anyone our little story. But, perhaps someday you will visit me and tell me about this friend of yours?" He looked over the buttons, rubbing the pattern on the front. "British officer, interesting, gave you the entire waistcoat. He still breathes on this earth, Miss FitzSimmon?"

"Yes, I pray God he does, Mr. Revere. And it is Mrs. FitzSimmon."

"Well then, Mrs. FitzSimmon, you will call in three days, Saturday afternoon, and I will present you with a lovely collection of coins for your purse, and a few for my own.

"Enjoy our currently very muddy town. I would apologize for the state of our streets, but if you are going to become a New Englander, Mrs. FitzSimmon, you must learn to enjoy them with pride. Why, before you go, I will tell you one of my favorite local stories.

"A man was riding on one of our well-kept streets in the early spring, when the ice melts and the mud feels like it goes from the surface down to the depths of hell. Well, this man sees a very nice hat just sitting there in the middle of the road. He hops off his horse and leans down to pick up the hat. When he does so, he sees a man staring up at him from the center of the road. 'Sir,' said the man to the head in the road, 'are you all right?' 'I'm fine,' the head replied, 'but I'm just a bit worried about the horse I was riding.

"Enjoy New England, Mrs. FitzSimmon, dusty and muddy. Remember what I said, and learn to be proud. Of course, at the same time you also must be humble. It's the riddle of our region. " He put his head back into his work, and Rebecca left the workshop, chuckling about the horse the "head in the road" had been riding, and knowing that she had just met someone truly special.

The two weeks in Boston were fun. Rebecca was feeling good to be well-fed and rested. The weather was clear and warm, without the damp heat she had expected from a coastal town in summer. Wearing the fashionable gowns made recently for her, Rebecca let Jenny show her around and help her buy the things she would need for her household.

Michael Daggette's sister, Claire, had written back to Josephine to say that she was expecting Rebecca anytime, and was very pleased to have her stay. The first floor shop was available, and it would indeed make a fine studio for a portraitist. The light was good in the back room, and there was plenty of storage space to do whatever she wished.

The Daggettes were wonderful hosts, and during Rebecca's time in Boston, Josephine introduced her little cousin to all her friends at "teas," as they jokingly called the gatherings where the ladies talked too much and drank brewed chicory, until the Madeira came out later in the afternoon. She got to know the husbands too, though most were captains or in trade, and often sailing, busy in shops or traveling. A few were with the army further south.

The second anniversary of the signing of the Declaration of Independence was celebrated on the fourth of July, in front of the Town House on State Street. Bonfires and fireworks burned and flared until late in the evening. The revelers rejoiced at a level of boisterous joy that Rebecca had never seen. She supposed that some people back home would love to indulge in this degree of celebration, but none did that she knew of. Bostonians were generally serious, political, hard working people, and Rebecca wondered if such people were more likely to give themselves over to Dionysian revels than people back home. Perhaps those who were less serious about day-to- day life were less serious about their joy as well.

She also wondered how a former British officer and aristocrat would fit into this world of fetes and long days of work. But then she remembered that John FitzSimmon would fit into any world that struck his fancy. And since she had tied her fate to his, she would learn to fit in as well.

"If only I can get rid of Manning and get on with this new life," she said to Jenny as they packed her purchases for travel, "it promises to be very interesting."

The heat had built up over the first weeks of July, and by the fifteenth it was hot. Rebecca found herself surprised that it was this warm, since the week of her arrival had been nearly chilly, but she remembered what Mr. Revere had said about the constantly-changing weather, and she vowed to learn accept it, if not embrace and love it. She fingered her shiny gold coins as much for the pleasant memory of their interesting meeting as for the hope they represented.

The coins were perfect, and Revere had them ready precisely when he said he would. Most were Dutch guilders, but there were a few British gold crown pieces, and some doubloons, cut and whole. Rebecca had asked the silversmith what gem he had discovered in his button. He laughed and showed her an exquisite emerald, not very large, as it had to have fit in the button, but flawless and a beautiful true green. He had the coins all ready in a leather pouch, and the gems were wrapped separately in wool flannel.

Paul Revere had handed her the two packages and told her to have a wonderful life. "If ever you have the leave to tell me the story of how you and this man became acquainted, and how you, the pretty American from Philadelphia, came to have these gold buttons," he nodded his chin in the direction of the pouches in her hands, "I would be most gratified." He came out from behind his work table and gave her a wonderful fatherly hug, and kissed her soundly on each cheek. "Well done, Rebecca FitzSimmon; whoever he is, he will be proud of you."

There was nothing Rebecca could add. She curtsied

politely and said a heartfelt "Thank you, Mr. Revere," and then she walked back down the narrow dirt road to Faneuil Hall. At the market, she bought cheeses, bologna, dried apricots, figs, cashews, candied fruits, chocolates, and a cured ham for Claire Daggette and her son, Peter.

They set off for Beverly in the new carriage that Michael Daggette had promised his brother's widow. The Daggettes planned their return by ship after a few days of visiting. It was Rebecca's first glimpse of New England's towns and farms. She was struck by the similar pattern in each. The towns each had a central green, surrounded by a church and neat houses placed close together and arranged symmetrically around the town center, with farmland beyond. It was obvious even at first glance that these people – her mother's people – would know nearly everything about their neighbors, the good and the bad. It would make sense that tradition held that neighbors be around to help when needed.

Rebecca sat by the open window and watched clean doorsteps and dusty roads, fishing vessels that dotted the small harbors, and farmland defined by stone walls and scattered throughout with large stones and dead trees. This land was so different from the perfect, orderly farms of Pennsylvania. She asked Michael Daggette what he thought caused the differences.

"It's the rocks, Rebecca. Every year, new ones come up in the spring, like the sap in the maple trees, or grass in the pasture. Makes it hard to remove them all, so they take out the ones they have to, and leave others for another year. The trees, well, they get girdled 'round the trunk. It kills the branches and stops the shade. Then they leave them where they stand, till they're good for firewood."

Rebecca went back to staring out the window at the sun-mottled forest floor and the fields full of young corn, some with beans running up the stalks. Maybe, she mused in the afternoon heat, these yankees worked only as hard as they needed to. Maybe they understood the futility of doing the impossible. She wondered, though – how does one know when something is impossible? Father never admitted it; he hammered at all of us to do things we could not. If the parents here are like the fields they farm, willing to let fieldstones lie, how is it their children are so industrious? There was much to consider now that the fates had declared she would live among people so like hers, and yet so very different.

Chapter 19

They left Boston and headed west along the southern edge of the Charles River, stopping for lunch at Angier's Corner in Newtowne, where Michael Daggette had business with a Timothy Jackson whose land was nearby. Rebecca was careful not to listen too carefully, but she was sure she heard one of the men mention muskets, shipping and Washington. She was glad Nat was getting supplied by these men. They seemed to know what they were about, unlike her father and Coffee Joe.

Rebecca consulted a map. Newtowne was away from the coast and quite a way from where she needed to be. She worried awhile that the Daggettes might not be as efficient as they had first appeared. Rebecca became frantic at the thought that the hard journey had all been for nothing, and that her sense of well-being and willingness to adjust might have come too soon.

Finally, after what seemed like half a day, they turned sharply north at a road sign marked "Lynn, Marblehead and Salem," and soon after, she began to see the sea birds and open sky to her right. Toward the road's end, the view was full of the ocean, many inlets, and small harbors and ships. Feeling better after an early dinner, she asked about their route. Michael explained that with the weight of her baggage, it was easier to avoid the ferries and toll bridges. There was so much water to cross, traveling along a coastal route, that it would have been a colossal waste of money to pay for all of the toll roads and ferries. Rebecca realized that by taking the more roundabout route, Michael had been able to conduct his business along the way as well. "The frugal yankee is not just a myth," she laughed to herself, vowing to save her worries for real things.

Riding through the farmlands of Essex County, Rebecca began to get an idea about how this world of sea and land worked. It was clear that with separate town centers, these little farming communities faced in on themselves and away from the sea, almost as if they were unaware of the vast ocean just to the east. She was sure, having grown up in a large port, that once she saw the towns that faced the sea, that orientation would be completely reversed. Moving east toward Salem, they passed places with names like Gallows Hill, still famous from the witch scare nearly one hundred years earlier. Rebecca didn't want to hear about witches and hangings, however, and so she let her cousin's words float by as she examined the rocky land. They headed west just far enough to find bridges that crossed the multiple large rivers, and then, finally, turned straight east into the town of Beverly.

Rocky outcrops and salty wind let Rebecca know when they were approaching the sea. On this hot July day, it was soft and sweet-smelling, but she was not fool enough to think this wind stayed that way in winter. Watching the town grow in front of her, she considered that entering a port town from the land was much like entering a house through the kitchen door. The best side was not forward, but the visitor could learn about the residents by the state of the garden and the laundry hanging at the back.

Inland, the town showed prosperous farms, with salt hay tall and soon ready for harvest. There were lively families in their gardens, and blueberries grown as hedgerows in front of white or sea-gray houses. The native bayberries were tall even where the sea winds would dwarf a less hardy plant. Rebecca was delighted with the apple and peach trees, some in orchards and many in home gardens. The civility of the town spoke to her, and she prayed that it was real.

Like Boston, and the larger town of Salem they had just skirted, Beverly was a port town. Shipyards hugged the harbor, which also had ferries that rowed and sailed across the Danvers River from Beverly Harbor to the deeper, and busier, port of Salem. There, smugglers and privateers were prospering, taking goods off British vessels in what should have been unequal battles. The Americans, with ships built right here in Essex County, prevailed in spite of the odds stacked against them. Rebecca knew that John's brother Jason was one of the Salem privateers, lucky and skilled, with a mast that flew the Union Jack when it needed to.

The busy streets around the harbor had elegant homes with symmetrical architecture, large windows, and chimneys on each of the four corners, showing that there were multiple, generous fireplaces giving heat throughout the winter. Rebecca sighed, thinking how nice it would be to live in such an orderly town, even though the houses lacked the extra chimney and the semi-separate kitchen that was so common where she grew up.

Not only the architecture was different. She knew she was different than the adventurous girl she had been. Not only were there physical changes that were becoming obvious, but she was more certain of who she was, and what she wanted. None of that meant that she understood exactly what her remarkable marriage would be, or who her extraordinary husband might turn into. But Rebecca could tell, from strangers' reactions to her, that she had acquired an aura of confidence. She was glad for that. As unsure as she felt about being the stranger for the first time in her life, and as scared as she had been about the journey north, she had successfully fooled everyone into thinking she was the master of her fate.

Claire Daggette lived not three blocks from the water, just north of the deep river the town shared with Salem. Her house was set back from the busy main street by the little shop that Rebecca intended to use for a workshop and refuge. The front of the pretty house faced a small side street, where there were roses in bloom. The woman herself was younger than Josephine and Michael Daggette. She was too young to be widowed, but in a world of sailors and fishermen, Rebecca was sure that was not uncommon. This world would make being a pregnant woman alone less odd. She reminded herself to put her wedding ring on her finger by tomorrow.

They were just sitting to dinner when Claire's son Peter came in. He was a tall fifteen, full of energy and quick intelligence. The meal was as elegant a dinner as Claire could serve to her Boston in-laws. They started with mulligatawny soup. Rebecca had never tasted the combination of ginger and curries before, but found, within a few bites, that she liked it. The rest of the dinner – cabbage stuffed with cranberries and spiced meat, haddock, roast beef, and apple pie – was more familiar. Rebecca was sure that Claire, who did not seem to have help in the kitchen, could not serve such a dinner every night. When she looked at Peter, she was assured that she would not often be so full too often, as his eyes were fairly bursting by the third course. She smiled at him knowingly, happy that she had found a new brother.

Rebecca was shown her room above the living room. This front room had probably been Claire's room, which she shared with her husband. Now, it had an empty feeling, as if it had not been recently slept in. It looked over the front yard and the small street, and it was possible to just see the main street and the blue of the ocean to the far right, if one looked out the window. Her boxes were brought in from the carriage, which was then driven by Peter to the livery stable. Claire walked her in-laws to the harbor in the warm summer evening. They were to spend one night in the Blue Heron Inn that had just opened across the river in Salem.

"Claire, Rebecca is a charming girl, but understand she is wrapped up in something ugly." Josephine spoke quietly to her sister-in-law as they walked to the ferry.

"What could that sweet girl have done that would follow her here?" Claire was half kidding, being fully aware of how circumstances push and pull even sweet people.

"I don't believe it was anything she did, or maybe it is, I don't know. But someone may be following her to do her harm. She said his name is Manning. I only hope it is her youthful imagination."

Claire thanked Josephine for the warning, voicing her reassurance that it was most likely Rebecca's imagination. Josephine did not need to be burdened with worry. She kissed her in-laws good-bye, thanking them again for the carriage and horses, and waved them off as the ferry was rowed across the river.

Claire had been less protected from the world of smuggling, both of goods and of information, than her wealthy relatives. She was less convinced than Josephine that Rebecca's fears were part of 'youthful imaginings." She wasn't sure how much she needed, or even wanted, to know about the girl's problems, but it was essential that she keep Peter safe. Having his father's name already made him too famous with the British revenuers on the blockades. The boy refused to use his middle name, and would insist on heading out on any ship that would take him. And right now, as Essex thrived with trade and building, the boy was welcome as an extra hand whenever he wanted to ship out.

It was important, Claire pondered as she walked home, to find out the nature of Rebecca's situation, before her new tenant's problem interfered with her attempts to keep Peter safe. She got home to find the food stored, the dishes washed and cleared away, and the floor swept. At the table sat Rebecca and Peter, deep in conversation over tankards of last fall's cider.

Claire poured herself a draught and sat with the young people. She listened to Rebecca's tale of betrayal by Coffee Joe and his comrades, and their manipulation by E.P. Manning. Rebecca pulled out a sketchbook to show them the man in black's likeness.

"Rebecca, what makes you think he will follow you here?" Claire spoke as soon as Rebecca finished her story.

"I don't know for certain that he will. But as he knows about John FitzSimmon's brother Jason, Manning will probably expect John to be in this area."

Peter, whom circumstances had pushed to become wise before his time, sat quietly absorbing the story before he joined the conversation. "Does Manning care that you are here, or is it only John?"

"Pete, I don't really know the answer to that, but he has a strange reaction to me. He has told me that if he sees us together, he will see us hanged. He has never explained on what grounds – I suppose my treason, and John's by extension, but he has never said he has the proof. And he has never threatened me singly with hanging. I really don't understand the seeming obsession."

Claire finished her cider, and stood to clear the three tankards from the table, proclaiming the evening's chat over at the same time. "Rebecca, you must be tired; Pete, it is time you got some rest. It seems to me it will be important that this Manning fellow not know that Rebecca is here in Beverly. Pete, that will mean keeping a sharp eye out, and leading him away or hiding you" – she nodded to Rebecca – "if necessary."

Claire turned to her son. "Pete, I don't need to remind you that a man like that would have no trouble turning you over to the revenuers if he could, so no shipping out, not even on overnight runs, until Rebecca is safe and Manning is gone. Right?"

She lead the way to Rebecca's room to show her where extra candles were stored, and to make sure she had water and clean towels. Just minutes later, clean and clothed in a fresh nightrail, Rebecca relaxed in the soft luxurious bed, under clean crisp sheets, feeling like she had found a safe haven, but for the first time since the sudden separation from Simm, she was hit by a nagging sense of loneliness.

Claire Daggette's home had been a safe harbor in her turbulent world. Claire was an ally, aware of men like Manning, and able to rally her forces to protect her son and their new friend. But as comfortable as her cousin's home had been, there was just too much staff for her to feel safe. Manning had proven to have such a way with cooks and maids, they told him stories just to show off, or prove him wrong. What he could have done to Josephine's kitchen staff, given a chance, she did not care to think.

Unfortunately, he had done just that. Catching the scullery maid out at the pump getting water for the morning coffee, he asked kindly if the master and mistress were at home. He had watched the house for a day, and had seen Josephine and Michael arrive from the pier the afternoon before.

"Just so happens they are back and expectin' their coffee. I best get in, sir."

"I'm sorry to have interrupted your work, mistress."

The girl was charmed to have been so spoken to, and stopped to chat for that extra minute. "They were gone, see, up to our North Shore to see cousins and drop off that young lady – another cousin. But they're back now. I'd better go, 'scuse me." And the young girl curtseyed, and fled into the kitchen. The man in black sauntered out of the small kitchen yard, and went directly to the wharf to purchase passage on the packet to Salem, where he knew that a Jason FitzSimmon and his family lived.

Rebecca settled into a pleasant pattern with Claire and her son. She set up her workshop and was having the Daggettes pose for her first portrait. She was rather pleased with the piece, even though it was quickly done and was not an elegant work. The portrait caught Claire's good humor trying to bubble to the surface, and young Peter's spirit. She was working on a more difficult painting, too; this was of Simm as a Roman Centurion. She remembered the uniform from her travels in Italy, and had a sketchbook of such costumes from museums her aunt had taken her to during their year abroad. The background would be the rugged shoreline of the New England coast.

His face and stance were harder. She could feel his eyes on her as she had worked over the bread dough, and she knew he had maintained the exact stance she needed for the portrait, but her back was always to him. Finally, out of exasperation, she showed Pete how to stand, and did a series of pencil sketches of him standing in a doorway. The first layer of portrait was covered and drying, waiting for the next layer of color, when Rebecca declared herself happy with her first real attempt at her Roman. She went upstairs to change for dinner and glanced out her window at the street below.

Looking over at the busy road had become a habit in the weeks she had lived in Beverly. The street lead to the river and harbor and was a constant source of entertainment, with all sorts of people walking and riding by. This evening was no different. There were fishermen on their way back home to their evening meal, women carrying packages heading to and away from the pier, children running home before they were missed, and, right on the other side of the window, two men having an argument.

The sounds of the road and the closed window muffled their words, so she saw, rather than heard, their disagreement. She could not see much of the man whose back was toward her, so she watched the other man, in horror. After a few minutes the first man, wearing the rough leather clothing of a traveler or a workman, walked north, away from the town, his stride powerful and quick, leaving the other man to stare at his back.

Rebecca stepped behind her curtain so this other man would not see movement from the second floor. It was E.P. Manning in darkest black, his clothing cut in the latest style. She quietly backed away from the window, and went down to tell Claire and Peter that the man had arrived. She did not immediately find them, but heard them in the front yard being as loud and conspicuous as they could be. When Peter saw Manning standing at the street, he had called to his mother. They went outside to get a good look at him, and decided to themselves it was obvious. They certainly annoyed him, standing in the yard, Claire telling her son, as loudly as a normal mother would be, to trim the flowers before the first frost, an event that, Rebecca was sure, even here in northern Massachusetts, would not occur for at least two or three months. Certainly, E.P. Manning would never associate Rebecca Willent with these crazy locals. She wanted to hug them both.

In no time, the man in black walked away, and Claire and Peter came in to their dinner. Rebecca had meanwhile set the table. "Daggettes" – she raised a glass of fresh milk that Claire insisted she drink each day – "I salute your sense of volume and humor. That man did not know what hit him. He is so used to everyone being scared and quiet around him. Thank you, you don't know how much I appreciate you." Rebecca took a great swallow of her milk and sat down. Claire served dinner, and they all enjoyed telling and retelling their impressions of the incredulity and disgust so apparent on Manning's face.

The next morning dawned cooler than Rebecca had expected. There was not yet even a hint of frost, but a fresh breeze blew from the northwest. She grabbed her new rust-colored cloak before she went out for her morning walk. She climbed above the town onto the headlands that overlooked the harbor and the little village nestled at the water's edge. It was her daily walk, and she had learned to watch the clouds and winds for changes. Today, the sky was bright blue, and the sea was choppy with whitecaps on the waves as they danced along the shore. She watched the early boats come in with the morning catch, and the lobster boats trundle along, pulling in their traps. She felt part of the this world; she thought of how many of the workers, sailors, fishermen and their families she had gotten to know through Claire and Peter.

Claire had understood Simm's direction that Rebecca get to know the local people before Manning or his helpers came to know and befriend them. Claire and Pete had made sure that Rebecca quickly became part of the community. She attended church with the Daggettes, she sewed and knit for sailors and soldiers, and she cared for mothers' children while they ran errands in the afternoon. She attended coffees and knitting circles. And, in between the obligations that defined her busy new life, she painted.

Her walk over, Rebecca headed back to her workshop to tackle that Roman soldier. Working on him brought Simm closer to her and made her miss him less, and yearn for him more. At least she was able to do more than conjure his image from her memories. Here he was, right out of her sketch books. Soon, she would take the painting to the hill and paint the houses and the sea as his background.

She turned the corner to find Peter leaning against the workshop door, chewing a stalk of fresh grass. Rebecca was about to ask what he was doing there when he grabbed her elbow and pushed her through the door of the workshop, closing it quickly behind her. She hung her cloak on a peg and turned to lock the door to the street, as was her habit, until she was ready to greet the interested passerby. She went into the back room to find the portrait of the Roman soldier already uncovered, and the man in leathers from the evening before staring at it.

Rebecca inhaled sharply, carefully putting her brushes back in their jar she approached the man who stood there, not saying a word.

"Now I suppose we will need to build a portrait gallery to house such overstated nonsense."

"John FitzSimmon, that is not overstated nonsense. Let me fantasize. I've been alone for a long time now."

"Sorry, I've been a'wandering, taking care of a few things." There was a wry sadness in his voice as he pulled her into his arms and covered her mouth with his. "Oh, my lady, I have missed you beyond distraction and worry." He cooed in her ear between kisses.

Rebecca separated an inch to speak. "Sorry, I did write, but I could not post the letters ... had no address." She pulled him close.

Peter strode into the kitchen. His mother looked up from the book she was reading. "Pete, you have the look of a cat that found a dish of cream! Why are you so pleased with yourself?"

"I found Rebecca's Simm; he is in her workshop now."

"Well, I don't hear yelling and screaming from over there, so I guess you did good. Wonderful boy! Where did you find him?"

"He's staying in Salem at that new inn. I rowed over this morning to see if it was the man in her sketches. You know that portrait that Becky had me posing for over the last few days? Well I'd got to know that face really well, staring at her sketches while she paints me, so I was able to see that fellow we saw yesterday with Manning was him."

"That lovely man in those leathers?" Claire looked like she was admiring the memory.

"He's taken, Ma, and anyway, you're too old."

"Who taught you to be cruel to your Mam?" Claire teased Peter. "Well you'd best go find something useful to do. I expect they will be awhile."

Simm held Rebecca in his arms, thinking how absolutely precious this moment was. Now that he was certain she was safe, he allowed the fear that had dwelled just below his conscious thought to emerge, and it nearly overwhelmed him. That same fear had come alive each night in the shadows and in his dreams, but he had carefully ignored it, knowing it was based on the unknown, not on some special ability to see the future. He ignored the burning desire that having her in his arms inevitably aroused. Instead they stood, still as statues, inhaling the essence of the other, hands in the other's hair, immersed in the joyous reality that each of them was actually here in the same place.

Rebecca relished being enclosed in Simm's strong arms. She let worries about the past float away in the feeling of safely that being held gave her. She knew that she wanted more of him than this simple hug, but feeling his hard body against hers was almost overwhelming and almost enough. She made no move to alter it.

Finally, it seemed they must move into the bright sunshine of the late summer day. Rebecca was the first to breathe, pushing herself onto her own feet. "Simm," she started, wondering if her saw her as changed as she felt, "do you want to come in for some coffee? I'm sure Claire would love to meet you. By the way, how did you end up here?"

"Pete. That young man came to my door as I was finishing breakfast. He held a piece of foolscap up to my face. Said it was to compare. He didn't say with what. He stared at me a minute or two. Then he asked if I was John FitzSimmon. He didn't look like the type of evil accomplice Manning would hire, so I admitted that I was, and he grabbed me and rowed me over, barely speaking more than a work or two, just insisting that I needed to come to Beverly. I thought I was being kidnapped, but was surprised when I saw I was being dragged to the same house where I had confronted Manning yesterday. Then I did become a bit concerned that Peter might be working for the man. But then he pushed me through the back door, into your little workshop here.

"I looked around till my eyes adjusted to the dim, and I explored a bit, uncovering your work until I recognized the style. Now I think the boy deserves a medal; he just saved me weeks of searching. Then you walked in." He put his hand on her cheek, gently feeling the soft skin with his fingertips. He moved his hand into the edge of her hair, twirling the soft hair that was escaping from the plait she had carelessly pinned up that morning for her walk. "The New England air must agree with you – you fairly glow with health. I could be a bit jealous that you have not been pining away for me." His voice had that teasing tone she had gotten so used to over the year. "I think I'd better slip away – I have some people to meet this afternoon."

"Not Manning!?" She wasn't sure why, but her instincts told her that Manning would be more dangerous for Simm than for herself. Remembering the anger the two men showed in the street the day before, she knew that she should be the one to handle Manning, and would have to do so without telling Simm first. He would never allow her to put herself in danger again.

"Not Manning, I promise, not unless he pounces on me again. This is about a potential purchase and investment I would like to make. Meet me tomorrow for dinner. I hope to have news. Have Pete bring you; he knows where the inn is. I'll ride you back after. You can promise your landlady that

I'll not keep you out late."

"Simm, you should meet Claire. I suspect she would think less of you if you did *not* keep me out late. We are married. remember – unless Reverend Reed was a fake."

"I will meet her – she sounds like a good friend and a good person – but not right now. I must get back." He put his tricorn on his head. Rebecca stared, realizing she had never seen him in a hat that was not decorated with regimental ornaments.

"Tomorrow at six, then." He pulled her hands to his lips, and kissed her knuckles with a determined glint and promise. Then he walked out the small door that led to the house and alleyway, and was gone. Rebecca felt suddenly bereft and cold, and shivered slightly. She rubbed her hands over her crossed arms, and followed Simm out the door, but she went into the kitchen to see her friends and to thank Pete especially.

She spent the afternoon working on a ship's portrait, and when that was set to dry, she took up her Roman again. Having seen Simm again helped, so she worked from recent memory as well as from her beloved sketches. She cleaned her hands carefully when she was done, with time for a walk and a visit to her new dressmaker before dinner.

Lydia Varon had recently come to Essex County from Charleston, South Carolina when her loyalist customers deserted her, and then threatened to hang her for her Patriot tendencies if she had stayed in business. Instead of sticking it out and putting her friends and family in danger, she had booked passage on a ship north, and now lived with an old widower uncle. Lydia was skilled, with a good eye for color and line, and Rebecca looked forward to needing her next whole wardrobe. Right now, however, Lydia was working in a beautiful homespun that Rebecca had found at a weaver's shop in Gloucester. The fabric was light wool and silk, spruce-green with flecks of black in the wool.

Lydia had joined Rebecca in marveling at the workmanship of the fabric itself, and had worked to create something special for Rebecca from the fabric. When she had ordered the new gown, Rebecca had had no idea when she would wear such a special piece, but now she had the occasion, and she wanted to check and make sure it would be done for the next evening.

The shop's closed sign was just put in the door's window when Lydia saw Rebecca, and motioned her into the little dress shop. There were samples everywhere, hanging on hooks, birdcage skirts, manikins and dressmaker's dolls. "Look, Becky!" Lydia motioned around the busy room. "Every smuggler, I mean privateer, brings me fabrics on commission so the ladies in town can buy from me. I've never had so much variety. But I do love your homespun – look how it came out!"

Lydia reached into a small cabinet behind her little desk and brought out the soft green wool. It was stunning. The wool was edged with lace; it was so beautiful that Rebecca was afraid to ask where it came from. The skirt was closed, giving it a gracious solemnity. "Are you sure it will fit? I am increasing, though I don't show too much yet."

"I think it should, but here, we'll just try it." Before Rebecca knew it, she was down to her shift, with the new, soft gown being poured over her head and shoulders. As predicted, it fit perfectly and would for another few weeks, at least. The waist was high and covered with a triangular piece that, cleverly, was not sewn down. It looked merely decorative, but the result was that it was concealing. The heat required that she wear it with a hoop skirt, and that would add to the illusion of a slim Rebecca. She was delighted. She bought some new gloves to cover whatever paint she might have under her fingernails, thanked and paid her friend, and cheerfully walked toward home, carrying her goods.

The streets were nearly empty, as most people had already found their dinners, and it did not take long for Rebecca to notice that she was being followed. She hurried her footsteps along the short walk back to the Daggettes. Frankly, she hoped it was just E.P. Manning and not some new problem. At the corner of Water Street, she saw Pete heading right toward her.

"Hey Becky, let me take that package." He turned to the person following her and politely, if not a bit sarcastically, doffed his hat. "Good evening, sir." He turned and shepherded Rebecca into the house.

"Pete, I didn't look – that was Manning, wasn't it?"

"In the desiccated flesh."

"He didn't try to grab me, did he?"

"No – just seemed interested in seeing where you went. Which must mean he hadn't spotted you before. It's perfect."

"Peter, you scare me. Why is it perfect?"

"Well, Simm is back and he can protect you from that thing."

"Oh, right, yes, that will be it." Rebecca nodded, absently. Unpinning her hat, she took her packages and carried them up to her room. "Tell Claire I'll be right down for dinner, would you, Pete?" She called down over her shoulder.

"Peter is right," she told herself sternly in the small mirror brushing out her hair. "Simm would like it so much if I let him take care of Manning. The problem is that Manning will have him killed. I saw that raw hate in his eyes yesterday.

There doesn't have to be a why, just as I cannot say why I love him. It is – for whatever reason. I have to do it myself. He has found me, he has seen Simm. And it will have to be within the week, whatever it will be."

She opened a dresser drawer, and checked the stiletto knife Nat had given her almost one full year before. It was as new as it was when he gave it to her. She re-covered the knife with her unused pads.

Rebecca dressed carefully the next night. She knew that she could wear rags and it would not matter, just as it would not matter to her if Simm appeared in ill-fitting homespun. But she wanted to make him proud that she was his. She felt the baby move as Claire buttoned the back of the green dress.

"Sit, Rebecca. I'll brush out and pin your hair."

"Claire, I think I just felt the baby move. She's excited, too."

"A she? Why do you think so?"

"I don't know, it just seems that way."

"Well, they're usually one or ta'other." Claire chuckled, and Rebecca joined in.

On the way to the ferry, Pete fell in with some friends, and Rebecca did not want to tear him away to babysit her again. She stopped him long enough for detailed directions to the inn, and got on the small, stable boat for the trip across the river. The inn was easy to find. It was in a new building right on the post road that led north to Portsmouth and south to Boston. She had heard some talk about funding a new bridge over the river to make travel on the road safer. Now, however, when the water was too high it was necessary to go the long way around. The new bridge would have a significant span, she thought, as she looked at the old one on her right.

The sun was still in the sky, but dark was moving in from the east as Rebecca entered the busy inn yard. She didn't know where to meet Simm, so she sat for a minute, enjoying the feel of the place. Being on the main road, the inn did not hurt for business, and the stage from Portsmouth pulled into the yard just after Rebecca sat down. She watched various well-dressed men descend from the coach. They men shook hands, and all looked pleased with whatever transaction had taken place.

Rebecca recognized Simm before he turned around. His dark hair was pulled into a fashionable queue. He wore the homespun of the finest gentlemen. His shirt, as always, was the whitest white linen, his waistcoat blue velvet brocade, patterned with leaves and flowers. He wore those boots Rebecca remembered so well, and his breeches were a good colonial buff. This was an enormous transformation, even from the civilian she had met that first summer, but here was also the same Simm as there always had been, a Simm she really did love. There, she admitted it to herself. It wasn't just that she madly desired him and let him take her beyond ecstacy. She did love him; maybe she had for a while now. She pushed the deep thoughts back in and smiled in the direction of the man looking at her with a pleasantly-familiar hunger.

Simm said good-day to his associates and grinned at Rebecca, pointing the way into the inn, taking her arm as they entered. They were shown to a reserved private dining room, just off the taproom. She was wearing that color again, and he almost wept with the wonder of her loveliness.

"Rebecca?"

"Yes, sweet man."

"Am I sweet? A bonbon of some sort?"

"That's my secret, I'll show you later."

"Fair enough. I admit I'm intrigued. What I was going to say was that I love that gown. The fabric is unlike anything I have ever seen."

"It's actually a local weave, from a shop in Gloucester. I consider it quite a find – silk and wool. Since it is a local manufacture, I had the decency not to ask where the fiber came from." She looked across the table and smiled. "John, it is really very, very nice to be sitting here with you. I just wanted to let you know that, in case you doubted that I might feel the same after all this time." She stood from her chair at the table while she was talking and moved over to where he was sitting, legs stretched out pushed out from the table.

Simm sat up to make a lap and pulled Rebecca into it. "My Lady, your hair looks so pretty, are you sure you want to sit here now? The waitress will be here soon." He ran a finger over her neck and teased at the soft skin just above her breasts, barely covered by the lovely gown. She kissed him soundly on the lips and hopped off.

"I may sit decorously over here, but I'm not done with you, FitzSimmon. I love you, ya know?"

Simm filled his lungs with air as a man saved from drowning might. "Oh Becky, I do know. I've always known, at least since you stitched my back together on the stone kitchen floor. I recognize why we have never used the words. It is hard to speak of deep things, when the only thing you and I were ever sure of was being unsure. In case I forgot to show you, I love you too.

The food was brought in just then, and they ate in companionable silence. As the dishes were cleared, Simm poured them brandy and moved to sit on a small couch in front of a welcome fire.

"I love it here. It was a wonderful idea to move here. But I cannot believe I'm enjoying this much fire, and it is still August." She untied her boots and curled her feet under her as she curled into Simm on the couch. He put his free arm over her shoulder, pulling her even closer. He kissed the hair on top of her head.

"Becky, I'm sorry, I'm going to have to ask you to stay at Claire Daggette's for a while longer. I bought a house today, but it is not finished except for the framing and the roof. It needs shingles, walls, plaster, paint, floors, ceilings, windows, a well, furniture, curtains, things like that.

"A little fixing. I understand it. No problem, as long as I can see you." She saw a worry cross his eyes, and knew it was Manning pushing them apart again.

"Manning." Simm spit out the word, below his voice.

"Don't think about him now, we'll deal with it when it comes up."

"No, I just saw him, in the taproom. When the girl came in to get the dinner things."

"Sit here. I make him less angry than you do. I'll get rid of him." Rebecca pulled on and tied her green boots. She walked into the taproom, head up, like she regularly walked through rooms filled with noisy drinkers.

Simm watched her handle the room. "Maybe that's what she had to do these last months; what do I know about what she suffered on the road?" he asked himself as he watched Rebecca approach and talk to the man in black.

"Evert? That is your name, right?"

The man was shocked to have Rebecca use his first name. He nodded reluctant agreement.

"I really think you should finish your drink and leave this

pleasant inn. I'm sure there are drinking places more suitable to worms." People started to look in their direction, so Rebecca allowed him to finish his drink. She spoke in a voice so quiet he had to strain to hear. "Manning, I'll put this plain and only once. You will leave this establishment right now, or I will announce who you work for and what you do. Before you choose to defy me, remember these are Marblehead and Salem privateers – John Glover's men and their relatives. Think back to Washington's retreat from New York and his little swim across the Delaware back home. Think about the men who rowed through wind, rain and snow, and then decide if you want those men to know who you are.

The man turned to leave, bowing his acquiescence as he withdrew. "Manning!" Rebecca got his attention and he turned back to her. "You are really too much, following us up here; it has to stop. I will meet you one week from tomorrow on the Beverly beach at sundown. Anyone can tell you where it is, just north of town on the way to the Farms. Now, if I were you I'd disappear for a while. We will meet next week."

Rebecca almost collapsed with relief that her counter-attack had worked. She was terrified of that man, but he had to be stopped. Simm stood at the door, almost invisible in the shadows. He had snuffed the candles, and the room was dark except for the fire which had died down considerably. He watched Rebecca charge into battle and make her foe retreat. He wished he could have heard what she said, but she was right – the man was slightly more rational when it came to Rebecca, even though he seemed to want to do her harm.

"My lioness, how did you make our enemy retreat?" he asked as he closed the door and led her back to the couch.

"I told him that I would tell a room full of seamen who had fought with Glover and Washington that he was the King's agent, here to cause trouble. I also told him it would behoove him to disappear. I don't know how long he will stay gone, but it will be nice for a while." It was a shame she had to lie to Simm again, but he would stop her from meeting Manning, and the man's presence would cause festering problems until he was removed. She snuggled close to Simm, turning her face to kiss him. After a few minutes of drinking brandy and kissing, Rebecca got up and checked the doors. Sure they were both locked, she came back to the couch and sat back against Simm. The room was warm. and her head was woozy in a delightfully fuzzy way.

"You are sweet, you know." She pushed him back on the couch and started to kiss him along the neckline of his shirt, unbuttoning his waistcoat as she descended. She nipped at his nipples, circling each with her tongue, pouring brandy on him and licking if off.

"I didn't know, but I'm thinking that you think I am *a* sweet; are you trying to eat me for dessert?" Simm almost grabbed her wrists to stop her, to push her down on the couch and ravish her, but she seemed to have a plan, and he was curious to see where it might lead. Anyway, he was already almost in the throes of orgasm, and not thinking clearly.

"Yumm."She worked her way down past his shirt, continuing to pour drops of brandy on his hard chest and hips, licking it off him, kissing and sucking his body as she worked her way to his breeches, relishing the earthy human smell of him, reveling in his feel and taste.

"Rebecca, I don't want to stop, you sweetheart, but are you sure?" He forced himself to offer her an out he really didn't want her to take. He fell back into luxurious arousal when she did not answer.

Rebecca did not reply. She simply answered by continuing

to unbutton Simm's breeches and allow his manhood to spring free. Then following the directions the sailors on the *Papillon* had not known she'd overheard, she cupped his dangling bits until he gasped, and then working up her nerve, she grabbed her glass and swallowed brandy as she put her lips on his throbbing essence. She was careful to tease him with her tongue and lips and teeth until he groaned and started to beg before she used real friction, loving the power she had to bring him to such heights of ecstasy. Twice she pulled away to tease with her tongue on the quivering tip. As his moans increased to a new pitch, she took him fully in her mouth, sucking and swallowing.

Simm shattered. He was slightly aware of Rebecca actually not letting him spill on her beautiful dress, but that was the only conscious thought his brain would generate. As he finished thrashing, and his mind began to clear, his muscles once again belonged to him. Rebecca kissed her way back up to his neck, buttoning his shirt and waistcoat slowly, leaving wet kisses behind as she went. Simm's head lolled back, enjoying sensations he had made himself deny missing. He wanted to return the favor, but he sensed Rebecca didn't want him to. He knew she would let him, but this new chapter in their lives needed to be played with delicacy, so he left her alone.

She swallowed more brandy, relishing his release as he had told her he had with hers. When he was done and relaxed again, she went behind the little curtained area in the corner of the room and washed her face and took a drink of cold water. Then, feeling more herself, she sat back on the couch, knowing she would have to explain how she had acquired that skill.

Simm took the minutes she was out of sight to clean

himself, and button his breeches. He was sitting, comfortably relaxed, on the small blue couch when she returned. "Rebecca, there probably is not a man in the world who would be upset that his wife would do that. But could you tell me how you came to acquire that knowledge without me? Honestly, I am afraid of the answer, but better you tell me." He put his arm around her again, teasing the escaped tendrils of slightly damp hair that stuck to her neck. She was feeling a bit distracted by his gentle touches, but she was determined to tell her story.

"It's not some evil event, really. Don't be so tense." She had reached into her small reticule and was holding a small book. "First, here is the letter book I wrote for you on the journey. I tried to write every day or two. All in all it was a pretty easy trip – people were helpful, and mostly very kind. As for your request – " she took a deep breath – "I was on a little ship from New Jersey to Boston for what seemed like a year. Actually it was from June twentieth to the first week of July. We sailed in and out of every cove between New York and Boston, and then, after the slowest trip I could imagine, we could not dock in Boston, because some blasted storm kept us anchored at an island in the harbor, in dense fog, for nearly three days. During that little voyage, I read every book in my stateroom and sketched everything on board, except the sailors. Being a bit outside the law, they requested that I not actually 'commit their likenesses to paper.' I quote. Anyway, I took to eavesdropping on their nightly brag sessions.

"Being sailors, these were usually a bit raw for me, but one night when I was particularly bored, I listened and memorized what the – again, I quote, 'best whore in Boston did one night.' I'm sure she had much more practice and so was far more skilled. So you see, the only knowledge I had for that was the sailor's description of what the hard-working whores of Boston did."

Simm sighed with pleasure and relief. "Mrs. FitzSimmon, I have to say, honestly, that was plenty of knowledge; if you'd had any more, you're likely to have killed me." He kissed her neck, letting her know that he was nowhere near death.

"Simm, I know we have to stay separate for now, but promise me I'll see you soon. Right now, I think we should start back. I should attend church in the morning, and I'm tired." Rebecca was not sure why, but she did not want to tell Simm about the baby yet – maybe after Manning was gone.

So much about this evening had been perfect. She had an appointment to see Manning, and hopefully to remove him from their lives, and they had been nearly as close as husband and wife could be, and she hadn't revealed her changed body.

"You can see me in the morning," Simm replied. "He can't grab us at church. Which church are you attending? I will meet you in front."

"Oh, Simm, that would be so wonderful, so normal, just walking into church with you. We attend the Third Church. It's just past Claire's house, on the post road; it's brick with a white steeple."

The week flew by almost effortlessly. The next morning, Simm met her group outside the church in plenty of time to walk Rebecca to the pew. Rebecca introduced him to the few interested neighbors who gathered after the meeting. There were few of the town's leading citizens at the small brick church. The men Rebecca was sure Simm needed to meet mostly belonged to the First Church. It might not matter, after all, she reminded herself – she didn't know what town they were to live in.

Simm could tell Rebecca was hiding something. He was wry about at least being able to spot that much. He didn't think the secret would need to be kept for long, so he chose not to confront her. He acknowledged her need to do things her own way. His journey had given him plenty of time to consider Rebecca and her quiet secrets. It was who she was, and who she thought he was. He was sure that she would get used to trusting him in time. Right now, he would leave her to keep the knowledge of the baby a secret from him, until she was comfortable with his knowing. The why of it, however, he did not understand. Honestly, he mused as he put his arm around her to walk her back to Claire Daggette's for a simple dinner, did she think he would not notice the changes in her body – a body he had memorized and dreamed about since she had walked away from him that first morning?

Anyway, she was more beautiful enceinte than she had been as that young, desirable stranger. Rebecca and her secrets he understood – belonging to opposing armies had not been a natural beginning for lovers. Simm hoped that, in time, she would trust him with her demons, before they grew into devils. Now, his own worries nagged at him. He had signed a note for Bill Packard's shipyard and half-built house. Packard had taken all his ready cash, and moved to Canada with his loyalist in-laws and family. That was all well and good, and his men said they would work on the house when they could, faster if he found the cash, but otherwise between paying jobs. How could he bring Rebecca to live in his little salt-box in the dunes? More importantly, how long could he stand living apart, if he could not get the house finished soon?

After dinner, Rebecca walked him north to the crossroads where he and Sisyphus, his new young stallion, would ride off to his new house. The evening was warm with the hint of a salty wind blowing off the water. The sun was low in the sky, with the dark blue of evening climbing upward. They watched gulls heading inland for the night. Rebecca stared into Simm's bright blue eyes, still shocked that they were so near being together forever.

"I will miss you. Knowing that you are closer than ten miles away, maybe that makes me miss you more."

"Then I will miss you more than you miss me. Rebecca, I will try to see you for church again next Sunday. In the meantime, I must get our house built and the business started."

"I will obediently stay away so you can work. Maybe I will spend the week finishing the Roman."

"Good, because I have decided he will hang in the front hall of the house."

"Perhaps you expect too much." Rebecca lifted her face to his, reaching to cradle his face in her hands. He leaned over to kiss her, deepening the kiss until they both felt their legs unsteady beneath them. Then, satisfied that he'd shown her how much he still desired her, he mounted the young stallion and headed to his small home in the tall dunes.

Chapter 20

Monday and Tuesday morning, Rebecca had Peter help her onto the headlands above the beach with the portrait. There, she framed the headlands and ocean behind the soldier. The white- capped waves on the gray sea, and the rocky outcroppings, captured the feel of the warrior's journey and new world, she thought. As the last bit of the outlines were finished, she was not displeased with the affect that was beginning to take shape.

Tuesday afternoon, Rebecca and Claire went to their weekly knitting bee. The town of Beverly was engaged in a friendly contest with Salem, and a few of the other large towns, to see which could knit the most socks for the soldiers. So far, they had knit over two hundred pairs, but most of the women did not care about winning as long as they had a good visit and did a little knitting for their cause.

Usually, Rebecca had very little to contribute to the conversation. She had little news about her own life, and no family in the region to gossip about. She did lift her head out of her thoughts when one of the women started talking about the new owner of Packard's Shipyard.

"Don tells me they call him Simm, but he should be a Fitz ... I guess his brother took that nickname. Anyway, it seems he gave Packard all his money and can't pay the men yet. They like him, and want to work for him, but they have to eat, right? So they've all agreed to give him a few hours here and there. Poor man, he'll never get that house finished before next summer at that rate."

"Peter," Rebecca called when she and Claire got back from the knitting bee, "do you know where Simm's house – I mean the saltbox – is?" The boy nodded. "Good. You are taking me there tomorrow.

Wednesday night Simm walked into his house and was hit in the face with a petticoat. He did not know it was a petticoat, though he was pretty sure it was a linen skirt, a garment of some sort. He threw it on a chair, put his dinner plate on the table and fumbled around for a light. He got the lantern lit and the fire going, then sat down to his dinner. The linen thing, he now knew, was, in fact, a petticoat. The dinner appeared nightly, supplied by his foreman's wife, Susan Trask. The petticoat he was unsure of. It weighed more than the simple garment should, quite a bit more, so he pulled his lantern closer to examine it.

Firstly, he acknowledged that Rebecca had made it. It smelled like her, and the needlework was good but not professional, and so it probably was left here because of some secret lining or message. Intrigued, and amused by the wonders of his new wife, he set to work to unravel the puzzle. From the outside, it looked like a normal petticoat – not one he would have chosen for beauty, but functional. He supposed it was for housework or traveling, and wondered if perhaps Rebecca was upstairs in his house. Two steps up the ladder showed him that it was not so, so he returned to his puzzle.

He turned the garment inside out and found, carefully stitched into the gathers, a row of pockets, each with something round and hard in it. There was no opening, so he sliced the pockets and took out perfectly real-looking gold coins. He decided to consult that little diary to see when these were done. He removed the coins, charmed and impressed with the quality and the number. He shook the petticoat to make sure it had revealed all of its secrets and it rattled, just slightly. He laid it out flat and found the small pocket, lined with muffling sheep's wool, that contained twenty-two small but perfect gemstones. He knew they were perfect; he had chosen them in Antwerp, four years ago.

"Ah, Becky" – he raised his glass to her, alone in his small hut at the edge of the sea – "you are not only beautiful, but clever and frugal. Girl, you barely spent a gold piece, and all the jewels are here. You are right, though; now I can hire the men to build you your house!" He was pleased that she had left him such a delightful puzzle, and pleased that so many coins left over meant it had been as uneventful a journey as she had implied. If it had been more dangerous, more coins would have been slit out of their pockets and used. Simm poured another glass of Susan Trask's dark ale, and sat at the fire to read Rebecca's tale.

Rebecca felt there was no way to prepare for her talk with E.P. Manning. She knew only that she needed to protect herself physically; after all, the man had tried to have her raped, and had been complicit in her tarring and feathering. She dressed carefully, wanting only to evoke the girl he had been obsessed with in Philadelphia, not the woman he had barely noticed in Salem and Beverly. They said that clothes make the man, but how easily man was deceived by clothes. Not finding what she wanted among her current clothes, she went into the boxes of her clothing. She pulled out the gown she had worn the day she sat on the pier and sketched what turned out to have been Jason's FitzSimmon's ship. That seemed an age ago, if was yesterday.

It had rained during the day and the evening, and though it had been warm, it was damp. Now the wind blew chilly off the bay. Partly to protect herself from the cool drizzle, and partly to hide her shape, she pulled out the blue cloak from its crate. She had not seen the cloak since she had packed it in the spring, but there it was – the most perfect blue, the color of the sky just after the sunset, dark and a bit mysterious. She had forgotten how much she loved the garment.

She checked the pockets for moth holes, but the herbs and cedar had done their job and all was fine. She pulled the stiletto knife out of her top drawer, glad that Nat had given it to her, and taught her slightly how to use it. It was four inches long and very thin. Last winter, the few times she had felt the need to wear such a bodice knife it had fit into her boned corset without a problem. Now, it dug into a midriff that had expanded out and upward, into her ribs.

"Well, I can't let that happen!" she said to the baby within, as she pulled the knife away from her expanded middle and out of the corset. She contemplated the hidden pockets of the cloak. They were too deep, which would make the knife inaccessible. A few minutes later, after sewing a new bottom edge to the pocket at her right hand, she went downstairs. Claire was in the dining room, reading a novel by a dying fire. "Claire, I'm going to the beach north of town. I am meeting Manning. I've not told Simm; it would put him in too much danger." Claire understood that women could approach such men without as much danger to themselves. Such men did not see women as threats, as they did other men.

"I was wondering why you were in such a mood this afternoon at dinner. I thought dear Simm was going to shake out your secrets. He is very tolerant, Becky, but I wouldn't live my whole life putting him through this, if I were you.

There is really only so much a man can take."

"I know. I fully intend to tell him everything from now on, but I can't let him be the one to confront Manning."

"And the baby? You are getting too big to hide."

"As soon as Manning leaves, I will tell Simm everything, I promise."

"Don't promise me. I will be your friend forever, dear, but I think you had better promise John FitzSimmon. He's not as all-knowing and omnipotent a being as you have created. He's worried himself nearly sick over you. You don't see how he craves your trust, but I see it, and I recommend that you try to trust him."

"You're right, Claire. I will just finish this last thing."

"Since you agree, I am sending Peter to Ipswich to bring him down. If you finish with Manning before he gets there, good. But if you need help later, he will be there."

"Thank you, Claire." Claire Daggette was right. Rebecca knew that, and it would be good to have Simm there at the end, as long as Manning was gone first. That's what mattered.

The full moon was rising out of the ocean as the sun set. The moon filled the sky, but clouds left over from a rainy day blocked much of its light. Rebecca headed onto the beach north of town at the appointed hour. She scanned to rocky shore for Manning, sure that he would be as anxious as she to hold this meeting. She saw him walking toward her from a sandbar on the other side of the beach. She stood still waiting for his approach, feeling in her pocket for the knife, felt assured when she clasped the hilt of the fine dagger, checking the movement from its sheath. Comforted by the safety it provided, she waited, going over in her mind what Manning might want from her as payment for leaving America.

As she had hour after hour during the past months, she went over what had happened at the man's behest. They had assumed that his actions were due to his hatred of the Howes and their plans for conciliation, and that had fed his hatred for those who worked on that project – Simm and his colleagues. Manning had claimed that his animus toward Simm was merely because Simm had bested or stopped his plans at every turn.

Following them to Massachusetts did not fit that pattern. The Howes' attempts at conciliation had failed. Right now, the war raged on in the northern and Mid-Atlantic colonies, with no clear winner, and it seemed certain to spread south. So what was Manning's reason for following Simm, now that he wasn't even a member of a regiment?

She refused to wave as he rose from the gray mist and fog. He seemed to be an extension of the rocky shore in his black breeches, black boots and dark cloak. If he had a light colored shirt or cravat, they were so well hidden under the outerclothes as to be of no consequence. He loomed larger as he approached. Rebecca checked the handle of the blade one last time, and pulled her hands from the pockets of the familiar cloak.

"Hello, Rebecca, you look lovely in that color. I barely recognized you in those new shades you've taken to wearing."

Rebecca wanted to laugh in his face. Of course the cloak made her beautiful. It was designed to deceive. It certainly had done its job. And here she was again with the blue cloak, and what she hoped would be its final, unpleasant chore. She steeled herself to talk to him.

"Hello, Mr. Manning. I think we must cut the pleasantries short, and ask what can Major FitzSimmon or I do to make you leave here?

"Well, Mistress Willent, of course none of this has been directed at you, and I am sorry you found yourself in the way so often. So I don't believe that there is anything YOU can do about my problems with Major FitzSimmon."

"Manning?" Rebecca began as she slowly sat on a large boulder that seemed to have been left there for her. She watched as the tide edged in and the strand line grew closer. She waited for an answer. Cold from the rock seeped into her, but instead of feeling the chill, she felt powerful, deeply connected to the power of the wind and sea. The strength of a rock that had been left on this spot so long ago, and withstood innumerable poundings by the sea and storm, appealed to her. She paused just a minute to finish her thoughts and started again.

"Mr. Manning, you have insisted that your argument is with John FitzSimmon. Yet all the attacks were upon me, aimed at me. I was not simply in the way, as you implied. There was one when, as far as we both knew, the Major was out of town in New York City. So, do explain to me how that attempted rape, if you recall, was an attack on the Major?"

"Miss Willent," Manning began to whine, rubbing the small pocket of his waistcoat, "believe me when I say that I did not orchestrate that attack on you. Truly, young lady, to think I would instruct such ruffians to behave in such a way is incomprehensible." He gained speed as his voice got higher, and Rebecca chose not to listen to his babbling.

"Manning!" Rebecca called out to make him stop. "I repeat! is there anything I can do to make you go away – from America – and leave Major FitzSimmon alone?"

"But Becky dear, you can't do anything because it has nothing to do with you." Manning nervously patted the big pockets in his knee length coat.

"Am I just an instrument then? Something you taunt and injure, to punish a good man who can only look on in a blind rage or find me bloodied after the perpetrators have fled?"

"Oh Rebecca, you mean much more to me than that. Why, if you would come with me to London, all my colleagues would be so envious. You are such a pretty young thing, so fair, so innocent, you could be mine, and I would take such good care of you, put you in a nice house in Town. When the FitzSimmons are finished, there will be just you and me."

Rebecca was not surprised. His words did not shock or surprise. She felt the rage boil to the point where everything moved slowly. Truly, it was a relief to have the parameters she had struggled with so clearly presented. There could be no ambiguity about Manning's rules for the future. Either she would leave with Manning, and he would destroy Simm, or she could stay here with John and he would destroy them both. The only way to accomplish the better and third choice, that he leave them alone, was to leave E.P. Manning dead. There seemed to be no alternative offered other than that third one.

With clear determination, Rebecca pushed herself off the boulder and walked over the wet sand, over to the man in black. He started in surprise, but quickly regained his composure and stepped toward her to welcome the young woman into his life.

Rebecca moved into his arms as he enfolded her in a flabby, weak embrace. She lifted her lips to his, as she slowly and carefully felt for the thin dagger from the pocket inside the blue cloak. In one beautifully smooth motion, the knife left its sheath. She held Manning close in a false hug with one arm, while with the other she pushed the knife under his ribs and straight into his heart. She heard him gasp for air as she stepped away from him.

Manning fell almost instantly onto the wet sand. He looked up at her, shock registered on his face, as his body lost life and his heart spilled blood into the incoming tide. He motioned her closer and she felt she owed him his dying words. When she was close enough, sitting on her heels in the sand, he whispered his dying words: "That Rebecca, was well-played."

Rebecca was sure that the man had something in those pockets worth getting at. She waited patiently until she was sure he was dead, revolted by touching him, even in death. She reached into the pockets he had continually patted and pulled out official-looking documents. She checked his other pockets for money or identification. Removing those would not make him harder to identify, but could make it seem he was killed during a robbery.

Peter had left the house minutes after Rebecca. The dim light of the setting sun and rising moon lit his way north to Simm's cabin. It took the boy only seconds to catch his breath before he spoke.

"Simm, it's Rebecca! She has gone to the town beach to meet Manning. Mother sent me to tell you. You know the spot? It's covered with boulders, not too good for pulling up boats, very handy for smugglers."

Simm nodded as he pulled on his leathers. He put a pistol in his pocket and strapped on his sword, feeling more completely dressed than he had in quite a few months. Luckily, the horse was just outside the door in a lean-to. Simm didn't bother with a saddle for the short ride – just a bridle and reins. "Pete, go to sleep. I'll tell your mother that you're fine and you'll be home in the morning."

The moonlit sky made the ride safe, as Simm and Sisyphus raced the seven miles. The horse had no trouble getting up the hill overlooking the beach. Simm stood on the headland, looking down at a man on the ground and a woman kneeling by him, seeming to be listening to him. He heard yelling and turned to see two men walking up the beach toward him. They did not appear to be friendly, so he cocked his pistol and checked his sword at his side.

Simm got to the bottom of the hill as the first man swung at his head. He ducked and ran at him, pushing him down into the sand. The daylong storm had left even the uplands of the beach wet and muddy, so in a short time all three men were sandy and damp. Finally, Simm was able to catch his breath and stand a short distance away from the two men, who were both doubled over trying to regain their breath and composure in order to resume the fight.

"Gentlemen" – Simm spoke politely as he could while trying to catch his breath. He pulled his pistol from his pocket and continued – "I don't know why you've decided to attack me, so if one of you could speak, I would appreciate an explanation."

"You FitzSimmon?" the first one who caught his breath asked.

"Yes, I am. Is that a good reason to attack?"

"S'posed to kill you."

"Oh, I am enlightened. You work for my good friend Manning. From what I can see, the man has already returned to the sea." Simm pointed his pistol and sword at the men, "I think you should row away from here in that little dory you came in on. Nice solid boat out there anchored, should take you far enough never to be seen in these parts again. I recommend it."

The men had moved down the beach as Simm herded them with the pistol and encouraged them with the sword. Soon, they were rowing furiously back to the little ship anchored beyond the rocks.

Rebecca put Manning's papers carefully in the secret pockets of the cloak for safekeeping. She took off the cloak, rolled it up, and left it on a dry rock above the strand line. Then, dressed in her simple house gown, she approached Manning's body, ready to push it beyond the rocks so it could be caught by the tide.

She carefully climbed over the slippery rocks, heading back toward the lifeless body. In the distance, she heard shouting and the sound of fists against flesh, but concentrating on the task before her, she put one foot carefully in from of the other and began to push the body into the deep current.

The moon was higher and smaller in the night sky, telling Rebecca how long she had been at the shore since the sun went down. She pulled and pushed the floating body past the rocks and sandbars that would trap it close to shore. Finally, past the last sandbar, she pushed Manning into the waves and watched the tide pull his body out to sea.

Now she turned to stumble back toward the land, to dry stockings and her warm cloak. As she stepped out of the deep current, the ocean swirled around her and she quickly realized that she had been standing on a sandbar. From this point she would have to head into deeper water, to try to swim in her heavy skirts if she didn't want to let the rising ocean carry her out to sea. She kept the vision of her dry shoes and warm cloak foremost in her mind.

Rebecca pushed herself into the cold ocean. The chill ate at her, and she barely had the strength to find the land.

Without the energy to swim in the rough waves, she let the swirling tide drag her toward the shore, using her last strength to hold her head above the water.

Numb with cold, she lay face down in the sand. Part of her just wanted to stay there and let the powerful ocean pull her back into the deep, cold water. Numbness engulfed her – numb not only with cold, but with the realization that she had just killed a man. She climbed out onto the shore just far enough to escape the incoming tide and let the weariness overtake her.

"Becky! Becky, are you alright?" Simm sat down in the wet sand next to her and pulled her into his arms. "Oh my god, sweetheart, you are so wet you're shivering. Lets get you home."

"Simm, I killed him." Rebecca could hardly get the words out. She was so tired and the cold was eating at her.

"Manning? Good, I approve – don't think any more of it. Now, where did you put him? I don't want those two buffoons finding their boss. Is that what you were doing in the water, pushing him into Neptune's arms? Honey, I did see you, but I couldn't help sooner. I'm sorry, he had sent two men to try and kill me."

"I – I pushed him out into the current, he'll head south, m-maybe wash up in the harbor or down in Boston, tha'at would be good?"

"Yes, darling that'll be good." Simm wanted to say that hell would be too good for the man, but this was not the time. He stood, lifting her in his arms as he got up. He whistled for Sisyphus, who trotted over obligingly, and waited patiently. Simm lifted Rebecca onto the horse and swung up behind her. "Becky, lets get you warm, I'm taking you back to Claire Daggette's. I need to tell her Pete is fine."

"Simm, my cloak is near one of the big boulders on the beach – you need the documents in the pockets." Then she drifted off to sleep in his arms.

The streets were quiet and nearly empty. Only a few walkers on their way home from dinner were about to see the unusual couple on the dark horse. Sundays were strictly governed by custom and law, so most townsfolk were indoors with family or already asleep. Sisyphus took them the short distance to the Daggette house without incident. Simm left the horse in the back and scratched on the kitchen door. He carried Rebecca into the kitchen where Claire Daggette waited, stirring a pot of soup.

"Hot water, please, Claire. She is cold and near sick."

"It's on the hearth, lots of it. I'll go and get the tub." Claire Daggette dragged the big wooden tub into the kitchen. "Rebecca, drink some of that soup, it will perk you right up. Simm, ladle some into a mug for her while I fill the tub."

Everyone did as they were bid in silence, until Simm remembered he had a message for Claire. He told her that Pete was staying the night in his cottage, and that he would send the boy home in the morning. He helped Claire fill the wooden tub with steaming water, and helped Rebecca out of her wet skirts and into the tub. Claire helped her wash the salt off and rinsed her hair, while Simm drank the nourishing soup and carried on polite talk with his hostess.

As Rebecca revived, it was clear she wanted nothing more than to go to sleep and put this day behind her.

"Simm?" she remembered, "you really have to get the blue cloak I left on the boulder." She emphasized the word "blue" so he would know to look in the pockets. Manning's papers contained one secret she wanted him to know first. A little while later, her hair in a towel with a warm robe over her nightclothes, she walked him to the door.

Simm pulled her into his arms and kissed her gently, holding her against him for long minutes before he spoke, "Becky, I will be back at mid-morning. Sleep as late as you want, but after that we are spending the day together. I want to show you the hut, and the new house and shipyard." Rebecca leaned against his hard, warm chest, feeling safe and comfortable. She didn't want this rock of stability to leave, but he kissed her on the forehead and left, closing the door behind him.

Simm rode by moonlight. Stopping first at the beach, he looked around the large boulder near where Manning's body had fallen, until he found the wool cloak. Once again, he noted that the weight of the wool, and the design of the pockets, made it impossible to feel the papers hidden inside. Breathing in the smell of Rebecca that permeated the soft wool, he pulled the warm garment over his own shoulders against the chill of the night.

He let the horse go as fast as he wanted once they were beyond the town buildings, and they soon made it back to the little house on the river. Charging hard across the marshes, Simm let speed and wind deplete the anger and worry he had stored in his gut. But he was angry at Rebecca for not telling him that she was going alone to confront Manning. What possessed her, after everything they had gone through? What if the man had killed her? And where did that knife come from? He hoped the man had revealed something of why he felt such hatred toward them, because now that he was dead, he would not talk.

But the man's death opened so many possibilities. With Manning's threats and obstacles finally gone, Simm could start to create a life with Rebecca, and she could begin to trust him with more than her lovely body. Which led to the other question. Why was Rebecca waiting to tell him about the baby? Was it not his? Had something happened on her journey that she was afraid to tell him? The coins and her journal did not lead that way, but why wait? He feared that he would toss with worry all night, but instead, he walked silently into the small hut and found the boy asleep in front of the fire. He climbed over him and up the ladder, where he fell on the soft mattress and was immediately asleep.

Rebecca woke the next morning, sure that something terrible had happened, but she could not place what it had been. The memory of E.P. Manning's threats teased at the corner of her mind. After a minute, the full image of pushing Nat's knife deep between his ribs and stopping his evil but still beating heart rose before her. As she woke, the full event came back to her and she swallowed hard, trying not to vomit. That worked just a minute, and she found the chamber pot just in time.

She washed and started to dress in a plain daygown, something suitable for staying in, or for going to the workshop and working on a painting. She tied the underskirts, thinking that something had not jogged out in her memory. Nothing seemed different. Everything felt the same as it had yesterday when she dressed to meet Manning. Slowly, she replayed the evening. It was when she leaned over to straighten the quilts that she found the bricks that Simm had heated and put in her bed. She put her head in her hands and started to cry over her foolishness.

She stemmed the cries, and stared straight into the small mirror on her wall.

"Why did I put myself and my baby in danger? Why do I always need to do things alone?" She chastised herself, vowing to ask for help from her dearest friend from then on. "And why, oh why, didn't I invite him to stay the night?"

The girl in the mirror nodded, and smiled at her forward thinking. Rebecca went to her clothes press and chose the gown the mantua maker had told her to wear in fall. She could see why now. It was cut to hide an expanding midriff and larger breasts, but more than that, it matched the energy of the bright September morning, a day of new schools for children and bright beginnings. The dress was soft wool and raw silk, a soft, golden yellow with a bluish green stripe. The gown was open from above the waist, and the stomacher and petticoat were of matching green silk as pretty as the gown. Glad to have a reason to dress in her finest, she gave herself the order to march forth into the new day, threw back her shoulders, and went downstairs to breakfast.

"You alone, Becky? Thought that Greek god of a husband would have spent the night."

"I'm afraid I was too tired for company, He is stopping by mid-morning." Rebecca sat and helped herself to popovers and honey.

"What happened between you and Manning?" Just as Rebecca was about to tell the story, the door flew open and Peter rushed in.

"Ma, I just rode the most beautiful horse over here from Ipswich. She is with foal, but is still the most spirited horse. Her name is Artemis, and she flies like the wind. Rebecca?" Peter barely stopped for air, "what happened with Manning? Simm came back intact, though I think he favors his left leg, and you are still alive?" Peter made that last statement sound like a question.

Rebecca rolled her eyes, and motioned for Peter to take a seat. "I met Manning on the beach as planned, and as he talked I realized there were two choices for me. The first was that I leave here and go with him to London, where he would put me up and he would take care of me, so to speak. To fulfill that choice, he said he 'would destroy the FitzSimmons'. I don't know what 'destroy' meant – destroy financially, destroy John's reputation, or if he intended to see him dead – he just said 'destroy.'

"I decided on different choice – a world without E.P. Manning. I'm afraid I killed him. I would rather have not, but he didn't offer a real alternative. I doubt anyone will report him missing. And I think he will not wash up here in Essex." Rebecca stopped herself from hysterical giggles, taking a few deep breaths until she calmed down.

"Ma," Peter broke the mood by changing the subject, "Simm says I can work at the shipyard over the summer and weekends now, when I don't have school. And if I work hard, and we like each other, he will take me on at the yard as an apprentice, and I can learn to be a shipwright. You know I love boats and ships, and you don't want me to go to sea. Do you think I could?"

Claire said that she would think about it and discuss it with Simm on another day, not today, but her happy, smiling face showed what she thought of the idea.

"Rebecca," Claire turned back to her friend, "I saw that man on the street, and in the stores these past few weeks. He was already stirring up trouble. I am sorry you killed him. Not because his death is a bad thing, but because it is hard to kill and, if the killer is a good person, he or she always pays a price. But – and please believe I am speaking from my heart – that man needed killing. So I may be sorry you had to kill him, but I am glad you did." Claire rose from her seat and pulled Rebecca into a thorough bear hug.

She turned her head and spoke to her son. "Now Pete, we won't speak of this to anyone. If the man's body does wash up, you and I won't even take notice of it. We only saw him the once, walking down the street. We didn't see him confront Simm. If anyone saw that incident and mentions it, we didn't notice it. Right, son?"

"Right, Ma." Peter nodded at his mother and stood behind Rebecca to give her shoulders a friendly squeeze.

Feeling cared for and valued, Rebecca went upstairs with warm water to wash the honey off her fingers and finish dressing for a day with Simm. She carefully washed her face and teeth, brushed her flyaway hair into some sort of order, plopped a cap over it and grabbed a light shawl in case the wind was cool. Rebecca had entered her workshop to check on a few paintings when the door opened and Simm came in. He'd left the door open, and she could see two horses saddled and ready to ride.

"John," Rebecca almost whispered it, not quite believing they were now free to do something as simple as leave the door open. "Could we leave the horses for a while and just walk the quay? I feel as though we have never been able to show ourselves."

Simm knew precisely what she meant. He tied the horses to Claire's back porch, and took Rebecca's arm for a simple walk to the shops on a Monday morning. And it was a beautiful morning. The storm of the day before had blown away, and the September morning was clear and warm. There was a brisk wind blowing from the west, and although it spoke of colder weather to come, it did not harbor any chill. It seemed so familiar, and yet so unknown being in public with the woman who was his wife. He was sure the townsfolk who knew them both, separately, might wonder at their reconciliation, but it was better to look happy than to offer explanations. So they said hello to people they knew, and introduced the other as needed.

Rebecca brought him to her new dressmaker Lydia's shop. Then they visited Mr. Bennett, a portraitist, who bemoaned Rebecca's talent as wasted on a girl who would choose to paint pretty pictures of her children and friends over the great art she was capable of creating. Simm commiserated with the older man, expressing sympathy for the wasted talent so many girls had, since they were not given the chance to fly independent of men. But he promised he would not thwart any endeavor his wife might pursue.

Simm was no stranger to the merchants of Beverly and, Rebecca supposed, Salem as well. She noticed that more than one of the wealthier gentlemen greeted him, and said good-day to her with great respect. This world of merchant aristocracy was strange to her. Although her uncle had been a merchant, he had died when she was still a small girl. Now Simm would associate with the Derbys, the Crowninshields, the Cabots – all the important men in the county. Had he already entered that rarified world while she was worried about Manning spotting him?

Could she adjust to being the wife of such a man, farm girl that she was? She had known farmers, merchants and ministers, her neighbors, her aunt and her friends, the wives of merchants. She reminded herself that she was not only a farm girl, but educated to Amalia's world as well. After all, Simm had found her sketching his brothers' *Good Queen Bess*. Hadn't she always been drawn to the elegance of these beautiful ships, and their symmetrical perfection?

Now she stood in front of the rows of wood and brick shops on the quay in Beverly, Massachusetts, six hundred miles from home, and considered her life. Listening to Simm discuss shipping rate changes due to the continued blockade, she saw the future in a flash, all of it surrounding John FitzSimmon. In that moment, she saw children, ships masts and wind-swept salt hay. She moved imperceptibly closer to Simm, and squeezed his arm beneath her hand, which had laid calmly on his white sleeve. With that came the realization that whatever changes might come her way, she truly did love this man, and this man was her path.

Now, she couldn't wait to tell him. Suddenly, she was anxious in a way she hadn't been. The week since their dinner had been almost too long. In that week, she had found him, although it seemed he was not so very lost. Her moment of light had made her feel a bit dizzy, and she needed to interrupt him so they could leave. But she did not know how to address him in public. Some wives used their husbands' last names. That seemed too formal. Some wives even used "mister," but that would never do for her. She made a decision she hoped was the right one,

"John, I hate to bother you, but I think I need to get out of the sun and sit down."

Simm excused them, explaining they had a luncheon waiting for them, and took his leave of the men he was chatting with. He took Rebecca's arm and they strolled back toward Claire Daggette's carefully, on the shady side of the street.

"Becky do you feel alright? Are you ill? You look a bit piqued?"

"Simm, it'll pass, just give me a minute." She took a deep breath to calm nerves that suddenly made themselves known.

"I need to speak to you. Can we get the horses and go somewhere?" She looked pleadingly into his ice blue eyes, feeling like he might not forgive her for keeping so much from him, but needing to trust him with everything, from now on.

Simm led her to Claire's porch and sat her on a chair while he got her a drink of cool water. Claire looked up from her darning and nodded but said nothing, letting Simm do what he thought best. She did glance out the window to make sure Rebecca was not ill. Satisfied that it was the sun or nerves, she went back to her handwork.

Rebecca approached Artemis, feeling like she was reconnecting with an old friend. She patted the mare's neck and underbelly to feel the small foal growing within, getting strength from the wonderful horse to tell Simm all of her secrets and fears, before this ride would end.

Simm wished he could tell Rebecca that he already knew what she needed to say. He understood that it was essential that she do it as she had planned. He knew the moment was important to her. It was important to him that she willingly tell him the important things in her life.

He felt like a simple man. He watched her talk to, and nuzzle, his beloved horse. He wanted to pat his wife as she had just patted Artemis, and let her know that he would love and support her no matter who the father of the child might be.

Simm mounted Sisyphus and followed her out the post road toward the north. As they left the town, Rebecca gave the energetic horse free rein, and the ladies took off like the wind. Simm followed at a pleasant trot, not wanting to race, or to intrude on one of Rebecca's rare flights of fun. Soon, she found a meadow with a fresh water stream, and stopped to let the horse drink. Simm and Sisyphus rode up soon after. He dismounted and came to where she was standing, staring at the distance.

"Rebecca, I know you want to talk to me, and I am going to sit here quietly and listen, I promise. But I must say something first. I have been a soldier since I was sixteen. I understand far better than most, that in wartime things happen that are no one's fault." He looked at her with a wistful air. "No pair of foolish lovers could have been more entangled by being on opposite sides of a war than we. Please know that whatever you tell me, I understand whatever you have had to do. And remember, I love you."

"I will now be quiet and let you speak." Simm sat on the grass in the warm meadow, listening to the quiet buzz of bees in the wildflowers, and waited for Rebecca to begin.

"I know, looking backward, that I should have told you that Manning had agreed to meet me. I did a foolish and dangerous thing. I might have been killed." She gulped air, hoping the next words would be easy. "I might even have killed the baby, by being so selfish." She whispered the last so quietly, the words were almost swept away by the wind. Rebecca looked at Simm, waiting to see if he would respond.

Simm said nothing. There was no reason to chastise her for what had already happened. Rebecca continued, "I know, I just told you that I'm pregnant. John, I should have told you right away, it just didn't seem to be the right time, with Manning still to be dealt with. I saw a doctor when I was in Boston. He said I am fine, and the baby will arrive in December or January. I was sick at the beginning, especially on the ship, the *Papillon,* for all those days. I covered up the pregnancy by claiming it was seasickness. I'm not sure anyone on board cared. Mostly they were concerned with outrunning or avoiding the blockade, and meeting up with the smaller boats in the coves and inlets."

Rebecca stopped talking, waiting for Simm's reaction to her news. He stared into the distance at the blue, late morning sky, waiting to see if she would continue.

When it was clear that she had finished, Simm turned onto his side and pulled himself onto an elbow. He did not want to sound angry, or imply anything that might anger her, but he needed to ask the question that had been nagging at him. He took a very deep breath and plunged in. "Becky, I need to ask just one question. I said at the beginning that war creates chaos out of normal lives, so if someone other than myself is the father of your child, I will raise it as my own, but I need to know. Is that the case?"

"That someone other than you is the father?" Rebecca was almost angry at his words. She bit her tongue, and stopped herself from reacting when she realized that Simm was not accusing her of anything evil. He was asking if she had been a victim of an event over which she'd had no control, like those men in the woods, or the sailors those first few days and nights on board, if she had not spent so much time leaning over the side of the boat.

She stood up, and walked the few steps to where he was lying on the grass. She sat close to him and looked deep into those bright blue eyes. "Simm, I would have found a way to tell you. If I had been attacked, you would know, you darling man," she took his hand and placed it over her abdomen. "Simm, this little one is yours and only yours. I can absolutely promise you that she will have the ginger hair you've threatened me with."

"I threatened you with red hair?"

"Well, a long time ago, you mentioned that all first girls in your family are gingers."

"That is undeniably true, but it seems a cruel fact with which to threaten a young girl."

Rebecca put her hand on his cheek and smiled back into that familiar face. "I think it is a girl, and if she is a redhead, she is certainly yours. If so, we can name her Elizabeth and call her Libby, after your mother. Did you know that lots of babies are being named Liberty, Freedom, Independence, and such? We could name her Liberty, and call her Libby, then pretend to your family she is an Elizabeth."

"But, mother would delight in her being Liberty. I really must make sure you meet her someday soon. As for going to Britain –"

"Yes?" Rebecca sat straighter as Simm became serious again.

"I read the documents you saved from E.P. Manning's pockets. And you were correct in meeting him alone, and very right thinking he had to be dead, if we were to have a life together. It took half the night, but I think I know what he was after." Simm stood and walked over to Sisyphus. He took the saddlebags off the horse and brought them over the where they were sitting. He reached in and pulled out a soft, clean horse blanket, Susan Trask's fresh cider in a stoppered bottle, and meat pies.

" A picnic lunch, thank you!" Rebecca took the blanket and opened it onto the ground. She found the mugs at the bottom of the bag, and set the food out. Unable to wait, she started eating while Simm told the rest of his story.

"I told Susan we would need food." He motioned to the picnic lunch, and stopped her from asking why he would think so. "I think you need to hear why it turned out you were right. Manning told you that he would take you to London to be his mistress, yes?" Rebecca nodded, her mouth too full of pie to answer. "Well, that is only partly true. It seems, from my own research on the man, that he does not actually like girls, which explains quite a lot, but he did intend to bring you to London, as bait.

"Manning didn't want his ruffians to hurt me, just to bring me along if they caught me. Or if they didn't catch me, he knew I would follow, to rescue you in England. Then, once we were both in London, he planned to create some sort of show trial of the beautiful American spy. His plan was that you would be sentenced to hang for treason. Then, because you were my lover and wife, carrying my child would be a great bonus, I would be charged with treason for helping you and hanged as well. Or maybe even only I would hang; they often commute sentences of pregnant mothers.

"But Manning wanted something bigger than us. Having either one of us dead really meant nothing to him. His goal was to discredit my older brothers, both of whom sit in Parliament. He might have hoped to blackmail them. Can you imagine the scandal for MPs who have a younger brother who is about to be charged with treason to the crown and hanged? Can you imagine what those brothers would do to keep the family name clean and that brother alive? Then, with the FitzSimmons under his control, the Whigs would have lost important votes in both the House of Commons and Lords, and Manning and the King would be even more powerful. Unfortunately, it would have worked."

Rebecca had been listening carefully, following Simm's reasoning as he went through the plot against them. She jumped in at that point. "Simm, he said that he needed to 'destroy the FitzSimmons.' I thought he meant you, but I think you are right; this was to destroy the political careers of all his opponents."

"Luckily for all of us, Becky, your instincts were good. If I had been there with you, or instead of you, he would have brought out his henchmen and grabbed us. But because it was an assignation, he came alone, thinking he could simply trick you. As I said, he didn't like, or think much of, women.

"You not only saved us, but you saved the careers and reputations of some very good men. I think a simple 'thank you' is not enough." He leaned over to kiss her. She moved into his arms and deepened the kiss. He rolled her under him and ran a finger slowly over the sun-kissed skin peeping from the distractingly low neckline. He let his fingers run along the fine stitching on the bodice of her gown. He gently cupped her breast in his free hand, teasing at the nipple through the layers of gown and shift.

Rebecca moaned gently as Simm began to tease her breasts. She opened her lips to his and drank him in. She felt him harden as he leaned over her. She breathed his essence deeply into her lungs and found that her body remembered belonging to him, in a way that God and law could only whisper.

Simm began to talk to her as he stared into her smokey blue eyes. "Rebecca, what I would love to do right now is to undress you layer by layer. I want to remove every last secret with every stitch of clothing. Then, with the sun bleaching away all our pasts, I would like to explore all my favorite spots on your beautiful body, from the tip of your head and your earlobes to the tips of your toes. I want to discover and rediscover all that was familiar, and the new luscious, voluptuous curves you have developed since I saw you last." He put his ear on her abdomen waiting for the slight movement of his child within.

Rebecca was sure they had teased at their reunion long enough. She ached for him, but wasn't sure she was willing to shed her clothes in a hay meadow so near the road. As Simm described undressing her, she wanted to show him her new shape, something she had been shy about until that moment. She looked up into the brilliant blue sky, and lost herself in the wonder of being with Simm.

She put her hands up and pulled his mouth to hers. Deepening the kiss, Simm ran his hand over the gown, feeling the shape of the women within. He put his hand on Rebecca's leg and slowly moved inside her skirts, feeling her arousal and listening to her breath quicken. At that moment, a large black dog trotted over and dropped a stick as large as a small tree trunk at Simm's side.

Simm picked up the stick and threw it for the dog to fetch. "Becky, where Gall is, his family will not be far behind. Here." He pulled her to a sitting position, fixed her shawl over her shoulders, and put her cap back over her flyaway hair. Rebecca stood and fixed her skirts, feeling very kissed, but instead of any sort of chagrin she felt rather proud.

"Gall? What a strange name."

"Like black ink from an oak gall," Simm mumbled into her ear, not wanting the Trasks to appear any sooner than expected. He got up to walk off some of his physical discomfort, while Rebecca fixed her skirts and bodice. He trotted away from her, where Gall could see him, and he whistled for the dog. As the black beast gambled over with his stick, a smiling matron and her freckle-faced daughter came into view.

"Well, if it ain't our Jackie! And you must be his Missus."

"Jackie?" Rebecca was amused and vastly curious.

"Well, we didn't want to call him *Mister* FitzSimmon,

even though he is the boss, and John, well there are too many of those, and of course, no one hardly calls him that. I don't like the children calling men by their manly nicknames, so the kids and I call him Jack. I know, it ain't his name. But he comes in here to buy out Packard – makes a new life, needs a new name, has a new wife. There Mari – Mama made a rhyme.

"I'm Susan Trask, by the way." The woman held out a large, friendly hand. Rebecca shook it. This is my last, Marigold, Mari for short. I confess the others are all Stephens and Matildas, but by the eighth I needed something prettier, so she is my flower. The girl rolled her eyes, and smiled at Rebecca with an understanding beyond her years. "My husband, Tom, is the foreman at the shipyard."

Rebecca finally remembered where she had heard the name. "Trask – Susan, you made the cider we just had, and the pie. Lunch was delicious, thank you, Ma'am. I'm Rebecca, by the way. Becky if you like."

"Very welcome, Becky. Come talk to me soon about the baby. Don't look surprised! I can always tell, usually from one month on. I'm the local midwife, as well as a great cook and sometime dog walker. We live on the hill right above Jackie's little hut. Visit anytime. Come along, Mari, let's leave these two to their afternoon." She whistled and tapped her leg, and the good-natured black monster named Gall followed.

Simm waited until they were out of sight to grab Rebecca, and burst into a fit of laughter. Rebecca was shocked. She had never actually seen Simm relaxed enough to laugh hard, certainly not like this, but she joined in, relishing the sheer joy of the moment. "What kind of dog is that? If he is a dog?" Rebecca asked through her giggles.

"It's a Newfoundland. Named after the island where those behemoths rescue sailors from the frigid sea. Gall is very friendly, if a bit alarming. Susan is just like her dog. I could not live up here alone without her. You will see, she is a very valuable neighbor and friend. Her husband, Tom, is my foreman at the shipyard; I am lucky to have him. He worked the yard for Packard, and could go off on his own, but with such a big family, he is happy for steady pay. By the way, Susan really is a very successful midwife. All the neighbors mention it when they speak of her."

"Then she will be mine. Simm, my love," Rebecca began rather slyly. Simm pricked his ears waiting for the question. "How is it that you talk to neighbors about midwives, when you did such a good job not knowing I was pregnant?"

"I confess to knowing the minute I laid eyes on you in that little workshop."

"Did Claire or Pete tell you?" Rebecca knew she had been clear that she wanted to tell Simm herself.

"No honey, no one told me. You had changed too much not to be. You forget that I am a child of a crowded estate, with marriages and babies, puppies, kittens, lambs and foals being born all the time. Also, a regiment on the move has wives and camp followers. Soldiers being soldiers, there are babies created, and born along the way. When I saw you, I saw the changes between April and September. What I don't understand is why you did not feel you could tell me." Simm looked at her for the truth.

"Manning. If we could not get rid of him, I wanted you free to run from me. So, then, I was shy until today." Rebecca was relieved to put that fear to word and to rest.

Simm kissed Rebecca, holding her tightly to him for a moment, before he took her arm and walked her over to the horses. They mounted, and Simm guided the way to, and through, the new house, the shipyard and, finally, the small saltbox in the dunes.

Rebecca was awestruck. She knew she should have expected that each of Simm's purchases would exceed her expectations. The house they would live in was not yet finished, but the exterior would be completed before the weather shifted. It was a symmetrical L-shaped structure, with two central chimneys and a wide front porch that was already welcoming. She could envision the rooms full of warmth and laughter.

She found she was choosing colors as Simm spoke to some of the workmen and introduced her to the crew. She smiled politely, not wanting to admit that her mind had drifted into questions of smuggled imported versus domestic fabric, and the current question in colonists' minds was made very personal right here – was there yet fine-enough domestic fabric for John FitzSimmon's house?

The shipyard was on the river, no more than a mile from the house. Rebecca had never gone so close to ships being built. There were no fewer than twenty men busy at various tasks, two ships nearly finished, and wood of various types and colors. These were sorted by size and shapes and stored in piles, or already on the ground, laid against a chalk outline of the hull of the ship.

She walked through the yard, aware and careful of where she put her feet, but mostly aware of the respect and comradery that Simm received from his men. She had noted his effect on those who worked for him in Philadelphia, but not with such pride. Now she was more than proud of how he put together the crews on both the house and at the shipyard. She found that his command of his world made her love him even more.

As they toured the shipyard and met the dubbers and sawyers, carpenters and caulkers, she wanted to pull Simm aside and tell him what she had discovered here in Ipswich that she could not have realized in Pennsylvania. She smiled a secret smile and was pleased to meet the workers. Finally, with the tours and introductions over, it was time to see the little Saltbox where Simm was living.

The house was nestled in the dunes, almost on the grounds of the shipyard, and within shouting distance of the Trasks's house. But it didn't feel part of the busy world around it. Perhaps because it was nearly one hundred years old, built by of the first settlers of the town, it felt like it came from another time. The front of the house faced the small estuary that fed the Ipswich River. It had two stories in the front and one at the back, with a shed built at the back to hold things, like snow shovels and rakes, that would not fit in the house. Simm had built a lean-to onto the side of the house for the horses, and they walked them in, fed and watered them, and toweled them down.

Simm took Rebecca's hand and led her into the house. There were only three windows on the first floor, and very little light came down from the second floor. The effect, however, was not darkness, but a pleasant closeness. Rebecca saw that the fireplace, for heat and cooking, took an entire wall on one side where windows might have been.

Simm lit a small fire for hot water, and soon they were able to wash and have chamomile tea.

"Becky, Are you hungry? We have another pie from lunch, and some chicken and dumplings Susan seems to have left us while we were touring the shipyard."

"A small bit of the chicken, I think. If I get too hungry, I feel sick. It doesn't do to wait till the clock says to eat."

"Modern man's obsession with clocks and time-keeping. We should all eat when we are hungry, but it might destroy civilization as we know it." He served them both moderate helpings, and they sat to the early dinner.

"Things might not be so easy when I assume the cooking. I don't recall having things ready ahead of time." Rebecca looked into the past, remembering their year at the farmhouse.

"Well, it turned out that you had other concerns, as I discovered." She nodded in response, and they ate in comfortable silence. Simm lifted her empty plate, and kissed her lightly on the lips. He put the plates down near the hearth, and poured two small glasses of wine. He turned back expectantly, not sure what Rebecca was ready for, though he sensed she was far more comfortable in his company than she had been the week before. Without turning back to gauge his reaction, she took her wine and led the way up the small staircase to the second floor.

Their were two rooms off the staircase. Each had one window and a slitted vent on the back wall that could be opened on hot days, and closed tightly on cold. One room was full to the low ceiling with wooden crates and clothing. The other had a beautiful bed that took up the entire room. In fact, the room fit the bed so well that one had to step onto it from the open door. Rebecca went into the first little room. She kicked off her shoes and unbuttoned her waistcoat, untied her skirt, and slipped out of her gown. She picked up her glass and, wearing only her shift, stepped into the narrow hall.

She looked across at Simm. He was on the bed, on his side, relaxed, leaning on one elbow drinking wine. A familiar expression on his face brought tingles from Rebecca's scalp to her toes. He smiled and motioned for Rebecca to join him on the bed. She handed him her glass and jumped onto the bed, wondering briefly if that would be possible a few months from now. She sat with her legs folded, considering the man lying next to her.

She took his wine and put it on the windowsill behind the headboard, placing hers there as well. She slipped out of her shift and lay on her back on the soft bed, her head resting on a pillow. Then she took his free hand and placed it on her belly. She lay still, saying nothing, just letting him explore all his favorite spots, and giving him plenty of time to delve into all her new luscious curves.

Later – much later – Simm asked if Claire would worry about her staying away, and Rebecca answered that Claire would think she was unnatural if she came back.

"Then let us shun civilization twice in one day, and be natural." Simm laughed as he pulled her back to him.

Chapter 21

December 27, 1778

The days before Christmas had been busy. The new house was finally finished; the furniture was in, and the chimneys drew as expected. Rebecca had packed and moved her things from Claire Daggette's, with the agreement that the herbs' seedlings would be collected in the spring. Peter had immediately moved his new tools into Rebecca's rooms, now vacant. In payment for her cleaning out so well, and more quickly than his mother had expected, he'd offered to drive a cart with her and her last few things over to Ipswich, ahead of schedule. He'd waved happily as he turned the team to return them to the stable.

Now Rebecca walked into her new house. The walls were painted a golden yellow, with stark white trim around ceilings, walls and doors. It was a color she had not expected to like, but the silent gray skies of the early afternoon made her pleased with her choice. She had surprised Simm by stenciling a pattern onto the walls of each room. He had been pleased with the results, but kept reminding her not to work so hard. But, she thought as she completed more and more of the rooms, these stencils were now the fashion, and were a wonderful way to use her talent. It had only taken a few weeks, and as the workers were finishing the last details on the house, she had worked in rooms they had already completed.

The stenciling had been fun. By Christmas day, she had finished all the upstairs bedrooms and was almost finished with the downstairs. The stencils were made up of animals and flowers for some of the patterns, and an eagle design for the edging in the dining room. The main, public room of the house required something extra, and Rebecca had spent the morning drawing and cutting out a new stencil with flowers and leaves in a wreath design.

The sun was still high in the sky as she painted, glad to be using the natural light through the unclothed windows. Standing on a low stool, she was just finishing the wreaths around the front windows in the parlor, and was ready to bring her brushes into the kitchen for cleaning, when she noticed a puddle on the floor. Rebecca looked around to see if her paints or paint water had spilled, but everything was as it should be. She started to walk toward the back with her supplies to grab a towel from the closet when she doubled over in pain. She sat down hard on the floor to catch her breath and think of what to do.

The house was empty, and John was not due back till mid afternoon, following a meeting he had scheduled with Captain Crowinshield after lunch. Between pains, she looked around for paper and pen. If there were some in the near empty house, none was available, so Rebecca took a brush and the spring green she had mixed for the leaves of the stencil, and painted a note on the floor near the front door.

J., Baby coming, gone to Trasks. R.

Rebecca grabbed her heavy cloak, and then waited between pains to pull on her warm shoes. The crunchy, week-old snow was not yet deep, but the house was set back from the road, and she dared not labor under a misapprehension of finding someone nearby. She breathed deeply, and walked out toward the main road. The day had turned, and new snow was beginning to fall, but it was not heavy, and Rebecca refused to worry as she trudged through the icy drifts. Again and again she paused to let the labor pains pass. They were not so strong as to be overwhelming, and she kept the goal in sight.

The few minutes it took to reach the Post Road had brought the storm full blast, and the snow was now coming down hard. It was getting hard to hold her head high enough to find the way. She stood at the juncture of her drive and the road, trying to catch her breath and get her bearings, when Mrs. Cummings, just on her way home from the shops, called to her.

"Mrs. FitzSimmon, are you a'right? Come here girl, let's get you inside." She ushered the nearly-frozen Rebecca into her small house, which was still beautifully decorated with greens and candles for the season.

"Mrs Cummings, the baby is arriving any moment. I think I need Mrs Trask."

"Susan Trask? Oh, that's right, let me see who can I send. But you, let's get you settled." She helped Rebecca out of her wet cloak and took off her stiff, frozen boots. The house only had two rooms – a great room with fireplace for warmth and cooking, and a back room for sleeping. Rebecca looked around. If she labored here, it would deprive this sweet old woman of her comfort, but she could not force herself out of the chair she was sitting in, let alone back into the storm.

Once Rebecca was settled with a warm brick at her feet, Mrs. Cummings left to find someone to take a message to Susan Trask who, amazingly, arrived not thirty minutes later. She knew that once the storm moved in, one of her "girls" would foal that night, so she'd packed her things and waited for a messenger or an arrival.

The boy had come in, breathless and near dead with cold. Susan Trask got the message that Rebecca was down on the Post Road at Emily Cummings's cottage, so she set her girls to revive the tiny messenger with hot chocolate and biscuits while she ran to the yard to find to find Tom, and the harnessed draft horses.

"Tom, Rebecca FitzSimmon is at old Mrs. Cummings. I don't how that happened, but the boy who helps her just ran up with the news."

"I'd best come with you. Should I collect the boy, and bring him back to his mother in town?"

""Yes, I expect there's time. First babies are never so quick."

Tom Trask went into the house to bring the young messenger and ferry him back to town in the cart. Then, with his passengers buried under skins and wool blankets, he skillfully drove his team of sure-footed draft horses through the blizzard into the town. The boy jumped off at his own home, with grateful thanks to be getting out of the storm. The Trasks then rode the short distance to the Cummings house.

"Sue, I'll wait with the horses till you come out and tell me what you intend to do."

Susan climbed out from her covers looking like a monster awakening in his cave. "Oh damn, Tom, I should have brought Marigold. Well, husband, I guess you will have to do for an assistant." And with that she strode to the front door of the little house, not quite sure what she would find, but she rarely did.

Rebecca heard knocking, and felt a cold blast of wind hit her as she leaned back in the warm chair near the fire, trying not to make a nuisance of herself. Mrs. Cummings was as kind as could be, but had no idea what to do, and the wind was picking up with the increasing intensity of her labor pains. Finally, that knock came, and then the familiar face of Susan Trask.

Rebecca, who had clearly been stoic enough to get down the road in the burgeoning blizzard, burst into tears as Susan walked into the room. Mrs. Trask summed up the situation in a second – the small room, Emily Cummings's only room, and the new mother, alone here in the storm.

"Becky, we have to move you. How often are the pains?"

"I don't know, I haven't been counting, but not too bad, I can talk between." She caught her breath and waited out the hard cramp, not wanting to scream or cry in front of kind Mrs. Cummings.

"That's good." Susan continued talking soothingly as she put Rebecca's feet back into the nearly-dry boots and wrapped her in the heavy blue cloak. She walked Rebecca to the front door and called to Tom at the road. The foreman came over, and picked Rebecca into his arms and put her into the back of the cart. Susan climbed in after her, covering her and telling her how everything was going to be just fine.

"Tom," she spoke to her husband so that Rebecca could not hear, "I don't like this. Let's get her back to the FitzSimmon house. I don't know what's set up there, but it's closer and this storm is not letting up."

Tom turned the large horses down the drive toward the new house. The building was dark against the white snow and the fading afternoon light. The horse cart took no time getting back to the house, and the door was open to their entrance.

"Tom, light, fires, heat hot water." Susan shivered in the cold empty house. "Then take care of the horses."

"Yes'm." Tom Trask knew better than to contradict Susan when she was working.

She helped Rebecca up the front stairs to the best bedroom. The bed was made with warm blankets and clean sheets, the fire was laid, and the wood box was full. Susan started a fire while Rebecca took off her shoes again and sat on a step stool as the next pain overtook her.

The two women could hear the clang of pots and fire starting coming from the kitchen below as Susan helped Rebecca off with her cloak, gown and undergarments, leaving her wearing only a warm shift and wool socks.

"First we walk for a while, just in front of the nice fire." Susan held Rebecca and helped her pace for a while. She left her for a minute to collect old towels from the kitchen, and then came back up. Finally, when Susan determined that Rebecca should rest and get ready to push, she added layers of old, soft towels to the pretty bed, and helped Rebecca into it.

"Now, you're comfy, we wait. Just breathe, Becky." Susan climbed onto the bed behind her to rub her back for a while, then fixed pillows for the younger woman to lay back on, in between pains. And between times, relaxed and warm, comforted by the presence of Susan Trask, Rebecca slept, willing herself not to worry about Simm out in the blizzarding cold.

Simm had left the meeting, pleased with the work the men had done in planning the new bridge for the head of Beverly Harbor. He pulled his greatcoat closer and rebuttoned the collar over his tricorn. The storm had already dropped nearly an inch onto the ground, but it did not concern him as he turned Sisyphus north.

For the first part of the trip the road was fine, but as he veered closer to the edge of land, and nearer to his own home, the ground became too slippery for the young stallion. Simm dismounted and walked the horse over the dunes toward his stable and home. The dark-cloaked man and the black horse made a moving shadow in the ever-whitening afternoon to anyone who was out and cared to look.

He arrived at the yellow house from the rear and stabled the horse. Simm took his time in the dry barn. He dried the stallion and found his warmest blanket. He checked food and water, and spent a minute feeding an apple to Artemis. He enjoyed the peace of the icy snow hitting the roof of the well-made stable and, with both horses warm and fed, he walked back out into the storm to find his wife.

Simm entered the house by the kitchen door. The house was cold, and no candles were lit. He found a lantern and lit the wick. He carried the light though the near-empty house, wondering where Rebecca was in this storm, but not alarmed by her absence. He smiled at the stenciling and paintings on plaster she had done in the main rooms of the house, pleased, once again, that they would not be visually burdened with the stylish, heavy wallpapers and their scenes of faraway places. In the front room, he stopped and stared at the nearly-frozen puddle of water on the floor. Confused, he went to fetch towels and started to wipe the floor. He walked toward the front stairs, thinking that Rebecca might be upstairs asleep and had not heard him calling, and almost missing the green paint on the floor.

Simm saw green paint, still wet with ice crystals beginning to form in the cold house. He went to collect his rags from the parlor floor to wipe up the green before it dried in place. Walking back into the hall, he placed the lantern on the floor and went on his knees, ready to clean the paint before it dried or froze in place. It was then he noticed the green was a note to him from Rebecca.

Relieved that she was with Susan Trask and worried about how she left the house, Simm grabbed his heavy woolen cloak and fisherman's knit cap and went back out into the storm. He trudged down the long drive, hoping to see Rebecca somewhere so that he could help her. At the main road, he turned toward the Trask house and his shipyard. Travelers heading into town passed him, but he paid them no mind, as he was determined to get to the Trasks's and find Rebecca.

Simm ran the last rise to the house on the hill. He was tired, wet and nearly frozen from the storm. His feet had not thawed from his walk with Sisyphus across the beach, and now the additional wet and deeper snow slowed his journey. All this only served to make Simm more anxious for Rebecca, and he pounded on the door, demanding that someone let him in.

Tom junior opened the door, and nearly jumped as the wind off the ocean hit with a full blast.

"Tom, don't be afraid, it's me, John FitzSimmon. Is Rebecca – I mean Mrs. FitzSimmon – here?"

"No, Mr. FitzSimmon. My Ma and Pa left with Joseph Grimley a while ago. I don't know where they went."

"Damn! Sorry, Tom, I didn't mean to swear. The team isn't here, is it?"

"No, Sorry. I saw Pa driving them when he took Ma and the boy to town."

"Thanks, son, I'm sure everything will be fine, thanks." And with that Simm turned back into the storm for the walk back to town. "I assume the first stop should be the Grimley place, to see if everyone is there."

It took the better part of an hour, but Simm discovered that little Joe Grimley had been sent by Mrs. Cummings to find the Trasks, and that they had driven him back into town. Simm was sorry to pull Mrs. Cummings away from her warm fire, but he needed to find that the Trasks had been there. Mrs. Cummings had not offered further information, but assumed that with the powerful storm moving in they had gone back to Mr. FitzSimmon's new beautiful house.

Simm went out into the wind and snow again. This time he retraced his steps from the main road down his long drive. Although the wind was causing almost immediate drifting it had not quite covered the hoof prints and cart tracks left by Tom Trask's powerful Suffolks. This time, there was smoke rising welcomingly from his chimneys. Simm climbed his front steps and entered a warm house. Tom Trask was boiling water and folding clean towels and blankets in the kitchen.

"Well, man, it's good to see you. From what I hear, little Becky's been a bit worried about you out in this storm." Tom welcomed him with a friendly wave. "Good pull on the chimneys, Simm, nicely-built house. Congratulations are going to be in order all around!"

"The baby? Rebecca? Tom! where are they?"

"Calm down, Johnny. Susan has delivered hundreds of bairns. Take off your wet clothes and shoes. The party is in your room, so changing is out of the question. But sit here in the kitchen and warm up – after you tell the ladies you're in out of the storm, of course."

"Thanks, Tom, you are a good friend, I'll just go up now."

Simm climbed the stairs two at a time, and called out that he was here, out of the storm, before he had reached the second floor of the house. "Ladies, I'm here and I'm just fine. Susan," he asked, "how is Rebecca?" he opened the door a crack to wave at the two women in the room.

"Jack, now she is fine. This is no place for a man – now you go get some warm tea into you in the kitchen, and I'll find you later." Susan shooed him out of the room.

Simm was no stranger to births. As much as women wanted to shoo men away, often that was not an option. He had observed a thing or two in all those years. He knew worry when he saw it, and Susan Trask was more harried and worried than she was trying to let on. He also could not help but notice that Rebecca was alone with Susan in the room. He knew, from an interesting life, that births were generally communal experiences, with the young girls working on towels, water and food, and older women helping the mother. His Rebecca was doing this with only one other woman. Mrs. Trask needed someone to help Rebecca and get this job done. He obediently went down to warm in front of the fire, but as soon as he found warm wash-water to clean his hands and face, he bounded back up the stairs.

"Susan," he said loudly as he knocked forcefully on the door, "you should not keep me out of that room. I am not just a ship builder, I am a soldier. I may not have delivered the hundreds of babies you have, but I have delivered my share. The wives always think the commanding officer can do anything. I will be in that room. And I need warm socks." Simm paced in front of the closed door, taking turns yelling and mumbling, depending on the level of noise from within. Finally, when no one answered him, he announced that he was coming into the room.

Simm opened the door. He saw Rebecca sitting up, limp and sweaty on the bed, with Susan Trask's head under the covers telling her to push. Simm walked in and closed the door. He smiled at his wife, who was weakly trying to sit up among soft pillows. She leaned back against the headboard, letting her tired head fall to her chest. She looked up to see Simm barefoot, sitting on the edge of the bed and pulling warm socks over his chilly feet. He heard Rebecca moan a laugh as Susan chastised him to get out of the room.

Simm spoke to her directly. "Susan, I know you are doing a fine job. But you are here alone and Rebecca is nearly spent. That walk to Mrs. Cummings must have sapped whatever strength you had left." He looked at his laboring wife, her hair still wet from the snow, and now with sweat running down an exhausted face. "Susan, you don't have to tell them at the midwives' guild meetings, but I am staying."

Rebecca had been trying. Lying down had hurt during the pains, and had produced weak pushes. She knew she needed to sit up, and for awhile Susan had been behind her, helping. But now she was on her own, so that the midwife could monitor her progress, and she could barely sit up, let alone push again. She was aware of John's voice coming from the hall outside the bedroom. She wanted him to just go away and not see her as the mess she felt she was. Then, like the man he was, he walked into the room to get dry socks.

The next pains swept her away, and she lost track of where John was. She heard Susan tell him again to leave the room. And the next thing she knew, there were strong, familiar arms holding her up. She leaned backwards onto his hard chest, breathing when he breathed, drawing strength directly from him. She heard Simm's voice in her ears, telling her to push, and in between the pains she heard him telling her to lean back onto him. She followed Susan's directions with new strength. So, cradled in Simm's strong arms, and with his strength willing her to continue, Rebecca pushed those final times until she heard the wail of a healthy baby.

Susan Trask told her sister later that she hadn't been sure if Rebecca had the energy to finish her labor, and that she was worried that she was going to lose her. But the girl's reaction to Jackie was immediate and powerful. "Maybe we should let fathers in?" Susan asked her sister, and both women laughed.

Susan sent Simm down to the kitchen to get the warm water and towels that Tom had prepared. "Well, Johnny," she started, as she took the water and started cleaning the tiny girl, swaddled her, and handed her to Simm. Susan moved on to clean and straighten the bed, and then help Rebecca wash and change into a clean, dry nightrail, with a warm robe over her shoulders. "You were right that we needed more people around for a birth, but at least everyone we had was an expert." She kissed Simm on the cheek and, leaving him with his wife and child, went down to the kitchen to get a cup of tea.

Simm turned to look at Rebecca as he added new logs to the fire. She looked beautiful, glowing with success and radiating joy, as the tiny girl with wispy red hair contentedly suckled, demonstrating that someone in the room knew what she was about. "FitzSimmon, I love you." Rebecca gently curled the child's silky fringe around her finger. "She doesn't have much hair yet, but I believe it will be safe to call her Elizabeth."

"Elizabeth Amalia!" Simm responded, "it will give her something to live up to."

Simm climbed onto the bed, and put his arms around both of the beautiful women in his life – the one he had just met, who had already claimed his heart, and the other, a gift from the gods, who had fallen into his life from above, been cruelly yanked away, and returned to him by a kind fate. A powerful feeling of love, and a promise to protect them, roared from deep within. He knew, at that moment, that should his family ever need to face the cruel winds of fate or foul weather, they would do so together.

A bit of history from Fate and Fair Winds

The British military occupation of Philadelphia began in the fall of 1777 and lasted until the late spring of 1778, when General William Howe was recalled to London. It was completely unlike the military occupation of Boston that preceded it. While Boston had been closed, starting in 1774, to punish the residents for the destruction of the tea, Philadelphia was the self-declared capitol of the rebellious Colonies, and was held as a beautiful captive rather than as something to be punished. It was also an elegant place for General Howe's troops to take up winter quarters. During the same winter, the Americans under General George Washington were a tattered force hunkered down at Valley Forge, twenty-two miles away, living under very different circumstances.

Several biographies describe life in Philadelphia during this period, among them *Beauty and the Traitor; The Story of Mrs. Benedict Arnold*, by Milton Lomask (Macrae Smith, 1967). For many in the town, having the Redcoats staying there was like a visit from old friends. With the Congress and the hardline Patriots gone, the remaining residents held a series of parties and teas to entertain the newcomers. Hairdressers and dressmakers from London even relocated to Philadelphia for the season, hoping to attract new customers. The Patriot army was never far away, but it did not hold the immediately-surrounding areas, as it had in Boston, and was in no condition to besiege the city. The atmosphere in occupied Philadelphia contrasted markedly with that of occupied Boston, where food, fuel, housing and opportunities for entertainment were in very short supply, thanks mostly to the physical isolation of the peninsula where Boston was located, the continued closure of the port, and persisting

Puritan views that were foreign to Philadelphia's residents. Philadelphia remained cosmopolitan throughout its occupation, and commerce continued to flow to and through the city, by land and sea.

I have tried to build on Philadelphia's well-described atmosphere during the 1777-78 British occupation, although I confess to changing one thing about William Howe. He and his staff did not take up residence at a local household. Instead, they found a nice house and temporarily evicted the residents. Still, I could not resist having this elegant general and his staff as a larger part of my story, and so I split up General Howe's staff, some of them staying as guests at a well-appointed town house, and others moving into a farmhouse just beyond the city limits as paying tenants, not confiscators.

George Washington had observed the Boston occupation. He was keenly aware of what had worked for the Americans–biding time until the Fort Ticonderoga cannon arrived and were emplaced above Boston and the British fleet at Dorchester Heights, and what had not–attempting, with a large but undisciplined, and cannonless, mass of armed men to intimidate the British, who knew that attempts to storm their impressive fortifications would be futile. Washington knew that a siege of Philadelphia was not possible, but he wanted something he had lacked in Boston, and that was to have "eyes and ears within the town."

So intent was he on having a civilian spy network, that it was in place before the British Army began to quarter in the city. That was how Rebecca became a spy for Washington. He wanted his people to watch, listen and learn, but never to put themselves in danger, which essentially separated intelligence from sabotage or raiding. A very readable book about this aspect of General Washington's tactics isThomas B. Allen's *George Washington, Spymaster: How the Americans Outspied the British and Won the Revolutionary War* (National Geographic Press, 2004.)

I have timed Simm's travels to actual events as much as was possible. There were ongoing negotiations between the Americans and the British involving cousins John and Samuel Adams, and the brothers General William and Admiral Richard Howe. The Howes had a generally sympathetic attitude toward the Americans, probably because their older brother, George, had been killed in America during the Seven Years War against the French. (He is buried near Albany, New York.) All three Howes had served with Americans during that conflict. Richard and William are reputed to have told King George III that they would not serve him in America unless it was as part of an effort to avoid an all-out war.

Unfortunately, the actions of Parliament toward America, and the attitudes of some Americans toward the British, made negotiation nearly impossible. That said, the final breakdown of talks did not occur until well after the American victory at Saratoga, in mid-June 1778 when Howe learned that a French fleet was en route to America. For the novel, that meant Simm left New York and returned to Philadelphia in time to save Rebecca in the woods – a lucky break for the characters and the readers who follow their story.

A final word is needed regarding the behavior of Simm toward his young paramour. An early reviewer felt I had done a disservice to the eighteenth century by allowing an older man to take the virginity of a young girl in such a fashion. I will not defend Simm too much, since he did make sure Rebecca's life would continue along the path that was already set out for her. However the reviewer's defense of that century's integrity misunderstands it. The 1700s brought fabulous inventions and innovations, from clockworks, mechanical looms and digging machines, to the use of unprecedentedly large debt to finance both overseas business ventures and wars, that changed how and where people lived and worked, and even how they socialized with each other. The eighteenth century, especially in John FitzSimmon's London, and also in America, despite official disapproval in Boston, saw the rise of gentlemen's gaming clubs, the codification of horse racing rules (at the Jockey Club, established in 1750), and a culture in which men and women took unprecedented risks and bet on everything that could have a disputed outcome.

The century also witnessed the rise of popular fiction in the form of novels, and some of the most popular ones, among both men and women, were risque even by our standards, and made everything a fair target for lampooning and ridicule, including morals and codes of conduct. One of them was John Cleland's 1748 work *Fanny Hill*, the first erotic novel in English; two others were Henry Fielding's *A History of Tom Jones, a Foundling*, published in 1749, and Laurence Sterne's *Tristram Shandy*, published in 1759 and followed by sequels. (*Fanny Hill* was banned in Boston until 1966.) As did their British cousins, the American people of 1777-78 had access to these books and read them, whatever they might ultimately think of their characters or messages. These were not a staid or uncurious people; the world was topsy-turvy, and they accepted that, along with the notion that they should have the liberty to make intimate choices, even if other people, or even empires, objected.

And so, dear reader on that note, I hope you have enjoyed reading Rebecca's and Simm's story as much as I have enjoyed writing it. Please visit me at *doryshistoricals.com* for tidbits of real history and fictional romance.

Dory Codington is a student and teacher of history and sometime guide on Boston's historical Freedom Trail. Her primary interests lie in using historical references and her imagination to understand the daily lives of those who lived during significant periods in history. Dory currently lives in Massachusetts with a husband, a daughter, a son and a tortoise.

Edge of Empire books take place during America's Colonial, Provincial, and Revolutionary Periods. *World Turned Upside Down* is how many people in America and Britain felt about the outcome of the American Revolution. Lord Cornwallis's troops stacked their muskets, when they surrendered at Yorktown, to a song by this name.

Books in the series are:
Cardinal Points
Beside Turning Water
Fate and Fair Winds

Other books by Dory:
Through the Eyes of a Poet:
The Life and Writings of Kate Fort Codington

Visit **DorysHistoricals.com** for the latest news and historical tidbits.

www.ingramcontent.com/pod-product-compliance
Lightning Source LLC
Chambersburg PA
CBHW051510250626
47156CB00001B/40